Low Key Connections

Low Key Connections

James Krake

James Krake

1

John

Normally when you find a girl in your bed in the morning, you at least have some fond memories of the night before. Or so I'm told. I'm not talking about beer goggle regret of rolling over and finding a few too many rolls beside you. No, I couldn't have even dreamt of more out of this girl. Long, slender legs tangled up with my blankets. Her belly had a twist to it where she had latched onto my pillow. All I could see beneath her golden hair was her parted lips and a little drip of drool as she snoozed without me. Completely out of my league and yet there she was, half naked in my bedroom.

But, I had not slept with this girl because I had not even been in my apartment all night. Despite what the rising sun had to say about the time of day, I was only just then going to bed. I'd been drinking for the past twelve hours, staving off a waking hangover purely by liberal application of more alcohol; but, for as worn out as I was, what really stupefied me was her tail.

The entire night had been a little strange, but not this strange.

The engineering college of d'Amaranth University is a soul crushing, life devouring nightmare of a program for six weeks out of the year: the two midterms and finals each semester. It's pretty reasonable otherwise, winter ice notwithstanding. As much as I'd like to, I don't slouch on studying for my tests. I very studiously track down upperclassmen and buy their last year's exams off of them. This isn't cheating, it's just reference material. Hell, the professors post example exams from three years back. Between those and the homework, every problem on the exam can be singled out, taken apart, and memorized.

Some might say studying this way doesn't actually teach anything. To that, I say, "Neither does a business major."

The cramming process is akin to taking a pint glass and pouring beer into it until the head overflows. You cram as much in as possible, until the beer is level with the lip, and then it's just a matter of delicately walking it to the table without spilling too much. It doesn't matter in the least if you spill it afterwards, you've already gotten the grade.

As such, the Friday night after any exam week has most of the student body stuffing their guts with beer until all that crammed-in knowledge gets spewed into a toilet. Or better yet, until it gets sweated out beneath the sheets with the fairer sex. I thought the latter option wasn't in the cards for me, so I studiously worked on the former. This was the bleary haze in which I met the man who would become my landlord.

With club music pounding through my skull and mint liquor shots burning up my blood, I had found myself alone in a booth. Something had happened in the conversation, and I wasn't quite sure what. I had missed some key sentence, and the flow had poured away from me while I was ordering another beer to chase the shot down. My friend Lance had opened the set with these two girls (I never quite understood how so many nursing students could be smart enough for medicine and yet not be nerds), but at some point he had vanished with the tall girl. Then I was alone with the short one.

There was nothing wrong with the girl, but she just wasn't the kind of bubbly extrovert that could keep a conversation flowing when I was so mentally blown out that I was nearly asleep with my eyes open. I'll never know if she said something, or if she just went to the bathroom or what, but next thing I knew, the bar staff were cleaning up empty glasses and I was alone.

Then The Guy joined me.

I think I thought he was the girl's friend, but really he was my friend. It's easy to buy friendship with a pitcher of beer at the right hour of the night. He looked like he had just stepped off a stage play. Gold rimmed sunglasses, greased back hair, and a popped collar beneath an embroidered jacket. He had a flair of presence, and two watches on his wrist. I was trying to figure out if they were silver or stainless steel (whatever they were, they looked more expensive than Rolex) when he stuck out his hand and said, "A pleasure to meet you, John."

"Likewise." I shook, but had no idea who he was. He hadn't introduced himself or maybe he had and I hadn't heard.

"What are you studying, John?"

I drank some of his beer as payment for the question, and told him, "Engineering, mechanical. And you?"

"People," he answered, and laughed. I didn't understand

the joke, but I laughed too. "What do you want to do with your mechanical engineering degree, John?"

"Get a job, I guess. Automotive is always hiring. Steady pay, steady hours."

"Sounds like a dream job."

"Not in the least, but hardly anybody gets a good job. All you can ask for is good pay. Better than... I don't know, going into petroleum and living in a Louisiana bayou or something. Hey, what beer is this?" Normally when I was drunk, the cheap beer started to taste like water. This one tasted sweet, almost like honey. It was good.

"Lager. And you wouldn't want to live in a bayou? That's where the last North American monsters can be found, so says the tee vee at least. That's the last man versus nature adventure to be had, ain't it?"

"Well, there's bears."

"Ah, bears too! But, then again, there's oil rigs in Alaska, you could get paid to move out there. I hear there's no taxes either."

I refilled my glass. "Negative taxes, even. They pay you to live there."

"You just have to deal with winter and bears, right? But, that's the price of excitement, right?"

I laughed. "There's winter enough here, man. I bet Alaska would actually be more pleasant, just... you know... no city life. No supermarkets and movie theaters and... and... no high speed internet."

The man's smile was contagious. "Well, I suppose a city has adventures all of its own." Then the lights came on. The waning crowd all blinked and groaned, but bouncers had started yelling at everyone to get out. The clock had struck two in the morning, and like a belated Cinderella, the magic was coming to an end. Cash out and get out.

I figured Lance had gone home with the tall girl, so I stepped out on the street with The Guy. Early November, Halloween already a distant memory as ice froze leftover jack-o-lanterns solid. The sky above was a blaze haze. The only stars were planes, while the horizon seemed lit by the fire of endless urban sprawl. There was a Canadian pot farm lighting up the southern sky like the rising sun, but that was nothing new.

"Well then, your night's not over yet, is it?" The Guy asked as he sauntered out beside me. I shrugged, he grinned. That was more or less how I ended up on the fifth story scaffold of an old apartment building. The thing was ancient, back from the glory days of Motown, and recently bought up by a developer. Everything within the art deco facade was getting stripped out and rebuilt to include proper utilities. The original architect never imagined a need for actual air conditioning ducts, which caused the renovations to be an endless scraping away of the innards. Maybe one day they'd finish, but that night we were smoking cigarettes between whipping tarps.

"Aren't you cold?" The Guy asked, pulling his sport coat tight around himself.

I had a flannel on. "Got a liquor coat on. I'm fine." I couldn't taste the cigarette, just the warmth in my chest as I stared at the city.

"So, do you find your college years exciting?" The Guy asked, leaning against the outer railing. In the gloom of the night, he condescended to lower his sunglasses and watch me with his emerald eyes.

"Could be better."

"How?"

"Could have a girlfriend. Maybe I should have joined one of the fraternities."

"They're not all they're cracked up to be. What else?"

"You know, I could have signed up to study abroad."

"And why didn't you?"

I leaned down on the railing, watching my smoke fly away without me. "Because when I looked into it, the coursework seemed to be a joke. By the time I realized freshman and sophomore year were a joke anyways, it was too late. Just kinda flew right by me."

The Guy didn't laugh at me, he nodded and very empathetically said, "Funny how life does that to you, ain't it? It feels like one day you go to bed, and when you wake up, whoosh! The years have gone by without you. Let me tell you something, John. I'm a bit older than you, so let me talk as your senior. The trick is you need to have a goal, and you need to be doing something... adventurous."

He kept saying that word. He was spitting it out like punches in a fight and didn't even know what it was doing to me until the whole thing burst out of my drunk lips. "Yeah, you see, the thing is, the only person I know that ever went on an adventure is my fucking brother, and he died."

"I'm so sorry to hear that, how did it happen?"

I shook my head, which made the world spin. Next thing I knew, I was sitting on the scaffolding, back to the building and sucking on the burnt butt of my cigarette. "We don't know. It's been three years now. Bank says his account hasn't been touched. Police report turned up nothing. He either died and didn't get identified, or did a really good job changing his name, but I doubt that."

"Why?"

I flicked the dirty filter off the side. "Because he would have told me to come join him by now. Our parents are one thing, but if he's alive, that means he ditched me."

The Guy nodded sagely and eased himself down next to me. He turned his head up to the colorless sky and slowly produced a flask from inside his sport coat. "I'm a bit envious of you, John. I don't have nearly as good a relationship with my brother as that. Of course, being adopted will do that, but still... sounds like you would have liked to go with him, yeah?"

"To his grave?"

"Not to his grave, obviously. But on the adventure! To go out and experience something you couldn't imagine in a re-built wreck of a town like this," The Guy said, gesturing with the flask at the cityscape.

"Hey, the city's on the upswing."

The Guy shrugged. "Only because billionaires are pumping millions into the real estate." He slapped the scaffolding with one hand, and handed me the flask with the other. He had honey liquor in it, which went down far easier than any other shot that night.

"You've got a bit of a point though. The only adventure in this city is going to the ghetto where there's more lots than houses, and frankly I don't feel like getting shot over pocket money." I passed the flask back.

"You know, I blame the internet," The Guy said, and paused to swig. "The internet killed the thrill of discovery. Why go to yonder hills when you can just search it up on Google and learn that fucking nuclear glow south of us is a marijuana farm, and you can buy their bud at the corner store for five bucks a gram? There's no impetus to act when learning is trivial."

I stared at the static light show, finding that my drunk mind was working more than I thought it would be working. "Is that stuff really only five a gram? That's pretty cheap."

The Guy groaned and rolled his head back again. "You wanna see the stars, John? I want to see the stars."

My cell phone bathed me in light as I tried to google the price of the farm's bud. "You can't anymore. Too much light. Everywhere you goddamned go. I went to a dark sky light preserve thingy once, tried to get a look at the Milky Way. You know what I saw?"

"The Milky Way?"

"No, I saw the fucking city glows across the horizon from forty miles away at two in the fucking morning. We could only see the planets because of–" I shook my phone at him, "–A fucking app."

"That's terrible. It's inhuman. Unnatural. Anti-Earth. Could you imagine going back a thousand years and telling people one day they wouldn't be able to see the heavens?"

I lit another cigarette, I still had The Guy's pack, and sent a cloud of smoke up to join the night haze. "You know, that's the kind of adventure I could get behind. Take the bridge over to Canada and go real far north. I could go hunting for the aurora borealis."

The Guy whistled. "I've seen them. They're beautiful."

"One bad blizzard on my way could kill me though."

He slugged me in the arm. "That's what makes the adventure

worth doing, doesn't it? Besides, that's just a challenge. You can prepare for that! Why don't you do it?"

I shook my head and puffed my cigarette. "School. Not enough time off."

"What about Christmas break?"

"I'm supposed to go back and see my parents."

"Bah, do you always do what your parents want you to?"

"If I want them to keep paying my tuition, I do."

"So you can get your degree to get a stable job with the easy money, find a girl and settle down and blow your brains out at the age of fifty?"

I nodded. "Yeah, exactly that. My whole life plan," I said, holding my cigarette out like a stick of incense.

The Guy jumped up and clapped his hands together. "John, I swear, I've never met a man who needed an adventure more than you do. You gotta go on one."

I grunted and held my hand out for the flask again. "We literally just went over the problems, didn't we?" The honey liquor still went down easy.

"Yeah, but that's where I come in. Let me ask you, what's it worth to you? If someone were to get you the girl and the adventure both? And I'll do you one better, you won't even have to drop out."

"And how are you going to do that?"

He grinned and cocked his head. "What's it worth to you?"

"Hard to say when I don't know how good the girl is or how crazy the adventure is. If it's... I dunno, Christine from econ class and we're roadtripping north, I'd say that's worth maybe a couple thousand, but mostly because the actual trip is so expensive."

"Christine is a troll."

"Like I said, mostly because the trip is expensive... Now, if it were Hilde, and shit, I don't know, the two of us had a boat to cruise around Greece, that would be worth... You know, I can't actually answer that because I don't remember how much is in my bank account right now."

"Not one to go into debt?"

"Absolutely not. Debt is slavery."

"I like that attitude. Gimme your phone, let's make a deal. Come on, I've gotta download an app. I'm what you'd call an entrepreneur. I see a gap in the market, I'm here to fill that gap, which happens to currently be you."

I frowned, trying to figure out if that was a euphemism, but I unlocked my phone and handed it over to him.

"Think of this like a matchmaking program, alright? It's going to scan your data and build a composite of the kind of girl you're into and then I'll put the two of you together." My phone glowed across his face like a magic orb as he pondered the arcane.

"Why do I feel like I'm buying a mail order bride from Russia?"

He grinned at me. "Because you only understand the world through movies and memes, kid. Those aren't even real anymore. What I've got is better. And as for the adventure, well she'll bring the adventure. Here, just sign here to pay in a month, after services rendered, after satisfaction guaranteed. No card needed, no nothing like that. And of course, this is my app, so you can contact me through it. What do you say?"

He handed my phone back to me. The app looked straight out of the 90's with huge impact fonts, flashing fireworks, and a green accept button half the size of the screen. "And why should I believe you?"

He slapped his hands together with a flourish over mine. The light went out. "A demonstration then," he said, and jumped off the side of the scaffolding.

I jumped to my feet, grabbing for the tail of his coat as he vanished like a rock down a well. The cigarette vanished, I dropped his flask, and I found myself staring down at his grinning face one story below. He wasn't a red splatter across the sidewalk, just a douchebag with a magician's flair. "You fucking crazy bastard."

The Guy laughed. "Showmanship!"

"I'm out." I shoved off and went back to the ladder down.

"What, were you not impressed?" The Guy asked as I climbed past him

"I'm going home, going to bed," I said, and tuned him out. My head was starting to pound. The booze was wearing off as dawn approached, which meant the cold of the night could bite into me.

Last thing I heard from him was, "Be seeing you, John!"

Which, eventually brought me back to my shitty little one bedroom apartment, occupied by an unknown blonde. She had a leathery, black tail that swished and flicked with her dream, nearly as mesmerizing as a hypnotist's coin, but I stared at my phone instead. I had apparently hit the accept button when I lunged to grab the seemingly-suicidal maniac.

That might have explained the girl, but it definitely did not explain the door across from me, where the alley window should have been.

2

Lily

Lily held the god's contract in front of her, squeezing the parchment between her fingers. It was heavy. The paper stock thick, the ink laden, and the gold gilding genuine. It was also, as far as she could tell, a complete lie. She felt stupid just looking at it, knowing her name was on it. Why she had thought anything else would happen was beyond her. She even knew she had been dealing with one of the trickster gods and she had been stupid enough to think that she was the one profiting from the scheme rather than getting victimized by it.

She groaned and knocked back her goblet of wine, wiped her chin clean, and slumped on the table. Just beyond the door, the bar was roaring with people. Drinks were being ordered and songs slurred. She could hear Mary cracking the bung off a fresh keg and the chef screaming at the bus boy to scrub faster. She was surrounded by the most boring variety of chaos she could imagine, a slush whirlpool of drunkards and bastards one step from under the boot of the elves.

And her five minutes of break was almost over.

"Lily! We need you!" The crying face of her newest co-worker burst into the breakroom—a closet beneath the steps really. Amy had fire-tipped hair that should have belonged to a warrior tribe, but Lily could foresee the problem even before the petite girl got the words out. "There are these really tough looking guys that stole the drink platter from the next table over and they're trying to get into a fight."

Lily groaned and tucked the letter into her dress. As she stood up and adjusted her bodice, she went through the mental steps of composing the customer service smile she needed to go diffuse the situation. Her face burned at the indignity of putting on a smile at almost midnight, but she needed the job; especially if she was going to have to pay rent on a magic portal.

Out from the backroom, with Amy clutching at the tails of her sash, Lily strode out to the warzone that was Thorn's Tap Root and Room. Oil lamps flickered from all the movement in the establishment, sending up tongues of soot that found ever new crevices to stain between the plaster and timber. She scanned from one table to the next. She spotted cowed construction workers buried in their own mugs with gnarled hands too tired to throw a fist. There were two djinn in the corner taking turns fiddling, but they weren't looking at each other. She followed the gazes of the blue-skinned devils over to the crowd of men standing. They weren't in smudged linens. They didn't have the slumped shoulders of beaten down workers.

She stared at no less than six suited up men. Too well

dressed to be mercenaries, too brawny to be merchants. Those that had horns kept their hair greased back so thickly their hair might crack if they got knocked around. Thugs, the lot of them. Except, half of them still had their tankards in hand. She recognized those men as regulars and she didn't recognize the ones with their hands free to fight.

Lily cleared her throat and put her hands together with a slight curtsy as she said, "What seems to be the problem?"

The thug that seemed to be in charge, or at least the designated talker, stepped over to her with an exaggerated swagger. "Well, if it isn't the little runaway princess."

Lily didn't lose her smile, but she said, "Don't call me that."

The thug who hadn't named himself hooked his thumb at one of the regulars, a stitcher by the name of Finnegan who was one of the most reliable tippers in the whole city. He had a bit of a compulsion about arithmetic that helped him play the role of anesthetist on good days and poisoner on bad ones. The thug said, "I was told, by word of honor among men, that this fine establishment wasn't supposed to have these sorts here."

Lily felt the tug on the back of her dress as Amy shrank. She said, "I assure you the only business that occurs here is that of eating and drinking. Anyone is allowed to come here to do that." All of the regulars knew that the bar wasn't a pleasant place by chance. It was because everyone was expected to come together and make sure unwelcome muscle didn't ruin it for the rest of the customers. As Lily kept smiling at the thug, she noticed the regulars putting their drinks down.

The thug laughed. "Is that so? Then why is it so hard for me to get a good mug of wine around here?"

"If you drank more, they'd start tasting good, I assure you," Lily said.

Another of her regulars snorted. "Maybe if he drank it instead of throwing it on the ground."

The thug rolled his eyes. "There was hair in my mug," he said, pinching a bit of Lily's hair between his thumb and finger.

"Get your hand out of my face."

"Been a while since your brother's been seen around here. What's he been up to, Princess?"

"You must work for Urdao, which means you're talking a lot of shit for somebody whose best fighter is enslaved digging a ditch right now. Now get your hand out of my face before I have it broken, okay?"

He let go and stepped back. "Peace doesn't last forever and your brother ain't here, Princess. Safety is only as good as the violence you can call on. We're not here to start anything, but it's time you people start thinking about what has to be done and who the real enemies are."

Someone slammed the front door of the bar shut and bellowed, "Guards!"

Fifty chairs shifted as everyone turned back to their tables at once. Urdao's thugs immediately started moving, flowing between the tables to the side-exit as the regulars took over their table. Everyone had just settled down when the door opened again and two steelfaces stepped in. They moved with as much swagger as the thugs, but their bodies were stouter for all the leather and metal cladding them.

Lily cleared her throat and put the smile back on her face, not quite sure what expression she had given the thug. As she approached the elven guards, she asked, "Is something the matter?"

One of them lifted his visor, exposing the baby face beneath, which meant he might be as young as a hundred years old. "Sounded like a bit of commotion in here. Just a wellness check as it were."

No one had actually raised their voices the entire time, but engaging the lie was a terrible idea. "Nothing out of the ordinary, sir. I'd offer you a drink, but I hear Captain Simmons has been cracking down lately. I wouldn't want to get the two of you in trouble," she said, peering over their shoulders to the cobblestone road beyond. There were two young men with their heads down and their shirts disheveled. Coerced confessions if she had ever seen them.

The guard grinned. "Drinking on the job do be disallowed, that's true. But that doesn't mean we can't inspect the wares. You know, plenty of fine establishments have been selling spirits as wine. Very naughty to dodge taxes like that."

Lily sighed. "Amy, could you get a pitcher of the house red?" she asked, and saw her coworker had already run to the kitchen. Her gaze moved instead to one of the tables with only two people at them. They got the message immediately, fleeing to the bar counter before the guards could single them out. Lily wiped it off for them and seated the two guards. Then, she spent the rest of her shift doing her best to never respond to them with more than a single word answer. Everything went fine, but stressful, until they finally left to continue their patrol and Lily's boss emerged from the shadows.

Mitchell Thorn was a thick and swarthy man, originally a sailor and with enough scars that most assumed he had been a pirate, even though most had been mishaps while cooking and butchering. His only real injury was the loss of half his tail, but no one ever asked why he wore closed pants. His connections made people think twice. "They ruined our tips," he said.

Lily's smile finally shattered as she slumped right down to her tail almost touching the ground. "I hate when they do that."

"Amy had a breakdown in the back," he added.

Lily's shoulders slumped further, her gaze loosely stuck to the door as people began vanishing into the night. "Well that explains why I had to cover all her tables."

"Do you need an escort home?"

Lily glanced to the one table that hadn't vacated yet, with a pair of bruisers she had known for a decade. Both were sipping ales and playing a game of reversi. "I'll be fine, goodnight Mr Thorn," she said and waved goodbye. When she stepped out of the bar, the two men conveniently finished their game, paid their tab, and followed her out. They stayed behind her a polite distance, shadowing her all the way back to her crummy little apartment. She was thankful that they weren't grumbling about how shoddy her home was anymore. That had taken months to achieve.

She waved at them and they nodded to her before melding into the night as soon as her door was shut and barred. Her apartment had almost no furnishings, she couldn't afford any. It was one of the cheapest rooms in the city and smelled the part, but there was at least an odor of fresh hay from the adjoining stables that night. While it wouldn't be so bad as to drive her back to her brother's protection, it just wasn't the kind of place she could bring people back to. The literal only upside was that the mudded timber walls blocked noise well. She sighed and unlaced her corset, draping her accessories across her kitchen table, beside the complimentary copy of reversi the god had given her as part of the contract. He had claimed it was proof that he could go back to Earth, but she wasn't convinced that he hadn't simply invented it. She picked up her contract letter again and sighed.

She froze when she opened the door to her bedroom. The door beyond was anything but her bedroom. Sure, it had a bed–a huge pillow like a sultan's harem chamber–but also clothes everywhere, overflowing from dressers and armoire. Men's clothes. There were strange cables and boxes that glowed. The air was crisp and refreshing and strange machines buzzed or whirred.

She glued her face to the nearest window–real glass–and gawked at the brick city covered in ice and sunlight. Her heart leapt up her chest as she spun around and threw herself to the bed. The god hadn't lied.

3

John

"What is this, Jotunheim?" a girl asked.

My eyes shot open. It helped that my hangover was setting in. I think just about any noise would have been enough to wake me up to a pounding headache. A girl's voice never would have ranked as a possibility. Lurching from my living room futon, I spotted the source of the anomaly, bent over with her head in my fridge. She was wearing one of my t-shirts, which was almost enough to cover her hips like a dress. I did catch a glimpse of white cotton beneath something black before she stood up and looked at me.

The most beautiful woman I had ever seen in real life stared at me from over the top of my fridge door. Her blue eyes went wide as she locked eyes with me. "I'm sorry."

"Can I help you?" I vaguely remembered the night before. I had stumbled out of my room and sat down on the couch and then nothing. My moment to think had turned into hours of sleep and now the blonde intruder was in my kitchen.

She blushed. "I was exploring."

"My kitchen?" The only thing in my fridge was half a dozen eggs, mismatched beer, and condiments. Maybe a leftover box of pizza.

"Technically, yes."

My head was pounding. I needed water and a handful of ibuprofen. Unfortunately, she was between me and salvation. "What are you doing in my apartment?" I didn't remember any damage to my door and I didn't have a balcony to break in through. Given that it was a one bedroom apartment above a cupcake shop, most people didn't even know it existed. It just didn't make sense.

She cleared her throat and stepped around the fridge door. She said, "Technically, it's my apartment too."

I scratched my head and tried to remember any emails about this lately. "Are you my landlord or something?" I was pretty sure I rented from some old retiree, but maybe the guy had a daughter. Still, intruding like this had to be some kind of illegal.

The blonde girl frowned. "You signed the portal agreement, didn't you? This is your house, right? I'm your new room-mate, Lily."

"Hi, John," I said, shaking her hand completely on auto pilot. My brain caught up with the conversation as soon as I let go of one of the daintiest, most gentle hands I had ever shook– and yet I still noticed some roughness on her fingers. "What's a portal agreement?"

She looked at her hand, then at me. I saw her nose sniff.

Then it was my turn to blush as she looked up and asked, "Do you maybe need a moment to get your day going?"

"Just a moment and don't leave. I'll have to call the cops or something," I mumbled as I squeezed by her. I slapped the faucet on and grabbed some pills. After gulping down some water and splashing my face, only a few more details of the previous night came back to me. That Guy had said something about a portal, hadn't he?

With my body marginally improved, I slipped back out of the kitchen and found Lily in my living room, staring out the window on her tiptoes. It reminded me of when my parents took my brother and I on a cruise, almost a decade ago now, and he and I both had struggled to see over the railing as the ship set sail.

Neither of us had a tail peeking out from beneath our shirts, swishing through the air.

Now, if it had been like the kind of dress-up furry tails that people wear to Renaissance Fairs and the kinds of weird events I don't think about, that I would have understood. She would have just been weird and probably fit right in with the computer science majors. Hers was wagging though. It was either the greatest piece of animatronic cosplay I had ever seen, or it was real.

While I was reeling with that, she turned back with a grin on her face to ask, "Is that snow outside?"

It was like some kind of naive fairy had dropped into my apartment, but damn if she didn't have a smile that could derail my thoughts. I wanted to take a picture or get her number, or something. Nothing like that would be appropriate at the moment. Regardless, I patted my pockets looking for my phone as I said, "Yeah, it's November. What do you expect?"

She shrugged. "I'm from a temperate climate. Cold has always just kind of been a vague idea for me."

I couldn't find my phone. That was enough to draw my eyes off the gorgeous blonde as I started searching the couch, the mess that was my kitchen table, and so on. "Are you from Florida or something?"

Lily laughed. "No, I'm from Alfheim."

"Ha ha," I said, deadpan.

She pouted and planted her hands on her hips. "Don't laugh. I'm from Blue Rock Bay specifically, the domain of King Charles Blattmeister. Now why don't you tell me just where this is? I know it's on Earth."

Still devoid of a phone, I tried to see if she was pulling my leg. She seemed serious. "King Chuck Sword Master? What the hell kind of name is that?"

Her face colored and she stiffened like a hissing cat. "Blattmeister is a title!"

"Who bestows a title on a king?"

"He wasn't king when he got it!"

"Are you like a big fangirl or something? Is this some tv show I should know about?"

Her anger vanished as she meekly asked. "What's a tv show?"

I had no idea how to respond to that and we both just stared at each other until I brought us back on track and asked, "How did you get in here?"

"Through the door?" she said, staring at me like I was the idiot. When I gestured at the multiple locks my front door had, she added, "Not that one."

Then I remembered the other door in my bedroom. I ran down the hall and threw open the door to my bedroom. Everything seemed normal at a glance–although my phone also wasn't on my charger here–except for the wooden door that barely fit into the frame, apparently magically inserted into the drywall. I said some ungentlemanly things as I approached it like a wary wolf. I went to one side, then the other like it might be painted on, Looney Toons style, but no luck. I even cracked my window open and tried to peer out the screen to the dirty alley. I was definitely on the second floor of a building with nothing but air on the other side.

And yet there was a door that kept sucking a draft as I stood next to it.

Lily shouted from the kitchen, "Can I have one of these beers? I'll pay you back. Promise!"

"Go ahead," I said, unable to take my eyes off the apparently magic portal in my bedroom. When I touched it, it was rough wood and completely physical. It swung back and revealed a new room on the other side. The floor was wooden and the walls plaster. I could see a little wood-burning stove next to a crummy pile of kindling. The room smelled of smoke, but also of horses and salt. Memories kept swelling up through my mind as I took a hesitant step through. My foot didn't plummet through the illusion.

The old memory of the cruise was suddenly stronger than ever, bursting into my mind with every whiff of ocean breeze that seeped through the rough window slats. It made me miss my brother again, however the rational part of my brain was still in charge and I whirled upon the juncture.

I stood one foot in, one foot out. I wobbled my weight and

didn't notice anything different. Staring at the door frame, I tried to see if there was some kind of seam, a visual glitch like in a video game. Even running my nail across the frame I couldn't find anything though. The weirdest part was that I could touch either wall and the thickness was only about as much as a sheet of drywall.

"Where the hell is my phone? I gotta get a video of this."

Lily asked, "What's a phone?" as she leaned against the hall door with a can of beer in her hand.

"Are you serious?" I asked as I once again became conscious of how messy my room was. Clothes were strewn across the floor. My textbooks were everywhere. Even my box of tissues was very suspiciously placed beside my computer.

She nodded. "I only sort of know what it is based on the name. The translation spell is not quite helpful enough. Like, the fridge in there, I pieced together it's a cold box machine, yeah?"

I had to take another look at what was allegedly her apartment before I answered. There were no lights, no appliances, no electricity whatsoever. The tools she did have were very fine and I was sure they could easily sell for far too much money as hand-crafted traditional luxury items, but they weren't technological. Her pans were cast iron, which has its uses of course, but no non-stick to be seen. Her wood-burning stove wasn't even level and I could see smoke stains where it leaked from the pipe. Worst of all, it felt like the middle of summer heat without so much as a rattle of a fan, much less an air conditioner.

The other side of the portal was the dark ages.

"A phone is a pocket computer for talking with people, taking photos, videos, and the internet," I said, walking into the middle of her living room. She had fresh vegetables laid out, still speckled in dirt.

"And the internet?"

"I'll tell you later," I said as I turned around and spotted her door. I was standing where open air in an alley should have been, but I still couldn't believe I was in some other world. I had to see it.

Lily came running. "Wait, wait!"

I froze with my hand on the door. "What?"

"Your clothes."

I checked them, but they weren't stained or anything. "Oh. You don't have t-shirts, do you?"

"Yeah, no," she said. "We have tunics and trousers. Whatever fabric this is, is way too soft. This is going to sound bad but I live in a cheap side of town. I'm barely above the trenches. If the guards see you walking around like that, with round ears, they'll arrest you for being a thief."

Lily did not have pointed ears, which raised some questions about just what she was. However, I could solve the immediate problem. "Thankfully, denim is super old," I said, and took my shirt off. I wadded it up and chucked it over her head, back to my bedroom, before throwing open the door to Blue Rock Bay.

A magical city of fantasy did not sprawl forth about me, spotted with lustrous birds and covered in the wafting scents of a thousand exotic meals filtered between the rolling hills of a medieval metropolis. Well, it did, from what little I could see beyond the gigantic troll face staring at me with myopic eyes, each nearly as big as my own head. The beast was hunched over and shaggy with fur like a mammoth. Every panting breath punched me in the face with the sweet rot of tooth decay as yellowed tusks spilled out of its blubbery maw.

Lily came barging out. "You get your filthy animal off my street!" she yelled, throwing herself across the narrow balcony railing to swing her fist at some kind of dapper-dressed monkey-man smoking a cigarette on the other side of the alley. The bipedal creature jumped and the troll-like animal swung its head to look at him. The animal stood on all fours and wore a yoke harness. Down a slope to my right was a muddy trench where other troll-beasts dragged sleds behind them.

I saw one of the creatures lash out and snatch up what looked like a rat the size of a dog and devour it mid-stride. Nobody looked twice at the grisly sight. In fact, most people were joining Lily in sticking their heads out windows to rain curses at the monkey-man. Someone must have identified him, because the whole street took up a cry of Shitheel Hanz until he started beating the troll-beast with a cane to usher it back into the slow-moving trench.

Aside from the lack of a trunk, I would have said it was a relative of the elephant except for aspect. It had human fingers on the fore legs. Thick as car pistons and probably tough as stone, but I could see the musculature webbing flex every time it walked on its knuckles the way a gorilla would.

"Lily; problem."

She stopped her grumbling to ask, "What? He's leaving and I don't see any pie piles down there. Doesn't smell like it either..."

I glanced over the cobblestone with her, but only briefly. "No, I mean your clothes. You're in my t-shirt."

She blushed. "I never asked if I could borrow..." Her gaze

snapped to the windows across from us where some middle aged woman was snickering and looking at the two of us.

"Little early in the night for that, ain't it, sweeties?"

Somehow, I understood what she said. I also realized the shadows of dusk were starting to streak across the city. The problem remained. "Didn't you just say to not–"

"I know!" she blurted as she darted back into the apartment to hide the fine fabric that was a bargain bin cotton t-shirt from Earth.

4

～

Lily

Lily sat on the couch in John's apartment, staring at her knees and fidgeting as her new roommate dug through closets. What had seemed like a simple night gown was nothing more than one of his spare shirts and it barely came down to her thighs which had been fine while she thought she was alone in the apartment. Her work uniform was still strewn about in the bedroom, but that had become ground zero for his attempt to help.

After running back inside from lastkan troll, he had come inside so seriously she had thought he was about to scold her. Day one and the secret had nearly gotten out because of her. Instead, he had asked where her bedroom was. That was where all of her clothes were, but the door no longer led to her bedroom; it led to his. As he pointed out though, the alley outside his bedroom still existed, which meant her bedroom should still exist.

There just wasn't a door to it anymore and that was a mechanical problem; his speciality.

"Just going to put a load in first," he said.

She flinched as he walked out of the bedroom with a wad of dirty clothes in his arms and she blushed because her mind had gone somewhere dirty that he clearly did not mean.

When he saw her staring back at him, he arched an eyebrow and added, "Of laundry?"

A moment later he showed her how the washing machine in his closet worked, how it would do all the soaking, the rinsing and even the drying, so long as she added just a little dollop of detergent. When it started spinning and humming, with a clanging sound like an apprentice blacksmith rattling inside, she couldn't take her mind off how beautifully unfair it was that he had a machine more effective than a nobleman's maid staff.

In fact, just about everything except floor space seemed to laughably dwarf the living standards of everyone but royalty.

John rose, still half naked and completely unashamed of his trim physique. He cleared his throat. "You're free to use this if you need it, but it can be a little rough. There's a setting for delicates but I honestly don't know what setting wouldn't rip all the threads out of your dress. Cold wash maybe? I'm really not an expert on that."

"But isn't that a mechanical problem? Your specialty?"

He coughed and looked away. "Fashion is not a mechanical problem. This though, is." Then he picked up some kind of plastic device with a spiral bit of metal at the end. He pulled the trigger and it buzzed to life, making the bit spin so fast it became a blur.

"Is that some kind of torture device?"

"No... wait, technically yes but that's not fair. Lots of things make good torture devices. This is a power drill. Your wall is plaster slats right? I'm going to punch a hole through it between the beams to see that your room is still there. I can't imagine what would be there instead. Then we'll just have to knock it down or something."

Not for the first time, Lily wished her room had a real window. It was a huge security risk in the city of course, but she missed the big bay windows and balconies she had grown up with. "Okay," she said, stepping back to let him through as she wondered whether they were offending the god. He had put the portal there for a reason. She just didn't quite appreciate the insinuation, even if John was totally her type.

She stole in behind him and gathered up her dress. Before she could escape back to the living room to get changed, she noticed that John was standing in the portal moving the power drill from one side to the other.

"Do you hear that?" he asked.

"The buzzing?"

"No, listen," he said, and moved it through the portal a few times. The noise shifted.

"Do you think the magic is doing something?"

His brow pulled together, and then he repeated the experiment while also moving his head to either side of the portal along with the drill. "No, I think the drill is hitting a different RPM. And I don't know what that means." He might physically be her type, but he might also be a little weird.

"Good luck?" she ventured, and slipped around the corner.

She had one of her corset laces gripped in her teeth as she tried to tie up her sleeves and skirt when he walked back into the hall.

"Your room's there. Just need a hammer."

"Just be careful please?"

He hesitated with a little claw head hammer in his hand. "You own the apartment, right?"

Her brother owned it technically. "Yes."

"Then as long as I don't hit the support beams it's fine. Or would you rather abandon your entire room?"

She hesitated long enough to catalog how much of her jewelry was hidden in her bedroom and sighed. "Do you think you can?"

John looked at the hammer and shrugged. "Let me see."

Lily finished lacing her dress and followed him back through the portal in time to see him staring at the wall, hammer hefted overhead. He slammed it down hard enough he could have caved a soldier's helmet in. A little pile of plaster fell to the ground at his feet. Half a dozen more strikes and Lily was afraid her neighbors would come complaining, all for him to have put a spider crack through the plaster and apparently hurt his hand.

"Wrong tool for the job," he declared, shaking his hand out.

"What do you mean?" Lily asked as he retreated to his bedroom. She peered at the wall and spotted a perfectly circular hole straight through the wall, and beyond that her undisturbed bedroom. It was exactly as she had left it except for what looked like a scroll left on her little writing desk. While her apartment wasn't exactly a fortress, and her lock sometimes didn't even hold up to a sturdy shake, there was a guard for the complex perfectly willing to put a crossbow bolt through a would-be thief's back.

If someone had slipped in to leave that there, it was either from her brother, or the god, and she didn't know which she was more eager for.

Unfortunately, when she returned to John's apartment, he was just sitting at his computer. "I need a sledge," he said, tapping away on the keyboard.

"Okay, how are you going to get that?"

"Lance has one."

"Who's Lance?"

"He's my friend. He might also have my phone. I was drinking with him last night, last time I know for sure I had it."

Lily leaned over his shoulder to look at the glowing panel that was his computer. It was filled with updating text like magic, but she was sure it was just a piece of technology like nearly everything else in his apartment. What he had pulled up looked something like a playwright's script.

KingOfKings said, "Can I borrow your sledge?"

ScrumLock said, "We breaking something?"

KingOfKings said, "Yeah, a wall."

ScrumLock said, "Awesome. When?"

KingOfKings said, "After lunch?"

ScrumLock said, "Aight."

John looked her over and meekly shrugged as he asked, "You hungry?"

She was only a bit peckish at the moment, but the prospect entailed exploring Earth. "Your friend isn't with the authorities is he?"

John blinked. "No. Why?"

"We lose the portal if they find out about it."

The two of them stared at each other for a moment, until John said, "Well that explains that, somewhat. Wait, do you have the rules to this or something?"

Lily put her hands on her hips. "Well I'm glad at least one of us was sober at time of signing."

"In my defense!" John declared, waving a finger in the air. "I had to be drunk to believe signing a contract for a magic portal would be real! But I also was an idiot to not get a copy. Wait a minute..." He spun and tapped away on his computer for a moment. The screen changed and he swore under his breath. "I thought maybe a copy had been emailed to me."

"Email?"

He sighed. "Happy to explain that to you, but Lance is a good guy and we need to get halfway across town to meet up with him for ramen. Do you like ramen?"

"Sounds great," she said with a smile and with no idea what ramen was.

He repeated his meek shrug. "So I know that was a really complicated dress for you to put on and all that, however you need to change clothes if we're going downtown d'Amaranth."

Lily deflated as she finally understood why he was acting that way. "Why didn't I think of that?"

"Also," John added as he rose and stuck his head back through the portal. "Okay, thought so. Do you normally use a public bath?"

She used a private bath in the apartment complex. "More or less."

"Do you want to use my shower?"

Lily hesitated while the translation spell pieced together the meaning of the word for her. Moments later she was immersed in steaming bliss. Forgotten knots in her muscles were evaporating as she scrubbed down with an endless supply of lathering soaps and shampoos and the hot water just didn't stop pouring across her. It even pooled up around her feet, filling the bathtub basin as she sang one of her favorite tunes.

Eventually, she left the warm embrace and wrapped herself in a fluffy towel that reached from her armpits to her thighs, clinging to her as she wrung out her hair. He even had combs to borrow. She changed into some of his spare clothes he had prepared, even though she had to cuff the legs of the pants, the sleeves of the shirt, and she had no choice but to tie it together in the front because buttoning it would have been a baggy disaster.

She stepped out of the bathroom beaming and found him waiting in the hall. "I didn't know you were a singer."

She retreated. "Sorry, I forgot you would be able to hear that."

"No, you're actually quite good. Sorry I don't have a hair dryer by the way. You're going to need a coat though." He tossed her a knit hat that she reluctantly put over her wet hair, then he dug out the heaviest parka from his closet.

While she was lacing up her own boots–she luckily still had those–she eyed the thin jacket he had taken out for himself. "I know I saw snow out there, but how cold is it going to be?"

John laughed. "Well, Alfheim feels kind of like Florida to me, and this is Michigan. I'll be fine. I've got thick blood. You'll freeze like a popsicle without that though."

Lily's mouth watered at the idea of the frozen treat. When she stepped outside with him and was hit in the face with the full brunt of early winter and lake-effect snow, she cursed the comparison.

5

John

I couldn't take my mind off the fact that the drill RPM was different in Alfheim. Well, what amount of my brain that was free and not thinking about Lily beside me. I wasn't even enamored with her, I didn't think, but I was constantly about to grab her by the arm and save her from breaking her tail on ice, or falling in a storm drain puddle, or just getting jostled off the sidewalk into a snowbank. None of that ever happened, but she was so busy gawking at all the wonderful sights of d'Amaranth to pay attention to where she was going.

At least, when she wasn't hugging my coat around herself and trying to keep her teeth from chattering.

Objectively speaking, d'Amaranth wasn't an ugly neighborhood. In fact, it had managed to avoid a lot of the glass-and-steel homogeneity of modern architecture simply because no one had ever rebuilt anything. We were practically Art Deco, like a lot of the historic buildings across the bridge in the rest of Detroit. That didn't mean name brands franchises hadn't slotted themselves into every nook and cranny with their crap Americana signs. And that was ignoring just how many windows were broken and boarded up, the tarp covered roofs of half-derelict homes, and the very questionable quality murals and city-claimed graffiti pieces. d'Amaranth was a fine island in the summer, when everyone was on summer vacation and the traffic let up. The first winter snows had turned it all to crap as far as I was concerned.

I kind of felt bad for Lily, getting a portal from Alfheim to d'Amaranth of all places. She could have gotten a city that was actually nice. Not that I could name one, but that was a personal problem. She didn't seem to mind though.

And I still wanted to know why the power drill changed through the portal. If I had been able to find my phone, I would have searched up the schematics for the drill. There was no way it was that complicated of a design. The lithium ion battery plugged into the bottom. Pulling the trigger applied DC current to some kind of electric motor which spun the drill bit. I had been holding the trigger all the way down, so it should have been at max torque, so any mechanical changes should have been ignored more or less. It was like passing through the portal sucked some charge out of the battery or something, but if that had happened then it would have stayed different when I brought it back to Earth.

It sort of felt like there was a magnetic field over there maybe.

Come to think of it, why did I assume I could survive over there? I should have treated it like stepping onto an alien planet. Who was to say the oxygen was right? Too much carbon dioxide maybe? Why would magic just magically make those things align?

"What is that?" Lily asked, coming to a dead stop as she stared across the road.

I winced. "That is called a painful car," I said, looking away from the exchange student who had decaled his anime waifu across a sports car that cost more than my degree.

"No, not that, that!" Lily said as she pointed to the fudge shop beyond the car.

It wasn't exactly a local specialty, just a branch location from up north. We were also about to go to lunch, but I wasn't an idiot. "You want some?" I asked, and started into the traffic. When I saw the expression on her face though, I slipped my hand into hers and made use of my personal jaywalking experience to move us across the street with the kind of confidence that warned drivers I actually wanted them to hit me so that I could sue them for the rest of my college tuition.

I was a little worried we were too early in the day, but they were open. "It's on me, pick out whatever you want."

Lily gaped at me about as long as it took for her to realize there was a heater blowing warmth across the doorway. Then she bolted inside and let out a little moan like when she had stepped into the shower. I didn't think she realized I had heard both of those and I wasn't about to complain. Either way, the salesperson welcomed us in. I got myself a little bag of sugar-roasted almonds while Lily practically glued herself to the display. She shifted from one spot to another, debating between peanut butter or butter pecan. She wavered between rocky road and mint. Things got a little dicey when she started getting free samples.

Eventually though, she settled on getting the original fudge flavor instead of salted caramel. However, by that point I was starving and they all sounded good to me so I interjected and just got one of each flavor. I was buying them anyway. So what if they tasted like the premonition of cavities.

It took two blocks for her to actually swallow and not have a lump of fudge packed into one of her cheeks. She asked, "Don't take this the wrong way or anything, John, but are you rich?"

I laughed. The fudge had cost a little over twenty bucks. I spent more than that at the bar last night trying to get a number. "I am quite poor actually. I'm a college student. I'm not even an employed college student right now. I'm coasting off money from working over the summer."

After a moment, Lily asked, "Is this poor people food here? Back in Blue Rock Bay, these kinds of sugary treats are for the lower nobility or for guys who really need to apologize."

I couldn't say that was particularly wrong here on Earth, but that didn't matter. "It wasn't much, so long as you don't want a box every single day. Also, I definitely assumed you don't have US dollars?"

"I've got silver," she answered, hiding her mouth with one hand as she chewed a lump of fudge.

I was strangely jealous of that answer, but didn't feel like explaining fiat currency at the moment. "I'll cover lunch too, while we're here on Earth. I'll need your help over in Alfheim though. I don't have any silver."

"What kind of money do you use if not gold and silver?"

"Government backed paper, I'll explain later. We're here," I said, pulling open the door to Big City Ramen. It was a little slice into an ambiguous commercial building, with a seating area done up in black and silver, decorated with anime fan art. The kitchen spewed as much steam into the seating area as it spewed shouts from the line cooks. It was damn cheap for the amount of food it gave though. The two of us slid into a booth, and I habitually reached for my phone. Which I didn't have. I was starting to feel like I had some form of separation anxiety.

As I got us a booth, Lily asked, "So ramen is a type of spicy soup?"

"Yeah," I said, then took another glance around the shop. I had only realized subconsciously but there was nobody eating ramen at the moment. There weren't even pictures of it, and I hadn't explained what it was. "How did you know that?"

"Oh, it got translated for me as *suppe*."

"What do you mean translated?" I asked as the waitress brought us over waters.

Lily laughed. "Did you think I just happened to speak your language? And you mine?"

I sheepishly shrugged and mumbled, "It works that way in the movies."

"It's part of the portal contract. Both of us have the babel spell put on us. Pretty standard for the gods."

"You keep saying that. Who are they?"

Lily winced and hesitated before saying, "Can I explain that over in my world? Remember my comment about the authorities? It's problematic. As for the spell though, imagine if you knew what cinnamon was, but had never smelled it, or rather, you didn't know you had smelled it before because you hadn't been told that was cinnamon. If you got asked to think of what it smelled like, you wouldn't be able to, but as soon as someone tells you that the smell is what it is, everything clicks, right? You knew the whole time, you just didn't have the word association."

"So, Lance will be able to understand you?"

Lily held up her menu as the waitress came back over and ordered herself a bowl of shoyu ramen. I said to make it three, because Lance was coming and the worst case scenario was taking it home as leftovers. The salty broth was great for hangovers. When the waitress left, Lily grinned. "I can speak with anyone on Earth, and you can speak with anyone in Alfheim. So long as we stay up on our rent."

"Rent?" I asked, just before the door bell clanged. I looked up and made eye contact with Lance.

"What up?" the rugger asked as he sauntered over with a fifteen pound sledge hammer in one meaty fist. He set it down on the table and almost squeezed in next to Lily before he saw her. "Oh, my apologies," he said before putting the sledge on the ground and then shoving me over to fight for table space.

Lance was as big as a bear and as strong as one too. As strong as a black bear at least, maybe not a grizzly. It made him an absolute terror on the rugby pitch, but what scared the hell out of me was how he could drink all night then wake up at dawn to workout. He had joined us still in a hoodie from the gym and I was grateful he smelled like soap instead of sweat. The man was superhuman, not the least reason of which was he still managed to make raid night for our MMO guild.

"The name's Lance," he said with a big grin as he held out his hand.

Lily was still in my parka, but she let it slip off her shoulders to extract her hand before shaking his. "Lily Hagen."

"So, how'd you two meet?" Lance asked, but he wasn't looking at either of us. He was staring at her hand after she let go.

"Just this morning. Actually, Lily, you know more of what's going on than I do. How are we supposed to be explaining this?"

Before Lance could shoot me an insinuating grin, Lily said, "We're roommates."

Lance tapped his finger on the sledge. "You're not asking me to turn two apartments into one, are you?"

"No, but you won't believe me until you see it for yourself, okay? Also, you're going to be sworn to secrecy," I said.

"How secret?" he asked as the waitress brought over our bowls. The steaming scents of chili oil and pork belly wafted over us, the aroma pungent in the dry winter air.

It made my stomach growl and I saw Lily gawking at it. "You know that thing we talk about making if we ever had some private time with a CNC mill? That secret."

"Oh, that's fine then. Thanks for ordering by the way."

"No problem, hey Lily, do you know how to use chopsticks?"

She shook her head. "I've never used a pair in my life."

I flagged the waitress back down for a fork as I asked, "Lance, what do you mean by that's fine then?"

"Don't worry about it. It's fine."

"Before I forget, do you have my phone?"

"No? Did you lose it at the bar?"

I buried my face in my hands as hope wavered. I looked up when I heard the mess of slurping going on across the table from me. A few tepid bites to explore the meal had become ravenous gulping until the spice caught up with her. I was waving the waitress back over to order us some beers as she tried to snuff the fire in her mouth with water, to little success. "Man, I cannot afford to buy a new phone right now," I grumbled.

"Where do you think you lost it?" Lance asked as three beers were set down between us. We all cracked one, but Lily was almost desperate to cool her tongue off.

I grabbed some of the chili paste and spooned it into my ramen. "Last night I was drinking with this weird guy after you went home. It must have been then. We may or may not have done a bit of urban exploring up some scaffolds. I feel like I would have remembered dropping it though. Maybe I left it there when that idiot jumped off the side."

"He jumped off the scaffold?" Lance asked.

I rolled my eyes. "He just jumped from one level to the next to scare me. The asshole."

Lily cleared her throat and managed to compose herself. "John, that was when you signed the contract, wasn't it? You realize that was our landlord, right?"

I stared back at her, replaying the memories from last night. Things were coming back clearer, or maybe my brain was just filling in the gaps with plausible nonsense. I mostly remembered The Guy's grin. It was a salesman's grin and he had sold me on his ideas and then I had gotten an app on my phone and then when I went home I had a girl sleeping in my bed.

And I didn't remember checking the internet as I stumbled down the nighttime streets. I was battling my drunkenness to get home safe without taking a bite out of the concrete after slipping on ice. The last moment I had my phone for sure was with him.

"He robbed me."

Lily said, "He gave you an unbelievable opportunity."

"He still robbed me though!"

Lance held up his hand. "Can someone fill me in?"

Lily turned to him and asked, "Did you ever want to go on an adventure?"

"Life is one big adventure, and I love every minute of it."

Lily went from looking like an assistant salesperson to outright floundering. I didn't know enough about the portal to help her, so I just waited until she recovered. "Well, I mean a more literal adventure. Seeing new lands, meeting new people–"

"You mean like taking a vacation? I still want to go to Oktoberfest. The real one."

I said, "Allow me. Hey Lance, how much would you pay to go be a hero and fight monsters?"

He entered one of his moments of deep scrutiny. "Well, I figure it would take several thousand dollars to buy enough body armor and ammunition–"

"We're not hunting people down. I mean sword and sorcery type stuff."

Affability returned in a flash. "Oh, like full dive VR kind of thing? If it was legit, I'd probably zero out my bank account. Did you sign up for some kind of brain implant trial or something?"

"Easier to show you in person," I said as Lance flagged down the waitress to order another bowl of ramen.

Lily leaned across the table to whisper to me, "Are you sure this is a good idea?" I nodded. "If this goes wrong, the portal will get shut no matter where we are. I could get stuck here, or you in Alfheim."

"Look, it's more likely to go wrong if I were to try to hide it from Lance. We're tight."

Lance cleared his throat, and probably heard everything we said. "So, Lily, are you a student here? Where are you from?"

I could see a tint of red in her ears as she said, "No, I'm from Blue Rock Bay, or at least close enough. I'll show you when we get back to the apartment."

"Blue Rock Bay? I haven't heard of there," he said.

Lily grinned. "You should visit some time."

"Could be fun. How are the beaches?"

She wilted. "Private, or covered in canal sewage."

Lance lit up. "Oh, is it like Venice? I always wanted to go to Venice."

After a moment of thought, Lily said, "Not quite that many canals, just a few for shipping."

I could sense that the conversation was getting a bit danger-ous to have in public. Given that Lily hadn't just outright said she was from a different world, I followed her example. Before Lance could ask questions like what state it was in, or what river the canals fed into, I jumped in to say, "We should cash out, the sooner we get back to the apartment, the sooner you'll understand. Also, we still need to take that wall down."

Lance shook his head. "Sorry, we'll have to wait a bit longer. Hilde's about to show up. Oh, hey sis!"

The doorbell rang as the silver-haired beauty of the fencing team strolled in with her gym bag over her shoulder. She was tall, lean, and smoking hot in a very literal way. A cloud of steam still billowed off of her as she unzipped her running jacket. Despite having bare skin from her socks to her hips, she still managed to run hot despite the early winter. I might have thought she was superhuman, but I was actually just convinced she had run from morning practice to join us.

That in itself was rather superhuman.

She was pulling her hair tie out as she dropped her bag against the booth. "Hey bro, John." Then she noticed Lily and froze.

It was my turn for red ears as I introduced her. "Hilde, this is Lily, my new roommate. Lily, this is Lance's older sister, Hilde."

Hilde's attention snapped to me, her gaze burning. "What do you mean roommate? That sty you live in isn't even fit for visitors."

Lily tried to say, "It's not that messy." She was completely ignored though.

"It's a long story," I said, but it really wasn't. I just didn't know how to explain it yet.

Lance said, "How about we explain everything back at the apartment? It seems complicated?"

Just then, the waitress arrived with the fourth bowl of ramen and I saw Hilde look at me, at Lily, at me again, at the food, glare at me again, then turn to Lily. "Hilde, lovely to meet you. So sorry to hear you have to put up with my friend."

"It's no trouble," Lily said, and she didn't quite shake Hilde's hand. In a very antiquated but dignified manner, she took Hilde's hand and did a sort of seated curtsey.

Hidle seemed even more confused than I felt, but her brother was signaling for our checks. "Well, I won't hold up the party," she said, and picked up her steaming bowl of ramen. Lily and I both stared as she drank the broth then vanished all the noodles and fillings into her stomach. In a flash fit for a sumo wrestler, she set a nearly empty bowl down beside ours before our checks had even been returned, bearing the most blissful grin I could imagine. "Now, John," she said. "I am very, very interested in your explanation."

6

Lily

The adventure came to an abrupt stop when the four of them returned to the apartment. There was of course a delay as both Lance and Hilde went through many of the same experiments that had interested John when he first stepped through the portal, but she had to stop them from running out the door. First, she explained, "We need to get into my bedroom. My brother has some spare clothes in there. Can't have you all running around in your otherworldly clothes and drawing attention, right?"

But, they couldn't just break down the wall because it was the middle of the night in Alfheim and, to everyone's dismay, was apparently twelve hours different and thus not quite dawn. When the lastkan trolls started their work, then they could break the wall down. Any earlier and people would be ready to lynch them.

There was a narrow window which would let in the dawn,

but in the night, there was almost no way to even see the peaks of the city sprawled out between them and the shore. That didn't stop everyone from impatiently crowding around and staring regardless.

"My phone just bricked," Lance said, holding his little communication device up and jabbing buttons repeatedly.

Lily rose from her seat in her kitchen, where she had been nursing what John called an energy drink. The device looked just like all the other gadgets and gizmos that dotted John's apartment, and apparently the entirety of Earth. She had seen the two of them using it at the ramen shop and it had clearly reacted to his fingers, but now only the black mirror looked at them.

She still couldn't believe the quality of the soup. It was incredible and disappointing at the same time. The vegetables had no flavor. The meat was tough. The noodles reminded her a bit of calamari. However the broth had a depth of flavor she had never tasted before, despite the pathetic quality of the foodstuffs. The drink had been a delight to her tongue, even if she could feel her heart rate elevating unnaturally because of it.

"Lily," John said, his gaze narrow. "Did the contract say anything about not bringing phones through?"

She tilted her head and pondered, conjuring up the words within her mind. "No, it was entirely written in elvish. A word like phone wouldn't have been in there. But the god did say you would have a different set of explanations. I think he called it localization?"

Hilde broke away from the two men fiddling with the device. "Elvish? Does that make you an elf?"

"Oh, no no no. Here, one sec," Lily said, and stepped

through the door to the bedroom, to put the wall between her and the men. She turned around and loosened her pants to slip them down. She had to loosen her underwear as well, which raised one of Hilde's eyebrows for some reason. Then she pulled her tail out, slipping it around her hip and swinging it free. "See?"

Hilde's expression morphed a few times before she actually chose a sentence. "No. I'm sorry, I guess I could have guessed you weren't an elf because your ears are round. But, what are you then? I obviously thought you were a human when we first met."

"Well, I'm mostly human," Lily said as she started to button her pants once more, but thought better of it. "Close the door?" she asked as she picked up her one remaining dress. "Can you give me a hand with the laces?"

Hilde's eyes flashed over the dress. "Sure, but, you're mostly human and a little dash of what?"

"Succubus." She stepped out of the pants and took off the shirt and got her petticoat on all before Hilde came to terms with the statement.

"John!" she called, throwing open the door. "Your room-mate's a—"

"What are you doing!?" Lily shouted as she yanked Hilde back in and slammed the bedroom door shut, her cheeks burning.

"Get your hands off me, demon!" Hilde leapt back, her hands in something resembling a fighting posture. Her weight was all wrong from the waist up though. While she had landed in good foot positions, she clearly had no idea what to do with herself.

Lily sighed. "I'm not a demon, I'm a demi-human. Are you going to call trolls, djinn, and centaurs... okay, sorry, I'll give you a pass on the djinn. But I'm demi-human. Demi. Means part! Like I said, I'm mostly human!"

"And part demon!" Hilde squawked.

The door popped open and John stuck his head in. "What are you shouting about?"

"Get out!" Lily snapped, yanking the door shut again. "I'm not dressed yet."

"That's my bedroom, you know!" he protested.

Lily's heart leapt in her chest as she wrapped an arm around her chest. It felt like her whole body was flushing and that energy drink certainly was not helping. "What do you think you're doing? Why did I even ask you for help?"

"John's room ain't a locker room," Hilde protested.

"Well excuse me, but my bedroom is currently behind several inches of plaster. That's the whole reason your brother got invited."

"And what are you going to do after that? Suck their souls out?"

Lily recoiled. "You think I'm going to do what?"

"Did John sign his soul away for this portal?"

From the other side of the door, John chimed in, "I'd contest the contract. I was drunk. I couldn't consent."

Lily huffed. Setting aside the fact that there were no soul lawyers to appeal to, no judicial court that would hear the case, she set her eyes on Hilde. "You're literally repeating centuries old slander. Succubi were made by Lord Dionyssus during the war. We acted as camp followers. We don't and never have stolen souls. What did happen was several women lost their husbands to succubi, because we—well, my ancestors—were tailor made to relieve psychological stress. That's what we do."

"How? By sleeping with them?"

Lily felt her cheeks burn and her throat clench. After a moment, she cleared her throat. "Technically, you're not wrong. But it's not soul theft! In fact, it's an in demand skill. The elven nobility pay good money for girls like me. They say the king has fourteen girls in his bed chambers to keep him rested."

Hilde clicked her tongue. "Rested? Yeah right."

Lily stamped her foot. "I don't steal souls! I'm not that kind of demon, even if I was full blooded!"

"Hilde," John called. "Stop harassing my roommate. We'll take it up with the god when we find him."

Lily groaned and pinched the bridge of her nose. "You know, nothing like this would be happening if John hadn't lost his phone. The contract with all the details that you Earth people need to know is on that. Seriously though, just treat me as human? I'm not planning to sleep with any of you."

"Weren't you sleeping in John's bed when he found you?" Hilde asked.

Lily spun on her heels and finished getting dressed. "That's different."

"Sun's up, getting to work," Lance said.

Lily frowned as she laced her corset—not so snug it was hard to breathe—and tried to figure out what time it was. She hadn't heard any temple bells, so it couldn't be dawn. If Lance thought it was dawn then there had to be light coming in. She swore and yanked the door open. "That's not dawn!" she cried.

Lance put the sledgehammer through the wall like a battering ram. He obliterated plaster, snapped boards and had to plant his foot on the wall to yank the head back out. John had to grab his arm to stop him, before asking, "What do you mean not dawn?" He pointed to the slatted window which definitely had a yellow glow coming from it.

Just to be sure, Lily ran over and opened the shutters. Pushing the panes apart, she stuck her head over the sill. The light wasn't coming from the horizon, slashing the city with warmth. There was only a minor light, far overhead as one of the other realms twisted through the branches of the world tree. The planetary barrier shone like mother of pearl, scattering a distant sun back across Alfheim in a glow as fleeting as a summer rainstorm. "It's just a light-storm," Lily said, pointing to what she thought might be Muspelheim, but she had never been an astrology expert despite everyone assuming she was all her life.

The two guys exchanged glances and John asked, "What's a light-storm?"

"Just wait for the bells? Please?" Lily asked, before there was a rough knock at their door. "Hide."

She recognized the man outside her apartment at once, and undid the chain. Rather than let him, she stepped out despite her half-dressed state. "Good morning Finnegan."

Finnegan was far too useful to her brother's organization to be working mere security, unless he had lost a big bet with the usual guard. That, or things were getting dicey with the other gangs and mercenary groups. "There something going on?" he asked, jerking his head toward the door.

"Just some friends," Lily said, clutching the hem of her skirt with both hands. Her smile felt false the moment Lance went back to hammering a hole in the wall.

Finnegan's eyebrows went up, and the corners of his lips went down. "And where'd you meet these friends?"

"They come well vouched for, don't worry. You can tell my brother that."

Finnegan sighed and crossed his arms. "You know we all want to give you some space to live, Princess–"

"Don't call me that."

"But, we still gotta keep an eye out for you, you know? I have to tell the boss something about what's going on. You're waking the whole building up."

Lily sighed as another sledgehammer blow cracked through wood behind her. She could hear the snapping and cracking and feel the vibrations through her feet. "I'll explain it all to my brother in person when he's back in town. Is that alright?"

Finnegan sighed in turn and scratched his receding hairline. In a lower tone, he added, "He'll be back sooner than expected, we think. There's some things we need to know about Lady Virent's excavation."

Lily tilted her head. "The shrine? What about it?"

Finnegan nodded. "For some reason, it seems like half the Black Fingers have gotten arrested and sent there, all together. It's more than a little suspicious."

That just made the posturing in the tavern all the more strange. She crossed her arms and declared, "The less of them on the streets the better, right? Like you said a moment ago, I'm out of my brother's business."

"You'd think it would be good, but they're not incompetent. They have to be up to something. And Lily, what am I hearing right now? It sounds like you're knocking a wall down in your apartment?"

Lily cleared her throat and stopped meeting his gaze. "Don't worry about it. The noise will be over in just a moment. If the landlord has an issue with it, the landlord can come in for an inspection. Okay?"

Finnegan groaned. "Your brother's half a continent away!"

"Lucky me. Be seeing you now!" Lily said as she slipped back into the apartment.

John and Lance had opened the hole up enough to duck through and both had made it into her bedroom. She chained the door shut again and ran to join them. While Lance was playing the part of a tourist, John had gone right to the writing desk and picked up the envelope. He held it toward her and said, "This is addressed to me."

7

～

John

"This abbreviated contract is to highlight some of the key information that will be useful to a newcomer to Alfheim, but is not itself a replacement for the official contract. Please see the Low Key Connections App for full legal details."

"Thank you for renting this gateway! You are one of the first tourists given this opportunity and I hope that it will become a permanent affair. If there are any problems, please use the Low Key Connections App (Hereafter "the app") to contact your landlord. As the temporary owner of this gateway, you have been granted certain blessings, rights, and responsibilities. You have surely already noticed that the language barrier is no more, for you, but not for anyone else you bring through the portal. I ask that you use your discretion and play the proper role of tour guide whenever you introduce a newcomer to the wonderful world of Alfheim. While translation is not provided, there are certain mandatory medicinal effects. Please fret not, although you may experience some nausea and discomfort in the first few days. This is to prevent any fresh soil contagions and symptoms will abate quickly."

"This gateway is for private use only! Any interference from relevant authorities will result in the contract instantly becoming null and void. Due to the circumstances of the magic, no promises can be made or kept with regards to return to proper realms. Which is to say, if the gateway is shut while you're in Alfheim, you're stuck in Alfheim. Please exercise proper discretion with introducing people to the gateway, but do not be afraid either. Anyone is eligible for a portal of their own and you will receive a referral bonus for any successful adopters."

"To maintain this connection requires a rental fee, at the end of each month, of ten thousand US Dollars, or five hundred gold coins. Details to pay can be found in the app. So long as this payment is made, you may use the gateway in any way you see fit, provided all uses remain private. Thank you for your patronage and welcome to Alfheim. Adventure awaits!"

"P.S. If you want to find me, head to Drithugel Manor and ask for Thomas Smythe. I do have your 'arcane relic'."

To all that, all I could say was, "Motherfucker."

There was really only one way for things to play out after that. We had to go to Drithugel Manor, which Lily described as the only friendly manor in the city. While Lance and Hilde were trying to fit themselves into spare clothes that were too small for either of them–Lily's brother was larger than expected but only about as tall as myself–she sat down at her kitchen table with me. "That's where Lady Virent lives. She's something of an egalitarian because she's young. Youngest of the high elves in the city, or so they say. She wasn't alive during the wars so she doesn't resent demi-humans much."

That news sat with me about as poorly as her brother's dirty shirt fit me. I really wanted to toss it in the wash. "I don't think you've told me much about this war?"

Lily sighed and crossed her arms, but she didn't seem annoyed by the question. Judging by how she fidgeted and glanced away from me, she was just uncomfortable with the topic. "Technically there were like seven, plus a few dozen armed conflicts here and there. If you hear someone talk about the war, you know, the general title war, they mean the campaign to... well... kill all full-blooded humans."

I sat and stared at her and she didn't say anything. Eventually, Lance emerged from the hole in the wall, dressed like a serf. He wandered over as I asked, "You want to run that by me again? Who exactly won that war?"

"It's hard to say that someone won, but humans kind of sort of definitely lost. But that was over a hundred years ago. There's no bounties or anything for humans now, just the gods."

"The gods."

"Yeah, like our landlord."

My jaw nearly dropped before I said, "You mean like the one hiding out at a high elf's manor?"

Lily gave a very strained smile. "She's a progressive? I guess?"

I turned to Lance. "This might be a disaster. Just like Lily is hiding her tail on Earth we need to somehow hide that we don't have tails."

Lance patted his rear. "These are pretty tough work pants, plus the tunic covers my hips. I think I'll be fine."

"Dude, we might get arrested and executed."

Lily almost leapt out of her chair to say, "You won't get executed! And unless you do something stupid, you'll probably not get arrested either. The guards are known to be too lazy to actually arrest people. They just..."

I arched an eyebrow at her. "They just what?"

She glanced away again. "Beat people up and leave them behind."

Lance laughed. "I'd like to see them try."

I groaned. "Lance, don't get in a fight with the police."

"Town guard," he corrected. "That's totally different from men of the polis."

"Excuse me," Hilde said, sticking her head through the hole in the wall. She was blushing. I'd never seen that before. "Do you have any longer skirts as options?"

Lily swept across the room. "Not here. How short is it on you? We can let it down a bit."

"How?" Hilde asked, and stepped out for us to see her. The hem of her skirt didn't even make it to mid-thigh, though the frill of her petticoat did. There was something about the dress that messed with my head, maybe it was the way it tapered in for her waist, but the dress seemed far more indecent than it objectively was. And by indecent, I mean the kind of attractive that could make a man walk into a light pole because he was too busy looking at her. I wasn't even entirely sure why, because I had seen her in athletic shorts that came down only a finger's width lower than her butt and this covered way more but still.

Lance snorted. "You'd fit right in at the renaissance fair."

Lily just stepped around her and did something to the fabric without saying a word. A moment later, the hem of the skirt was a bit lower and yet she was glaring at me. I hadn't even said anything! That didn't stop her from souring the mood.

I left the table and stuck my head out the window. There was an actual dawn now, rosy sky and everything. "Guess it's my turn to get changed. We don't want to be here all night."

"Day," Lance said.

"It's our night."

"This is going to get confusing," he said, and I nodded agreement.

"Do I look alright like this?" Hilde asked as she twisted back and forth, looking herself over.

While Lily gave her assurances, I crawled into my room-mates bedroom and picked up the rough clothes she had laid out while I had been reading the contract. Getting changed into trousers and a tunic was easy enough, but I found myself staring at the bed the whole time. If it could be called a bed. Really, it was a box filled with loose straw and a few bags of what were probably also straw. The pillow seemed to be a lump of feathers. A few experimental prods and I could imagine how comfortable Lily had been the moment she flopped onto my bed.

The tech differences between Earth and Alfheim really shouldn't have been surprising, but getting confronted with the past left me with a certain kind of awe and curiosity. I wanted to see what else the world had to offer. As I climbed back out of the bedroom, I simply made a mental note to at least get an air mattress or something. "Lead the way? To Drithugel Manor."

"Is your phone really that important? I can understand wanting to speak with our landlord, but..."

All three of us humans said, "Yes."

Blue Rock Bay had already woken up by the time we emerged. While Lily was signaling the guard who had shown up earlier, and engaging the crude lock, I watched as all manner of workmen and house wives began flowing into the streets. I saw men with axes, woodcutters I assumed, piling into things that I could only describe as land barges. They were too big to be called carts and besides the size, they didn't have wheels. They were strapped to the backs of those giant creatures that Lily had called lastkan trolls. Little, impish drivers cracked whips and the creatures lumbered away from poorly-marked loading stations.

It wasn't just woodcutters though. I saw every conceivable manner of medieval occupation. There were troops of armored guards patrolling the city over bridges and motley-dressed merchants hauling barrels over to stalls beneath tapestry-like awnings. I heard the clang of hammers and smelled burning coke. As Lily took us aboard one of the bizarre troll-buses of the city, my nose was stabbed by sewage but also tempted by bakeries and, as we approached the western sea, the scent of salt and of fish.

Everyone around us was talking, so much and so fast that I couldn't keep up even with the translation spell. Most was small talk, weather, greetings, jokes, and grumblings. Once, we saw a man leap from a second story balcony with nothing but a pair of silk shorts as a woman chucked stale bread at him and cursed him out in three different languages.

It finally, really, started to sink in that we were in a fantasy world, with magic and elves and who knew what else. Lance, Hilde, and I were all gawking like tourists, but I think I was the only one to notice Lily stealing uncertain glances at me. On some level, she blew me away even more than Alfheim. I could rationalize that because she had basically co-signed the contract with me, her ability to help pay the rent was critical to me seeing Alfheim but I knew that was just rationalizing. She had gone all on her own into Earth, following my demands and now here we were, barging around her city again following my demands.

I took my eyes off the rolling hills and slimy canals. I sat on the bench beside her. "I didn't even ask if you have classes or a job or anything."

"Not today, no," she answered. I saw her scan the crowd on the troll barge before she turned back with a smile. "Though, I have to admit that I'm getting pretty woozy, even with that energy drink."

"Oh, yeah. About that. Did you like my bed?"

She blushed. "You could probably sell that to a nobleman."

My bed was the cheapest mattress money could buy, short of a flat packed futon roll. "Well I do hear that mattress stores are a good way to launder money, but that might have just been a conspiracy theory... Speaking of, actually, are we allowed to bring things through?"

"I don't see why not?"

"We should check when we find our landlord. I've got some lucrative ideas. From what I can tell, this world is pre-industrial." Just about any trash from a dollar store could probably fetch a good price over here. I just had to figure out what the best option would be.

Then I noticed the way Lily was looking at me, and I remembered why I had brought that up in the first place. "Right.

I saw what you normally sleep on. Especially with our day and night apparently backwards, you can feel free to use my bed. It's nothing special but it's got to be better than a box of straw and rough blankets. If, for some reason, we're trying to use it at the same time, I can just crash on the couch."

"You know, right now, that actually sounds like the nicest offer someone has made to me in a long time," Lily said.

I almost missed the driver announce our stop.

8

～

Lily

Drithugel Manor looked like it had been cleaved in half. While the old wall still cut between it and the city, a newer wall separated the actual manor from what had been a private courtyard. About ten years ago, Lady Virent had made it a public access park and the landscaping had been deteriorating ever since. Some locals tried to tidy it up here and there, but the sheer damage the local children wrought on it was insurmountable.

Lily was staring at one particular tree, with a huge scar where a branch had once connected, when one of the butlers finally approached. The scar brought back memories of course, because she had been the one to break it, just about the year before her brother formed the Blutengels. The butler cleared his throat. "Should I say that Lily Hagen has come to pay a visit? Or the Iron Princess of the Blutengels?" the older man asked, his face lacking even a hint of sarcasm.

She spun on him with a scowl. "Since when are Lady Virent's servants so loose lipped?"

The man was unfazed. "My apologies. Could you please inform me as to the nature of your visit? My lady is quite busy today, very tight schedule. I'm sure you understand how it is."

She sighed. No one was particularly close to have overheard and even then, she knew she couldn't actually escape her brother's influence. Not in Alfheim at least. "She can spend all the time she wants at that dig site. I'm not here to see her at all."

"Then I hope you enjoy the park," the butler said, promptly turning away.

"Hey! That doesn't mean I'm not here on business!"

The butler bowed, his expression unchanged. "My apologies. But, if you aren't here for Lady Virent?"

John stepped up with a casual grin. He might have been close enough to overhear that, and yet he looked entirely ignorant of the disdainful look over the butler gave him. "An acquaintance of mine by the name of Thomas Smythe. He's the one we're here to meet. Could we get a message to him to come out or something?"

After a moment of awkward silence, Lily held out her hand and introduced him. "This is John. He is something of a business partner with me. I'd also like to see Mr Smythe."

There was a ripple through the butler's greying mustache that managed to give Lily the impression of him clicking his tongue at them, even though he didn't make a noise. "I'll see if we have such a guest available at this time," the man said, and left the two of them alone in the courtyard.

Lily sighed and slumped onto a bench in the shade beneath an oak tree. John followed after her, but didn't sit. He scanned the little expanse of nature around them. Lance had ended up on the opposite side of the park and seemed to be giving a child a ride on his shoulders. Lily could imagine how they had managed to communicate with pantomiming. "Wait, where'd the other one go?"

John glanced around too. "There," he said, pointing to where Hilde was standing on tip toes atop an old bench to peer over the dividing wall.

Lily groaned and forced herself back to her feet. "Hilde, are you trying to get arrested?" she asked as they walked over.

"I'm just looking!" she protested, not even turning around.

John asked, "What am I hearing right now?"

Lily inclined her head and listened to the clash of metal. "Sounds like sparring."

Hilde grinned down at them. "There's actual sword fighting. Not a fight, it's practice sparring. But it's real swords!"

Another energy drink sounded very good to Lily at that moment, even though the last one seemed to have left her a little extra parched. The ache at her temples was slightly peculiar for mere sleeplessness and it bogged down her thoughts. "There isn't an adult woman wearing a mask there, right?"

Hilde glanced again and said, "I'm not sure I'd call her adult, but yeah there's a woman in a mask."

"Get down!" Lily blurted. "That's Lady Virent you're spying on."

"Company," John said, stepping between the two of them and an approaching guard.

The house soldier eyed them over with an arched brow. "That's private property, you know."

Lily grabbed Hilde's wrist and yanked her down. With a quick bow, she said, "Sorry, she's new."

John crossed his arms with a shrug. "She's just a sword nerd. No harm intended."

The soldier nodded and hooked his thumb into his belt, but he didn't leave them be either. "I saw you were talking to Mr Fischer. I suppose you're probably waiting to hear back from him but I think I'll ask you to wait outside the park. That understood? The troll-man too."

John looked to Lily for direction. She sighed, lacking the energy to argue. "Just make sure Mr Fischer knows we're just outside?" she asked, and only got a noncommittal nod. While the idea of sitting back down on a bench sounded like bliss, she shuffled her way back to the main gate. John disentangled the children from 'the giant' while Hilde distracted a pair that looked like they might cry.

Lily yawned as John held out an arm with a small child refusing to let go of his elbow. "I'm not a tree, kid. Shouldn't you be helping your mother or something?"

The kid, with his feet dangling almost two feet off the ground, retorted, "I'm an orphan. Shouldn't you be at a job instead of flirting with girls?"

Anger flared up and blotted out her fatigue for a moment. She walked over and smiled at the brat, but she was well aware how forced her expression was. "You're an orphan? Around here that must be Old Lady Aruna's home, isn't that right? I happen to know her quite well. Should I go tell her what you've been up to this morning?"

Some of the color drained from the boy's ruddy face. "Who are you?"

"Me? I'm the Iron Princess of the Blutengels." While just about every rumor about her was unfounded, she most certainly was one of the orphanage's primary donors, or at least the Blutengels were. Her brother had been recruiting the older boys for years.

"Like hel–"

Without changing her smile, she plucked the handle of her corset blade and pulled it free just enough to let the boy see the edge while hiding it from John with her hand. "Try me." The boy dropped from John's arm and grabbed his friends. All of them gave quick and supplicating bows before scurrying away.

John rubbed his shoulder and asked, "What was that about?"

As she watched the kids run off, she realized she didn't really know why the comment had so gotten under her skin. "There's a cafe across the street," she said, heading out of the park.

9

⌇

John

"So, how are we supposed to pay?" Lance voiced the question on everyone's mind. Everyone's except Lily's. We were sipping mediocre black tea with no sugar, no honey, no nothing, while Lily's cup cooled off, untouched. We were getting side eyes from the waitresses meandering between tables. Everyone else getting their morning started was getting laughs and smiles in exchange for tips. My snooping had confirmed that everyone else was paying with these copper slugs that must have been a low denomination.

Thoughts of smuggling the copper back to Earth for scrap value aside, we humans had no local currency. The only one who did had put her arms on the table, buried her head, and fallen asleep on us. Since we were waiting for that Mr Fischer to show up anyway, we had intended to let her sleep as much as possible.

Then Lance finished his cup, and Hilde finished hers and

I was only pretending to drink mine. Obviously, we could just jostle her awake but I was uncomfortably aware of how long she had been awake and how little sleep she had gotten because of me. We should have let her nap. The fact that she had shown this much patience with us was remarkable and I really didn't want to return the kindness with anything less.

Theoretically, all we had to do was wait and let her pay for the tea–which couldn't be too expensive–until Mr Fischer came back to get us. Then I could meet with That Guy, get my phone back, and sort out some of the nuances of this rental agreement. It wasn't like I was going to go in screaming at him. As far as I could tell, while the portal was expensive, it was a pretty good deal. How exactly did you put a price on a portal to another world anyway? I could imagine that the central bankers would pay way more than me for such a portal and yet That Guy had offered it to me instead of oil sheiks.

Then a pair of men walked up to our table. One looked normal enough, an incubus I had to assume because he was in Alfheim and didn't have pointed ears. The other was blue and almost as large as Lance. It wasn't like I could say the other guy was ugly or stupid or anything in particular, but he had an enormous jaw like a Hapsburg and a sort of vacant look to his gaze. Both of them walked up to our table wearing reasonable clothes, which I tried to calibrate my brain to indicate that they were wealthy people. The poor people of Blue Rock Bay were in pretty rough linens, with single-stitched fabrics. Given that Alfheim was pre-industrial, everything had to be sewn by hand and that made enough sense to me.

Then the incubus sneered down his nose at me and asked, "Who the hell are you?"

I considered what I could say, and couldn't figure out anything good to say that was honest, so instead I sneered back and said, "What business is it of yours?"

Both Lance and Hilde seemed to catch on that the guy was being rude to us. Even if they didn't know what his words meant, as any scientist would say, most of communication was in body language and they understood that just fine. It only took a moment before they were sneering back at the two men looming over us. The incubus said, "If you're just her friend, you should get out of here, you twerp."

"Twerp?" I asked, and I felt myself gripping my tea cup tighter.

Lance leaned across the table to ask, "This doesn't seem friendly."

The incubus ignored him and made a shooing motion at me. "We're here on behalf of the Black Fingers. You understand what that means? Unless you want to make your life hell, get the hell out of here."

I motioned to Hilde and she started trying to wake Lily up, but it was a difficult challenge. I didn't take my eyes off the guy talking to us because I could see that he had a short sword strapped to his hips. It wasn't a proper weapon, not the kind of thing that would end up in museums about the medieval age, but it was perfectly lethal–I assumed. Working off the assumption that he was just some thug in the area, I glared back at him and said, "We're just here for a little bit. Why don't you give us some time?"

I didn't want to get in a fight, especially with someone armed when I wasn't. Double-especially when I didn't understand the criminal understandings of Blue Rock Bay. The only person at the table who might was passed out and not providing her opinion, but that just meant I had to not deliberately offend the locals. If we had intruded on someone's territory somehow, which I doubted because Lily would have said as much, we just had to give them a modicum of respect. We were just random people as far as they were concerned.

Then the incubus sneered down at me and said, "I told you to get lost. You and your oaf friend. Get out of here."

Lance perked up at that, catching the intent if not the meaning. He asked, "How do I say 'fuck off' in the local tongue?"

I ignored his request and reached over to grab Lily's shoulder. Before I could jostle her awake, I felt a hand on my own shoulder. The incubus grinned at me. "No, no. You and the guy leave. The girls can stay with us."

The emotion I felt had to be rage, but it wasn't fury. I was too calm for that. So, I gently took my hand off Lily and turned to face the thug. Then I stood up. Lance rose, facing the blue man. I had half a head of height over the incubus as I glared back at him. "How about you and your friend fuck off?"

Lance snorted. "That how you say it?" he asked, and repeated the elvish command.

The incubus stopped grinning at me. He looked downright morose as he shook his head. "You must work for her brother."

Then some homeless man sitting against the wall of the cafe shouted to ask, "If you're going to fight, why did you get so close to him? You've got reach, you should use it!"

All of us glanced over at the man. His clothes were in tatters and his beard was such a dirty mess I almost couldn't see a face beneath the brim of his hat. When I looked back at the incubus, I instinctively looked to his chest because we were almost bumping against one another. That was when I saw the knife in the guy's hand.

The incubus asked, "Do you want to be a part of—"

I sucker punched him. It was just a left-handed jab, I popped him in the cheek. The other people in the cafe scattered as I followed up with a right hook into his gut that drove him staggering back. Beside me, a table practically exploded as Lance slammed the blue man into it. Everyone was shouting and people leapt over chairs and tables to get away from the fight. That included Hilde and Lily. She was practically dragging the blonde away which let me put my focus back on the guy with the knife.

I had staggered him but not enough to make him drop the knife. Lance had been atop the blue man for a moment, hammering blows but now they were rolling into tables. I heard the serving girls screaming, not in fear but in rage. I half expected to get beat over the head with a broom as I focused on the knife like it was a hypnotist's coin. The incubus was snarling at me and swearing, but when he took a stab all he hit was air.

"Oh, just kick his knee out," the peanut gallery shouted.

And for a moment, the knifeman took his attention off me to shout at the homeless man.

I snatched his wrist and clamped hold of it. Then I kicked his knee out as hard as I could. Pain exploded in my shin but the thing that cracked wasn't inside me. The knifeman crumpled, his eyes bulging. The moment I felt him fighting my grasp though, I slammed my free fist into his nose. Blood gushed and I tried to punch him again. I only hit his elbow.

The incubus rolled back and I had to let go if I didn't want to end up in a grapple with a knife. I snatched up a chair instead, hefting it like I was ready to go into a wrestling ring with him. When he got to his feet, we snarled at each other. I was already breathing hard. Then his expression changed. The fight went out of him as he looked over my shoulder. A whistle blared behind me and the knife fighter dropped his blade. I saw him make a few glances but he didn't cut and run so I slowly put the chair back down. When he put his hands up and sighed, I finally turned around.

A half dozen chainmail wearing elves had surrounded the cafe. Most had truncheons in hand, one had a sword drawn. The man I assumed was the captain of the squad looked me over and asked, "Weren't you just in the manor park?"

"Hey, they attacked us."

The old man laughed and slapped his knee as the incubus spat blood out and said, "He threw the first punch."

The elf just rolled his eyes. "It's not even the evening. You're all sober. What is wrong with you?"

At that moment, Lily intervened. "We are so sorry. Things got out of hand when that man pulled a knife out. We can talk this out, can't we?"

The incubus snorted. "Can't a man defend himself when he's assaulted in broad daylight?"

"You're screwed now, kid," the guy with the dirty beard said. He had been sitting on a rain barrel, but slid off and wandered away, waving over his shoulder. Apparently, I had been mere entertainment for him.

I stepped closer to the guard, slowly and with my hands in the air. "Sir, if you'd been here, you'd understand. Any man would, I think. A couple of strange men show up and say to get lost and leave the girls for them? Them's fighting words as they say."

Lily turned around, her mouth slowly dropping open as her ears went red. The guard showed no reaction at all. "Take a look around you, idiot! You broke half the restaurant! You're under arrest and you'll be lucky if they can get even half this cost out of your sweat!"

Lily started talking so fast she sounded like a babble. I heard her trying to sum up the costs and make promises of paid installments. I almost made the mistake of offering to pay it off, before I remembered I only had US dollars. I cleared my throat and lamely asked, "Can I get a lawyer?"

One of the lower ranked guards stepped over and slugged me in the gut. While I was reeling and fighting to not vomit, they twisted my arms behind my back and started tying them together with rope. I tried to think of a way out of this, but I was way out of my depth and it seemed like even cooperating wouldn't keep them from beating the piss out of me.

Just before they hauled the four of us off, Lily stamped her foot and shouted, "I want to speak to Lady Virent!"

The guards paused, looked at her, and then continued arresting us.

10

~

Lily

This wasn't Lily's first run in with the law, not by a long shot. That did not make her an expert in it though. She didn't know who was on the pay, which judiciaries were lenient, none of that. She didn't need to know it. Not only was she known to be out of her brother's organization, but even before separating, the bribes were kept private. There were specific men employed in the organization to keep track of it all and she needed one of them fast.

"So, they're going to get let out, right?" Hilde asked. "You said most guards can't be bothered to actually arrest people. They just rough them up..."

Lily winced and glanced up and down the street again. She should have been able to spot whoever was tailing her, but she couldn't. Normally, they were very discreet but after that kind of commotion, someone should have been there for her. The fact that nobody was there made her feel very alone. She chewed her nail as her stomach twisted into a knot. When Hilde touched her shoulder, she said, "Normally, yes. Did you see the green sashes at their waist though? They're Lady Virent's personal guard."

"Then what are they doing arresting people?"

Lily arched an eyebrow for a moment, then shook her head. "She's allowed to. In fact, that's the exact problem. One of her duties is a prison warden and everyone knows they're desperate for more hands to press into service. Those people definitely will arrest and imprison without trial. I just didn't think we'd get into a fight on practically her front porch!"

Hilde planted her hands on her hips and said, "Well it was because of you!"

"How was it because of me?"

Hilde jabbed her finger into Lily's shoulder. "Get lost and leave the girls. That's what they said. Then they mouthed off about what big shots they were—"

"Black Fingers," the dirty traveler said. He had reappeared, leaning now against a street light. Lily had suspected previously, but now could clearly see he was missing an arm, which must have made him a beggar.

She suppressed her scowl of frustration and fetched her little coin purse from the folds of her dress. "You helped my friend. Thank you," she said, and tossed him a silver talon. That would be enough to get him cleaned up.

He snatched it from the air with a stupid grin. "Very kind of you, young lady. I'll happily hang onto this until your friend is tossed into the arena. I bet I can make a lot more betting on him again."

Lily rolled her eyes. "He's not going to the arena. Aren't you from around here?"

"Can't say that I am."

"He's going to be sent to the ruins of Pravati's Temple, like everyone else. Go use that to get yourself fed and cleaned up."

The man whistled and scratched his beard. Rather than leave though, he asked, "And here I thought you'd be worried about a gang of violent criminals coming after you."

Lily shook her head. Out of the corner of her eye, she spotted Mr Fischer finally emerging from the courtyard to look for them. "That's none of your business," she said, and gestured for Hilde to follow her over to the butler. "Is Mr Smythe here?"

The butler sighed. "I think it would be best if you came inside?"

Lily whispered a translation to Hilde and got an uneasy nod of agreement. Moments later, the two of them were left in a small sitting room in one of the corner turrets of the manor. They were just high enough to see over the wall and while no servant was given to them the room shared a fireplace through one of the walls. A tea kettle simmered, but she could only take a furtive glance to the room beyond the fireplace. It was too dim to tell what kind of room it was, or if anyone was in there.

Hilde peered out the window as she asked, "Is this Lady Virent going to meet with us?"

"I don't know," Lily said, going through the motions of pouring herself a cup of tea.

"Is this Mr Smythe going to be of any help?"

"I don't know."

"Well there has to be something we can do, right?"

"Let me think!" she snapped. After a moment, she dropped

into one of the old chairs and apologized. "Okay, worst case scenario here is they spend a day digging up rubble, more or less. I can get ahold of my brother and he can help."

Hilde seemed about to say something, but the door flew open first. An elf in a maroon robe carrying a goblet of wine barged inside, demanding, "What's with the long faces?" He grinned and kicked the door shut behind him.

Lily asked, "Mr... Smythe?" The man's face was different, elven, but she recognized the body language.

He grandiosely waved his goblet around and said, "Here, you can call me Mr Landlord, if you'd prefer. Certainly not my other name, if you please. Never quite know who's listening in places like this, now do you? Where's good old Johnny boy though? Off on an adventure already?"

Lily took a breath and stood back up. "You could say that. He just got arrested for getting in a fist fight with some thugs."

Mr Smythe, Loki, burst out laughing. "Well, I hope he won at least. Wait, arrested?"

"Excuse me," Hilde said, stepping over. "You're speaking English?"

"Möchten Sie, dass ich Deutsch spreche?" Loki responded.

Hilde winced. "Ich Deutsche nicht so gut."

Lily sipped her tea, listening as the translation spell worked overtime, and watching as her landlord almost swooned over the silver-haired woman. She asked, "Does Lady Virent know?"

Loki spun around with a grin. "She does not. Wonderful, isn't it? I've got a whole fake identity cooked up to be right under their noses. I must say though, it's a shame your room-mate got this close and then got... pulled away while I was in the bath."

Lily didn't see a speck of moisture on him. "Are you able to help? Or do I need to find my brother?"

He turned to her with a very serious and dour look. "Lily, I'd like to think that before I was your landlord, I was your friend. A family friend even." He had known her family for centuries, technically. "And it would be very hard for John to pay his half of the rent if he's digging holes, now wouldn't it? Lady Virent will be here shortly, I think, and I will do my utmost to persuade her to leniency."

"She's on her way?" Lily asked.

He winced. "Yes, but not because of you. She's coming because of the man in the other room," he said, pointing toward the fireplace. After Lily and HIlde exchanged a glance, he strolled over to the adjoining door and threw it open. A scant bit of light passed into the gloom, but he opened a lantern to flood the disused drawing room.

Lily stopped halfway through the door. There was a corpse laid on the table. She recognized the man. Not well, but enough to know he worked for her brother. A member of the Blutengels had been stabbed through the throat, given a bib of blood. Her hand reflexively went to the knife hidden in her dress, but she only squeezed it as she composed herself. "That... explains that."

Hilde gasped and turned away, getting a comforting hand on her shoulder from Loki. The god wasn't fazed by the death, inured over the ages as he was. "The guards found him round the corner just a little bit ago. Given the circumstances, I think there's a relatively strong case for self-defense. What do you think?"

Lily pushed herself over to the man and began checking the

corpse over. She didn't need to identify the cause of death, that was plain enough. She even spotted the part on his vest where they wiped the blade clean. That would give a good measure of the blade size. She made a mental note to bring that up as evidence. While it was just the three of them, she slipped her hand into the man's pockets to make sure he didn't have anything on him Lady Virent shouldn't get. She didn't find anything, which should have been obvious to her. When she had asked to leave the group, her brother had done everything he could to accommodate that. There was just the obvious issue that she was still, and forever would be, a target to get to him. Thus, a security detail that was meant to stay out of her business. Nowhere in Alfheim was safe, and she had just gotten John nearly killed. She wanted to go running to Earth and never come back. She wasn't so childish to think she could actually do that, but she chewed her lip until she bled regardless.

She definitely had to make things right, and get John out of prison. Lance too.

Hilde stood against the wall, one hand covering her mouth to hide her trembling. "Those thugs at the cafe were literally killers? Just what the hell were they doing there?"

Loki said, "Technically speaking, they were doing politics. A very crude sort I must say. I meant to say this to John, but you'll have to suffice miss..."

"Hilde."

"What a traditional name! I can see already how you were drawn into this. I surmise you're my new renter's friend? I'm quite certain he would have mentioned you if you were dating."

Hilde scoffed. "He's my brother's friend, but we're on good terms and all that. This just sort of happened."

"Then, I shall entrust this with you," Loki said as he pulled a disassembled phone out of his robe pocket and handed it to her. "Do not power it on. Computers break over here, but so long as there's no charge then it's just a bunch of silicon and metal. Really though, I thought we'd have a day or so to at least plan. I didn't want to spoil the adventure of exploring the city and all that. I must insist you realize how different personal protection is treated over here though. I know back at d'Amaranth University, you can get expelled if they catch you with a weapon and all that, but here? My dear, if you don't have at least a knife you're just asking for trouble. You're at the mercy of those around you! And if you don't have pointed ears then the guards are of very little use."

A spark of realization struck Lily and she spun about to face the god. "Hold on, isn't this weird? I thought most of the Black Fingers had been arrested recently? By Lady Virent no less? How do they have the manpower and the balls to do something like this?"

The door swung open and Lady Virent stepped through. "A very good question. Desperation perhaps?" She was a high elf. Anyone could tell at a glance. Even if the lacquered mask didn't give it away, nor the extended length of her ears, then it would be in her posture. Upright, but graceful. She glided into the room in a way that exuded authority right until she wrapped her arms around Lily. "I always forget how much you've grown!"

Lily awkwardly spied over Lady Virent's shoulder and saw Hilde hiding the phone in her skirt. Loki also seemed unfazed, so she eased up a bit. "Auntie, you know we grow up faster than you elves. I'm not a kid."

Lady Virent released her, but kept her hands on Lily's shoulders. "You're only twenty! Even by demi-human standards you're a child."

"Am not!"

"I suppose you're right. No child would be composed next to a corpse of a man they knew. I'm sorry."

Lily slumped and apologized. Loki laughed, forcing life back into the conversation quite intentionally, or so it seemed. He had a jester's mirth as he gestured with his wine. "Would that matters not be so serious all the time. We might actually have peace in this city, cousin."

Lady Virent sighed and planted her hands on her hips. It made her dueling saber wave, which seemed to capture Hilde's attention completely. In fact, the human appeared to be sizing up every part of the elf's outfit. The high elf was in military dress, which meant a green tailcoat and double layered pants tucked into leather riding boots. It probably seemed far more in line with Earth fashion than the dress she had on. Lily could only shake her head as Hilde subconsciously tugged the hem of her skirt down a little more. "You're not hurt, are you, Lily? Your brother's rival groups are so troublesome to deal with. They are like a morphing chimera, latching onto one revenue stream after the next whenever we find a way to squeeze them and if we get too rough then they run wild with incendiary pamphlets, shooting their recruitment up faster than we can arrest them."

The look on Hilde's face changed, her eyes narrowing and focusing on Lily. She realized she'd have to explain everything sooner rather than later, but while in private. "I'm fine, Auntie. Actually, the entire reason that I'm fine is because of my friends and business partners. They're the ones that got in the fight with those men and your guards locked them up too." She stared up at Lady Virent with the most child-like, innocent expression she could muster.

One of the most powerful nobles in the realm cracked on the spot. "I'll see what I can do to get your friend out. What's his name?"

"John, and the large man is Lance."

Loki slipped around to say, "You'd like him, actually. Wickedly smart, even with a flagon of wine in him. He's got a mind like a scholar, the body of a warrior, and a whole world of possibilities ahead of him. Get him out and he'll be quite in your debt. Wouldn't even bat an eye at solving some of those mechanical problems I know you've been having."

Lady Virent said, "I wasn't aware you knew him as well... cousin."

Loki snickered. "Actually, I only met him a night ago, but he came very highly recommended."

Who had recommended him, Lily never learned because the two elves, at least by appearance, headed back into the hall after some promises of hospitality. Maids came in to escort Lily and Hilde to proper rooms and a pair of guards stepped in to see to the corpse. For the moment, they had to wait.

11

∾

John

I had been robbed. Abused, lied to, and robbed. With no trial, no investigation, no judicial process whatsoever, the elves had tossed me into a fenced off ruin along with dozens of other imprisoned workers–no better than slaves. The whole place was nothing but toppled stone, charred debris, and throat parching ash. I hadn't understood what was going on at first because no one explained anything. There were just people milling about, or shoveling dirt into carts. I saw two men pretending to dig out one of the foundation blocks, almost directly under the gaze of a squadron of crossbowmen who apparently didn't care that they were faking the work.

Or maybe they didn't care enough to realize the work was being faked.

The dig site was a furnace beneath the sun, which beat down on me with a nearly tropical force. Everywhere I looked, exposed stone radiated heat and if a man happened to be sweating nearby, I could see the wavering haze of steam boiling off of him and his toil. What was worse, the only food and water was controlled by what amounted to a prison quartermaster who very brusquely explained the commerce of the dig site.

If we wanted water, we needed to bring either one block, or ten buckets of dirt to the dumping lot. If we wanted food, it was five blocks or fifty buckets. If we didn't want to work, then we wouldn't be fed. An elegant system to say the least.

For the first few hours, Lance and I just sat in a spot of shade wondering if help would come rescue us. Then we convinced each other that it would be worth the effort to get some water, before we sweated ourselves to death. That was when we learned that the bucket counter was corrupt. Just glancing around the dig site–even if I hadn't figured out what had burned down in the first place–I could tell that most of the men were in some kind of alliance. Prisons always had gangs, that was common sense. Thankfully, there was no hazing we had to go through, probably because of all the armed guards watching us.

Until we realized that twenty buckets of dirt shoveled out of the debris and brought to the next yard over only counted for ten, because we hadn't packed them to overflowing. Instead, we had filled them up just as much as anyone else and pointing that out got us nowhere. The other prisoners were older or had been there longer, or were more famished than us, or any other excuse the bastard felt like coming up with.

Ten was enough for one of us to get a water ration though, which Lance gave to me. There was something off about the taste, and I prayed it wouldn't send me to the latrines. Still, it revitalized me enough that we set about bringing one 0f the foundation blocks over. I could hardly understand how they had collapsed, but it must have been from the fire. The only other explanation I could understand was that the imprisoned workers had knocked them down willfully. It took some straining, some leveraging with a crude shovel, and finally an improvised pulley, but we pulled the block out of the cement-like ashen mud and got it onto a cart. They couldn't talk their way out of giving Lance his drink.

For a while after that, I meandered through the digsite, trying to find someone who would talk to me about how I could get a hearing with the warden. The prisoners ignored me. The guards laughed. After a while, I found myself sitting upon a crudely exposed mosaic near the center of the dig site. Given the rough layout of stones, I figured it must have been the center of the prayer hall, if it was anything like a Christian church.

The image of the mosaic seemed something like a star, and it took me a moment to realize the inslaid and inscribed circles and geometries had been constructed of gold. If it had been silver, I would have thought it was some kind of magic circle, rather than a mere prayer device, but maybe that was foolish of me.

Around the time the sun was directly overhead, I found Lance again, sitting next to the blue skinned thug that had attacked us of all people. They both had wooden mugs and were grunting a conversation to one another. I had figured we were lucky that no one had bothered to check in our pants and see that we didn't have tails like all the other workers, and doubly lucky no one had noticed Lance couldn't speak elvish, but here he was faking it.

"Making friends?" I asked, eyeing the drink. It wasn't the water we had gotten earlier.

Lance nodded and gestured to the blue man. "This is Molsen."

The blue man nodded. "You fought well," he said, with an ambiguous sneer.

"Black Finger," Lance said, pointing to the blue man, then he repeated it while pointing to several dozen other prisoners. When he stopped, he had pointed out almost two thirds of the people around us. The idea of spending the night in the dig site was starting to sound like a death sentence.

"How is it that you accomplished more than I did, but I'm the one that speaks the language?"

Lance shrugged and scratched the stubble on his chin. "Yeah, about that. I've been listening the whole time, you know? You say you're speaking elvish but it sounds like mangled German to me, mixed up with a bit of something else. And if you think about it, doesn't that kind of make sense? It's not like the people who came here a few centuries ago would have just abandoned their own languages, right? I think I've figured the basics out and it's not like Molsen here is speaking poetry or something."

Taking a gamble, I crouched next to the blue man. He was staring at the dig site with a listless expression, like he was stoned or might nod off in a moment. I asked, "Can't the four of us just agree to not press charges against each other?"

"Three of us," he said. "Ricky ain't here. Ricky had the knife. Ricky went to the arena."

Lance said, "Gladiators."

I said, "Well, let's not also do that."

Lance laughed. "Oh come on, that could be fun! Better now while we're fresh than after a week of labor. Don't you think? We could win our freedom!"

"We haven't even been formally charged. We don't have a sentence. They're just detaining us arbitrarily right now. Obviously, I'm hoping Lily can do something on the outside for us but holy crap; don't we get a lawyer or something?"

Another man walked up to us and said, "Not very fair, is it?"

I immediately sniffed danger, but I couldn't sense if I was the one in danger or if I was useful to put someone else in danger. The feeling was complex to say the least, or perhaps I was just wary of men that looked like generic salesmen. The last one had trapped me in a contract for a magic portal afterall. This particular fellow was on the shorter side. His skin tawny and his hair already graying. His mouth never stopped smiling, which stretched his early wrinkles almost into a jester's grin but maybe he was just an affable guy.

"I've been in a lot nicer drunk tanks," I said, rising to meet him.

The newcomer swept his arm around the dig site prison. "It's dehumanizing, isn't it?" he asked, taking in all the other prisoners we were sweating beside. "Don't you think it's insulting that they have basically enslaved us to dig out a relic our people very deliberately tried to keep out of elven hands. At the least they should be digging it out themselves, no?"

I could surmise that the temple, before it had burned down, had been for the demi-humans. What a relic was could be anything from a magic weapon to a pinky bone of a saint. I said, "The management seems very strange, to be honest. If the workers here neglect their duty, they will go hungry, which at first will motivate them to work. But if they miss two days—because of sickness perhaps, or injury—then they are two days unfed. You can't dig like a healthy man on an empty stomach like that. The most you can do is try to survive. You'll end up like... that guy." I pointed to a nearly skeletal man with gray whiskers down past his shoulders.

"I couldn't agree more," the man said, crossing his arms and nodding along. "In fact, we've been organizing a bit of a slow down, almost a strike. The idea has been to stretch the dig to the breaking point until we had an edge."

"An edge?"

He nudged me. "An innocent man to twist their conscience."

I gave him a leery gaze. "What is this, a prisoner's union?"

He shrugged. "Would that be a bad thing? We have rights, don't we? We're living men, afterall. More than that, we are providing utility to these captors. If we weren't here then all those guards would have to break their backs to get this done. I say that gives us some negotiating power."

He made a fair amount of sense, and I found myself nodding along. "I guess that depends on what you're trying to negotiate for."

"Oh, nothing much! Nothing much at all!" he said, throwing his arm around me as best he could. Our height disparity made it difficult, but he carried on confidently. "You see, the warden comes almost every day, and she's been ignoring our demands thus far. You're new. A new face, new consideration. You can help us!"

"And you'll get me a hearing with the warden?"

"With Lady Virent? On my honor, or my name's not Hanz Grimner," he said, sticking his hand out. Hesitantly, I shook.

He spoke for what felt like an hour, but the sun hadn't budged much by the time one of the guards started banging a little, iron gong. He had been giving me a big sales pitch the whole time and probably would have made for a good cult leader if he became so inclined, but I was a bad audience for him. He kept referencing the conditions in the city which I really knew nothing about. All I could do was pretend like I was a local because he was the one that was going to get me in front of the prison warden.

Some of the prisoners meandered over to one of the gates, where the gong was being rung. The whole area had been walled off with crude fencing. The gate didn't even have a hinge let alone a lift like a portcullis. Most of it reminded me of Roman military fortifications, but an illustration couldn't compare and the ancient Romans certainly didn't have a fifteen foot troll on hand to pull the gate out from the dirt for them.

One of the guards tossed the troll what looked like a bloody sack of fur. It happily snatched it and started gorging itself on the entrails of some animal as the elven procession strolled in. The guards that came in, flanking a woman, were of a different breed. Straight backed, sharp eyes, hands resting on swords, and very clearly signaling they had no interest in talking things out. The woman in the center had to be the warden, Lady Virent apparently. She was the only one wearing a mask. While the other elves had metal visors, she had an ornamental piece fit for a theater stage except it had a neutral expression rather than a caricature. Between that, and rolling brown hair past her shoulders, she fit the description.

"Line up. There's a man here I'm looking for!" she snapped, and her cadre of soldiers spread out in front of the mass of prisoners. Everyone started shuffling into something approximating a line until I felt a shove against my back and stumbled forward.

Hanz sauntered out beside me with his hands in his pockets and a grin on his face. "I am honored that you've finally taken the time to notice our plight!"

Everyone was looking at us, both wary prisoners and confused elves. I scanned the crowd behind me and spotted Lance, watching with a frown. He eased his way up front as I turned to see Lady Virent sizing the man up. "Who are you?" she asked.

Hanz chuckled and strolled before the crowd. He raised his voice for everyone to hear and barely looked at her as he spoke. "Hanz Grimner, and I think I speak for most people when I bring up just how inefficient and unjustly this place is being ran."

For some reason, the elf locked her eyes on me. "And you're with him?"

I didn't know what else to say but, "More or less?"

"For how long?" she asked.

The whole crowd seemed to get awkwardly silent as I answered, "Earlier today?" I didn't honestly know how long he had been talking to me. "He said he could get me out of here."

The elf lifted her head up, glaring down at me like I was human scum. "He can't get you out of here. Only I can do that. And please, rest assured, lying scum like you... I have better places to put you than a low-security labor camp."

"Excuse me?" I asked, and even Hanz suddenly separated himself from me.

The elf turned and pointed at me. Speaking to her guards, she said, "Bring him, him, and… him to the arena," she ordered, somehow singling Lance out from the crowd.

"Excuse me, what?" I begged.

"We're here to negotiate!" Hanz begged.

"I don't know what she said," Lance said as he was shoved out from the crowd.

For some reason, the masked elf turned back to glare at me and added, "Lying bastard." And then for the second time that day, I was cuffed and forced into an armored carriage to be hauled across the city to places unknown and I severely regretted trying to cooperate with Hanz. The silver lining was he looked even more broken and despondent than we did.

12

~

Lily

Lily had slept blissfully in one of Lady Virent's guest rooms. Hilde hadn't done quite so well, but both of them eventually were rested and ready for the day properly. The day, at that point, consisted of the evening and the looming night, but at least for Hilde it was the equivalent of waking up early.

The two of them were dressed and taking a quiet dinner—which Lily was pleased to see impressed the Earther—when secondhand news came in about John. One of the butlers stepped inside and stiffly told them, "It seems that your friend has shown his true colors after detainment. I regret to inform you that he is in fact a conspirator with the Black Fingers and has since been transferred to the gladiatorial arena."

Lily dropped her spoon back into her bowl of seafood stew as she stared at the butler. Obviously John could not have been working for the Black Fingers. He had never set foot in Alfheim before. Loki was nowhere to be found however and there was no chance she could explain a magic portal to another realm given the circumstances.

Thus, as the sun began to set, she found herself collapsed in one of the viewing chairs at the arena, in Lady Virent's booth but without Lady Virent. Lily was barely able to muster the willpower to watch the fights occurring beneath them. In fact, a form of low grade despair made her sag into the thin cushions and stop thinking. Being kept up all night also had a say in the matter. The opening trumpet blasts made Lily open her eyes and feel the aches in her body. She had slumped over on the couch. She remembered it had felt so soft, but after who knew how many hours, it felt like stone. She grumbled and began shifting about, stretching limbs and wiggling toes–her shoes were discarded in front of her. First she noticed that a blanket had been put over her, which surely put her into a deeper sleep than she had planned.

Pyoter, the old veteran who had replaced the poor fellow who had been murdered, was reading a book next to the door into the private booth, quite primly dressed in a shirt and vest. Most people would never expect the sheer volume of knives he had hidden about his wiry body. "No sign of the boy yet, princess." The Blutengels had moved out in force to retaliate against the Black Fingers, despite the men responsible already being imprisoned, but his presence gave Lily a sense of security nonetheless.

"Don't call me that," she grumbled.

"Would you care to watch the opening fights? There are some honor duels I think. Private affairs to whet the appetites of everyone."

Her head ached and just looking at Hilde's rapt attention

on the spectacle made her feel doubly hung over even though she had barely drunk anything. Fatigue alone was making her ill. "Just some water."

Pyoter snapped his book shut and strode across the room to the liquor cabinet. The actual stores of spirits were low, but servants had provided a carafe of water and an amphora of house wine. Private booths had certain privileges. He poured her a cup and brought it over before resuming his post at the door.

The water helped, but as soon as she heard one of the duelists shouting and their weapons clanging, she remembered what had brought them to the arena. She bit her lip, staring at the bottom of her cup, and she must have shifted somehow.

Hilde rose and walked over to the booth's bannister with a carefree grin on her face. She stretched her arms overhead and had the energy to do a twirl and that seemed to confuse her. "That's funny. I feel really good. Maybe that's just because today is a Sunday and I'm not hungover?"

Lily winced. The two of them had technically shared a bed, even if it had been large enough for four people and she was reasonably certain they had kept to their own sides. It had really just been a nap. Even Pyoter seemed to notice something was wrong with the pep in Hilde's step. The human looked as perky as if she had gotten a full night's rest.

At some point Lily was going to have to explain what was going on, but the more she could delay that, the more she would.

"Should I ask why a god is following you, Lily?" Pyoter asked as she stood up.

She stopped short of putting her shoes on. "Which?"

"The one-armed one."

Lily blinked. Hilde was listening, but if the Earthling understood anything, Lily couldn't say. The human had moved to the balcony to watch the fights. Lily dropped her voice and moved closer to Pyoter. "You mean that traveler?"

He nodded. "Finnegan noticed him at the dig site too, lingering around. He might be working with the Hindi. Unless you know otherwise, you need to be careful. That dig site is filled to the brim with our enemies, and I wish I could say that was a good thing for us but we don't know why so many have allowed themselves to be arrested."

Lily could think of a much more plausible explanation why a god would be sniffing around her roommate and his friends, but not one that she wanted to share with her brother's underling. On top of that, she felt like an idiot for not realizing who that dirty traveler had been when they met. "Keep him away from me, will you?"

"Of course. What's a god going to do anyway? He's probably just here to gamble. It's something of his specialty afterall."

Lily joined Hilde at the balcony and looked around the stadium. The lower seats were filling up quickly, more people squeezing in or sneaking through back entrances. The arena had been subdivided to five slices, loosely marked out by lines in the sand. Armed guards stood about the fights, making sure the separations were respected and stepping in to stop a fight whenever mercy was called for.

"These fighters aren't very good," She said, leaning with both arms crossed on the balcony. It was an eye-catching posture but, with ten rows of seats between the ring and their box, no contestant was likely to call for her favor.

"Why do you say that?"

"They're stiff. They stand up straight. They're hacking at one another's faces mostly. Is there a problem of honor about cutting your opponent's leg?"

Lily checked the remaining fights, seeing Hilde was right. "So you don't wear pants for nothing."

Hilde's face flushed. "Why do you keep bringing that up?"

Lily snickered. "Relax, it's not exactly lady like of me to see it as well. By the way, I'm not going to be expected to wear pants over on your side, am I?"

"You'll be able to wear pants, but nobody is going to make you, except maybe the cold weather."

"That's what socks are for."

Hilde rolled her eyes. "If you can find socks thick enough, I'll be impressed. Even my athletic socks leave me shivering. But you know what? I want to see you pull it off... with the four of us... We're going to be able to do that, right?"

Lily winced and forced herself to nod. "Look, the way this works is they send out the new arrivals for friendly matches first. Just light clubs so they can show what they're made of for real betting the next day. The bookies would riot if it went any other way. Your brother and John might get some bruises, but nothing serious is going to happen to them before everything closes down for the night and we can explain the misunderstanding to Lady Virent."

"Can we trust her?" Hilde asked.

"Her heart's in the right spot," Lily said. Lady Virent was the only high elf in the city that had been open to legal equity with demi-humans prior to the more successful military actions by groups like the Blutengels. She had always been a reasonable person, even if her first obedience was to the king. It certainly helped that all of her business occupations were almost completely supported by the lower classes. Everything was just a simple misunderstanding because Lady Virent thought John had betrayed Lily, and that could be cleared up.

"They're coming out," Hilde said, pointing to where a new batch of prisoners were emerging from the gates. The guards marched them over to the viewing boxes and announcers started their spiels about upcoming bouts. The headline would be a river dragon, but that didn't matter.

Lily bent over the railing and squinted her eyes, not believing what she saw. While the crowd was exactly as she had described, a bunch of dirty prisoners with clubs and shields, John and Lance could be seen in the middle. They did not have clubs. John had a spear and Lance had a battle ax. The blood drained out of Lily as she struggled to accept what she was looking at.

"Lily, that doesn't look right."

Lily sank to her knees. John and Lance were going to get killed. The only reason they would have actual weapons would be if they were being put into a live fight. She couldn't imagine what named gladiator would accept a show bout against two nobodies though.

Pyoter leaned against the bannister and crossed his arms. "Are your friends gullible?" he asked.

"Ignorant."

Pyoter clicked his tongues. "Bastards," he said. Hilde shot him a reproachful glare and he corrected himself. "Not them, the organizers. They need volunteers for the exhibition matches, so they offer time off sentences. Ignorant newcomers are easy prey."

Lily pulled herself back up and stared down at John and Lance awkwardly waving to the crowd. They kept glancing at the men around them until the guards starting shooing everyone back inside the gates. The two of them were going to die and she couldn't even think of what she could do to help. The gears in her mind slipped and sputtered and left her numb.

"They're going to get eaten by a monster," Lily said.

Hilde winced. "They have to fight an animal? I thought you said it would just be a show off thing?"

"So did I."

"Well, what kind of animal?"

Lily shrugged, watching in vain as the other prisoners were returned to the sands for their individual bouts. John and Lance were nowhere to be seen. "I don't know, a few wolves maybe. I'm afraid they're going to be fed to the dragon though."

"Like a big, flying, fire breathing thing?"

Lily let out a weak laugh. "No, the river dragon. No fire. Just, like, a couple thousand pounds of muscle, scale, and teeth. They eat horses, you know?"

"So, more dangerous than a horse. We talking like a puma? A hippo? Or a bear?"

The translation spell just made Lily more confused as it tried to supply her brain with what a hippo was. "What? Hold on, shouldn't it be puma, bear, hippo? Hippos are more dangerous than bears."

"Well, yeah if you're talking about a scaredy cat black bear. But what about a grizzly?"

"Hilde, hippopotamuses are several thousand pounds of muscular, territorial herbivore."

Hilde frowned and rubbed her chin. "Well, this dragon

sounds kind of like a hippo. This is fine. You see, if they had told Lance to kill a person to survive, he probably would have let himself get stabbed. But an animal? He won't lose to an animal."

"Your faith awes me."

Hilde clicked her tongue and pouted. "I'm not the only one," she said, and hooked her thumb over her shoulder.

Lily followed the line and saw, practically beneath their viewing box in the stadium seating, the one-armed man hollering at the nearest bookies. "Let it ride, baby! I said let it ride. Put it all on the spear boy!"

Lily grimaced, looking at what should have been a proud god. A war god no less. Her eyes shot open when she realized what she was looking at. "Hey!" she hollered, almost throwing herself over the bannister. The bookie, a greased up rakshasa squeezed into a suitcoat, pounced over heads to face her. "Put it all on spear boy!" she shouted, chucking her own coin purse down to the ape demon. Then she glared at the one-armed god. "And you! Get up here!"

The god turned away from her, twisting a finger in his ear and pretending to not hear her as he squeezed through the crowd and moved closer to the gates.

Lily fumed. "Pyoter, get that man for me!"

He shrugged and bowed. "I'll let the guards know," he said, and headed out the door.

Hilde headed over to the liquor cabinet and poured two goblets of wine. "You sure you're not a princess or something?"

Lily glowered as she took the drink. "They just call me that to tease me."

"But they take your orders."

"He works for my brother is all. This isn't exactly a safe city."

"So I noticed," Hilde said as they sat back down. "Still, I would have thought John would be a bit smarter than this. A lot of book smarts and no street smarts, as they say."

"This is my fault," Lily said, sinking into her chair and gazing into the ruby wine.

"Trust me," Hilde said with a smirk. "You had nothing to do with John being a bit of an idiot. Just because he can ace an exam and is going to be rich when he gets a job doesn't mean he's not an idiot. My primary evidence? He's single. Oh? You were wondering about that, weren't you?"

Lily's face burned, but she had to admit the change in thoughts was a welcome one. "Well, I kind of figured he didn't have a lover in his life. A normal man would have mentioned that long before we made it into Blue Rock Bay. It can be a delicate question to ask though, can't it? I mean, if he did have a wife, what would she say about the two of us living together?"

Hilde's laugh was more like a snort, and she hid her face until she could suppress it. "The guy can't even land a date. Personally, I blame the J-pop idols he watches online."

"J-pop idols? He likes cute girls that can sing... okay, I guess that sounds pretty obvious when I put it that way," Lily said before letting out a wistful sigh. She slumped deeper in her chair and thought about the world beyond the portal, a technological wonderland where nobody knew her. John had made for a wonderful guide, setting aside the two of them had to pay the rental fee. The fact that she couldn't do anything about his fate had her almost grinding her teeth. One by one, the duels were getting cleaned up and bets paid out. For a moment, she imagined how it might play out if she were to charge down to the holding cells, but she'd never make it past the guards. The only thing she could do now was have faith.

13

∾

John

Lance paced the sandy room, holding a huge headed battle ax that must have weighed ten pounds and he couldn't take his eyes off of it. "Okay man," he said, "I know this is incredibly dangerous and we might both die right now, but come on. This is really fucking cool."

"Lance, if you wanted to fight with axes, we could go to a LARP. We are literally about to die."

"Nah, have you seen these people? This is like, dark ages man. We're both like six inches taller than their big people and properly fed."

I scoffed. "If high fructose corn syrup counts."

Lance swung the weapon around and pointed it at me. "Hey, don't you besmirch the glory of HFCS. How else would fast food be delicious? Besides, don't you eat a diet of chicken and energy drinks?"

"Point taken. But we're not fighting other people. We're in the monster exhibition."

He shrugged and grinned, putting the ax on his shoulder. "Okay, sure, but like, I've always thought that a monster probably can't be any more dangerous than, like, a pack of hungry wolves, right? And I can fight a pack of hungry wolves."

We were going to die, and my family would never know. I was pretty sure I was about to get torn to shreds for the entertainment of elves, then the portal would shut off. Hilde would be trapped here with Lily. I couldn't even take out my phone and try to contact the fucking god who got me into this mess and beg for help.

It felt like I was lurching from one stupid mistake to the next. I didn't know how to talk my way out of a fight over here, or maybe the first mistake was that I had gotten it into my head that fighting strangers was ever a good idea. I still couldn't believe my own reaction. Then I had fallen in with the wrong prison gang because I thought I could cooperate precisely long enough to smooth talk the warden but that had gone completely sideways in ways even the prisoner couldn't believe. Then Lance had demanded we do whatever necessary to not fight other prisoners and here we were. About to get eaten by a dragon as the reward for this stupid adventure.

This was exactly what happened to my brother. Well, probably not the part about getting teleported to another world. He had gone off though, something bad had happened, and then he had vanished without a trace.

Workers pulled the gates open. The heavy wood scraped between stone and sand and the sun glared down at us. The gust of heat dried out my throat and the crowd shouted for us to come out. I glanced back, but there was no going back unless I wanted to eat a crossbow bolt from the guard. "Jesus Christ... fuck, Jesus probably isn't even in this world."

Lance laughed. "Jesus technically isn't back on Earth either, right?"

"Man, I have so many fucking questions about how gods apparently work, and I'm not going to get any answers because I'm going to die here."

He clapped me on the shoulder. "Nonsense. You'll get plenty of answers after you die!"

That didn't make me feel better in the least. Picking up both a spear and a sword, not knowing which would be better, and marching out with my head held high sort of made me feel better. The arena was small, far smaller than the coliseum. There were four stone pillars the size of a boxing arena, a bit of space around them with high walls trapping us in a circle. Gamblers leaned over and shouted, the noise melding together into raw noise like an overclocked processor with an off-kilter fan.

There was no announcer, not for us. We were just sacrifices that no one cared about. The guards had even told us to not bother saluting or saying anything. Too many prisoners had used the chance to insult the lords, so that right had been taken away. Workers shut the gate behind us and then scrambled up rope ladders to get out of the way as hype began to grow. My heart was thumping in my ears as I edged into the sandy pit. I felt like some kind of game piece being shoved onto the board for the entertainment of the elves. The bloody patches of mud scattered around us were no game and pretty soon I was going to be one of them.

My one adventure and I was going to get ripped apart.

"Hey kid," someone said, and I caught his words because they were in English. I spun and saw a middle-aged man leaning over the arena wall, grinning at me. It was the homeless looking guy from the cafe. "Want another hint?"

"Yes, please."

"When it charges, it's going to break that spear, but it's still worth using. Then, no wind up. You don't need to wave a sword like a damn hammer. Just woosh, in for the kill."

I blinked and he was gone. Not magically gone, but sucked back into the crowd so fast I almost thought I had imagined him. I staggered away almost in a daze but suddenly I felt like I had a plan. Plans meant there was a chance they would work, and therefore that I would survive.

A scrawny elf leapt up to a little podium facing the rich people's booth. I had no idea who was watching us probably get killed, but it was easy to see they were rich because they had space to spread their fat asses. "It is time!" the elf shouted, lifting his head and straining his neck to scream over the roar. "For the Fight of Fate! Against! The Demon Of The Nile! A RIIIIVERRR DRAGON!"

Lance and I glanced at each other. We didn't need to say a word to know the other was shitting themselves at the word dragon. We only had a moment before the gate opposite us was pulled open. First thing I heard was the creaking of hemp rope, then the snorting of a monster within. The arena workers didn't even wait to get the gate fully open before they panicked and scrambled out.

The dragon let itself enter the arena. The thing smashed nose first into the wooden doors and threw them open like a boar. I saw the tusks and the blackened horn emerge first, protruding from scaled flesh. The thing jerked forward again and I heard some shouting and panic inside. The head emerged, large as a horse's and nearly as tall. Green like a crocodile, save for the black leather harness from which mooring lines tried to hold it back. One by one they went slack, its restrainers evidently giving up. The river dragon prowled out, serpentine body wiggling with each step as it snorted and sniffed.

Eyes like onyx fixed on us as they shut the gate behind it.

A trumpeter blasted as I scrambled to brace the butt of my spear against the ground and level the steel tip at it. There was almost an entire foot of blade at the end, enough to lop a man's head off, but it suddenly felt entirely insufficient. I needed a lance. I needed a fucking cannon.

"Looks like a crocodile mixed with a rhino," Lance said, giving his ax a twirl.

"Both of those things are man killers! This is at least twice as bad!"

"Oh, calm down, John. If you panic your brain will be useless."

"Why don't you use this damn spear then!"

"Nah, I need to hamstring it. Good luck bro, I know you can do it," he said, taking one big step to my side. Then he smacked the back of his weapon against a stone pillar.

He may as well have rung a dinner bell, because the river dragon sprinted like a drag car. The sand beneath it spewed backwards as it thundered forwards. I wanted to drop and run but there was nowhere to run and the spear was my only damn chance so all I could do was scream back at it. My heart pounded, my head swam, my senses slowed down in the panic and I saw it swing tusks at me.

In my mind a memory flashed: Hilde shouting, "Circle six!" There was no possible way she could have been in the audience screaming at me. It was just a memory, had to be. That one day taking fencing lessons from her just happened to pop in my head because the way the dragon twisted its snout to smack the spear away looked similar.

So, I responded with a circle six parry, a little flick twirl of the tip around the monster's tusk. I saw its eye go wide and it bucked its head up. The charge became a rearing up and I felt the steel catch the sagging gizzard hide beneath its neck. The whole mass of creature reared up in front of me, claws swiping the air until the spear shaft cracked between my hands. It stomped down as I fell backwards, almost trampling my feet.

Blood gushed across the sand as it shook its head and knocked the spear blade free. I had done it, just like the old man had said. I'd stabbed a dragon in the throat and...

The blood flow was already slowing to a trickle. I laughed, remembering the remarkable regenerative powers of crocodiles. Apparently this dragon had them even better: scar tissue in seconds. "Aw, fuck," I said.

Then Lance cleaved his ax into the thick muscles of its haunch. As soon as the steel bit in, he bellowed a war cry and wrenched the weapon through the wound. The dragon snarled and jumped back. It tried to snap at him, but couldn't push off fast enough. He leapt away, buying me time to scramble to my feet.

"It's healing!" I shouted.

"That's bullshit!" he shouted back, diving around one of the stone pillars. The monster charged him, smashing its tusk against the stone as it tried to gore him.

The crowd was going ballistic, throwing goblets of wine over their head with every attack. It really did not make me feel better that my death was good entertainment. I couldn't afford to take my eyes off the monster as we ran it around the pillar. The last thing we could let it do was charge again. I almost failed to draw the sword from the sheathe, the thing had rust spots that snagged the cloth liner, but then I had it out and over my head. I ran to the monster's backside and hacked at it.

It felt like I had smacked butter with a stick. It took me a breath to realize my sword was stuck in its hide. Before I could pull it free, the dragon's tail slammed into me like a linebacker. I felt the hit, the pressure, then I was on the ground. I swore, barely able to breathe as the dragon stepped around to bite my head off.

Once again, Lance jumped to my rescue. With a brazenness I couldn't believe, he swung right at its face. It jerked around with a snarl to bite him, rows of ivory daggers for teeth. His ax head bit straight into its eye. I heard the orb pop. Blood and ocular goop spewed out as the dragon screeched. Not a roar but a fearful whimper.

We had actually injured it.

God, I wish I could have looked over and seen the faces on the rich elves. I wanted to see them sit up and take notice that their prisoners weren't just rolling over and dying. I had to settle for seeing it after we escaped. I'd have to wait to see the warden's indignant face as she let us go.

I got back to my feet while the dragon reevaluated whether it was hungry enough to want to fight us. The monster found itself blind in one eye, an injury to deter any predator; but, it was as trapped in the arena as we were. It was also still wearing the restraining vest, still dragging rope around like anchors.

"Lance!" I shouted, darting over to grab one of the trailing ropes. The dragon didn't even react until I was already pulling on it. Then it charged at me.

Before it could gore me to death, Lance had the other rope pulled around one of the stone pillars. The impact slammed him into the stone and I heard him shout, but it jerked the dragon to a halt. There was no real way to win a contest of strength with it, but we didn't necessarily have to. We just had to keep it confused and bleeding and heating up.

The sun had turned the arena to an oven, but Lance and I could sweat. Our clothes were drenched already, but the dragon had no such relief. Just glancing at it, I could see the way its tongue swelled up and engorged with blood. Steam poured out of its panting maw as it looked between us. The moment it decided on me again, Lance ran a circle around his pillar.

When the dragon lunged for me, I dropped my rope and fell backwards. I heard the hemp snap taut and the crowd sucked in breath, but it didn't break. The fibers cinched tight and friction did the real work. The dragon grumbled and strained, digging claws through the sand and trying to march towards me.

What I would have given for another spear. Or a bow and arrow. Or a gun. A gun would have been really nice. Just a third person to stab it to death while we restrained it could have worked too. But we had none of those things.

Which meant I had to do it myself.

It wasn't going to bleed out. It would turn around and attack Lance before it overheated. All I had was the rusty sword in my hand, dripping blood, so that was what I used. Somehow

I walked over to it, trembling so much I felt lightheaded. All I had to do was stab it and kill it though, just like the old man had said: no wind up, just whoosh and in for the kill. It lunged at me as soon as I got close, jerking the rope taut as it reared up. Fat arms swiped through the air, grasping nothing. Spittle flew across me.

I looked where its heart should have been and threw myself into the lunge. The tip of my blade shot forward and bit into the hide. The chest hide was thinner. It didn't have that sodden muck feeling like when I had slashed its back. The steel just sank in. It jarred slightly, shaking my arms as it slipped between the ribs. Then it sank deep.

I felt vibrations through the sword as blood squirted out.

I never saw the tusk coming until it clipped me in the neck and threw me to the ground. A moment later, the dragon collapsed beside me, both of us bleeding out. That left Lance the last man standing and he wasted no time in hopping over, burying his ax into its skull with an overhead chop. Then he jumped on top of me, using his shirt as a bandage.

14

Lily

Lily needed to find a priest. She buried and stifled all the elation of seeing John kill the dragon–a full grown river dragon!–because there wasn't time. She had seen the blood and knew the guards weren't going to do anything to help him. She was the only one that would care. Thankfully, this was far from her first emergency and she didn't panic. She just sprinted out of the viewing box as fast as she could put one foot after the next.

She didn't even have time for Pyoter to return or John would bleed out. She needed a priest and a priest wouldn't bother without payment. Hence, she was chasing her bookie down and ready to throttle him. The man who had offered her ten to one odds was a rakshasa. The moment John had felled the dragon, his camouflage had failed like a snuffed candle. No one noticed until the one-armed god had ripped one of the coin purses from the demon's hands and then the uproar had started.

Evidently, only she and the god had been stupid enough to bet on two guys versus a dragon. Maybe the entire stadium would have thought otherwise if they had realized a god was banking on the prisoners. If there had been swords among the viewers, the demon might have been cut down then and there, but when all they could do was try to grab him, he proved as slippery as an eel. From her vantage in the booth however, Lily immediately saw his change of outfits. While everyone else stormed the main hall, he went running for the private halls and Lily went straight after him.

"Give me my money, you backstabbing monkey!"

"I'm not a monkey!" the demon shouted back at her, trying to keep his short-brimmed hat clamped to his head, lest his horns show.

The halls were sparse, save for guards and cup bearers running about. The games weren't over, so they were nearly the only people trying to evacuate the arena. When the rakshasa reached the servant staircase and began charging down the three flights to escape, Lily did something very unladylike. She threw herself over the railing, twisting around to land on top of the thief demon.

The two of them hit the wall and fell over one another, but her brother had taught her the basics of how to fight. Their tangle and tussle came to a stop when the rakshasa yelped and froze. She had his furry tail gripped in one hand and the edge of her bodice knife against the base. Her brother's gift, normally quite hidden in the corset of her dress, was always sharp enough to shave—or to take a demon's tail off.

The demon was face down on the landing of the staircase. He slowly spread his arms to either side and held up his hands. The display was grotesque, his wrists as flexible as an owl's neck. "I give, I give. You can let go, miss," he said as he stretched his neck and turned his head around to face her.

Lily wanted to gag, but she kept her voice firm. "My money."

"I can give you your money back. Look, won't even move. Your purse is at my hip. See there?"

Lily nudged it with her knee, not releasing the demon's tail. She could hear the coins clink but by the weight of it was merely how much she had put down. "Where's the rest?"

"I don't have the rest," the rakshasa said before yowling in pain like a cat. The knife had sliced into his skin, drawing blood as it worked down to the bone. "Stop, stop, please. Do you have any idea how hard it is to grow that back? You crazy woman. Didn't you realize I wasn't taking bets for the dragon? I'd go bankrupt even at one to ten odds on the dragon. Your money is all the money I took for that round."

Lily narrowed her eyes. "You were doing bets on the singles duels, weren't you?"

The demon snarled, champing his teeth and sucking breath through the froth. His eyes smoldered at her as he explained. "Yes, but the cripple already took that money!"

"I don't believe you. My friend needs a priest and that costs money."

"Stop, stop, stop, please. A priest? I can get you a priest. I know a great guy. Works real miracles. How about you get your friend and I'll take you there? A word of introduction eh? Worth a thousand coins in the wrong hands."

"Speak your name, demon. Do the Black Fingers know you're running scams here?"

"Fuck that chutiya! He treats me like scum. I'm not his fucking errand boy."

"You are scum," Lily said. "And I want my money, not some back-alley priest who probably can't even use magic."

"Look I don't have your winnings! I'm dirt broke just like the rest of the cretins in this city. Take your money back and go. Look, how about a little information, eh? The right words in the right ear at the right time can be quite valuable, don't you think?"

Lily huffed and snatched the coin purse off his hip. She didn't let go of his tail however. When it looked like he was smiling with relief, she sneered down at him. "What do you have to say?"

"The temple dig is rigged. That's why Urdao's men were all arrested. They're slow walking the dig to buy time so that the Black Fingers can steal the relic. They're planning a move and it's going to be at your brother's expense. Come on then, you gotta say that's worth something, right?"

The last thing Lily wanted to do was get involved with her brother any more than she had to. If she was going to be in Blue Rock Bay, she'd need their protection at this rate, but she didn't want to be in Alfheim anymore. She wanted to be back on Earth with John in one piece. She almost jumped when one of the arena workers cleared his throat on the landing above them. Lily's head snapped around. "Sorry, just a little–it's nothing."

From beneath her, the rakshasa spoke with a feminine voice to say, "Please sir, don't tell anybody about this!" 'she' pleaded.

Lily's head snapped back around to see the new guise of the shapeshifter; as pretty a girl as any nobleman could hope to court. And she was stradled atop of her, pinning her to the ground in private. Like a complete dupe, her grip on the demon's tail slipped and before she knew it the lying scum twisted his bones out from beneath her and bolted down the steps. Lily leapt up but only made it one step in pursuit before she realized the heel of her shoe had snapped upon landing.

"Is everything alright?" the workman asked.

She didn't have time. John was bleeding out. "No, I need to get a priest."

The man cleared his throat again and said, "Might I suggest the second floor? There's a green cross on your left. Perfectly discrete unlike the public healers."

She turned away so he couldn't see the blush in her face, then hobbled to the second floor. The door beneath the green cross was a shabby thing, squeezed in like a servant's quarter and totally missable if one wasn't looking for it specifically. The inside of the room seemed more like an apothecary than a medical suite. Even the priest seemed unfit for the job. Lounging across a couch was an elven woman with skin the color of chocolate. Lounging across her in turn was a shaggy wolf dog that probably weighed as much as she did.

"Contraceptive tea is on the shelf. Ten gold coins a baggie," the elven woman said, gently stroking her dog's ears to keep him from leaping.

Lily blinked, glanced over at the stack of contraceptives and just how many spots were empty already, then turned back to the elf. "Can you use healing magic? There's been an injury."

The priestess paused to puff on her delicate pipe, some herb smoldering in the pot nearly a foot away from her. "You're joking."

Lily stepped closer, getting a snarl from the dog that she ignored. "Please, he was a fighter in the arena! He was gored by a dragon."

That put some shock in her face. "Can you afford that?"

Lily chucked the purse at the elf, who snagged it out of the air. After a heft, she clicked her tongue. The dog hopped off and sat down so she could rise. The woman's dress was so scanty that it would have belonged in a brothel, but she made no move to even get a coat or cloak. "Fenrir, watch my stuff," she ordered and then gestured to the door. "Go on then, honey. Or do you need a new pair of shoes?"

"Not important right now!" she snapped, and ran back to the hall. After a moment of fretting and turning, she ran to the nearest guard for directions. The underbelly of the arena was set aside from where the attendees stayed, but wasn't actually locked off. It only took them a moment to run down to the basement where she caught up with Pyoter, Hilde, and then she saw them packing bandages into John's shoulder.

She froze, feeling like as much blood drained out of her as was out of him. "I-I got a priest."

Pyoter strode over as the elf knelt beside John. He grabbed Lily by the scruff of her dress and snarled. "Do not run off like that. You'll get yourself killed one day. You know that, don't you?"

She knocked his hand away. "That rakshasa would have gotten away."

"Forget the money! Your life is more important, Lily."

"John is about to die!"

The priestess peeled back some of his bandages and declared, "He needs vitae."

Lily shoved past her bodyguard to kneel beside her. "Can you fix that?"

"For the amount you paid, only if you have a donor," she said, and puffed again on her pipe.

Lance and Hilde were both watching Lily, and they leaned in when she clenched her jaw. "Is she a witch or something?" Lance asked.

"She's a healing priestess, yes. She says he needs a transfusion, but that's dangerous if the donor hasn't been tested. The process can be rejected and leave the patient even worse off."

Hilde and Lance glanced at each other then back to her. Hilde asked, "You mean a blood transfusion?"

"Vitae."

"Vitae is blood, isn't it?"

Lily grimaced, the translation spell floundering for her. "Sort of?"

Lance frowned and stared at the ceiling for a moment. "Well, shit. I'm A-, and he's A+. Is that the safe direction? Or is it the other way?"

Hilde said, "AB+ is a universal receiver. It's the universal donor, O-, that is screwed and can only get their own blood type. Why do you know his blood type?"

Lance scoffed. "Because it's good karma to donate blood. We went together like two months ago then got hammered on discount."

Hilde buried her face in her hands as her brother offered his arm.

The elf arched an eyebrow. "They don't seem to speak elvish. What is he doing?"

Lily took a breath to steady her voice. "Offering to be the donor."

"Well, it's more likely to work from a virile youth, but wasn't he the other fighter? Isn't he exhausted? I'm not taking responsibility for a fouling of his humors," the priestess said before taking Lance's hand and turning it over. She pressed it into John's palm, lacing their fingers together. Lance's brow knitted together. Then she clapped her hands on either side and began the magic.

"Real magic," he remarked as green light emanated from their grasp. "Kind of tingles."

"Most people find it painful," Lily said, not taking her eyes off John's pallor.

"Most people get lightheaded from a blood donation too," he said.

Hilde redoubled the pressure on John's shoulder when the bandages started to ooze red again. "He still needs a hospital."

"Are your doctors better than this?" Lily asked.

Hilde nodded. "Yeah, I'm going to go with yes on that."

The elf sighed, letting go of Lance's hand. "Technically, I reconnected his muscles, but he's not out of the woods."

Lance flicked some blood off his palm. "Right then, that's first aid. Time for the hospital."

Lily took a trembling breath and stood up as Lance hefted John onto his back, carrying the limp dragon slayer like a dozing child. She turned to Pyoter. "Can you deal with the guards?"

Her bodyguard crossed his arms and shook his head. "I can,

but what are you going to do with him? He's going to die at this rate."

"That's for us to deal with," she said, and turned back to the elf. "Thank you for the help."

The priestess sighed a cloud of smoke. "Girl, I don't like taking money for half-assed work."

"It wasn't, you did enough," she said, and led the way back to her apartment.

15

~

John

I woke up in a hospital room, and for a moment thought everything had been a coma hallucination. Maybe I had been hit by a truck that drunk night with the god. Staring at the fluorescent lights overhead gave such an opportunity to pretend nothing crazy had happened, but then the memories began to stitch together. It would have been easier if I had actually blacked out, but I wouldn't have survived if that had happened. I only lost enough blood to make myself woozy and confused and I had to be carried back to the apartment then on to a hospital.

I owed Lance my thanks, and sort of my life.

The first thing I moved was my eyes, rolling them around the room as I took in the beeping machines and the dangling IV bag. They had really pumped me full, somehow leaving me parched in the mouth but also in need of a piss. Then I started checking my muscles. Fingers and toes wiggled, limbs shifted, and I finally noticed the weight on my chest. There was a yellow thing on top of me. I had to extricate an arm and rub the crud from my eyes before I could make out blonde hair atop me.

I cleared my throat, and Lily woke up, some of her hair stuck in her mouth as she looked around. She seemed as confused as I had been, until she spotted me. "You're up!" she shouted, leaping to her feet and grabbing my arm.

"Where am I?" I asked, coming to realize they must have had me on very good drugs. I felt no pain. I barely even registered that one of the most attractive women I'd ever met in my life was chewing her lip and staring at me. I just kind of felt good, and tried to not think about the bill at the end.

Hilde waved a half-empty latte at me from the corner of the room, and said, "Gracefield Hospital," she answered.

I grunted and nodded. Gracefield was the only hospital on the island, of course they had brought me to it. "Right, well I guess that could have gone better," I said. Hilde laughed and I tried to scratch my nose. A twang of pain shot through my neck, and I remembered why I had been admitted. A fucking dragon had gored me.

"Try not to move," Lily said. "Here, is this the spot?" she asked, scratching my nose for me.

"Uh, yeah, it was. Thanks. Is Lance okay?"

Hilde rolled her eyes. "Lil' bro is fine. He's at rugby practice right now, since we had no idea when you'd get up."

I frowned. A moment later, my brain pieced together the problem. "Wait, doesn't that mean today is Sunday? So I've been asleep all night?"

Lily nodded. "I'm so, so sorry this happened. I should have been there. I should have known something like this would happen and been there to help. You... you got arrested and almost killed because of me!"

I blushed. I wasn't used to people apologizing to me, but I was saved by a nurse walking in. She stuck her head in and was taken aback. "Up already Mr Martin?" she asked, strolling over to the monitoring machines.

"Should I not be?"

"For the amount of painkillers you're on? I figured you'd be out till noon, easy," she said with a shake of her head that made her bundle of dreads bounce.

"Strong liver," I said with a shrug, and for some reason Lily turned away from me.

"I suppose so. A benefit of the collegiate life, hmm? But maybe no more falling off balconies, yes? I'd accuse you of drinking too much, but with these kinds of things, you probably would have been better off drunk."

"What's that supposed to–" The moment I shifted to offer her my wrist, to check my pulse, I felt the bruise. Felt like half my body had been paralyzed. "Oh god," I gasped out, sinking into the bed again.

The nurse laughed and took my pulse. "Just hold on, and the doctor will be in shortly. We've got you stitched up. Let me just check your blood pressure, okay sweetie?"

I noticed that Lily watched intently, following every action the nurse took. She must have been shocked to see a doctor, though the nurse wasn't really a doctor, that could actually lower one's chance of dying. Maybe Alfheim still relied on imbalanced humors and leeches and so on. I doubted they had antibiotics. They probably didn't even have germ theory.

When the door closed behind the nurse, Lily asked, "Why didn't she just use magic?"

Hilde and I stared at her. "Oh, you've gotta be fucking kidding me. I could have been healed by magic?"

She blushed and fidgeted. "Well, I mean, you were. Mostly."

Hilde nodded. "Yeah, when Lance dragged you out of the arena, your pec was in two pieces. This elf woman stabilized you before we got you back to Earth. You still needed like two liters of blood though."

"They've got magic but not blood transfusions?"

Hilde said, "They've got this thing for Vitae, but to be fair, I don't think blood transfusions between demi-humans would be safe. We also don't have refrigeration in Alfheim."

I sank back on my pillow and stared at the lights. "God damn it, now I have to go back over there."

"Oh, no, I wouldn't blame you if you didn't want to anymore. That was a huge mess!"

I shook my head–big mistake. "Nah, I have to go. If you're telling me there's fucking magic over there, I gotta go learn it. Besides, I've got an idea. Thought it up while I was stuck in the pit."

Hilde rose and said, "Well, we can talk it out over Bennies. Lily, you need a coffee or something?"

"That'd be great," the succubus responded.

Then the doctor came in and welcomed me back to the waking world. He chided me for falling off a balcony without the decency to be drunk at the time. Neither of us corrected him when he implied that Lily was my girlfriend, saying she was just a friend while wearing my spare clothes would have been worse. Then, he said, "We'll get you discharged just as soon as the painkillers wear off. You can pick up your prescription at your local pharmacy. I've got you here for a few hydrocodone and the rest will be high strength acetaminophen."

I held up a finger to stop him from leaving. "Did you just say I don't get to leave until the drugs wear off?"

The doctor winced and adjusted his glasses. "Sorry, Sir. Hospital policy. We have to do our part to fight the opioid epidemic."

"Mother fucker, you literally stitched my neck shut. You think I faked that to get drugs?" Then he was gone.

Two hours later, I was discharged and barely managed to negotiate my way to my drugs with a combination of stares, grunts, and shoving papers around. All of the pain was back, none of the shock to numb it. Getting hit by a steamroller would have been preferable. I stole a 2-liter of pop off the shelf to chug down the first pill and collapsed into a chair for the pharmacy.

"You good?" Hilde asked.

Digesting the painkiller was going to take at least half an hour, so no, I was not good. "Let's go get some food," I grumbled, and needed their help to haul me out of the chair. A bit like a zombie, they dragged me to checkout, then down the street to Bennies.

Of course, Bennies being Bennies at noon on a Sunday, I fit right in. When the old lady walked over to take our order, I grunted something resembling the phrase, "Smothered Grand Slam," which she somehow jotted down correctly. Decades dealing with hungover college students must have helped.

Eventually, a heap of syrup glazed breakfast appeared before me. The drugs were kicking in, taking the edge off, and Lily was actually jittering. Probably had something to do with the second cup of coffee she had gotten. I had to remind myself that it was the middle of the night for her, so of course she wasn't hungry. After shoveling half a waffle, an egg, and a quarter pound of cheesy hashbrowns into my stomach, I said, "Okay, so, spices."

Hilde arched an eyebrow at me, a piece of french toast halfway to her mouth. "On your waffles? You mean, like, cinnamon?"

"What? No, I mean like black pepper."

"On your waffles?"

"No, no. Fuck, no. I mean money." I groaned. "I mean selling spices like black pepper for money. Cut me some slack. Lily–" I picked up the pepper shaker and set it in front of her. "That right there is a complimentary pepper shaker. Salt too. Industrialization has made it super cheap. Alfheim isn't industrialized. I swear they don't even have iron, but iron is way harder to carry over. How much would pepper sell for?"

Lily frowned and picked it up. She gave it a shake to look at the black and white powder within, then she put some in her hand to give it a taste. "This is complimentary? Like, free?"

"Yeah, it goes good on eggs. How much?"

"This much? I don't know, maybe one gold coin?"

I glanced at Hilde and shrugged. "That's not bad."

I watched her face unfold, opening up as she thought it over and realized something. For a moment, she enjoyed the anticipation, drawing us in out of curiosity. "If you think that's good, I know something even better."

***

While Hilde and Lance vanished to the grocery store, Lily

and I were left alone in the apartment. I could see the droop in her eyes and figured she had to be exhausted. The energy of a newly minted caffeine addict could only go so far. In an attempt to subtly let her go nod off in the bed, I had taken out my textbooks and gotten to work on some homework. Overnight in a hospital and a prison the day before that had eaten up a lot of my weekend and classes weren't on hold for me.

She sat down across from me as I turned on some lofi music.

"You're really going to go back there? After what happened?"

For a moment, I fidgeted with my pencil. "Hadn't really thought about it," I admitted. "I still need to get my–"

"This?" she asked, sliding my phone across the table to me. "Sorry, I've been hanging onto it since the arena."

I snatched it and failed to turn it on. When I plugged it into my charger though, the screen booted, so it wasn't broken. "I guess I did almost get killed," I said, watching the battery begin to creep back to full.

Lily took a breath and composed herself. When she locked eyes with me, she said, "You got in that fight because of me. I'm sorry."

The thugs had told me to leave her behind. That was sort of the entire reason I had gotten into it with them. "It was the right thing to do."

"No, that doesn't... It's still my fault, and I'm sorry. I didn't warn you, I didn't think anything would happen in the middle of the day. Blue Rock Bay isn't exactly safe. To tell you the truth, that's sort of the entire reason I signed the contract, why I have spent months dreaming of seeing Earth instead of this mess that is my life!"

She looked in pain, and I was just doped up enough on painkillers to not feel it myself. Moving my left arm didn't feel good, but letting her beat herself up? "Hate to break it to you, Lily, but while d'Amaranth is an alright college town, I didn't exactly grow up in a good neighborhood either. Also, I'm a dragon slayer now!"

She sighed. "Okay, I'm just going to tell you right now, that if you try bragging about that, most women are going to assume you're a violent weirdo. Unless you kill a flying dragon, like Chad Paladin, it's really not that impressive. Wild boar hunts can be more dangerous."

I tried to respond to her. I really tried to take her words seriously. I had to ask, "There's someone named Chad Paladin?"

Her expression lightened up. "What's so weird about that? You've met people named Earl and King, haven't you? I mean, you have, haven't you?"

Technically speaking, paladin was a court rank from Charlemagne's court. "Have you met anyone else named Paladin?"

"Well, technically I haven't met him either. I guess maybe he took the name?"

"And you're sure his first name is Chad?"

She pulled back from me, her eyes suspicious. "That's what the stories all say. Hold on, are you trying to measure up or something?"

"No, no nothing like that," I said, but I was pretty sure that was a made up name. That just had to be someone else from Earth. If I had gotten a portal to Alfheim, other people must have too, and someone was out there living it up as Chad Paladin. It was like he was telling everyone who would know that he was from Earth. It was just about the nerdiest way I could imagine it, but who was I to judge? My brother and I had done exactly that kind of crap.

More importantly, I had to address her concern, and do it seriously. It would just be wrong to brush it off. "Trust me, Lily, I'm not going out there looking for a fight, but there's no way we're going to pay the rent on this portal with just hard work. First of all, I don't have a job right now. I work over the summer, not during the school year. Second of all, I won't be making that kind of money even after I graduate. If we want to keep the portal open, we have to get clever. Tonight, we'll go in, keep a low profile, see if we can make this work, and get out. I don't care who those guys are, they're in jail and they can't have that many friends."

She hung her head as I spoke. "I don't want you getting hurt again because of me. I came here to get away from that."

"Then I just have to not get hurt. Easy enough." Part of me was screaming that the obvious way to not get hurt was to not go back to the clearly dangerous fantasy world. I had a very good reason to go back there, sitting across from me though.

Lily sighed and straightened up. "Can you show me around Earth? Me, you, your friends, we can go to the market today. We'll probably have to bring some of my friends to be safe, but I understand where you're coming from. Just, I'd feel better if we let things in Alfheim cool off?"

I couldn't say no to her. I would have felt like a monster disagreeing with that. "Absolutely. I think we'll have to get a hold of our landlord and see what he can do to get you an ID card though."

Her brow pinched together. "Why would I need that?"

"So you can drink. It's the law here. Very annoying."

This time, when she sighed, she deflated. "I really gotta catch some shut eye. Sleeping in that hospital was terrible. I will figure that out later," she said as she shoved off the table and trudged to the bedroom. When she got to the door, she added, "I still owe you for protecting me."

Before I could pick an appropriate response, she shut the door.

Eventually Hilde and Lance showed up with a bag of groceries. They also brought Chinese food. While I was devouring mongolian beef to stave off anemia, Hilde asked, "So, you're letting her use your bed?"

I had to wipe sauce off my chin as I said, "You saw that moldy box she calls a bed, didn't you?" That reminded me I hadn't checked what the backside of the portal was like, but I was somewhat worried it would open to some kind of rift between dimensions filled with unspeakable monsters. Or, forcing the door might break the spell.

"So where are you going to sleep?"

I coughed. "Well, funny you say that. I could sleep on the couch, but since our days are opposite, we don't actually need the bed at the same time..."

"Lily is a really good girl, John. Don't make a mistake," she said.

I waved her off and gestured at the bag of groceries. "What's in there?"

Her smile was devilish. "Ginger."

We let Lily sleep until the Earth sun went down and caught up on seasonal shows until it was dawn in Alfheim. We didn't have to wake her up, the noise of the elvish city did that for us. Our offering to her fatigue was a can of double shot espresso, which apparently tasted like candy to her. Then, we all got dressed once more in Alfheim-appropriate clothes and headed out. A very dangerous looking fellow fell in behind us, without a word, but Lily waved to him and he waved back, so I figured she knew him.

"Your friend?"

"Let me put it this way. Before you get in another fight, with your arm about ready to fall off, let him fight?"

After another ride on a troll barge, we arrived at the dock-yard-adjacent bazaar. It was a bustling place of jam packed wagons and carts. Merchants had awnings and umbrellas meshing together like a canopy of motley sails. Without room for a horse to walk, I wondered how they ever got it set up in the first place. Some seemed to actually be permanent fixtures of the market, they were so burdened with random goods.

There were reed baskets, and paper parasols. We passed fruit merchants and fur traders. We had to weave around clothiers and jewelers, skirt vats of boiling soup getting hawked for coppers, and press through lines of shoppers trying to squeeze into the public bathrooms. I didn't even realize we had gotten to a spice merchant because all I could smell was human–well, succubus–sweat.

But Lily had gone right to the old lady surrounded by bags and jars and more than one thug, her grandchildren perhaps. I tried to recognize what she had for sale, but they were just so many colors of powders. I figured they were probably cut to dilute them, maybe with salt. Even salt was expensive though. She was selling it by the bag, using one of them as an arm rest while she puffed a pipe. "What are you buying, young lady?"

"Selling actually," Lily said.

The spice merchant tilted her head, making a circlet of brass discs dance across her forehead. It looked like a charm bracelet to me, but I knew I just didn't know fashion. "Sweetie, what makes you think I'm in the market to buy something? This is Blue Rock Bay. Nothing luxurious is grown here."

She grinned, sticking her nose up. "I have a source, but I can't show it out here." Then she passed the woman the smallest piece of ginger root we had.

The woman looked at it, uninterested and unimpressed at first. Then she rolled it in her hand, and dug a finger nail into it. The surprise had to be worth its weight in gold. I watched her sniff it and sit up straight. "You have more?"

Before I knew it, our group was split. Lance and Lily went with the old woman, vanishing into a warehouse I hadn't even realized existed in the market, so well hidden between the roads, and I lingered with Hilde and the thugs. I would have preferred going with her, but someone who could speak elvish had to stay with Hilde.

"You don't have any money, do you?" she asked, staring over at what appeared to be a permanent fixture of the market. It was a bar to be precise, with beer kegs tapped. I assumed they were warm, but they did sound better than not.

"Soon, soon we'll have all the money we could need, right?"

"If this works... we'll need to buy you and Lance new clothes, first. You look like a bum."

I adjusted the cape Lily had given me. It was a silly thing, but it covered the bandages around my neck. "I guess we'll have to go to a tailor. It'll be the first time I've ever done that, ever gotten something sized for me. I wonder how expensive it'll be?"

Hilde shook her head. "Given they don't have machines to make the fabric? Probably very expensive. Hey, why aren't we smuggling textiles?"

I shrugged. "And what would our explanation be if someone asked us where we got polyester from?"

Hilde scrunched up her nose. Then she saw something else. "Hide."

"What?"

"Guards, hide now."

I glanced where she was looking and saw half a dozen red bedecked elves marching towards us. My stomach nearly hit the ground before I could clamber around the spice cart. I got gruff snarls from the thugs. One of them almost tossed me back into the pell-mell of people flooding from the law enforcers, but I ducked around the corner of the warehouse first. I kept one eye peeking around the corner and watched as Hilde got very cozy with the thugs. I really hoped they were good guys. I knew they at least were succubi, and the city had an unmistakable tribal attitude.

The succubi stuck together. Of course, they'd still rob each other, but it had been my stupidity that had gotten us arrested. I had acted like I was still in a first world country where police could be held accountable. The scar on my neck would keep me from forgetting that lesson.

"Found you!"

The man's voice made me jump. He clapped me on the shoulder as I spun around. The pain blinded me for a moment and I stood there struggling until I could see straight again. It took me a heartbeat to recognize the grinning, bearded face. "You! The arena!"

"Keep it down, keep it down," he said, speaking in elvish. He craned his head around, peering over my shoulders as the red tabards came into view.

"Who the hell are you?"

"Me? Don't worry about me. I want to know who you are, you tailless idiot."

I set my jaw and stiffened. The memory that he had spoken in English resurfaced. The whole fight had grown hazy in my memory, a confused dream of fear and pain getting gobbled up by the drugs and bloodloss. "No, I need to know who you are."

The man wetted his lips and glanced around. He was dressed poorly, but better than me. It looked like the fabric had once been nice, silk perhaps, but had worn threadbare. Obviously, something bad had happened to him, because he was missing his right arm. I couldn't imagine what kind of work–in this poorly developed economy–a cripple could get. Rocking on his heels he said, "Here isn't exactly a good place to say that kind of thing, you know?"

"How did you find me?"

The man tapped his nose. "You don't stink like everyone else. You've got," he sniffed again, "coconut on you."

Coconut was the scent of my body wash. I hadn't even thought of that. It probably smelled like perfume. "You were speaking English earlier. How?"

The man shrugged and put his arm around me. "What can I say? I'm a polyglot, just like you. Well, not just like you. My spell is a bit better. You know how it is. What you should be worrying about is what great things the two of us can do. Or three, if your berserker friend wants to join us."

"I don't need your help," I said, glancing back at the elven guards. They were just about to pass us. Then I could let my breath out.

The old man laughed. "You needed it in the arena, didn't you? You would've died without my instruction. So, don't you see how valuable my time can be to you? Not just anyone can get sword instruction from yours truly. It'll toughen you up too."

"What? You've only got one arm!"

He smacked me in the back of the head. "That's why I'm an instructor! And I'm a damn good one at that. Listen here, me and you can do great things. You've got spark inside you."

I broke out of his embrace. The guards had just passed us. "Thanks, but I don't want to get in fights. I'm not here to get myself killed. No sword instruction is necessary."

The old man sighed and scratched his beard. "That's a damn waste, you know that?"

"Fighting would be a waste of my life... because I'd die. No thank you."

"Well that's weird, you portal kids are usually dying for adventure, aren't you? How did you get over here, anyway?"

I really needed to find That Guy and corner him about this contract. Everyone else seemed to know what was going on better than I did. "None of your business. I have my own things to take care of, so I'll be going."

"Before you go..."

I should have just left, I could feel it in my gut. There was a twisting worm of anxiety worse than walking into a lecture hall to discover the midterm was that day not the next week.

The old man asked, "Do you have an older brother?"

And then I was stuck. I had to turn back and give him my

attention again. I knew it was probably just a good guess, a bit of cold reading, any of the tricks a fortune teller would use. Still, I felt compelled to answer, "I did. Past tense."

That didn't phase the man. He just narrowed his eyes and nodded like a mountain hermit sage. "I suppose the guy I'm thinking of did go missing a few weeks ago."

Hope was not an emotion I allowed myself to feel. I was too rational and cynical for that. "Does that guy have a name?"

"He's got titles, and I suppose you do too, now. Don't you, Dragonslayer? Of course, a half-starved river dragon isn't a particularly impressive feat unless you're an elf who can't imagine the lower class can so much as lift their head up. But this guy? He killed a real monster, Wrathclaw The Red. They say he took down a cyclops too."

I stepped over to him and tried to loom, but he was as tall as I was. I settled for getting in his face. "Does he have a name or not?"

"Some call him Chad Paladin, but his name is Charles Martin." He laughed in my face as he watched my reaction. "Well then, would you look at that? You do know him, don't you?"

"Where is he?" I asked, grabbing him by his shirt.

Next thing I knew, he had touched my wrist and did something with a step and a twist. Then the whole market spun. I only realized I was moving when my back smashed through a fur trader's cart and landed in the street. I found myself blinking at the sky and surrounded by angry customers. My wound should have ripped open but somehow the stitches held. I supposed I had to be thankful he had flipped me onto furs. Anything firmer would have had me back in the hospital.

As the pissed off merchant hauled me to my feet and began

to swear at me, the old man shouted, "Come find me at The Last Resort!"

16

∽

Lily

Interdimensional economics was so lucrative it actually scared Lily. The way technology on Earth had made some things cheaper and other things lower quality confused her, but there was no mistaking the profit. Fifty bucks back in d'Amaranth, not even as much as the four of them had spent on ramen, had just been exchanged for a flavorful root which she had exchanged for enough gold to pay her month's rent on her apartment.

And they could exchange the gold for even more money than that back on Earth.

However, Lily hadn't returned after finishing the deal with the spice merchant. She had slipped further into the bazaar and quietly took out her broken shoes. There were stalls of every industry, and a few permanent buildings too. It only took a moment of wandering, of peeking above heads, to find a cobbler. The fellow was a gnarled old incubi with fingers so cut and scarred she wondered how there was feeling in them at all, he barely even had fingernails left. That didn't stop him from turning over the broken heel and fiddling out the broken pins.

"You didn't buy this from around here, did you?" he asked, holding the sole up to the light with one eye closed.

"My brother got them for me as a gift."

"This wood is from the western islands, isn't it? Very beautiful but that's the problem."

Lily suppressed a gasp. "You can fix it, can't you?"

The cobbler sighed. "A proper fix would be to replace the heel entirely. See here though? The edge that cracked off? Best I can do is put some lacquer in here to fuse the bits back together, hit it with a rasp and knife and hope for the best; but, that's just waiting for it to break again. You're a lucky lass you didn't twist your ankle off when this happened. What were you doing anyway?"

"That's none of your business," she said, wishing her cheeks weren't burning.

The cobbler shrugged. "Whatever you did, I'd have to ask you to never do it in these again. I wouldn't even dance in them, lest you lose a foot when it cracks again. I can shape up a heel for you but that brings me back to the first point. This is island wood. Mahogany if I'm not mistaken. There's none to be had here, as far as I know. Expensive stuff, fit for a lady like yourself. That's precisely why I can't fix it for you. You'd be laughed at if the heels don't match... and if I were to swap both out, why that'd destroy the gift completely. There's nothing too special about the soles, just a bit of dragon belly. You can get that anywhere for a price."

Lily lifted her head and nodded. "Just lacquer it together please. I'll be careful with them."

The cobbler sighed and turned around to his workstation to start scraping away at them. Lily pulled out her purse, not the one fat on ginger root gold, but her personal savings. She had more silver marks than she had gold coins, and not much of either. When Hilde called out to her, she jumped and spun around.

"Hey, if you have shopping to do, shouldn't you be dragging the guys with you? You know, to not repeat what happened last time?" she asked.

Lily winced. "Just had to take care of something," she said, gesturing to the cobbler.

Hilde crouched down, picking up a few of the sample shoes and turning them over. The cobbler shot her a few glances as she fiddled with the fabric and scratched at the seams. She looked up at Lily with an arched eyebrow. "Do you need new shoes?"

"It's fine, I'm getting mine repaired."

Hilde sucked in a breath till her bodice laces strained. She rose and clapped a hand onto Lily's shoulder. "You need to go shopping, don't you? I'll take you thrifting just as soon as we get back home, okay? We can bring John. The two of you are going to have to work out some kind of reimbursement for each other at some point."

"Thrifting?" she asked, just before everyone started shouting because a man had been thrown through a market stall and Lily immediately knew who was to blame. The whole conversation went on hold when John and Lance were reconvened with and they had to begin the process of outfitting everyone for Alfheim properly.

Everything went well, aside from John's near run in with the guards and they made it to a tailor Lily trusted. Then John sat down on a bench and scowled. While the seamstress tied Lance up with measuring cords, clicking her tongue and shaking her head as she struggled to find something that would fit him, John kept his mouth shut. He watched as the woman fussed and shouted and the two of them somehow managed to communicate mostly through complaints and her slapping his arms into position. And at the same time, Lily watched him.

Hilde laughed at the situation, but she was staring at her brother. Only Lily noticed the line of maroon appear across John's shoulder. "You're bleeding," she said, grabbing the collar of his shirt. The adhesive bandage was still stuck to him, but now it was mottled in red and just touching it made him grimace.

"We'll have to get back to the apartment and get a fresh one. This is what I get tangling with that one-armed bastard. Hey, side note, isn't it dangerous to be speaking English here?"

Lily rubbed her fingers around the seams of the bandage, pressing the glue back against his skin. Checking herself, she kept her answer in Elvish and said, "A little. You're sure he was speaking English?"

"The guy that tossed me in the gutter like a cigarette butt? And taunted me about my brother somehow? Yeah, he was speaking English when he felt like it."

She patted him on the shoulder and helped him pull his shirt collar back up. "It's possible he's another renter like us, right?" She knew exactly who that man was though. Every instinct in her said he would bring trouble. Gut feelings aside, John needed to heal, not to go chasing old gods.

"Maybe? But if he is, he must have had a different god open the portal. He said his language spell was better than ours. Hey, speaking of magic, can you do any?"

Lily sighed and sat down on the bench next to him, out of the tailor's way. "No, I wish. We succubi are completely incapable of all magical spells. We used to be able to work magic, but now all that's left is well... not relevant at the moment." She had to explain to him what resting with a succubus actually did, and do so properly. Public just wasn't the place and if she didn't explain it right, he might stop being so understanding. Really, Hilde had had the expected reaction. John was the weird one being okay with who she was.

"So who can? Elves?"

She nodded, watching the tailor pull out bolts of cloth and start marking them with chalk. "Yeah, they're the healers of this world. White magic, fleshcraft, grace, whatever you want to call it, they're the masters of bodies. That's part of why it costs so much to get healed. But, it saved your life, right?"

"But does it work well?"

"If you get a good one. Lots of healers are hacks. Judging by the fact that you're in one piece?"

John whistled and nodded, getting an unfocused look in his gaze for a moment. Before worries of anemia could begin, he said, "We have to get back soon. I need to sleep."

At the moment, it must have been approximately midnight on Earth. The fact that he cared about his own sleep schedule more than hers irked her for a moment, but she said, "Sure, we can have the clothes delivered to the apartment when they're ready. You don't have to immediately go to the Last Resort, right?"

"Not quite immediately. I'm going to prepare first," he said before he rose to his feet. He cleared his throat and tapped his bloody shoulder for Lance and Hilde to see. "Let's wrap this up and come back. I've got class in the morning."

Lance laughed. "Oh, right, you didn't give yourself a three day weekend. Rookie mistake."

John rolled his eyes. "Didn't exactly have a choice there. So, come on. Let's square up the cost of the clothes. Lance, if you're free in the morning, why don't you see if you can pawn one of these gold coins or something? It won't do us much good if we get a stack of gold and run out of dollars, right?"

"Sounds like a plan," Hilde said. She eyed some of the dresses as she rose, but didn't ask to buy any. If the spice trade kept flowing well, she'd be able to buy herself an entire wardrobe in the future.

After paying, the four of them emerged to the roads. John sucked in the air, filling himself with everything from sea salt to odeur of horse manure. The city had better smells elsewhere, of baking bread and brewing beer, but the market district was only ever one gust from smelling like the troll trenches. Thousands of people filled the city, milling around little pockets of noises where minstrels played, and Lily happily left it all behind to disappear onto Earth with a smile on her face, at John's side.

17

~

John

I was almost loath to leave Alfheim, even if it was to slump into slumber. The alarm in the morning came as surely and relentlessly as semester exams. With no care for my rest or what I'd rather be doing, my phone screeched across the nightstand and I had to go through all the motions of a regular day–bandage excluded.

Part of me wondered if I should email my professor and ask for the notes offline due to my injury, but shoved that off. If I didn't learn… whatever they were going to allegedly teach today, it would have to be another day. I could recover as easily in a lecture hall as in my apartment, probably even easier since I wouldn't be getting worked up over online video games.

I found myself completely unable to pay attention to the professor. The squiggles of circuit diagrams just seemed like random doodles of a child and my mind drifted. It was the smell. There was something artificial in the smell of the heated air. The whole room somehow smelled dirty and I couldn't put my finger on it. When I freshened up in the bathroom, it was little better because the porcelain simply stank of lavender chemicals.

It was around the time I was picking at the decaying foam of my chair's armrest that my professor put up the Maxwell equations next to a diode diagram. He was explaining how the electrical resistance of the LED produced the specific wavelength of light based on the composition of the diode. There was a fun fact about most LED lights being composed of RGB like the pixels in a computer screen, but only the local weed growers cared about that fact–chlorophyll actually needing full spectrum daylight to function, unlike human eyes.

I put my hand up.

"So, professor," I said, trying to formulate the question as fast as I was speaking it. "Looking back on everything, is there actually a circuit that cares what the fundamental constants are?"

Dr Tan blinked at me from behind his coke bottle glasses and pointed at the slide. "I literally just went over this. The fundamental constants determine the light emitted."

My cheeks flushed and some of the room snickered. "Sorry, I phrased that poorly. I mean is there a circuit that wouldn't work if you changed the constants on it, like the low and high pass filters or something?"

He shrugged. "You'd get different time responses, but unless you changed something about how electrical fields propagate, they would still work fundamentally. Most that would happen would be a change to manufacturing optimizations. You know, you want your wire gauge to be a different size, or your capacitors to be this way instead of that way. These concepts are very fundamental, that's why we're teaching them in the 101 course."

"What about circuit boards? Would they fail?"

"You mean processor units?" That made him tap his finger to his lips. "That, Mr Martin, is a bit beyond this class, but I appreciate that you're thinking deeply about the material. Let me think about that, yes? Why don't you come into office hours tomorrow and we can discuss? Because off the top of my head, the only thing I can think of would be a change to internal resistance. That is very much outside the scope of this course, and I don't want to confuse the other students. Come to office hours and I will confuse you there."

Office hours were the next day, so I packed my things up and, after class, I hiked to the student parking garage. Layer upon layer of concrete and cars, with the thickest ice rink imaginable at the bottom. The school had given up salting the mess, and switched to sand bags. People still took out the crossbar every week, but I had four wheel drive and plenty of experience.

I normally didn't like driving. Every winter, half the population forgets how to drive, gives up on parking legally, and gas prices go up. One of the upsides to living in d'Amaranth was walkability, but I couldn't walk to where I needed to go. It took me half an hour to get there, but I pulled into my parent's driveway around three in the afternoon; before either would be off work. Their forced happiness drove me up the wall.

They lived in a shit neighborhood by objective standards, but rather nice compared to what they could be in. Not in the ghetto, not in the suburbs, but stuck in between on factory salaries. I would have been worried about my car getting broken into if there was anything worth stealing in it.

The screendoor had been ripped open, the front door was stuck in the jamb. The house stank of dirty dishes, despite the three air fresheners–all dead–and the seven unlit candles with such wonderful pairings as pina colada and pine cone. Ignoring my sense of smell, I went to my brother's room. I was immediately reminded that it was his room no longer. They had wasted no time in rearranging the house and moving on. Legally speaking, he wasn't even officially dead yet and still they had destroyed what he left behind.

They had turned his room into an art studio for the worst fucking watercolor art I had ever seen. I swear my mother, it had to have been her, was following Bob Ross tutorials with acrylic instead of oil. Absolute heaps of square foot canvases bought from a dollar store and smeared less elegantly than an elephant could. More of her brushes were crusted with paint than were clean.

My bedroom hadn't been unmolested either. They had shoved all of Charles' furniture into my room. They must have thought there was plenty of room after I took most to my apartment. Still, they had left my shit alone, so I was able to get my old multi-tool and pry open the screwdriver nub. I had to crawl under my mother's shelf of paints, but I was able to unscrew the vent cap.

Inside was my brother's 9mm semi-automatic pistol. Fourteen round mag, one in the chamber. Black composite body, diamond pattern grip, burnished steel slide, and glow-in-the-dark iron sights. He had almost fifty rounds of ammo too. It was a good, simple gun, along with a hip holster. The idea of walking around in a medieval tunic strapped with a pistol felt a little incongruous, but not having protection seemed even stupider.

After sealing the vent back up, lest my parents realize, I headed back to my room. I dug out some spare hoodies and other assorted clothes, then went out to my car. I had just tossed everything in the back when another car pulled up. I didn't realize anything was amiss until I heard the scrape of rubber against concrete and the bang of the bumper against the curb. Only then did I realize it was my father.

My father had a face halfway between a boiled egg and a raisin, which stuck up above the roof of his rustbucket to squint at me. "John? Wasn't expecting you here today."

I slammed my trunk. "Just wanted to get some spare clothes. The engineering hall gets chilly." Specifically the computer lab where I had to do my simulation work. Of course, I had better clothes for that. These were destined for a more fantastical life, well, my fantasies at least.

My father nodded and scratched the back of his head. "Were you planning to stay for dinner?"

"No, I'm leaving already."

The relief on his face was evident. He had probably been planning to go out to eat somewhere and didn't want to pay for me, or something else like that. "Well, alright then. Study hard and don't forget to call."

"Tests were last week. Nothing to study for a while yet. I'll talk to you later."

"Right, you do that. Don't need to send a search party for you too. Can't have you flunking out of college. We're paying a lot of money to put you there."

I stared back at his grin, wondering why the hell he thought that was amusing. Then I jammed my key into the lock and got in my car.

***

I found Lily eating a plate of fried eggs when I got back around sunset. The room smelled smokey, but not cigarette smoke. "How did you cook those?" I asked, dumping the pile of clothes into my living room's recliner.

The succubus shrugged and pointed at the bedroom door. "I got a little breakfast fire going in my kitchen. You don't mind I'm eating here, do you?"

Did I mind having my bombshell roommate eating food on my couch, sprawled across the cushions in a night dress one step away from lingerie? "The table would be preferred. So, you used a fire to fry those?" She licked her lips and nodded. She was using one of my plates and forks, almost sheepishly turning away from me. "You know the electric stove is a lot easier, don't you?"

"The what now?"

Fifteen minutes later I had fried myself an egg to teach her how the stove worked. I was trying to decide how much fire safety warning she needed to be given since she normally worked with actual fire. I almost started a speech on how electricity could be called Earth's magic, when she asked, "Are you okay, John? You're really out of it today."

I blinked, completely losing my train of thoughts. "What?"

"You look upset. Did your boss yell at you or something?" She tilted her head as she spoke, getting a better look at me even if she had to brush hair out of her face.

I turned off the stove and tossed the pan into the sink to be cleaned later. "I don't have a job during the semester, only over the summer," I said, taking a seat at the table. I had to shove some old mail aside to get space–I really needed to clean up.

Lily sat across from me. "So, did your professor yell at you?"

I grimaced and started ripping my egg apart with my fork. With a gesture at the pile of clothes, I said, "I like Dr Tan. It's my parents that are the problem. Had to go back home today. By the way, help yourself if you need any of that. It's not exactly girl clothes, but nobody will think twice about you wearing guy clothes."

"I'm not worried about clothes. Hilde is going to swing by for shopping soon. Do you not get along with your parents?"

I normally liked the burst of egg yolk in my mouth, washing it down with some juice or coffee. Normally. "Not since my brother went missing. Turns out that family tragedy only brings you together if everyone is on the same page."

"That's... I didn't think you were... John, I'm sorry to hear that."

The way she was looking at me with so much sincerity made me fidget. "Hey, don't you work today? What do you do for a living?"

She blinked and straightened up. "Didn't I tell you? I'm a waitress at Thorn's Tap Root and Room. That's sort of on hold though, what with the fight and other things."

For a moment I tried to discern if that was a brothel or a strip joint, but her expression was too innocent to conclude that. Then again, she was a succubus. "So, that's more of an evening job?"

"Yeah, as long as I'm in before noon, the owner is happy,

but I'm expected to show up early at least some times to help with cleaning the place up. It's an alright place. It's safe."

I twiddled my fork against my plate, thinking about the weight of my brother's handgun. I had it strapped to my hip, hidden by my flannel shirt. It was completely rational to get a weapon for Alfheim. I'd already been in fights and nearly killed, and I couldn't just avoid the place. My brother might be alive there. I just didn't like the idea of shooting someone.

I liked the idea of getting stabbed even less.

I said, "I can sleep in on Wednesday, so I'll stay up late tomorrow and go to Alfheim and track down The Last Resort."

"Are you sure it's wise to trust that old man?"

"Well, given my injury and all, I need some more rest and recuperation. If I decide it's a bad idea in the meantime, I won't go. He knows something about my brother though. I can't just ignore that."

Lily huffed. "At least take your rest seriously? Please? If you can't do that, we can book another visit with a healer, I guess."

"Yeah, yeah, I won't go to the gym or anything. I promise I'll just be a homebody for a bit. I've got some games to grind." I stopped and turned to my bedroom door. My computer was in the bedroom. That wouldn't do. "I'll need some help rearranging things though."

Lily smirked. "Yeah I figure it's about time we figure out a proper living space, you know? The way I see it, my old bedroom can take a bit of furniture overflow to let us rearrange some things if we need to."

"Like what?"

"Well, I figure we should have the best seating arrangement all together, right?"

I arched an eyebrow. "You have better seats than I do?"

She hesitated and cleared her throat. "Cooking equipment?"

I shut my mouth before thoughtlessly retorting, then asked, "Do you have cast irons?"

She frowned. "Do you not?"

"I've got stainless steel, teflon, and unknown non-stick materials. Yeah, sure, let's compare kitchen tools but I think the only furniture we're going to move around will be setting up my computer desk in the corner here. Want to learn a bit about computers?"

"Earth's version of magic? Absolutely."

So I more or less conned her into unplugging the dozen different cables that kept my gaming station together, in exchange for rudimentary explanations about them. I sat on the end of the bed and watched her work, treating every bit like a novelty. It was a shame I hadn't gotten my hands on a real magic item yet, the portal notwithstanding. When everything was finally piled on the table and ready for us to carry out to the tv room, I promised her, "I'll get you set up with some video games if you want."

"Yes, please. I'll handle all the dishes in exchange."

"No, no you don't have to do that. I've got consoles I don't even touch. I'll teach you how to use the washing machines too and you'll realize how little effort it actually takes to keep a house in order over here."

She stared at me as I squeezed through the doorway. "If that's so, why is your place a mess?"

I hung my head and almost put a hole in my wall. "Never had a reason to. Starting now though, fifty-fifty? For as long as the portal is here?"

She smirked. "Sure," she said as we nestled the table into the least cramped corner of my tv room. It was directly beneath the AC wall unit, but I had months before that would turn on.

I'd have to show off the might of a global supply chain when it came to cooking, and then awe her with the power of a dishwasher. Maybe some other things too, but I'd have to figure those out. Before I could cook up some impressive display for her, my doorbell rang and Hilde arrived to sweep her off to thrift shopping and to awe her with secondhand capitalism.

Before the two of them left though, Hilde shot me a direct glare and stated, "You're coming. Right?"

18

∾

Lily

The thrift shop Hilde took them to had similarities to the market bazaar, in that every non-perishable good Lily could imagine was for sale. However, there was no bustle of people. Rack after rack after rack of clothes, in every make, fashion, design, and use that she could imagine, stood throughout the store like so many burdened pack animals and yet there were maybe half a dozen shoppers and three sales people.

Beyond the clothes were porcelain and glass dishes. There were kitchen appliances from outdated to kitsch. The middle of the store was strewn with furniture from a dozen different styles. There were even paintings, board games, and vinyl collections. A mountain of treasures Lily could barely wrap her head around and Hilde just waltzed over to the clothing racks and started rifling through them.

John stood back, shoulders slumped and eyelids drooping already.

Lily followed after Hilde, going at the pace of excitement rather than whatever drudge John had fallen into. She was practically tip-toeing as she tried to take it all in. Hilde pulled out a slim sundress with a rose flower pattern to it, the kind of art a nobleman would decorate a drawing room with. Lily gaped at it and reached. Hilde wrinkled her nose at it, said, "No," and shoved it back into the rack of clothes like a piece of trash.

Hesitantly, Lily reached out just to touch one of the shirts, and instantly part of the magic was taken away. There was a certain dryness to it, like she was touching paper. She'd been ignoring the smell as well, the whole place was a bit musty. It gave her hope that she could actually afford some of it, but it made her wonder what a fresh clothing store would be like.

"Don't," Hilde said as Lily tugged out a lace blouse. The human took a pair of jeans off the rack and held them up. "Most of the stuff here has been washed a thousand times. Shirt like that? You're better off buying in bulk. Here," she said and thrust the pants into Lily's hands.

Lily held her tongue and looked around the store again. John had meandered from the door and begun flipping through the music collection. She didn't really understand what a used vinyl was, but she wanted to. "Hilde, I know we just came into some money–"

"--And we're about to get a whole bunch more, as long as John doesn't do anything stupid again. Relax, I know you don't have any dollars. I'll cover it. It's just a thrift store."

Lily looked down at the tag on the jeans, ten dollars; just a few silver marks. "Your world is confusing. You know that?"

Hilde shrugged. "Commodities are cheap but everything

else about life is incredibly expensive. You wanna guess how much debt I'm in right now for my degree?"

Lily frowned as more clothes were piled into her arms, until her entire wardrobe at home seemed like a joke. "From the way you said that, I don't think I want to know."

"I'm a hundred thousand dollars in debt with student loans and I don't have a chance in hell of owning my own house until I'm forty. But that's pre-med for you. Here, try these on. I need to see how you look from behind. John, get over here for the second opinion!"

Lily tried to hide her blush and ran into the changing room. Pants were an immediate failure. No matter what cut, style, or fabric was tried, her tail was either immediately obvious or so pinched she had to strip back down. Everything from the waist up fit perfectly, but that did nothing to soothe Hilde's growing frustration. John just said it all looked good, so long as it was comfortable. That started an argument with Hilde that Lily missed most of because she was trying to tug tight-waisted capris back down her hips. When she emerged wearing a skirt that looked like a three-layered bellflower–and completely covered a pair of thermal shorts Hilde had found–Hilde declared, "Okay, that's it." She started piling the good clothes into a basket. "We're going to the mall."

John rolled his eyes and slid in beside her as Hilde took everything to the register. "For the amount of money we're going to be making, only buy this stuff if it's comfortable. You'll have better looking stuff soon enough."

"Is that your way of saying it doesn't look good on me?"

"You look like a dancer."

She hesitated. "Is that a good thing or a bad thing?"

John smirked. "Depends, are you going to drag me out dancing somewhere? Because then you'll be embarrassing me."

"Oh? But isn't dancing a mechanical problem?"

"Not even close!"

"But what if I need a dancing partner! My brother invites me to balls sometimes and I'm too old to be his dancing partner."

John stumbled over his words before he finally asked, "Who the hell is your brother? I kind of really want an explanation on that sooner rather than later."

Lily's grin vanished. "That's complicated and it depends on who you ask. I'll tell you about it when he comes back to town, if that's okay?"

"If that's okay depends on if there are going to be more people showing up to harass you."

Harassment was a light way of putting attempted kidnapping, but she didn't correct him. "The politics in Alfheim are complicated, but technically speaking, he's a hired mercenary for Lady Virent. He just... does some other things on the side that has quite a few people thinking he's something like a race traitor."

John frowned, but Hilde had finished paying for everything. "I guess that explains why you'd rather be over here. Let's talk in private?"

"Sure, we can do that," Lily said as the three of them left the thrift shop and returned to the cold of d'Amaranth streets.

Lily resigned herself to managing more surreptitious trades, perhaps using some of her brother's connections for better discretion. She didn't even want to know how much Hilde spent on her, just accepting the obvious lie that it wasn't much.

Everything had been packed into bags that felt like they would pull her arms out of their sockets before they got back home. Hilde didn't seem to mind the weight as she said, "Mall is on the other side of town, we can drop everything off then keep going. We can get you some proper shoes, some underwear, whole nine yards."

Lily winced. "I think we bought more than nine yards of fabric already..."

John said, "That's a... Oh, I guess you don't have football, do you?"

"You mean with the goalies and the ball you kick around? We have that."

Hilde grimaced, her cheeks extra red in the cold. "He means American football. Nevermind, it's an idiom I never asked to have jammed into my vocabulary. We'll get you everything you need to get around over here, except a driver's license. I don't know how to get you that, so you won't be buying any alcohol."

Lily frowned. "What does driving a car have to do with buying beer?"

John said, "Because of puritanical busybodies from like a century ago."

"You know, the more I learn of your world, the more questions I have."

"Hey! Your world is the one that arrested my brother and tried to feed him to a dragon!"

Lily flinched back. "Point taken."

When they made it back to the apartment, Hilde shoved the bags into John's hands and told him to take it upstairs. He protested and she declared, "Private conversation! Have some tact." That sent John grumbling up and left the two women on the sidewalk. Hilde had a smug grin on her face as she turned to Lily. "Anyway, the question I have for you: are you interested in John? Or are you just his roommate? I saw the way you were modeling yourself every time you came out and he did save your life sort of."

Three armed assassins at once and she would have had more control over herself. "How am I supposed to answer that? Am I interested in him? In the guy that got arrested for picking a fight with assassins he knew nothing about but were trying to abduct me apparently? For someone gullible enough to get duped into fighting a dragon but brave enough to kill it? Hilde, I've almost spent more time with him in a hospital than outside of one! How could I possibly have a sane opinion of him when I haven't had a moment of normalcy since I met him!"

Hilde waited to respond, making every excruciating moment pass until it was undeniable the woman was cutting right through the confusion. "Okay," she said, flat and condescending. "So we're going to the nice stores. Got it. And relax, if he drops the ball, you'll need nice clothes to find someone else, right? I know guys, you'll do great."

Lily huffed, scurrying after Hilde to keep up as the two of them headed back to the apartment. "If you know guys so well," she asked, "Where's your husband?"

"Husband? I don't even have a boyfriend!"

"The question stands."

"Oh shut it, don't snark back at me. You have no idea how hard it is to date in pre-med. Every guy in my class is drug addicted and don't even get me started on the fencing team! I'd sooner date the girls there than one of the guys."

Lily grasped for one response after the next, but ended up with nothing more than some snow in her gaping mouth. She changed the subject, "So the mall has cute clothes for cheap?"

As John started down the steps, Hilde said, "Not for cheap, but that's what credit cards are for. Money today when you'll make it tomorrow. Come on, let's get lattes first though. I don't need you falling asleep on me just because it's the middle of your night. Perk up buttercup. The day's just starting."

19

~

John

Unfortunately, against all the best of intentions in the world, I found myself up at one in the morning playing Reborn Isles. After so much time wandering the mall, my brain had nearly fried. I didn't have the energy to do anything productive, and thought I'd pass out asleep soon enough. So, I had put on a podcast, and then cracked open a beer and it just got worse from there. It wasn't raid night for my guild, but most of the usual crew were online and we just started jamming dungeons. I actually played better the drunker I got, according to my stat calculator addons, which encouraged me to drink more, which encouraged me to play more.

Lily woke me up by shaking my shoulder. "John, are you okay?"

I almost kicked my table over as I jerked awake, blinking and spinning around. Bleary and confused, I tried to get the taste of beer scum out of my mouth while getting my eyes to focus. The silhouette looming over me came into focus as I realized sunlight was burning in from the window. "Aw fuck, what time is it?"

"What is this thing? It says you died. Are you okay?"

Alt+tabbing to desktop I saw it was nine in the morning and groaned. I probably wasn't going to make it to Dr Tan's office hours. "What do you mean? This is my computer. I was playing Reborn Isle. Fuck, I'm going to be late for class." Of course, my phone was dead too, hence no alarm. I ran to the bathroom to scrub my teeth. By the time I came out, the new words had finished updating inside Lily's head and she had taken my seat at the desk.

"So you can have a lot of fun on a computer..."

I needed to get to the engineering building and sit through my philosophy course–which I had forgotten to read the passage on–which was even further than the engineering building. I could not just leave her with my computer though. I reached around her and locked the computer.

"Hey! I was curious about that." She even pouted cute.

However, her having access to my social media, or just my browser history, was not a risk I could take. I handed her my console deck and booted Cap-mon. "Knock yourself out. Don't take it through the portal," I said, and took the risk of leaving her alone in the apartment.

I used a pocket battery to charge my phone on the walk across town, stuck earbuds in, and started a YouHub stream of some philosophy nerd that had a ten minute talk on Intro To Descartes. Horrible quality, the guy was practically chewing on his microphone, but it let me fake that I had read the meditations. I actually liked the professor, so I felt bad having forgotten to do the reading, but no one in the class seemed to reliably read.

I couldn't pay attention in class no matter how hard I tried. The professor was talking about a priori knowledge and I was thinking about the fact that pantheon gods were–or at least had been–real. Philosophy suddenly felt like a bunch of made up bullshit compared to history, but on the other hand I wasn't sure gods could give life meaning if they were just people living and getting worshiped, maybe renting out magic portals.

Class ended before I could come to a conclusion and I headed back to the apartment. I found Lily in the exact spot on the couch I had left her, glued to Capu-mon. "Having fun?"

"No," she said, not looking up. "This fucking trainer is the biggest jerk I've ever met. He won't let me go to the next town until I beat him up, but he keeps beating me up!"

I glanced over her shoulder and shed a metaphorical tear that she had deleted my save file, but I hadn't actually played in months. She was at the second town, apparently inspecting every single tile in the map for secrets. "Let me guess, his little dragon thing keeps steamrolling you?"

"Yes!"

"Yeah, so if you go west of town you'll hit a dead end, but there's a spot where you can encounter rare monsters. Search there until you encounter a Fight-ape, and capture it. Fight-ape will wreck your rival right now, then you can progress."

By the time I had ordered a pizza for dinner that night, she had gotten the Fight-ape. I was standing at the door trying to tip the delivery guy when she came running over with the console. "John! John I did it, I finally beat that stupid asshole!"

she shouted, jumping onto my back and stuffing the game in front of me.

I took one glance at it and said, "You haven't won the fight yet, he still has his Falcano."

Lily blinked, looked again at the phoenix monster and ran screaming back to the couch to continue the fight. The delivery guy seemed more dazed and confused than I was. He asked, "Is she playing Capu-mon? That's awesome, I wish I had a girl-friend that gamed."

I shoved a fiver into his hand and said, "Jury is still out on whether she's any good at gaming. Thanks," and shut the door. Lily was nearly in tears as she tried to finish the rival fight, and I just sat down at my table and watched. It almost hurt to watch her be so invested in the game that she was frantic to beat it, because I could not remember the last time I had been that engrossed by a video game.

She fell onto the floor, holding the console up triumphantly, as I finished my fourth slice of greasy pizza. "I did it! I had to challenge him a second time after buying a bunch of healing items, but I did it!"

"Congratulations. You'll have to fight him again after the next city, so level up your monsters as much as you can. Want a slice?"

Lily sat down next to me, looking like she had just run a marathon. After eyeing how I was eating it, she took a slice and tried it. I blinked, and it was gone. Cheeks puffed out on pizza, she covered her mouth and said, "That's really good, can I have more?"

I slid the box over and let her eat the other half. I was text-ing Lance about plans to go to The Last Resort the next night when she finally cleared her mouth and asked, "So, I've been meaning to ask, what is that?"

She pointed at the 9mm I had left on the table. I hadn't really thought about it, because the ammo was all in my car, so there was no danger to it. "That? It's a pistol, and it's what I'm going to bring when I meet that old gambler... just in case."

She frowned. "Do you think he's the danger? Or are you worried about the other guys?"

"He did throw me through a market stall, didn't he? I've also been robbed and arrested and fought a dragon. My neck is still healing, so I can't exactly throw fists... so, I'm just being prudent."

"You might want to think twice about that. If he was speaking English, there's a real chance he's a god. You don't want to insult a god and he might take that the wrong way."

"He didn't seem like much of a god to me, and I'd rather have the gun than not. Hopefully, I don't need to use it. Besides, won't people in Alfheim be looking for swords and daggers? Not guns?"

"True, I guess, but it's a risk, you know? Whatever, just don't break the terms of the contract. Hilde is supposed to be shopping for more spices so we can get enough gold to pay the rent and stuff. Your clothes weren't cheap, you know? Whatever, I gotta go sleep. What time is it?"

"Almost sunset..."

Her shoulders slumped. "Shit, did I stay up all night?"

"Careful, you're going to end up a video game addict at this rate."

"Will not! Good night," she declared, and vanished into the bedroom. She left me reeling in shock that a girl from a fantasy world of magic and dragons was actually a nerd. Possibly almost as much of a nerd as I was.

But, if she was sleeping through her morning, where was I supposed to sleep? My couch wasn't actually comfortable if I wasn't drunk. Then she stuck her head back out the bedroom door. She didn't quite look at me as she said, "Just give me enough time to nap, then I'll go with you to The Last Resort, okay? You probably wouldn't be able to find it on your own, and you have no cash, and yeah. I'll help."

***

The biggest issue with putting on the tailored jacket wasn't the fit. It fit great, even if the stitching was a bit imprecise. It wasn't the weird powder they had on it, which was allegedly for sweat to protect the fabric. The issue was the shirt wanted to be buttoned almost to my knees, which made it look halfway between a tunic and a dress shirt. I barely understood fashion on Earth so I had no choice but to accept what I was told at face value.

The only change I made was leaving the shirt unbuttoned at the bottom, which gave me a disheveled look and exposed the button fly on the trousers, but I could reach the gun clipped to the small of my back.

Just as I expected though, The Last Resort was not a classy place. It was a dive bar with congealed sawdust across the boards like a beer cement. Smelled like a swamp, which I surmised was from the various inhuman creatures crowding the tables. Some of them I vaguely recognized from around the city, but only here and there. The Last Resort must have attracted them like an ethnic bar. Or worse, like a soccer bar and I didn't exactly know what colors to cheer for.

I saw one giant that appeared to be filing his tusks down, scraping a metal rasp to cut the points off. I took a guess he was a troll. On the other side were a group of short and stocky men playing cards: dwarves. No less than three people were black furred dog people, jackals perhaps. The fact that half of the people in the bar were succubi, a type of demon, actually came as a relief.

Even Lily seemed to hesitate as we looked around the room.

The bartender sized us up with one eye. Not because he was a cyclops but because he had lost the other to some ambiguous gash—scars now. "Well, I'm guessing the two of you are looking for someone?"

I glanced around, seeing half a dozen people watching me with frowns. "I do like dive bars, once you make friends with the workers, but I'm not sure my acquaintance is a particularly good reference."

The bartender passed a mug of beer to a lone dwarf, and said, "This is a local spot, and we like to keep it that way."

"I am a local," Lily said, glaring back at the man.

He arched an eyebrow. "Are you now? I haven't seen you before." He glanced at the dwarf and the burly guy took one look at her and laughed.

She planted her hands on her hips. "I work at Thorn's Tap Root and Room." The bartender paled and mumbled an apology, which satisfied her.

I scanned the bar, no sign of the old man. Upon second glance, I had to question whether the dwarf at the bar next to me actually was a dwarf. A female of the species maybe. "Is there an old guy missing an arm here?"

I heard no less than seven mugs get set down.

Then someone said, "Calm down, he's with me." A wrinkled old hand waved from the back corner, almost hidden between an unlit fireplace and the end of the service bar. Lily and I went over, and found the crippled gambler with a plate of ambiguous stew. I didn't even want to ask what was in it. It looked like meat slop and probably had more gristle than meat. Didn't phase the old man at all, he just swallowed, washed it down with some beer, and said, "What the hell is wrong with you, boy? You wait three days and then come at, what, noon? Who does that?"

I took the seat opposite him and Lily sat next to us. "You didn't say when to show up, just where."

The old man waved his fork at me. "Common courtesy says to show up as soon as possible. I thought you'd go that night! Looks like you made yourself pretty instead. Can you even lift your arms in that?"

I couldn't lift them overhead. "Should I be wearing a robe instead?"

"Or a gambeson at least. Don't you know the first thing about fighting? Or did your friend do all the real work killing that dragon?" he asked, then sized Lily up. "You're the lovely local, yes? Is he the rental owner? Maybe I should be scouting his friend instead. Seems he's got all the warrior blood. From the north too, by the looks of him."

I said. "We're here because you know where my brother is, was, whatever. What do you know?"

The old man grinned and jabbed his fork into another hunk of meat. "Got you interested, didn't I? But information isn't free. I'm looking to come to an arrangement with you, alright?"

Lily cleared her throat. "What do you want? Money? Or are you trying to make connections?"

"Nah, nothing so mundane as that. I want his love and adulation."

I stared him back in the eyes and said, "I'm not gay."

He grunted and scowled. "You modern people. Your language is crude and corrupted, you know that? What do you call it in this un-poetic shitheap of French you speak? I need your worship."

I rolled my eyes, and saw Lily shaking her head too. "What are you?" I asked. "A god?"

"Not so loud," Lily whispered. "Even if he is being rude."

He grinned again. "I'll have you know that I am no less than a god of war. Why else would my advice have been so good, hmm? And you, young man, as I've determined, are not the useless–divinely speaking–half breeds that fill this land, but a bonafide human. Just like the good old days, or even better, before the good old days in the days where I was in charge, but even still, back on Earth."

"So, you are him," Lily said.

"None other."

"I'm agnostic. What does worship entail? Need me to kill a deer in your name or something?

"Close. That would be a hunt god though. I suppose if you killed another monster like that river dragon it might count, but there's far easier ways."

"I'm not fighting a dragon again," I said, because if I had to, I'd just get a hunting rifle.

"You don't have to. Like I said, there's far easier ways.

Namely, fighting. There's some nuance, like I'll have to put my mark upon you–"

"Do not," Lily cut in. "John, you are already tied to our landlord. Splitting your devotion can be dangerous. The portal could break."

The god put up his hands. "You won't have to. It just needs to be drawn on you. So, you get my mark, you get in a fight, then I tell you how to track down your brother."

I considered asking for some kind of proof that my brother was actually alive. Doing nothing more than recovering his body... well, I'd get arrested if I did that. Finding out for certain was still worth it though. "Lily, I'm sorry but I kind of need to do this. Risky or not. You, god, what kind of fight?"

"One, more, depends on the quality of the fight. You see, worship is a funny thing, and not everyone's adoration is the same. Now, we gods all learned the lesson that focusing too much on the cream of the crop is a losing strategy, but that was in times of plenty. Times are lean now. You and your absent friend are some of the only humans in all of Alfheim–"

Lily interjected, "Some of? Excuse me, but how many bridges are there? Crossing realms is not supposed to be easy."

"What? Did you think there weren't other portals? Other survivors? Come on kid. So, you're some of the only humans in all of Alfheim, which means it's worth the investment to make you better, more able to exalt us. Do you follow?"

I said, "Only sort of. What are you going to do? Teach us how to fight?"

"I might as well teach a horse to sing. Why would I go to that much effort for someone who doesn't even want to be-lieve? I'll consider teaching you a thing or two when you realize it's worth applying yourself. Until then though, there's something a lot easier: virtue. Be valorous, be courageous, be honorable. That makes the reward all the sweeter. Nobody wants a coward or a sneakthief, not unless they're scraping the bottom of the barrel."

Lily scrunched up her face. "There are multiple gods of thieves."

"No, there are trickster gods, who take the thieves because no one else will worship them. All the real men end up singing names like mine. War god names. Sometimes harvest and fertility, but the youth is... it's the veal of the divine buffet, yeah? Not that there's any harm done to the humans in question."

I said, "Unless they get into a stupid fight because of you."

"Aye, unless that. I just wanted to stress that gods don't take anything of you that you have use for. We're almost like plants sucking up your carbon dioxide. What? Is that a bad analogy."

I had my head hung, pinching between my eyebrows. "No, sorry, that's just a me issue. Something about hearing a fantasy war god speak about chemistry just sort of hurts me inside. Go on."

"Right, so don't worry about losing anything. We gods are symbiotic, not parasitic."

"If that's true," I said, "Why am I being charged so much?"

The old man shrugged. "For the portal? That's between you and the other guy. You should have negotiated better."

"And if the other guy gets upset I'm giving you my... whatever, instead of him?"

"Is it in your contract that you have to wear his mark?" he asked, and I shook my head. "Then you're fine. Must be why he's taking so much money. Besides, I'm pretty sure I know the guy, and if he has something to say about this, I'll rip his beard out of his face and see how he likes that."

I scratched the stubble on my chin. "I think he was clean shaven."

"Bah, someone beat me to it then, that redheaded bastard. Still, don't you worry about that. So do we have a deal, Mr Martin?"

I stuck out my hand to shake the so-called god's. "How much time do I have to do this? I can't just randomly get in a fight."

The god clasped my hand and we shook. "You're the one in a rush to find your brother, aren't you? I've lived this way for a hundred years. I'm in no rush. Just, when you find the right guy, give them a good one-two. You know boxing, don't you?"

"I know what a one-two is. Who are you, anyways?"

The old man grabbed me by the wrist and twisted my hand over. He jabbed his thumb hard onto the back of my forearm. Runes remained when he let go of me: Norse runes. "I think you anglos pronounce it Tyr."

There was a feeling like a pinch across my forearm, and when he let go there was a dark mark. Something like a magical tattoo. Rubbing it eased the itch but didn't smudge the mark at all. It seemed simple enough and I didn't feel any different. Thankfully, the mark didn't look like anything weird, just some norse rune I could easily explain away. I figured that it wouldn't activate if I wasn't worshiping him, fighting. "Now what?"

Tyr shrugged and went back to drinking. "Now nothing. Not until you provide me some sustenance. For the record, I don't know where he is right now, or even if he's alive. I know how to get that info. It will take some effort however."

I snarled. "That wasn't exactly the deal."

Lily put her hand onto my leg. "I told you this was a bad idea, John. Let's get out of here."

"Go on," the god said, nodding to the door. "You don't need to rush into the fight. You didn't rush here. Besides, I'm an honorable fellow. It won't be much good to me if you go attack somebody. It's gotta be righteous, you understand. Tell you what, the worst case scenario is this: I'll need a week if all you do is sit in your house and sleep. You get in a fight before then, you come see me like a good little hero in need of training. Okay?"

"I can't believe I trusted you," I said, rising.

Tyr stared at me. "Your brother is here in Alfheim. I met him myself. Tried to recruit him just like I recruited you now. Problem is he already partnered up with that Egyptian fellow, Montu, and that was a direct clash. Definitely can't split that two ways. Me and a trickster? We're different enough, but I don't see eye to eye with Montu. The problem is, this was a year ago, before he was a dragon slayer and all that. I didn't lie to you John. This is just a partnership. And it's not without benefit to you in a very literal sense, you understand?"

"Yes, you'll be telling me how to find my brother."

He grinned. "That, and I'm going to train you up from soft clay into a fine specimen of a warrior. It'll take some hard work from you, but there's no greater teacher than me in this whole realm. Now then, I'll be seeing you."

I grabbed Lily's hand and tugged her back across the floor of the tavern and out the door. She didn't seem to mind and only when the door shut behind us did I become really conscious of what I'd done. "I'm sorry," I said, relaxing my hand.

"You really care about your brother, don't you?" she asked, not letting go of me.

"We were close, before he vanished. Now, I don't know what to think."

"We have that in common," she said, smiling up at me.

"Yeah? I guess you'd be surprised."

"No, I mean I too have an older brother that I hardly know what to think of."

We started walking back to town, hand in hand. "Am I going to meet him? Or just more of your muscular friends?"

I started when her hand slipped out of my grasp and she hung her head. "I think that would be difficult, at least for now. It would be best to keep my distance from him, I think."

"Back on Earth?"

"I almost wonder if that's not far enough, until things blow over at least."

I hoped that would be soon, but that didn't feel right to say, so I let the conversation drift to more mundane things about life in Alfheim. I had no idea how to get into a righteous fight though.

20

～

Lily

When the two of them made it back to the apartment, John bolted to get his phone with all the urgency of an addict. That made Lily frown and hesitate, but it also left her near the door of her apartment and she caught sight of a vaguely familiar man. She thought she had seen him at the villa or somewhere else friendly, but he was too young to be a regular member of the Blutengels. Despite that, he made the right hand signals to her.

There wasn't an exact translation and the meaning shifted with context, but she saw the blood on his shirt. He was telling her to stay safe and keep her head down.

She couldn't believe how bold the Black Fingers had gotten, or perhaps desperate. Bolting her door shut hardly felt like security. When she stepped into the bedroom, she asked, "This is going to sound weird, but could we move that dresser in front of the door?"

John walked back over, both hands on his phone. With a casual shrug, he said, "Sure but won't that be really weird if someone gets inside? There's a hole in your wall, remember? What are they going to think when the door is jammed shut but there's nothing on the other side?"

Lily bit back her curse and stared at the door out to Alfheim again. Of course, there was physical security. She was starting to think that relocating the portal to a door either in her brother's base of operations or maybe Lady Virent's would be better, but she also had no idea what kind of magic kept it there in the first place. Thinking about it didn't get her anywhere though. She couldn't come up with anything except waiting for her brother to come back from his journey and let him suppress the Black Fingers. With most of them imprisoned, this would be the best chance.

John cleared his throat. "So, it's the middle of the day for you, right? Not tired?"

She was actually feeling like taking a nap, especially if she could put all the blankets through the dryer first to get them warm and fluffy. "Not very, why?"

"House party? At Hilde's?"

"Yes," she said, half her mind rapidly thinking of what outfit she could put together from the assorted pile she had acquired. "One question though; what is a house party over here?"

Half an hour later, she still didn't really understand if a house party was like a friendly dinner, a gambling hall, or a ball, but the two of them were out on the street headed for Hilde's. While John was dressed like normal, Lily didn't feel normal. Despite having seen plenty of women dressed just like her, the sheer foreignness of the outfit–the oversized denim pants for example–was just weird to her. What she couldn't deny was the warmth. Secondhand boots lined with faux-fur kept the half-frozen slush off her feet and her body was wrapped in a voluminous, fuzzy wool sweater that was like armor against the wintery gusts.

The whole walk, while the two of them chit-chatted about the little things on Earth, she wondered whether it would be appropriate to peel it off once she got there, to wear nothing but the salmon-pink tank top Hilde had picked out for her. It had less fabric to it than some prostitutes Lily had seen.

Concerns of propriety vanished when the door to Hilde's apartment swung open and she saw the mess of people inside. With a dozen people crowded into the two-bedroom apartment, even with the windows all thrown open, they couldn't get the temperature down below a body-heat sauna. At least two girls had fallen asleep on a couch. They weren't quite cuddling but one was definitely using the other as a pillow. How they could be sleeping through pounding music as well as half a dozen people boisterously gambling on cards just a few feet away... she could only guess how many of the beer cans had been theirs.

"Holy shit," John said as he slipped his coat off. "You got it cleaned up?"

Lily did a double take at the apartment. There was junk everywhere, not the least of which were the half dozen cardboard boxes across the kitchenette for take-out pizza. She just couldn't wrap her head around the capacity for waste on Earth. Everything came in packaging and nothing was used to the point of breaking. Beyond mere clutter, one of Hilde's roommates seemed to be a seamstress, with mannequins and yards of fabric shoved into various corners, spilling out of closets, and looming in one of the bedrooms. There was a tv in one corner, almost buried by the mess, playing what looked like a movie about talking trees.

Those were mythological even by Alfheim standards.

But on the upside of industrial productivity, every beer was in its own can, cold as ice, and still carbonated. While the flavor wasn't the best, she happily slid in beside John at the card table. As far as she could tell, the house party had more in similarity with a raucous, post-battle celebration than anything than an elf would call a party, but that was fine.

"So, I met a god," John said. He lamely added, "In a dream, a very inspiring dream though. Check this." The other people at the table shrugged and didn't question him. Everyone peered over as John rolled his sleeve up and revealed Tyr's mark.

Lance whistled. "Don't tell me that's from the one armed dude?"

The other guy at the table asked, "Nice tat, where'd you get it?"

John coughed. "It was a back alley kind of place and I was drunk. Anyway, my shoulder is feeling pretty good actually."

Lily grabbed him by his shirt. "Do not push yourself."

John put up his hands and made promises as introductions were hastily made as to who Lily was. She was apparently John's friend from out of town and they had met online. Everyone took the story at face value, though anyone who could elbowed him in the side. It didn't take long for Lily to piece together what everyone was assuming about their relationship, but acknowledging it would be confirming something that wasn't actually happening. Denying it would probably just extra confirm it.

As the card game was set back up, and the rules quickly explained to Lily, John mused, "I have to somehow get in a fight this week."

Lily stared at him. "Just wait the week. You're still healing."

"I'm telling you, I feel fine. Look; I can raise my arm and everything," he said as he got his elbow up to shoulder height and no further.

"Can you raise your hand up any further?"

"Hey, Hilde, can I get a shot?" John asked.

The tall woman strode past and pulled open the freezer. She had poured a round of blue drinks before she stopped and asked, "Aren't you on super strong painkillers?"

Lance added, "From the hospital, not for fun," for the benefit of the other partygoers.

John's shoulders sank. "Oh come on, let me have some fun. Your liver grows back!"

"No," Hilde said, putting a blue shot down in front of everyone but John. "Bottoms up everyone, because if we flunk out of med school that's how you pay back those loans!" Half the table laughed and half seemed stricken with despair but they all took their drink.

Lily couldn't identify the flavor. It was sugary and sweet, fruity but also acidic, and it certainly did not taste like alcohol. "How strong was that?" she asked, licking her lips.

Hilde laughed. "Careful, we don't need you getting freshman-fucked-up on us." She left the almost-empty bottle beside Lily. While the game resumed, she read the label and did the math on how much alcohol was hiding in the sweetest drink she had ever tasted. The amount was almost terrifying.

"Sorry this isn't some grand adventure for you," John said, slumping down beside her to talk quietly. He kept his cards fanned out in front of him and in full view of her.

"John, you actually have no idea how nice it is to be among regular people."

"Don't get much of that back home?"

She grimaced. "Not for a long time and not because of anything I ever did."

"But because of your brother?" he asked and then tapped the card that was her best play at the moment.

"I can lose this game all on my own, thank you very much," she said, getting a grin out of him as she tossed the card down. "Also, yes."

"Well, I tell you what. This spice business plays out? We start banking some serious cash? I can take you to some real high society places. Across the bridge, Detroit, is a major city with major attractions. I think there's Michelin star restaurants... Hey guys, does Detroit have a Michelin star restaurant?"

The table shrugged and one by one they voiced their ignorance. John pulled out his phone and started searching as the front door flew open. A short girl came in groaning so loud even the drunks on the couch woke up. "I made a mistake!"

Hilde jumped up from the table. "What did you do?"

The new girl groaned and buried her face in her hands. "I fucked him again," she said, before spotting the liquor in front of Lily. "Oh, perfect," she said, grabbing it and drinking straight from the bottle.

"I'm not a mistake!" some guy shouted as he came stumbling

drunk into the apartment wearing a smelly fur coat and over-sized sunglasses.

"Katelyn, what the fuck?" Hilde blurted out as all the men at the table started cleaning up the game.

The short girl rolled her eyes. "I said it was a mistake, didn't I?"

"No, you, out," Hilde ordered, pointing a finger at the guy in the coat.

John cleared his throat and stood up. He put himself between her and the guy before leaning down. In a casual whisper, he said, "This guy's like a bull in a china shop."

"China?" Lily responded just before the translation spell pieced together the contextual intent.

John shrugged. "He's broken doors, at least one coffee table, countless mugs, and never pays for it. Honestly, if he's sticking around..."

The whole party began to grumble. Everyone set about picking up their things or getting new beers. Someone even turned off the music as the drunk mess continued to play out at the front door. Lily almost couldn't take her eyes off the guy in the fur coat. She had a morbid curiosity, like she was looking at an auditioning court jester or something. "How is he so brazen?" she asked.

"Lack of consequences," Lance said, and John nodded.

John put his hand on Lily's shoulder and squeezed it. With a pained grimace, he said, "We should have gone somewhere else. This is a terrible welcome to... d'Amaranth."

Lily put on a smile. "I don't think this is your fault. Besides, this is still way better than getting in a knife fight at a cafe, right?"

John laughed and nodded toward the door. "Come on. We can let the roommates sort this out."

Lily stood up and followed behind him as he tried to squeeze through to the door. She waved and said a few pleasant goodbyes as they got their boots back on. Lance jumped up to ask when they thought they'd have a gold exchange or maybe a trip to a pawn shop, which gave the guy in the fur coat just enough time to realize they were leaving.

"Hey, hey, hey, don't just book out because I got here!"

"Todd, get back over here," Katelyn said, stamping her foot on the ground.

He ignored her, tugging his glasses down to leer at Lily. "I don't recognize you. The name's Todd," he said, reaching his hand out toward her.

Reflexively, Lily slapped it away and that got everybody's attention. Todd looked more shocked than reprimanded while everyone's attention was on them. She was halfway to sneering at him when she realized she had just treated the drunk like someone in Alfheim. "I'm sorry," she blurted out, stepping back from him.

John cranked the door handle and popped it open. "Don't be," he said, making way for her to evacuate.

Todd laughed and turned back to the crowd. "Can you believe this shit?"

"You're an ass, Todd," Hilde said.

Lily took her attention off of him for a moment, turning to John. "He was just trying to shake my hand, wasn't he? I screwed up. Not even a week and I did something like that."

John put his hands back on her shoulders and looked into her eyes. "Don't worry about it."

Then Todd lurched forward. His feet flailed randomly as he knocked into the coat closet door. Before Lily could get out of his way, one of his hands swung out and grabbed hold not of her, but of her sleeve. Todd broke his glasses when he hit the ground but nobody had sympathy because he had taken one of Lily's sleeves with him.

John said, "Change of plans. Lance? Give me a hand?" Then he grabbed Todd by the scruff of his coat and Lance took a leg. The two of them carried the drunk into the hall and left Lily behind.

Hilde walked over and plucked at the torn wool. "Are you okay?"

"Oh, I'm fine," Lily said, ignoring the fact that her reaction had almost been to kick Todd in the face, which would have been entirely appropriate in Alfheim. "But, has John always been like that? Or did the other fight make him cocky?"

Hilde sighed as Katelyn shouted an apology from across the apartment. "He's probably showing off because of you."

Lily couldn't help but grin.

21

John

I really didn't have anything against Todd in daytime scenarios. It was when alcohol got involved that he went stupid. Of course, he sort of always was stupid because he was always thinking about getting alcohol. He said he was an engineer, but he was only getting an AES degree so he didn't have end of semester projects. That made him not an engineer as far as I was concerned.

Worse than that, he wasn't taking us seriously even after we slammed him up against the stairwell wall.

Todd put up his hands and stared at me with half-lidded, unfocused eyes. "Sorry man. I'll buy her a new sweater... You'll have to get me her sizes though." He grinned.

I groaned. "You stupid idiot. You are literally incapable of repaying me for fucking up the first time I bring Lily out for the night. You know that?"

Todd let out a simpering groan, his eyes raised. "How did

you find that smoke show? What dating app? You gotta tell me, man."

"Friend of a friend," I said, getting a snicker out of Lance. Then I remembered that there was something I needed and it was something Todd could give me. "Hey, Lance... what do you think counts as a fight?"

My friend shrugged. "Throwing hands."

Todd seemed to realize something had changed. He looked at me with a flicker of awareness as I asked, "And what would you say is a righteous fight?"

Lance arched an eyebrow at me. "Defense of self or others."

I shrugged. "He assaulted Lily. Damaged her property. Scared her. He broke the, what do you call it, non-aggression pact."

"Principle," Lance said.

Todd cleared his throat. "Hold on–"

I slugged him in the gut. I hammered my fist right into his stomach as hard as I could, which wasn't that hard. The hospital hadn't been that long ago. The rune in my arm felt good though. It grew warm and tingled for a moment as Todd fell to his knees, doubled over.

Then he vomited on me. An entire night's worth of beer, liquor, and what looked like chicken wings spewed across my chest and legs.

The fight was over. All three of us gagged and staggered away from the mess. Todd went stumbling down the steps and I was thinking about crawling into Hilde's shower when a flashlight swept up and hit me. A police officer stared at us, one hand hooked into his belt. "Did you just punch that guy?"

"No," I said. "He puked on me."

The police officer's brow pulled together. "Are you going to call maintenance?"

Lance took a careful step around the puddle of chunks and took a look at the cop. "You got a reason to be in here? This is a locked apartment building my dude."

The police officer turned away and mumbled something that I swore was, "I told you so."

Then a woman pushed into the bottom of the stairwell. She wasn't in a police uniform, but something about her sport coat said she was a detective maybe. It was probably the handgun she had holstered under her arm. "Noise complaint," she said as she marched ahead of the cop and joined us at the landing. I couldn't place her age to save my life, but she was wearing a Christian cross on a necklace. At first I thought that might be a good sign that nothing much would happen, that she wouldn't give us a hard time maybe.

Then I remembered the very clear warning in my portal contract against the authorities finding out about it.

Lance folded his arms. "Did that noise complaint come with an apartment number?"

The cop trailing behind the detective answered with Hilde's apartment number.

The woman didn't seem to care. She just walked over to me and looked me over. Then she sniffed. Her scowl was instantaneous, and I couldn't imagine why she had intentionally taken a whiff of fresh beer vomit. "You smell like my ex."

"Ok?" I asked, backing up to the wall to give them room to pass us.

"Get yourself cleaned up," she said as she headed up to knock on Hilde's door.

Lance and I stayed in the stairwell and eventually he asked me, "What just happened?"

"I don't know man, but I feel like I'm a magnet for trouble lately," I said, finally realizing that some of the puke had gotten on my arms. I tried to give it a flick off but there was nothing to do but wait for the shower. The rest of the party, mostly Hilde's fencing friends, came fleeing out of the apartment like cockroaches when the lights turn on. The music had already been turned down and now the party was truly dead. Nobody asked me how I had gotten puked on, they just used the next staircase to keep their boots clean.

Eventually, I tried to go back into Hilde's apartment to get into the shower, but the detective stopped me. "You go to the clubs around here, much?" she asked, keeping a good distance away from me.

"Sometimes," I said, obviously holding my arms up as filth dripped off of me. "Can I go get cleaned up or are you going to arrest me?"

"You ever run into a man there? Middle-aged, red hair, likes to wear sunglasses indoors?"

My blood ran a little cold as I worried she was describing my landlord, but I said, "I don't talk to middle-aged men when I go to the clubs. Now, if you'll excuse me," I said, and shut the door between us.

Hilde gagged when she saw me and fetched cleaning supplies. "Mistakes were made," I said as I peeled my sticky boots off. The tv had gotten to the end of the movie trilogy which I had been surreptitiously watching all night, and I was a bit loath to miss some of the best scenes but I had to clean up.

"Hold on," she said, dumping the chemicals on the ground

beside me. She came back with some beach towels and had me walk across them to get to the bathroom where I started stripping off. Lance caught her up to speed on what happened as she sanitized everything I had touched.

Lily stuck her head out of Katelyn's room. "John? You okay?"

"I'm fine, just gross," I said as I dropped my t-shirt onto the back of the toilet and turned the shower's hot water on. Then I saw her without her sweater on. I immediately did a double take at the slim tank top she had on. She may have literally been a gangster princess but at least she looked the part. I could still remember the disdain she had shown for Todd and yet when she looked at me there was nothing but worry.

I had to ask her out properly. Not just going to a friend's party. I knew my brother would probably have warned me to not shit where I eat, we were roommates afterall, but fuck that. This had to be fate or something. Or rather, the fruits of a conspiring god.

That didn't change the fact that I had to clean the puke off of me. There's always something a little off about showering in someone else's place. The elbow room is off, I think. I was knocking my elbows against the tiles and covered in soap when Lance reached into the bathroom to set down a glass of cotton candy vodka which I drank. I still had plenty of adrenaline in my system and the booze helped cool it off.

A few minutes later, I stepped out with a towel wrapped around my waist. "Guys, problem. What am I supposed to wear?" I could hear the wash turning over my jeans, at least I assumed my jeans were inside, but that would take hours.

Katelyn jumped up from the table. "Hold on, I got you."

She and Hilde were not on good terms, but I would owe her one if she saved me a long wait.

Lily came over and I thought she was going to thank me again or something, but she just grabbed at my shoulder and prodded the stitches. "You broke one."

"Which?" I asked, trying to crane my head down to see. She poked my wound right at the bottom and sure enough, one of the loops had snapped. "Uh, first aid?"

Katelyn stopped in her doorway, staring at me. Hilde had to open the closet to hand me the bucket of medical supplies. After improvising a replacement for the stitch–antiseptic, liquid bandage, and medical tape–I held my hand out to Katelyn for the clothes. She shook her head and handed them over. "I stole this from my ex. You don't need to give it back. The pants are another matter though. I need them for a photoshoot next week."

"I'll get them back to you as soon as I... can." She had given me capris in late fall. They would get me home at least. Once I was dressed, I asked, "Ready to go?"

Lily smirked. "It's a bit early."

"Maybe for you. You can stay if you want but I'm going to bed. When a drunk pukes on you, your night is scuffed. No more. Call it. Try again the next day."

Lily laughed. "Hilde, can I borrow a coat?"

A few minutes later, we had said our goodbyes and I had gotten Lance up to speed about revisiting Tyr. Then we were on the road together. Once we were alone, Lily asked, "Do your friend's parties usually go like that?"

"Destructive and violent?"

"Casual and fun... I mean before Todd showed up."

"Depends on the group. Most of those people passed out early, remember? We were mostly chatting with the alcoholics. The big irony of college. Those that drink the most get the least drunk."

"Well, I liked it."

When I glanced over, she was smiling at me. "I'll be sure to bring you to more then. You got pretty hooked on Capu-mon the other day, right?"

Lily blinked and her expression shifted slightly. She had a slight mixture of annoyance and determination. "Yeah, I'm stuck on a really annoying gym leader!"

I could take a few guesses which one she was stuck on, but I didn't just tell her to grind levels. "I can introduce you to some other games, other genres. I've got a whole pile that doesn't get enough use. But what made me think about it is that we probably missed Drunk Driving."

She frowned. "John, I've seen enough of these metal death traps to know that's a bad idea."

I snickered. "It's a game."

"Do you have a death wish?"

"No, I mean a video game. The actual game is just a kart racer and in fact you can't drink and drive. You have to put your controller down to pick up your drink and you have to drink if your kart gets hit, as well as you must finish your beer before you finish the race. And if you get hit after you finished your beer, you gotta crack a new one. Lots of fun. The best player gets the drunkest so it all evens out."

Lily nodded along until I finished. "I have no idea what you just described, but I'm in."

I mentally added that to my list of things I had to do, and

put it someplace below cutting deals with a pagan god to find my brother. At least my injury seemed pretty well healed thanks to the magic and in the worst event I could probably afford another magic healer. I just had to make sure I didn't drag Lily into my mess.

22

~

Lily

After John fell asleep, Lily opened the door to Alfheim and waved down her guard. It was a rare day, or maybe the Blutengels were worried. The man who walked over was Minotaur. No one knew his actual name, not even him. The behemoth of a man was a djinn at least three centuries old with a pair of ram horns adorning his head like a crown. That made him old enough to have been poisoned by the elves during the war.

In a voice rivaling the rumble of a troll's, he asked, "How can I help Prin–... Lily?"

She frowned and held out the tea cup regardless. "Drink this?"

The djinn took it daintily and arched a scaled eyebrow at her. The coffee didn't look very appetizing, she knew. The taste was another matter. Despite Minotaur's hesitation, he gave it a sniff, wrinkled his nose, and sipped it. "What is it?"

"Is it good?" Lily asked.

Minotaur sipped it again. "Not really. An acquired taste?"

"Maybe you're too big. It's like tea mixed with tea... compounded with tea."

Minotaur looked at the coffee again. "That's a lot of tea."

"Well, it's not actually tea. It can perk you up like tea though, and a lot faster. I'm thinking of selling it to the nobles."

"Oh," Minotaur said, nodding along. "I see now. Selling trash to rich people. Classic. Like that time someone convinced them caviar was expensive."

Lily pouted. "It's not trash! It's medicine at worst. And I have an exclusive supply. That makes it a luxury good. Huge mark up."

Minotaur nodded. "Right. Big money for the dirty water. The dirty water for the stupid nobles. Get the stupid nobles to give their money over. Money for the dirty water. Got it."

Lily groaned and took her tea cup back from the djinn. "You don't get it! It tastes good... after a couple cups. Look, I want to take this to Lady Virent and sell it to her first."

Minotaur nodded. "She'd buy it."

Lily checked her enthusiasm and asked, "And why do you think that?"

"Because she likes you. She'd buy your dirty water."

"Oh, would you just get somebody to escort me there, please?" she demanded before slamming the door shut. She turned to put the cup back in her wash basin before she realized the door had thudded against Minotaur's boot rather than the frame.

The djinn gently pushed the door back open and hunched down to fit his head into the apartment. "Who's the guy, Lily? And why is there a hole in your wall?"

She still hadn't put up a sheet to cover the wall. "Don't worry about the wall. As for John, he's my supplier."

"A business partner?"

Lily put the cup into her wash basin and reflected on the fact that she would probably never have to use it again. She had an automatic washer just on the other side of the portal. "Yes, just a business partner."

"That lives with you."

Lily blushed and fidgeted, trying to find an excuse. "Temporarily."

"And you trust him?"

"He's not with the Black Fingers if that's what you're asking."

"He could be with someone else."

"I know who he's with and I'm not at liberty to say. He's trustworthy, okay?"

Minotaur nodded. "I'll have to tell the boss."

"You let me tell my brother!"

Minotaur shrugged. "He'll be back soon. If you wait at the base, you can be the one to tell him."

"And if I don't?"

"I'll have to tell him. He's the boss. The boss has to know."

"John isn't a security threat."

Minotaur arched his eyebrow again. "He got in a fight. Got arrested. Got sent to the arena. Killed a dragon to escape. Then got in another fight in the market."

Lily clicked her tongue. "That second fight wasn't his fault. In fact, neither of them were."

"Right," Minotaur said and even though he nodded, Lily knew he didn't believe her.

"Can you get me to Lady Virent or not?"

"Certainly, Princess," Minotaur said, ducking back out and letting the door close.

Lily started forward, yelling at him to not call her that but stopped herself. She knew he didn't mean anything bad by it or anything he had said. She just sighed and readied herself to go back into Blue Rock Bay. The trip took more coordination than she would have liked. Her security detail ended up being two people, one of which openly wore brigandine armor. The other was younger and did his best to chat with her like they were merely friends and they were friends of a sort.

Her relationship with him could only be stilted by the dynamic of the Blutengels, but he was young and savvy enough to have a pleasant conversation about the recent games in the arena and about plays available both upriver and downriver. The trip was almost normal despite the rest of the passengers on the lastkan barge sliding as far away as possible. More importantly, nobody attacked them and Lily was able to arrive at Lady Virent's manor once more.

"Here for the layabout?" the guard asked, not taking his gaze off her protection.

"For Lady Virent."

The guard sighed. "Subject?"

Holding up a cloth bag full of coffee beans, she loosened the top slightly to let the strange aroma out. "Business."

That got her inside, and an hour later she had dined on tea and biscuits while perusing the elf's library. Eventually, a maid opened the door and said, "Miss Hagen?" That was all the alert she had to prepare herself, shutting the book and sliding it across the table as she sat upright. Then Lady Virent stepped inside. Her coat was loosened and unbuttoned, her hair in a messy bun. While the door remained open she moved purposely but as soon as it shut, she sagged.

Lily smiled. "Busy day, Aunty?"

Lady Virent slumped into the chair across from her. "Oh, Lily, you have no idea," she said as she adjusted her mask and shifted it enough to expose part of her face. She grabbed a chocolate coated cookie and stuffed it into her mouth with no delicacy at all.

For a high elf to expose their face was very taboo if it was in front of strangers. Despite things getting strained recently, there was a reason Lily still called her Aunty. "Something to do with the digsite?" she asked, pouring Lady Virent a cup of tea from the porcelain kettle. A hint of steam still remained.

"I put the wrong man in the arena..."

Lily grimaced. "You nearly killed my friend."

"He was betraying you!"

"He had no idea who the Black Fingers were! He had been falsely arrested. That was the whole... ugh! Why didn't you talk to me before putting him in a death match?"

Lady Virent leaned back with her tea, practically sulking. "I didn't put him in a death match. Just an exhibition. Your friend chose to risk his life."

Lily smacked her fist on the table. "He got tricked! Oh, forget it. Look, I don't even want to know what you were thinking because that's not why I'm here."

Lady Virent crossed her legs and asked, "It's not?"

Lily glowered for a moment, wondering if she should push the issue. Then she sighed. "I know it must seem strange that this guy you've never met before is my friend and somehow isn't part of my brother's group. That's what I'm here to clear up. Do you know what this is?"

When Lily offered the bag, Lady Virent tugged the opening of the bag down with a finger. The smell overwhelmed the tea. "Beans?"

"Not for eating. I mean, maybe you could eat them. But you steep them and drink the water like tea. Stronger taste. Maybe it's acquired. Stronger energy though. Can keep you working right through the night. I mean, you'll pay for it the next day, but you can. I believe nobody else in the city can supply this. It's a luxury good. Rare."

Lady Virent picked up one of the roasted beans and held it between them. "Where'd you get it?"

Lily swallowed the knot in her throat and said, "He has a relic." That wasn't technically a lie, even if she knew it was misleading.

Lady Virent narrowed her gaze, then took the lid off the kettle. "So you steep them?" she asked, dropping the bean in.

Lily nodded. "You'll need more than that. Mixing it with tea might be... distasteful."

The elf sighed and rang the service bell sitting beside the kettle. A moment later, the maid looked inside. "Hot water, nothing in it, please." A fresh kettle was brought and a handful of the beans were dropped inside.

For a few minutes of small talk, Lily couldn't take her eyes off of it because she didn't actually know if such a simple method would work. Hilde had shown her a sort of pass through contraption, and it needed a filter. Those had been ground up though, which darkened the color.

"How long do we have to wait?" Lady Virent asked, swirling the kettle.

Lily chewed her lip. "I'm not sure…"

Lady Virent arched a slender eyebrow, then nodded at the book. "Been brushing up on old German?"

The translation spell had proven more useful than she expected, but she didn't know how to explain that to Lady Virent. "Trying to," she lied.

The elf planted her elbows on the table. "Your friend… he wouldn't be a god, would he?"

"No, definitely not."

"Where'd you get the beans then?"

"From a relic… For our safety, I really can't say more. It's not the kind of information that I can let leak out."

"Lily, you know that my leniency with you, your brother… the people allied with him, it can only go so far as they are citizens of this kingdom. The gods are another matter. If you ally with them, there will be no mercy for you, or for me."

Lily gulped. When she had the courage to test her voice, she said, "I wouldn't do that, Aunty. I just can't tell you how John got his relic, okay? I assure you he is not a god though. By the way, how is your guest doing? He might be an interesting benchmark for the saleability."

"Mr Smythe? I think he's out at the moment. Last I spoke with him, he was going to negotiate a collection of wine purchases for me. He's proven to be quite a helpful fellow actually, in a somewhat imposing way. He conducts himself like a high elf, and speaks like one too."

Lily smirked. "So, he's been good company?"

"I certainly don't mind having him around. Now, how

about we try this bean water?" Lady Virent proposed, and poured both of them small tea cups of the brew.

Lily knew immediately that the color was wrong. She hesitated, then sipped it and almost spit it back out. Lady Virent kept herself more composed, but didn't say anything good about it. "Maybe it needs sugar?" Lily proposed.

"Honey is all I have here."

"Let's try it," Lily said, and both of them added a dollop of honey, stirred it in, and again found themselves not quite able to say they liked the flavor. Lily hung her head. "I'm sorry, I'll go back and double check the proper preparation method."

"You'll check with this John fellow?"

The tone in Lady Virent's voice had changed. Lily met it with an emotionless, "Yes."

"He's just a business partner, you say?"

"Well, after meeting you, he's a dragon slayer too," Lily said with a smirk.

"Bring him to me, won't you?" Lady Virent asked with a smirk. "Let him make the coffee."

Lily forced herself to smile even though she knew the elf was merely planning to meddle in a relationship that didn't exist. "Sure, I can do that."

23

∽

John

I woke the day after the party with a certain, hungover grogginess. The vestiges of alcohol damped my perceptions and dragged me into a familiar rut. I was too tired, even after coffee, to take much initiative until the malaise passed and by then I was through a normal morning routine. As though I wasn't engaged in a real adventure, I found myself at class and sitting through lecture.

Lily hadn't been in the room when I got up, nor had she returned before I left. She must have stayed the night somewhere else, and I couldn't text to ask because phones didn't work in Alfheim. As the day progressed, and my learning did not, I found myself agitated and restless. She hadn't left a note, or told me what she meant to do, when I could see her next. In fact, the only evidence of what she had done was some missing coffee beans from the pantry. That gave me a vague idea what she was doing, but I couldn't help but feel I hadn't taught her very well how to make coffee.

That couldn't be my fault. I wasn't a barista. Coffee was a means to an end, not some kind of modern alchemy. Certainly the internet was filled with tips and tricks, recipes and blends. I was sure there was no end of luxury and boutique coffee methods that could be employed to swindle the nobility of Alfheim, but the idea just didn't appeal to me. It wasn't an adventure.

It did seem to be better than my class on control systems. By the end of the hour, I and everyone else had quietly watched our professor fill four chalkboards working through a single problem. He had first written the original problem, something about the shock system for a car on a noisy road, then worked through simplified problems that he attempted to apply back to the full equation but twice he had made a mistake and been forced to erase huge sections of math.

I raised my hand and asked, "Is this going to be on the test?"

"Yes, you will need to understand these principles," he said.

"But our test period is only an hour and you haven't finished solving the problem."

For a moment, I had the rapt attention of everyone in class as we watched the professor sweat. As we heard the rumble of feet while other classes were dismissed, he meekly said, "Maybe it will only be one of the simpler problems. We'll finish this one next week, alright class?"

Feeling like just about the lamest variety of classroom hero, I exited the classroom and started making arrangements for the night. Lance was supposed to come with me to Tyr. He responded by asking if Hilde could come too. She started a group chat with our four numbers, although I didn't envy the flip phone Hilde had bought Lily, and then the fencer's first message was, "I want a sword."

Lance responded with, "John, she's out-nerding us. This cannot stand. I need two swords."

Two hours later, they carried in a stack of pizzas which we devoured with the vague hope that Lily would arrive sometime around sundown. We needed a guide of some sort, but I also didn't like the idea that I was tied to Lily. I didn't want her tied down to me if she wanted to go to Earth either. "We're like each other's travel guides, right?" I said around the time we were picking over cool slices of pizza and the ends of the breadsticks.

Hilde said, "I don't think it's really a fair comparison, between Earth and Alfheim. Don't forget you literally got arrested and basically sentenced to death."

"Yeah, but is Earth much safer? What if she ended up over in the penny lots?"

Lance said, "Honestly, Aflheim will probably be safer for us than Earth is for her... once we have swords. I think we'll be fine to head back to the markets, just gotta be careful and not trust anyone."

"Yeah, yeah, so long as after we do that, we go find Tyr," I said, and we all nodded. With the hope in the back of my mind that Lily would show up before we got out the door, we all headed through to Alfheim and got changed into local clothes. While Hilde took her time trying to lace up every new bit of her dress, I sat down with pen and paper to write a note. The first one I wrote I had to crumple and throw away, not because the wording was embarrassing or something but because I literally couldn't read my own handwriting. I had the lazy scrawl of note taking rather than a scribe's touch.

The second attempt took me much longer, to form the words properly. Just as I was getting to the end, the door opened. I swore under my breath, turning and expecting to see Lily in the doorway. Instead, almost the entire frame was filled by a blue skinned brute. I saw sharp eyes staring at me from beneath twin horns. The giant said, "I knew something was strange about you people."

"Can I help you?" I asked, my heartrate slowly rising. Unlike my friends who were trying to arm themselves like medieval knights, I still had a modern weapon. My brother's pistol was holstered beneath my tunic. Unfortunately, I wasn't sure I had enough bullet to deal with this beast of a man.

The horned giant shrugged. "Lily said you were friends, but I didn't expect you to be humans."

I knocked my chair over as I rose. "That's a dangerous accusation," I said, my voice almost trembling as I turned to face the man.

The demon lifted a hand and shook his head. "Calm yourselves. I'm a friend of the gods. For three hundred years I've served them. Unless you're agents of the Usurper, then I won't betray your secret. Besides, you're friends of the princess."

Lance folded his arms and asked, "Usurper? You mean–" He didn't get the rest of his question about before his sister clamped a hand over his mouth.

I stepped forward. "Do you work for her brother?"

"I work for the boss, yes. You can call me Minotaur. Everyone else does. I'll have to tell the boss."

I felt in my gut that Lily's brother finding out about us was an inevitability, but also that it was something she should tell him instead of some blue demon named Minotaur. "Can't you have Lily do that?" I asked. "Also, what makes you say we're humans?"

"The boss is busy. Also, we're speaking English."

Lance cleared his throat. "Yeah, I should have pointed that out to you, John."

That explained how Lance had responded to the Usurper bit. I cursed my translation spell for being too intuitive. "How the hell do you speak English?"

Minotaur scratched his chin. "I may not be as smart as I once was, but I am not a forgetful man. Many languages came over from Earth to this backwater. Now, why don't you come with me, humans? You want to buy weapons, do you not? You'll need them if you're to be friends of the princess."

Thus, the three of us ended up in an awkward procession not to the main thoroughfares of land barges and trolls but traversing a series of circuitous bridges and ruts. Some roads had proper stone arches to span the animal gullies below, but more often than not we had to pick our way over rotting wood. I was not surprised to see only hovels, workshops, and warehouses as we proceeded toward the southern shore. The stink of the city grew worse, as though the odors of life drifted down from the elven hills.

I kept myself occupied memorizing the path and keeping my head on a swivel. People kept looking at us from the corners of their eyes, but shying away from Minotaur. Hilde stayed close behind me, but Lance seemed unperturbed. "What did you mean you used to be smarter, by the way? You don't look old or anything."

Minotaur glanced over his shoulder. "I'm a djinn," he said, and didn't elaborate until after the four of us had stepped into an overstuffed weapons shop packed with secondhand goods. I wasn't an expert in weapons, but I could tell they had been bought and resold, probably scavenged from battlefields. Swords didn't fit their scabbards properly. Spear tips had been fitted to new shafts of mostly-straight wood. The shields were flaking one color of paint and revealing another beneath. The only good pieces of metal were kept on display behind the shelf and beneath them was the proprietor.

"New blood?" the white haired shopkeeper asked.

"Something like that," Minotaur said as he took a seat on a bench beside the front window. His frame blocked most of the light, barely letting us see by the oily candles. "Don't let them break the bank, but put it on the tab in my name"

"We can pay," I said.

Minotaur nodded. "Yes, I saw the dirty bean water Lily is trying to sell. I'm sure you can pay. That's why I'm putting it on my tab now. Safety first. Money second. Always."

Hilde almost stopped holding herself back and hissed in my ear. I translated to Elvish and pointed to the basket-hilt rapier the shop owner had. The man grinned and nodded, giving us a short speech on the qualities of the blade that went entirely over Hilde's head. She smiled like she was listening then stepped back with it in her hand. One flick and she frowned. We all watched as she gave it a brandish like a figure eight, then her expression soured even more. It didn't seem to pass her rattle test either and it did nothing to scratch the back of her nail when she tested the edge.

The shopkeeper was visibly distressed at her rank assessment, wringing his hands until he laid eyes on Lance. "You there, is there something you had your mind on? A nice sturdy weapon for a warrior like you?"

I didn't dare translate the question to English but when I gestured at the weapons Lance got the intention easily. He passed over the battleaxes, the zweihanders, the claymores, in fact he passed all the oversized weapons that could have felled trees. He didn't even take anything from behind the counter, but hefted a pair of handaxes kept on a side table. After checking their heft and their sharpness, he slammed one into a chunk of wood for testing. The board cracked in half from the blow. It had already been beaten up by previous use, but the pain on the shopkeeper's face was apparent.

"Sharpen it up for him. Clearly that fits him well," Minotaur said, and the man excused himself to the back with the pair of weapons. Then the djinn crossed his arms and said, "You wouldn't know, but it's common knowledge here. We djinn were made by the gods several centuries ago. We were smart and strong, a race of heroes but the elves called us demons. Because we wouldn't age and are quite difficult to kill, they arranged a betrayal instead. Long ago, the elven king broke all laws of hospitality in a bid to cripple us. When the poison was discovered, hardly any of the betrayers survived the night, but the damage had been done. To this day it lingers in our bodies, it pollutes our thoughts. It muddies us."

"And healing magic won't cure that?"

The djinn's grimace was sorrowful beyond what I thought his scaled visage could produce. "Three hundred years and we've never found a mage willing to try."

Alfheim was starting to sound a lot less hospitable, but I

had to remind myself that most of Earth was embroiled in centuries old conflict too. Every major flashpoint in the world had history behind it. Maybe things weren't too different and certainly it wasn't any of my business. I had to ask, "Is Lily, her brother I guess, still involved in some kind of war? She seems like she's on good terms with the elves."

Minotaur snorted and grinned. "Lady Virent isn't like most. Don't you need a weapon?"

I had a pistol already. "I'm good. Besides, it would be a little rude to show up to meet somebody with a brand new sword on my hip, wouldn't it?"

"Depends on the somebody. You've already been in a fight because of Lily. Don't you realize it's dangerous? How are you going to explain yourself if you get killed because you thought you didn't need a weapon?"

"How would I explain myself if I was dead?"

That seemed to stump the djinn and he sat there scratching his chin until the shopkeeper returned. First, the man set the newly sharpened axes on the counter in front of Lance, then he produced a new rapier for Hilde. He went on about the lengths he went to to procure the weapon from a failing noble house, the master craftsman who had made it, and so on as though Hilde understood anything coming out of his mouth.

I saw her grin as she held it though, and I figured she was finally happy with a sword. We'd have to smuggle more spice, or toys, or coffee or something through the border, but that was definitely easy enough to do. I put out of mind worries about ancient wars and focused on the moment. Which meant I was paying full attention as Hilde got into en garde facing the new test board. I saw the shopkeeper blanche as she lunged forward. The impact had two cracks. First, the split of wood around the tip as she sank it an inch deep. Then the crack of the rapier's blade.

Everyone but Hilde groaned, but all the apologizing she could do couldn't repay the man.

24

∽

Lily

Lily was on anything but her idea of a romantic date through the city. Her companion kept acting like they were on some honeymoon adventure. The people around them seemed to think so too, until they realized the man was wearing a leper's mask and then their looks became sorrowful for her. Not that the man was a leper, nor that they were dating.

Lily's reward for politely and safely staying the night at Lady Virent's manor, and entertaining the local kids, was a business meeting with her landlord that had spiraled entirely out of control. At first, it all had made sense. Loki, otherwise known as Mr Smythe, had enjoyed a fresh baked breakfast of gooey eggs atop steaming muffins with a side of dried fruit. While Lady Virent dined with them, conversation had been about local plays, distant weather patterns, and speculations of trade changes. He had even helped properly brew coffee for everyone, showing Lady Virent how tasty the drink actually was.

When duties called away the elf, conversation between Lily and Loki switched promptly to their chief issue. Lily had no legal identity on Earth, nor could they easily exchange currencies between the worlds. The contract would have to be amended to allow Hades to siphon power through it, despite not even residing in Alfheim. That was perfectly reasonable but there was a problem.

Lily couldn't change the contract on her own. They needed John to agree to it before the magic could be changed. Thus, they had to travel back across the city and find her roommate, hence the outfit.

Before they could reach Lily's apartment, one of the guard patrols sighted his porcelain mask and came marching over. "What's this about then? Who let you in the city?" the elf asked, wagging a lantern staff at the two of them but glaring at Loki.

The god, with a standing bounty on his head that could let anyone live in luxury for the rest of their lives, had the audacity to recoil. "What do you mean? I am a man of the cloth!"

"You're a leper," the guard said, sparing a glance for Lily before spitting out a wad of tobacco and facing Loki once more. "You got a permit to be in the city or something?"

Loki flourished his arms like a jester, flaunting the golden holy symbol he had about his neck that any elf would recognize. It was their religion's symbol. "I am no such thing as a leper, I am a servant of those unfortunate souls, come here to do charity. Day and night I toil to make their decrepit lives easier, to enable them a measure of dignity despite their disease. You think that because I adorn myself as one of them it is because I am blighted? Nay! I wear a mask to be as one with them. I have no desire to appear as some grander being. I am man just like they are man. Look here. My hands, my wrists, even my arms if you must. I have no lesion, no sores, no sickness or blight. I feel pain like anyone else. Do not scorn me for having compassion for the ill!"

The guard was clearly taken aback, put on the back foot as Loki thrust slender and soft arms toward his face. Of course, there was no sign of leprosy upon the immortal. "Well why don't you take the mask off then? If you're here for business instead of charity, eh? You're causing confusion. People are worried looking at you."

"It is a holy vow you ask me to forsake. I will be gone soon enough and nothing bad will have come to these people. How odious you are!"

At this, one of the other guards tapped the first on the shoulder and they left with collective grumbles. Loki laughed. "And they wonder why I've never been found in all these years."

Lily sighed. "Your brazenness boggles the mind."

"Come! Before they decide to find a reason to harass us once more," he said, sweeping back the little capelet his holy outfit was adorned with. His mirth vanished the moment the two of them arrived at the housing complex.

Lily had been worried the guards might accost her for arriving seemingly unprotected and she had no idea how to explain that she stood next to someone quite a bit more competent to protect her than even Minotaur. No one came forward to speak with them however. That itself was a cause for concern. When Loki stormed up the stairs and threw open the door to her apartment, she had to run after to keep up.

"What's wrong?"

"Shut the door," Loki ordered, taking off his mask once she did. He wrinkled his nose and sniffed, stalking around the kitchen before barging through to Earth. "Hello?" he called, hearing no response.

"John?" Lily called out, just before she found the note on her table. It was horribly out of place, written in some Earth ink and on immaculate white paper the likes of which he kept in a device beside his computer. Before she even finished reading the note, she took it through the portal back to where it fit in.

Then she had to reread the note as her grip squeezed down and crumpled the paper. "He just couldn't wait, could he?" she asked, snarling at the note. She had asked him to keep his head down! He had agreed! Now where was he? Cohorting with another god.

Loki plucked the note from her grasp, almost ripping it in half to get it. In a flash, he scanned his eyes over it and grunted. "I thought so. It smells like Tyr in here."

"That's because he cut a deal with Tyr."

"Why would he do that?" Loki demanded, falling upon the bed.

Lily closed the door to Alfheim and asked, "You know about his brother, don't you?"

"Are you saying Tyr offered to take him north?"

"So, you do know about him."

Loki leapt up with a scowl. "That is neither here nor there. What does he think he's doing? I thought he was a bit of a coward. He loathes adventure. Sees only the problems with it, the risks. Who is he to go running off without thinking about it? This isn't going like I expected at all. Come, you said he was with Tyr? Do you know where that vagabond is?"

Lily sighed. "If you're going there, take me with you. I have my own words to give John."

"Yes, yes, but where, girl, where?"

"The Last Resort."

The god let out a sigh. "Good, at least it's in Alfheim."

"How could Tyr be on Earth?"

The god shrugged. "It would be difficult, that's true. But as you can see, I've slipped through. Technically, he might find a way as well. I just thought it might be. Well, no, I'm being silly. He'd have to be given an invitation and my daughter is more likely to kill him than to invite him over."

Lily felt her stomach go cold. "You mean the authorities have already noticed us?"

Loki winced. "Maybe, maybe not. No way to really tell, now is there? Come, come, at the least we know she won't be in Alfheim and I won't have a very disagreeable family reunion, yes? To the Last Resort!"

25

∿

John

"The one-armed man?" the bartender of the Last Resort said as he lazily cleaned mugs. We had come relatively early in the day and business was quiet. "He's not here today."

I stared at him until it was obvious he was keeping his mouth shut. "Well, where is he?"

"Who do I look like? His keeper?" the man responded, snarling at me.

Minotaur loomed around me and put his hand on the counter. "The man would have left word about his destination."

The bartender balked, but retreated from the bar until his back was to his wine bottles. "I don't work for you, blue-skin."

"Actually," the djinn said, his voice low and rumbling. "You do. The Black Fingers are in no position to protect you, or to take your protection money. The Blutengels will be taking care of you from now on. If that's understood, then you'll tell us where the one-armed man went."

Around the bar, a few men looked like they might stand up and start something, but the bartender broke first. He put up his hands and everyone settled back down as he said, "Fine, fine, you demon. But it's no place to go blabbing about. Down the road here, off the main road, you're looking for the Rose Hips. But I warn you it's no place to take a lady."

Minotaur nodded and let go of the bar counter. "We'll be in contact about payment later," he said, and exited the building.

I quickly ushered my friends out the door behind him, catching them up on the conversation as we tried to keep up with the djinn.

Lance somehow managed to walk with his gaze seemingly on the sky and yet avoid stepping in any puddle, rut, or horse pile as he asked, "No place to take a lady? You think it's a brothel?"

"No way," Hilde said. "What kind of god would go to a brothel?"

The answer was evidently a norse god, because Rose Hips was certainly taken straight out of a red light district and dropped into one of the, otherwise, quaintest farm villages I could imagine. The windows weren't displaying the goods, but we could all hear the noise from the second floor.

Minotaur turned around, his head bowed. "We can find some place–"

Hilde laughed. "What? You think I'm offended by seeing half-naked women?"

Lance and I shrugged. "Earth is weird," I said, and stepped into the brothel. The odor of rose petals ground up into potpourri and perfume. The women, less painted up than I would have expected but this was an impoverished world, must have bathed in the perfume. Actually, I figured they probably did bathe in it. I could see a menu hanging on one wall that listed a bath for a certain number of gold coins, about halfway down the list.

I felt like I had brazenly stepped into a hidden paradise. Everything was cushioned–not that I was particularly impressed by that coming from Earth–and candles flickered in every sconce, nook, and cranny. Live music danced above heads and cherry red lips curled into smiles to laugh as bottles of wine passed from hand to hand while gold flowed out the back; from pocket and purse to hand for a kiss.

There was a girl, maybe a bit older than me, walking over. She sashayed her hips and I could barely understand how her clothes stayed on. Had it been Earth, I would have suspected glue and magnets, but her silk dress must have been magic. It was cut like the fabric cost a premium too: more skin than not showing. Her thighs were soft curves and gently tanned. Her figure was as perfect as shapewear pretended to be and she was smiling at me.

I was a rich man, too.

But I was rich because we had been clever, not because I listened to gut instinct. That had gotten me arrested. Tamping down base urges paid off immediately as the shapely succubus smiled at Minotaur and wrapped herself around his arm. The two of them fell into friendly conversation and it was clear they were already acquainted.

Hilde wasn't impressed. "I see more skin at the gym."

Then Tyr grabbed me by the scruff of my shirt. "Getting

a little eager, are you, boy?" the god asked as he dragged me back out the door. Hilde and Lance waved goodbye to me, vanishing off to the bar where Minotaur had already claimed the bartender's attention.

I turned on the god. "Woah woah woah, what's the rush?"

Tyr pointed at the sky with his stump. "The sun. You expect me to watch you run in the middle of the night or something? It's a wane moon and you don't even know what kind of animals are out here."

"Animals? I think I can handle animals. Or do you mean monsters?"

Tyr just laughed. "City boy, you don't know the difference. Let me tell you this, you run into a hog out there, you turn your ass to it and pretend your one night stand's boyfriend just showed up: run like hell."

I scoffed. "I'm pretty sure I can handle a pig."

Try rolled his eyes. "So look, here's the deal. Come around back. You ever chopped firewood before?"

"No."

"Well you're going to now. One hundred splits, I'm going to time you and watch your form. The madam will appreciate it too. Then it's running, and I will time you for more splits after. That'll give me a good idea what I'm working with, alright?"

"And then you tell me about my brother?"

He nodded. "And then I tell you about your brother, but don't worry. You'll realize this was important because there's no way you're finding your brother as weak as you are now. But don't you worry! Working with me you'll be a hero in no time. I bet you don't even feel where that dragon gored you anymore. Knew from the moment you came back over. I got this big rush. No idea how you got in a righteous fight that fast but I'm not complaining."

I'd split kindling for a camp fire once. As long as the ax was good, I was fine. And it wasn't like my speed actually mattered. If he said I was no good in a fight, what skin off my back was it? So I followed him out behind the brothel. Some of the windows were open and I could hear girls moaning. That got some blood going in the wrong direction. When he pointed at the cutting ax I wrung my hands around the haft. It was heavy. Brushing a finger across the edge showed it wasn't particularly sharp though.

"One hundred?"

Tyr nodded, and I set the first chunk of log down. The hewn surface was soft, almost fuzzy. I guessed that was from the crudeness of the saws. No one in Alfheim had a chainsaw to flush cut with. I had no idea whether a soft edge would make it easier or harder, but again, it didn't matter. I set it down on the cutting block, lifted the ax head high, and smashed it down.

The edge ricocheted off the gray slab of log. The handle almost wrenched free of my grasp. "What the fuck?"

"You weren't joking, huh? City boy."

"The hell is this?"

"Ironwood."

"For fuck's sake."

My next swing split it down the middle. It cracked like glass, straight down the grain lines despite the ax head only biting in a few millimeters. The impact left my hands tingling as he knocked half aside and lined up another split.

"That's one," Tyr said.

By the time I finished a hundred splits, blisters had covered both of my hands, sweat had drenched through my shirt and left me dripping after taking it off. I fell over like the pile of kindling I had made, ready to die if it meant a reprieve. The sun had turned scarlet as the sun sank, and then it went black as Tyr stepped over me. "I suppose we can skip the second round of splits, but I still need to see you run. Come on, get up. It's your upper body that's tired, not your legs."

"But my heart."

"But your heart," Tyr parroted back. Then he kicked me in the short ribs. "Come on, get up. War doesn't wait on punks like you. It waits on heroes and kings! Go on, down the road till the crossroads. Turn right at the sign. Cross the bridge, then turn right again. The road is dirt and mud, but will circle back around here. After you wade back across, you just come back here and I'll have a pretty girl serve you some wine, alright? Don't look at me like that. You aren't even bleeding because of the gifts I'm giving you and you don't even know!"

I couldn't even respond. I had to take so many breaths just to clear my woozy head. Then I said, "Better be one of the cute ones."

"Sure sure. And remember what I said!"

"Yeah, yeah," I said, getting back to my feet. I set my head and started for the road. "Right at the crossroads, across the bridge, right again, circle back. I got this." I took off at a slow jog.

Putting one foot after the next was almost relaxing, almost pleasant. There was a breeze to take the sweat off me and Tyr had been right: it was my arms that had gone completely numb, not my legs. In a sort of sleepwalk stupor, I jogged down the road until I could put my eyes on the crossroads sign. That leg of the journey wasn't quite a mile and my only lament was the lack of music.

After the turn, I had to take a few walking stretches. Tyr couldn't see me and his watch could be damned. I stretched and wiped my forehead off and tried to intermittently jog until I spotted the bridge. I found myself going faster than I had expected to, partly because whenever I slowed down an insect would attack me. Also, the sky was shifting through hues of lavender and violet, and I was afraid to be out with only the light of a sliver of moon.

The bridge was wooden, mossy, and rotting. Somehow the timber supported my weight, and I even spotted horseshoe marks that had chipped the surface. I figured it must have been made out of that ironwood stuff because it didn't even budge when I leaned over the railing. Fish the size of baseball bats stared back at me, idly fighting the trickling current. They were as fat as salmon and probably didn't have any mercury or microplastics in them.

I was just thinking that I should catch some over the weekend when I heard a snuffling. The thing snorted and I turned my head to see a boar staring back at me. This wasn't Wilbur. It wasn't Porky Pig either. Pumbaa might have been its younger sibling, but the thing staring at me wasn't going to break out in song and dance. The boar snorted again, scraping the ground with a hoof as it pointed tusks at me. Given its height, the tusks were perfectly lined up with my kidneys and were backed by as much muscle as a hippopotamus.

For a brief instant of coyote time, I remembered the actual context of what Tyr had told me not to forget.

The boar lowered its head, facing me with a hairy slab of hide like a battering ram.

I turned tail and ran like an angry boyfriend was after me.

It charged after me, throwing its body around in a raging pulse. The beast galloped and stomped, storming towards me. It could have flipped a car over if it wanted to, or uprooted entire trees, and all of its anger was focused on me.

I found reserves of energy I couldn't have even imagined. I'm not sure I even inhaled, but ran off of pure adrenaline. I forced my feet to fly until everything was burning because for every step, I heard the boar stomp twice. Only after nearly a hundred yards did I realize I was an idiot. I was running down a street: flat and even terrain whose only issue was some mud. I pivoted and darted off the side of the road and into the brush.

I had to dive straight through a hedge line, probably into some poor farmer's field. I nearly fell at the abrupt berm of dirt demarcating the middle, but for as much as I stumbled, so did the boar. It was too hot on my heels to turn down the hedge, making it bust through bushes–and I was worried I would trip–so I booked it across the field. The damn animal ripped a line straight through the clover. Shredded it to muck fit for a swamp.

But, ahead was the river. That was the only thing I could think of. The 9mm across my back was laughable, completely ridiculous, to use against a biological tank charging after me. I could shoot it in the face and I doubted it would even flinch. Thankfully, there was no berm between the field and the river. Unfortunately, there was the opposite: irrigation ditches.

I cut across them at an angle, vaulting them and making the boar circle round until I ran out of the little micro-canals.

Then I ran into the river. It went from a gentle one inch to four feet of body sweeping current in the span of one step. Sucked me straight under. I burst from the surface flailing and gasping, feet bouncing off logs and rocks as I tumbled, but floating meant I was moving without having to run.

So I twisted and got flat on my back, feet up. It let me lift my head and see the boar. The damn thing was staring me down, stomping its front hoof at what must have been the edge of its territory because it wasn't chasing me down. "Holy shit," I shouted, screaming at the night sky as I finally felt the burn in my lungs and my legs. The cold water took out my strength like a crowbar to the kneecaps. If the boar had kept chasing me, I wouldn't have been able to even crawl free.

I couldn't feel my legs at all in mere moments. When I bumped against the bridge of stones and logs that served as a fording point–presumably where Tyr had intended for me to cross over. It let me crawl out of the river like a drowned man. Eventually, I stumbled back into the Rose Hips, still dripping river water on the floor. Half the room stared at me when the door closed.

I lifted up my arms, looked myself over, and said, "Giant boar chased me into the river."

Tyr spoke up from beside the common room's bard–a decent looking guy with a guitar variant–and said, "Get the man a towel and a beer, on me."

The madame, at least I assumed she was by her age, hit me in the face with a piece of cloth I figured had once been a blanket. I was too tired to care if there were sex stains on it (I could almost smell the bleach) and just started wiping myself down.

When I sat down across from Tyr, he looked me over and blew air out from his lips.

"Well then, I suppose you want to know about Charles Martin."

Tyr got a pitcher of beer for himself, took a long drink, and began the story.

"Okay, so about three years ago, fellow by the name of Charles Martin shows up. This isn't Blue Rock Bay, not at first. He was in the middle of nowhere really. A bum town called Fisher's Crook. This was during the war, just a little border skirmish between King Richard Lazuli and the Anarcho-theists–"

"The what now?"

"Don't worry about them, they're just crazy bastards who dammed up a bunch of the rivers. Nasty guerilla war in the eastern mountains. Point is, the army was busy at the time and the farmers couldn't grow anything. All the water was getting flooded up in the mountains to starve them out. Anyone who could, shepherds and the like, they fled the area and took their money with them. Suddenly, the area was dry, poor, and half-defended. The fae-vermin started to multiply."

"What the hell are those?"

"Are you going to let me tell the story or not? You call them goblins. Nasty little things with half a brain between the lot of them. Some of them can talk, but most can't think past whether they should put the thing in their hand into their mouth. The problem is that the smart ones can lead the other ones. They're worse than wolves for farmers. They will steal cattle, goats, pet dogs, anything they can beat to death with sticks and rocks. Then, they drag it off and eat it. They get really bad if you kill the smart ones though, after they've taught the dumb ones where the farmers are."

"Wouldn't they be less dangerous if they're all stupid?"

"In a sense, in a sense. Easier to track down and kill, sure, but the dumb ones end up hungry because they can't plan, and when they're hungry, they'll eat anything. Rats, pigeons, and people too. Nothing haunts a farmer's nightmares more than the idea of finding a pack of goblins in their child's room, fighting over the scraps. So, when the remaining farmers–there were no shepherd flocks by this point, mind you–started noticing more attacks, they got real worried. They tried asking the king for help, because it's dangerous work going into a goblin den, but..."

"All the soldiers were fighting the war."

"And mercenaries like going to war too. Good money, good business, better to send veterans to kill your enemies than raw recruits and hey when it's all said and done, the more of them that die, the less you have to pay and the less likely they are to turn around and sack your city. So, the only option for the poor people of Fisher's Crook was to do something about it themselves. Half a dozen of them were killed trying to clear out, horrible stuff, but they knew it was risky. Goblin dens are tunnels, usually built out from some pre-existing building. In this case it was a burned down villa for some forgotten elf noble family. Probably one the king had put to death for one reason or another. Point is that they brought spears and pitchforks and that only worked until the tunnels were so short they had to crawl in. Then the goblins butchered them and ate them."

"Are you telling me my brother went in after that?"

"I am telling you that, yes. Or so the story goes. First he did some probing, some kicking around until he scared up a goblin and killed it. That gave him the rough measure of the things and the next night he went to get rid of the den. No, nobody but Charles himself can really tell you what he did, but what the farmers of Fisher's Crook say is there was smoke, and yellow lightning. They saw in the distance the flash and the bang of thunder, but the next day, when they checked the manor, the goblins had not been seared by lightning. No, they'd been punctured, like by tiny lances."

"So he used a–"

"Yeah, that thing that doesn't exist here. He had a couple other interesting things too, but no one ever found the magic trick he used, because–I shit you not–he buddied up to Montu, the Egyptian war god fragment–"

"Fragment?"

"Come back after your next fight and you might have earned that explanation. Point is though, he's like me. He trained your brother and when he made his debut, he was a hundred miles from Fisher's Crook in the great trade city of Poletau. He didn't fight with anything fancy, just a dwarven longsword. Now, those things are great and you should be angling to get one yourself, but every noble and their mother has a dwarven sword of some variety. But the things he could do with it blew everyone away. He took first prize at the martial tournament and turned down every offer to hire him. Now, the thing is, he couldn't take their offers because they would have found out what he was lacking in his pants, if you know what I'm saying."

"You did not need to ask if I knew what you were saying."

"Right, so the thing about Poletau is the diversity of interests in the city. Trade does that, it levels the playing field. Means there's a couple dozen little kings and queens instead of one big tyrant, so he didn't get scoped out before the tournament. And then? When he got the gold? He turned around and handed it to the dwarves again along with some blueprints for a couple of weapons. On the one, a compound bow complete with all the cams and pulleys to lock it out. And the other thing he wanted was a set of crossbows with pull weights so high a three-foot lever was needed to crank it back. They say they had to use sinew from sea monsters to hold the tension."

"I'm surprised he didn't spend the gold on a house or something."

"Your brother had bigger ambitions. The tournament money was piddling, compared to what he could do with Montu's help. In fact, he went on a little dueling spree after he made friends with an elf who could patch him up after each fight. That was just to kill time waiting for these man-mounted siege weapons of hiss. They covered the bar tabs, you know? What he really wanted was a bounty, and not just the gold of the bounty but the title it would give. He wanted to kill Wrathclaw the Red."

"And that's a dragon?"

"Was one, yeah. A big step up you might say. You could also say that, given the right tool, killing a twenty-ton ball of muscle and fire is easier than a den of goblins. There's only one thing you have to keep track of. It can't exactly sneak up behind you in the dark and shank you. Much the opposite in fact. Still, it was pretty dangerous and worth the ten thousand gold bounty–if he handed over the corpse which he didn't–so the day before his journey he had a party. Whole town, well not the whole town but a damn good portion of it, got in on the celebration. He shelled out good coin for the beer and the wine and a roast boar–like the one that chased you–and he was having a grand time by all accounts until he up and vanished."

"I thought you said he killed the dragon?"

"I did, I did and he did kill it. I just meant for the night. He and his healer, a beautiful thing by all accounts and one of the few high elves you'll ever catch without a mask on in public. Of course, I have my own speculation about why that is and it says rather ugly truths about the fairer sex, so I'll be keeping present company in mind and my thoughts to myself. Still, everyone who knows the story knows the two of them were lovebirds. Plenty of problems, but normal relationship problems. Her name was... ah, what was it? Adria I think it was. So Adria was a miracle worker at fleshcraft, which should have been a lucrative job, but the moment a child was involved, or a hint of a sob story, and she wouldn't take payment."

"She sounds like a good person."

"Aye, that she was, sure, but she was also a frivolous spender. Worked your brother to the bone at times but you know, two sides of the coin. She was a frivolous buyer of experiences, not of something useless like clothes. She lived life to the fullest and dragged him along with her at times. The two of them interlocked their lives and that night they tied the knot as it were."

"They slept together."

"Bingo. Big fight, right? Very dangerous. Now, he wasn't going alone. He would have only needed the one bow if he was by himself. No, by this time the war had ended–quite favorably for the king mind you–and mercenaries were back on the prowl. It was just enough time for their wallets to be feeling lighter than they used to be, and the genuine chance at taking down Wrathclaw brought in a dozen good soldiers. A whole troupe of them, all races; dreamers, dwarves, elves, you name it. Some people say even a goblin volunteered, but that's bullshit. They were the ones the heavy crossbows were for. Your brother didn't need them, he had Montu's blessing at the time, which meant he was the one that was going to go in and put it down for good."

"And he didn't bring his boomstick?"

"No boomstick, he did this the heroic way. After they got its attention, they peppered it with rope-carrying bolts. Nasty, barbed things they could yank on and drag it to the ground. Hiding behind walls of wet fur to stay safe from gouts of fire, they eventually got enough rope into it that it bled like rain. Plants still won't grow there, because the beast's blood was toxic. Then down it went, after torching a few of the mercenaries less keen than the others. They hauled it to the ground, but didn't kill it. No amount of bleeding would be enough to kill a dragon, not like that."

"They should have used poison or something."

"Pfft, shows what you know. Cutting through the scales would have sheared the poison off. No way to get enough of anything to hurt a twenty-ton beast."

"Oh come on, they use sedatives all the time."

"Not ones you can get here, idiot. This is a dragon we're talking about. Haven't you seen one? Even just flying in the sky?"

"Only the one in the arena."

"Well quadruple the size and give it wings and fire breath and twice the cunning! This is a big deal. Wrathclaw was known to kill entire herds of sheep in a day. He once attacked a military training ground and flew off with a horse in his claws! The arrows they shot just bounced off his ass–useless. But your brother, they brought Wrathclaw down. They grounded him, kept him from running away, and he walked out to fight the dragon one on one."

"But the others were holding it down. That's hardly–"

"It was man versus dragon! You gotta do something to level the playing field. Are you crazy? Even heroes need strategies."

"Tell that to Beowulf."

"Fuck that prince! He died fighting the dragon, remember? But your brother went in and dodged the last burst of flames Wrathclaw could muster, then it was his sword against the dragon's claws. With swipes able to break houses the dragon assaulted him, pounding and scraping, wrending and tearing. The dragon tore the ground apart as cut by cut Charles hacked through scale, through fat and flesh and down to tendons. Then it reared and–"

"Let me guess, he stabbed it in the reverse scale?"

"No! Who the hell told you that? His sword was dwarven and still had a sharp tip. When Wrathclaw reared he charged. Stabbed his blade right into the behemoth's belly and blasted his blade from breast to balls. He doused himself in the monster's guts and still dove to the side before it toppled onto him!"

"And then what? He kept the corpse? Sold it to dwarven craftsmen or something?"

"Aye, he did, only got a fraction of the bounty, most of which he gave to the mercenaries. There was more rejoicing, that time he didn't have to pay for it at least. The local lords footed the bill completely. Killing Wrathclaw was a boon to all the small people of Poletau and he was a hero, a true dragon slayer."

"So where is he? If he's so famous?"

"Well, that's the thing. He ordered himself a suit of dragonscale armor to be made from the corpse of Wrathclaw, and that's a plenty recognizable suit of armor, you'd think. So, why is it that nobody knows where he's at right now?"

"That's literally what I asked you."

"It's because of the time it took. You see, between the finishing of that armor and that first celebration, that was nearly six weeks."

"So what?"

"So, that means two moons had passed and then there was no doubt your brother had done the impossible. And I don't mean killing a dragon. Plenty of heroes have done that. I mean he was successful in his consummation. He had a child with an elf. Half-human, half-elf... you're an uncle to quite the aberration, John, and your brother has been in hiding ever since."

I rocked back in my seat and sat there. Tyr got another round of drinks as I processed everything. While the god had been speaking, I could treat it as a story. It was something that had been a little distant, a little fake. I had been trying to find the lie, the deceit and the falsehood. I finally realized that I had been listening the whole time expecting to be conned and instead I had been given the best news of my life so far.

I tried to rationalize the emotions in me before they got out of control. It was like I had been gilding a little machine, an action figure or a toy or something. A work of art out of ideas and facts. The whole time I hadn't expected it to work but now all the support had been taken away. The scaffolding of apprehension was gone. The fact didn't fall apart. It held up and that meant I could incorporate it as fact.

My brother was alive. He hadn't gotten himself killed on an adventure.

Just like that it felt like years of emotional mud came dislodged inside me, but before it could go anywhere, before I could even let my body cry, Tyr swore and darted from the table. He left me alone and confused until I saw Lily glaring at me.

26

〰

Lily

Lily relocated the two of them to a small table behind the Rose Hips brothel. It was shaded and private, and let her glower at her brazen roommate who was risking both of their fates without a second though. He wouldn't even meet her gaze. The strong hero that had protected her was nowhere to be seen. Had probably never been there in the first place. For all she really knew, Lance had been the one to fight off the Black Fingers and John had just gotten tied up in it.

That was probably going too far, but she had thought he would be above going to a brothel.

"What do you think you're doing here?" she demanded.

He shrugged and gestured to a cutting stump for firewood. "Met Tyr here. He gave me a bunch of training to do. Cut wood, run around, that sort of thing."

"What is this? The twelve labors of Hercules?"

For the first time, he looked back at her but his face was wrinkled in confusion. "Why do you know... right, same gods."

Lily crossed her arms and leaned back in her chair. "We're still part of the world tree, John, but you're going to get our bridge broken!" She still couldn't believe that Minotaur had figured them out and she definitely couldn't believe that he was nonchalantly helping Hilde with her German. She had no idea where the two gods had gone, but if Tyr wanted to lounge around a brothel that was his business. It didn't have to potentially ruin everything unless John stuck his nose into it.

With his gaze not on her again, he spoke almost under his breath. "Lily, I told you I was going to do this."

"You could have waited for me! Did you even know that one of the authorities has been snooping around? May have been in your apartment?"

He stared at her flatly. "If they had been in my apartment, the contract would have voided. And look, I'm not... we're not tied to each other, are we? You're the one with enemies skulking around, not me. They have no reason to bother me except what? To get to you?"

"John, that's just how stupid you are. You don't know anything about this place. Every elf you walk by from the nobles to the guards, they are all your enemy because you aren't one of them. That's what it's like here. It's terrible but it is what it is. Why do you think I wanted to go to Earth?"

"Well maybe I have my reasons for wanting to leave Earth!"

"Like what? You live in luxury! Was it so you could come here?" she demanded, gesturing back to the door into the brothel.

For a while, John didn't answer her. He leaned back in his

chair and stared at her until her indignation faltered. Then, he said, "My brother, who I thought died, is here. I don't particularly care that it's dangerous. I don't care that a one-eyed drunk is treating me like a video game character to dump fetch quests onto. Your clothes are itchy, your seats stiff, and your judicial system is a joke, but that's all crap I can put up with because finding my brother is more important."

Lily felt like she had been punched in the gut. "I'm sorry," she stammered out, her heart starting to ache in her chest as she realized he wasn't sullen, he was actually about to cry. Except now he was too pissed off and it was her fault.

He scoffed at her. "Betting money says my brother got the same deal I did, and his portal got found. I get it, Lily. We're walking a tightrope. I'm sure you'd feel better if I was just keeping my head down but that's something I can't do, okay? Why did you even come looking for me? Isn't this just making the whole situation worse? You're way higher profile than I am."

She jumped to her feet. "Right, I almost forgot. Before we realized... look, we have a way to convert gold to cash. We just need you to agree to the updated contract. It won't take but a moment. I'll go get him right now. Wait, okay?" she blurted out before darting back into the carnal house.

She didn't find the gods, just her companions if she could still call them that. Minotaur beckoned her over. "Where did they go?" she asked.

"Didn't say," the djinn answered. "I'm your guard now, Princess."

She glowered and Hilde said, "It was something about his daughter. They got a bit heated."

"We should head back to safety," the djinn said, gesturing to the door. "Gather your friend."

"He's not my friend," she snapped back. "Just my room-mate." She didn't know what to do, or how to respond to John's friends staring at her. Everything was suddenly going wrong. She could feel her grasp at normalcy crumbling apart. The portal was going to be found before she had even gotten to use it. She couldn't get stranded on Earth either. In a world of humans, she'd be a freak even if she was only a tiny fraction inhuman. She always had a tendency to wrap her tail around her leg when she got worked up, and she was definitely worked up now.

Then John was brought in from outside and the whole group began walking back to the city proper. She saw his face, drawn down and as lively as a rock. Her chest felt hot as she fought over words in her head. The whole walk back was quiet and stifled and she could feel the side-eyed glances coming her way from Lance and Hilde. It was obvious they knew she was the one at fault.

Even she knew that. She just couldn't bring herself to apologize.

The problem was bigger than him leaving the city once without her. The problem was that she had never really explained why her life wasn't normal and what kind of danger that entailed not just for her but for him too. She should have told him. He should have known before signing the contract and sharing a room with her. In a sense, their fates had become entwined under false pretenses.

The whole time the four of them sat upon a lumbering lastkahn troll back to the apartment, she chewed her lip without saying a word. He didn't speak either. Only when they were back inside, after Lance and Hilde left with some complaints about the time, could Lily work up the courage to speak. "Can I ask something?"

"You can ask. I can't stop you from doing that, can I?" he responded as he sat down at his computer.

"You didn't know your brother was in Alfheim at first, right? So, what did you want from the portal?"

He scoffed. "Hell if I know. I was drunk. Honestly, I barely remember signing the contract."

"John, I saw the way you were looking at everything. You never smile here on Earth."

"I smile here."

She could only remember a few times she had seen him smile, and it was only ever at her; someone from the other world. Lily moved over and sat down on his couch, almost close enough to touch him. Now that his desk had been moved out of his bedroom, the living area wasn't exactly well laid-out. "I'm sorry... you got matched with me."

He slid down in his chair, planting his chin in his hand as he clicked through the internet. "Why are you apologizing? You didn't choose me."

"Anyone who got matched with me for this portal thing, I'd owe anyone an apology because of who I am."

John sighed. "You haven't done anything, Lily. I'm not going to blame you because other people are after you."

She took a breath and braced herself. "I need to tell you at least the short version though. My brother has one of the magic swords and he, well, isn't using it to overthrow the elves. That has made quite a few people very... very angry with him."

He arched an eyebrow. "I'm not going to say they don't deserve to be overthrown but, what does that mean for you? They're trying to get you to get to him?"

She fidgeted with the hem of her skirt and said, "You know what you said about other people being after me? You kind of said it like I had nothing to do with it? That's not entirely true because I sort of helped my brother steal the sword in the first place. I mean, he won it in a duel technically but I was the one that figured out how the magic on the sword worked which let him win so... I haven't had an exactly normal life since then."

"So you've needed constant armed protection ever since then?"

She nodded. "Except when I'm here on Earth. That's why everyone calls me Princess, you know? Because I have to be protected like one."

"I thought they did that just because you're beautiful," he said, his voice as calm as if he were talking about the weather. When Lily's head snapped up and her cheeks flushed, he cleared his throat. "Sorry, I'm a little emotionally drained right now, so bashful I am not."

Lily almost choked on her own throat as she mumbled a thanks. "Right, well, now that you understand that it sort of is my fault. I would understand if you wanted to break the contract. I'm sure Loki would set you up with another portal with someone less problematic than me."

After a moment, she dared to look back up at him. He was staring directly at her and spoke only once they made eye contact. "I'm not going to blame you because other people are out to get you. That would be wrong. Look, I'm sorry. I guess I just don't know how to handle myself right now. It was a hell of a day, I got a lot dumped on me. Let me put it this way. I'm a pretty normal guy with normal desires most of all. I want a good job. I want a wife and kids. I want to die old, happy, and with grandkids. I've also got a desire to go on an adventure, to do cool things and meet new people. I just never took that desire seriously because it seemed to fly directly in the face of the more important goals. I had very close to home evidence that running off an adventure can get you killed so I stifled that for years. Now, today, right before you found me, I was convinced that not only did my brother not die, but he's over in Alfheim having the time of his life with a wife and a kid. My brain is kind of broken right now. I need to sleep and hope it makes sense in the morning."

When Lily didn't respond, he planted his hands on the arms of his chair and shoved himself back to his feet. He mumbled something and started heading for the bedroom. "Wait." Lily was standing, her chest tight. When he looked back at her, she almost forgot what she was going to say. "Tomorrow... I'm supposed to bring you to meet Lady Virent. She's going to apologize and if you want to go find your brother, she would be able to help."

John shook his head, eyes drooping. "I'll figure that out in the morning, okay?" he said, and went to bed.

Lily sat back down on the couch and pulled the throw blanket around herself. She was only a little ways from the bedroom, could slip through it and back to her own apartment. Her bed was still there, through the hole in the wall. She didn't go to it though. She felt too miserable to even get off the couch.

27

~

John

I found Lily curled up with my secondary blanket the next morning, face half buried in the guest pillow. On the one hand, I felt like I should be a proper adult and own an actual throw pillow for my couch. On the other hand, throw pillows were useless and she was clearly comfortable on a standard bed pillow.

I still didn't know if I was upset with her sleeping and had done almost nothing to help me sort things out but I was pretty sure rationalizing was not the correct way to decide in the first place. She had her priorities and I had mine. We were entangled with one another. Emotions getting high could only be expected and my sentiment from last night was probably correct. Give it some time and my gut would figure it out. Eight hours simply hadn't been enough. That time would come, and I knew something that would help speed it up.

After quietly slipping on my boots and tugging on a parka,

I headed out of the apartment. The winter bite had my fingertips burning before I even got my car to auto-start and I almost fumbled my phone's numpad, but when I slammed the door it was ringing. I almost missed the answer as the engine rumbled to life and then we had to shout at each other until the bluetooth system decided to properly connect. I was almost turning onto the business express when my grandfather finally, and clearly, said, "What do I owe the call to, Johnny?"

"You doing anything?"

"I'm at the butcher shop right now, picking up some pork butt. Woke up with a hankering for some polish sausage but I'm not sure I can find the right spices. Today's a cooking day. Why do you ask Johnny?"

I felt my throat almost catch as I tried to answer him. Things were tense with my parents, but I'd have to tell them eventually too. I just wanted to start with him. "I'll meet you at your place."

"Don't you have class?"

"Not today," I said, though I would have to watch my prof's recording later.

"Well, sure, Johnny! Would love to have you over. Are you coming now?"

I was passing over the bridge back to downtown Detroit. "If it's not a problem."

"Not a problem at all. I'll head right back."

"See you then."

My grandfather lived in the same house he had bought fifty years prior. Ever since my grandmother passed away, he had taken to complaining about it being too big and empty for just him alone, and the neighborhood had changed, he didn't like the tax policies, a thousand issues that time had caused but couldn't fix. The three-bedroom house maybe was too large for him, but he also said he was too old to go back onto a mortgage, so he grumbled and lived with his memories even after the old fruit trees in the back withered away.

It had my own childhood memories too and I had plenty of time to reminisce before he pulled into the weedy drive behind me. "Help me with the bags, would ya?" he asked, slamming the door on his old Camero. Then, one thing led to the next and I found myself helping prep a slow-cook brisket while hammering mixed drinks. When I had just about lost the nerve to dredge up family drama, he sat down at the table beside me. "So?"

I drummed my fingers on my glass and he gave me some time. Explaining everything that had happened with mere words was a daunting task I hadn't been thinking about. Now that I tried to form ideas into words, I hesitated. "I have been living through something quite remarkable."

"You get a girlfriend?"

"What? No. Wait, sort of. Maybe if things play out. That's only part of what I'm getting at. Look, I need you to believe me that what I'm about to tell you is not some prank. You're not being recorded. I'm not crazy. I have corroborating evidence."

"Johnny, calm down. Even if you were using me for a prank video—"

I put up my hands. "Appreciated, but really. This is between us and completely honest. And I'm serious about that, I signed a contract that if the authorities find out the deal is done."

I winced immediately when I saw my grandfather pale and pull back. "We talking ghost guns? Drug running?"

"Neither. Different kind of authority."

"Are you doxxing people online?"

"What? How do you even know what that is?"

My grandfather grinned. "The flyfishing group has a mentoring program so the community doesn't just die out. I've been brushing up on the latest trends and tech."

"Okay, we should talk about that some time, but let me just actually explain and don't interrupt me. I got drunk in a bar and met a guy who turned out to be from another world and I signed what I thought was a joke contract but actually gave me a portal to that other world. It's really expensive but it's legit. I went over there. I've brought things back and forth. I've brought people back and forth. I just can't show you a picture because phones don't work over there for something. I think electromagnetics are slightly different. But, what's important is that I think I found Charlie. At least, a rumor of him. Name is the same and the timeline checks out. I think he also went to this world and just lost his portal or something, but I think I can find him. I think he's still alive."

To punctuate my explanation, I fished out a silver coin from my pocket and set it on the table between us.

My grandfather picked up the coin and rubbed it between his fingers. He had to get his glasses out to see the embossment. Then he put it down and folded his hands together. "Tell me about the world."

I had been prepared for denials, to be told that I was just stressed out and hallucinating or something. So, it took me a moment to arrange my thoughts and explain everything that had happened. I leapt forward and back, swinging from one idea to the next as I tried to make a cohesive whole from what had happened and prove that the world was too complex and real to be just something I imagined or was making up to get money out of him.

When I was done, he nodded and asked, "So, what have you come here for? What do you need?"

"You believe me?"

He shrugged. "I'd believe you more if you could bring this roommate of yours but I doubt she'd want to show an old man her tail. But, yes. I believe you, Johnny. At least in part. I never told you this, but before your brother vanished, he told me he was going to go on a trip. That's why we all assumed he went off on some adventure and got himself killed—yet another missing person's case. The thing is that I never told you where he said he was going and now I hear you're going to the same place: Alfheim. I thought it was a video game or something. Maybe it was an allusion to Sweden—there's really quite great skiing there, you know. I told the police when the search began but they wrote it off as a slang reference. Now, wherever this Alfheim is, it seems you've found it too so I want you to realize that wherever this palace is, it's dangerous. Your brother never came back from it. You should consider and prepare accordingly. Maybe don't go at all."

"I have to go."

"Alright, I understand. You're a young man. So I ask again, what do you need?"

I reclined in my chair and killed my mixed drink. "First, I need you to cover for me with my parents."

He nodded. "I can cook something up for you. When are you going? Now? It's duck season, you know."

"I was thinking right after finals."

"Christmas? You mean you're going to miss Christmas?"

"And New Years, and maybe a few weeks in January. He's not exactly close to where my magic door leads to."

"I'll have to think of something good for that. But, with your relationship, would they even notice? Ah, I suppose they'd notice the holidays. Bad time of year, ain't it? I can figure out something though."

"And one more thing. I need a hunting rifle."

"I thought you said it wasn't ghost guns?"

I got up from the table and poured myself another drink. When my grandfather lifted his empty glass, I poured him one too. When I sat back down, I said, "I need a hunting rifle that can take down a hippo because there's goddamn dragons over there and one of them already gored me and put me in the hospital. I'd still be in the hospital if not for literal healing magic on the other side. So I'm hoping for that bear gun you've got."

When I tugged down the neck of my shirt to show the yellowed bandages, my grandfather leapt from his seat. "Jesus Christ Almighty, boy!"

"I'm fine. I'd just really prefer a big gun for next time, instead of a spear."

My grandfather darted around the table to prod at my injury like a sports coach, shaking his head every time I winced. "Come with me." The two of us descended into his basement, the decor switching from the kind of modern, flat-packed crap that fills dorm rooms for cheap, back to the 1980's. The bulb for his backroom is an exposed incandescent the color of a candle flame that's probably been there since the house was built. As he opens the display case for his rifles, he says, "Unfortunately, the 45-70 is no good. I broke something in the action a few years back and never got it fixed–I'm too damn old to be elk hunting. I can put it into a gunsmith but I can't make any promises it'll be back before then. What I can give you is this."

He handed me an M1 Garand.

"I'm not sure this is big enough."

"That was my father's weapon in the war. Your great-grandfather's. It's a damn sight better than anything you're going to get your hands on in the next few weeks, what with these damned waiting periods the government forced down our throats."

My great-grandfather served in the occupation forces, and I was always told to not ask how he got his own rifle back home. Still, if I wasn't worried about dragons, it would overpower most other threats. I just didn't know how I felt about that. When I was over in Alfheim, it was like I found myself in the flow of the world. It was a more violent place and I found myself more violent as well. Still, it was better to be violent than to be dead.

When he handed me a sleeve for the gun and a pile of ammo, I started packing it up. "I'll introduce you to the girl as soon as I can."

He laughed. "She must be something special. Just don't let her get you into trouble, you hear? Unless you love her."

"I don't know her that well, Grandpa."

"Hey, I knew it was love at first sight when I saw your grandmother."

"You saw her at a New Year's Eve party that you went to in order to meet somebody. I found a stranger passed out in my bed who was from another world. It's a little different."

"Bah, that's just like those cartoons you watch, isn't it? I know all about it."

"Grandpa, who the hell is this guy you're mentoring and what is he telling you?"

He laughed. "Wouldn't you like to know. Come on, there's food to be eaten," he said as he slapped my arm and pulled himself back up the creaking steps.

I ate my fill and packed up enough barbequed meat to last a week, or half that because I meant to share it with Lily. But, when I got back to the apartment, she was nowhere to be seen.

28

Lily

Roaring had awoken Lily. It was the kind of powerful, rumbling blast that no human or elf could make, only a troll. With her hair still a mess, she threw on clothes and stepped out in Alfheim. It seemed like half the city had gathered to watch from balconies and flat roofs. In the trench below, mayhem had broken loose and merchants were wailing as two lastkan trolls grappled with one another. Their yokes and reins had snapped off and dangled from their shoulders as they thrashed from one side of the transport trench to the next. Entire buildings shook as the two beasts drove their shoulders into the ground.

Lily had heard of what trolls could be like when in rut, but never in her life seen it happen. Anyone certified to handle the beasts should have known better than to let a rutting troll out of chains inside the city.

Everyone watching gasped as blood so dark it was nearly purple spewed into the air out of the neck of one of the trolls.

It wobbled and collapsed beneath the victor of the struggle–likely bankrupting whoever owned it. The other troll stood up, blood dripping from its teeth. Bells were ringing and the city guard were storming over. Soon they'd have the creature suppressed. And if not them, Lily saw Minotaur at the entrance of her little neighborhood, standing with a cudgel-blade resting on his shoulder. The hunk of steel was the kind of weapon only a troll or a djinn could use. Weighing nearly fifty pounds, it was more than capable of breaking a troll's bones and cutting off limbs if need be.

Lily's heart was racing from the excitement below, but she could tell it was over. The troll had won its dominance battle and would soon be taken away. It certainly couldn't make it through Minotaur to get to her. She stepped back into her apartment, thinking how she would tell John about what had happened, and got herself properly dressed for the day.

John still wasn't back from wherever he had gone, so when Lily had all her layers on for the day, she stepped back onto the balcony. The moment her hand hit the railing, and she saw down to the street, she stopped. Breath caught in her throat as she saw the djinn impaled on the lastkan's horn. Minotaur roared as he was tossed around like a puppet, but he had a dagger in his hand. As he was thrown around, he stabbed and stabbed, driving the metal through the troll's face until flesh and bone spewed out with blood. People shouted for the guards, and Lily saw the steel caps charging across bridges but they were too far away.

She was helpless. John could have done something, but he wasn't here. She didn't even know what he could have done, but she knew he would have done something. He would have ran down there to help. Lily felt faint as she slumped against the wall. Clutching a hand to her breast, she tried to force herself to breathe. Her thoughts barely let her do that, let alone get away from the violence.

She stood there like an audience at a theater as the troll faltered and collapsed on the ground. Minotaur fell away, bouncing across the cobblestone as his own blood spilled out. But he rose to his feet as the troll heaved and whimpered. He picked up his cudgel-sword, hot breath steaming as he roared. The steel swung up, then split the troll's face in two.

Only then did elves arrive.

Lily found herself running down the steps. Guards she could deal with. The apparent captain was swinging a lantern pole around while his subordinates carved open the troll's throat to bleed it dry. "Who aggravated this troll? That's a crime akin to arson!"

Lily shouted, "It was nobody here. Don't you see the other troll? The beast was in rut and shouldn't have been in the city." She grabbed Minotaur's arm and lost her train of thought when she saw the sucking wound through his ribs, a row of punctures matching it across his belly. All of them were oozing blood as he struggled to breathe. The djinn had his weapon wedged between stones, propping himself up on it.

"What proof?" the guard demanded.

She scowled at him. "There are a hundred witnesses! Pick one of them. He needs a doctor."

The elf spat on the ground. "He's a demon. He'll be fine."

Minotaur's wet hand closed around her shoulder as he gritted his teeth. "Eventually," he agreed. "But, I need rest, if you don't mind."

The elf turned his head up, looking at the dozens of other demi-humans glaring down at him. "We'll question you later, blue-skin," he said, and ordered half his men to round up the owners of the trolls.

Lily bottled her anger and hefted her shoulder. The djinn weighed enough to crush her, but she could at least help. "Come on, no time."

"I don't like this," Minotaur said as the two of them shuffled to the very back of the alley, where the shadows loomed deep and privacy was paramount. The buildings pressed tight and the puddles stank of blood and alchemy. This was where the closest stitcher-surgeon lived.

Lily pounded on the brass knocker, banging it in a rough approximation of the Blutengel code. "Henderson! Get up!"

Feet hit floorboards within, and she heard the old man cursing and swearing at her right until he opened the door and saw the djinn. "Oh, by the gods," he said, falling back. The doctor took the djinn into the back room, letting the demon fall across the low bed. "You might want to…"

She backed away rather than watch him slice open Minotaur's clothes. While the djinn thrashed and shouted in pain. There was a wash basin near the front, which she knelt beside. Soon it was polluted with Minotaur's blood. She tried to tell herself that the djinn was hardy. So unkillable even the elves could do little more than poison them for a time—although the time was measured in centuries.

She was sat with her head hanging when the doctor rejoined her. "What madman is bringing such violence this early in the morning? I haven't even gotten over my hangover."

"Is he okay?"

"Relatively speaking. There's blood in his lungs. That might take a few months to clear out, so he won't be running any marathons. Few new scars. I'd prescribe him bedrest but he'll just ignore me."

"I can't believe I walked away on him," Lily mumbled, not taking her eyes off the doctor's slippers. "Excuse me," she said, slipping past the doctor. She found Minotaur laid out with a bottle of liquor stuck in his mouth. His chest had been toweled clean and the wounds were little mounds of chemical dirt scabbing into his flesh.

The djinn pulled the bottle from his lips with a pop, some of the brew splashing across him. "Someone caused that. Never seen a rutting troll not calm down. Must've been poisoned."

Anger flowed up from the tips of her toes and swallowed her. "Somebody did this?"

"Somebody. Don't know who."

She clenched her hands into fists and felt her nails digging into her palms. "Where is my brother?"

"Coming, not here yet," Minotaur said, waving his hand at her.

Dr Henderson stuck his head through the door to complain, but she ignored him. "If that was intentionally caused–"

The djinn snarled. "If the Black Fingers did it, they'd have already busted in here!"

"My brother needs to know what has been happening!"

"And how are you going to tell him?"

"I... have ways!"

"Lily, stay where it's safe."

"There's no one here to protect me. The villa is safer than here."

"Go back through–" Minotaur's words were cut off by a gush of blood. He doubled over, spitting it out and pounding on his chest.

The doctor shoved Lily out of the operating room. She didn't stick around to see what the stitcher-surgeon had to do for the djinn. She left and slammed the door on her way out. Swinging by her apartment, she saw that John still wasn't back. She grabbed the phone Hilde had bought for her and sent him a text. "Gone to my brother's." Then she made sure she had her protection knife, and left.

The only way to get to the villa was through the magic door, and she made no detours on her way to it. Once again beneath the city, she caught herself before beginning the passphrase for the relic. It took her conscious brain a moment to realize what her instinct had picked up on, but she was already too close to the door. She had rushed down through the tunnels and sewers and made a mess of her dress, splashing through grime and the seeping puddles of a light morning drizzle. It wasn't the smell that was wrong, nor the temperature or anything else in the tunnels themselves.

She couldn't hear any rats scratching their claws against the damp stone.

Thankfully, she wasn't working so she didn't need to conform to uniform standards for a bar. From under her petticoat where her stockings ended, she drew an eight inch stiletto before holding her little oil lamp up to the door. There was a crack around the handle. How they had gotten enough force to do it, she couldn't imagine, but someone had tried to force their way through the door and destroyed it.

"Oh no."

The Blutengels would never do that. Without the right pass phrases, the door literally did not connect to any of the other doors, not that these brutes understood that. Evidently, they bought in on the urban legend that the doors remained connected to their previous destination. Someone had tried to get to the Blutengel base, probably precisely when everyone was busy with the troll attack.

Her best alternative would be back to Thorn's Tap Root and Tavern.

She spun on her heel, ready to sprint, then saw the body in her way. It was huge and stooped, shoulders almost against the herringbone vault. She swore, stumbling backward. The tunnel went on. It had branches, not that she knew all of them. She didn't parley, she ran. Following the trickle of water, she headed to the sea until she had to skid to a stop. Another figure was before her. She threw a glance over her shoulder and saw a rakshasa walking around from behind the broken door. The spindly little ape demon strolled toward her wordlessly.

She immediately understood how she had played into their plans.

She didn't ask who they were. It didn't matter and she was confident it was the Black Fingers regardless. Regular people didn't show up in desolate tunnels waiting for people to show up.

She glanced again at the two main hulks. They were bigger than regular bruisers; probably djinn. A rakshasa she could handle, maybe–not a djinn. She chanced it and ducked through the crumbling hole to the storm sewer. Instantly, the tunnel network split like meshed roots. She ducked this way and that in the darkness with only the flickers of her oil lamp to guide her.

"Come on back, Princess," the devil called, his voice echoing after her.

She needed a way up. Every dozen feet there was some gasp of air, or a reflection of light, but never more than a drainage shaft. She found basements and cellars with walls collapsing around fresh-dug warrens. The stench of beer slop began to stick in her nose, the kind of dregs that breweries threw out and was barely fit to feed to pigs. People used these areas of the tunnels, but they weren't people she ever wanted to meet.

If people descended to the darkness to drink, smoke, and fornicate though, that meant there was a way up. She found the crude ladder in a shadow. It was equal parts missing bricks, wedged lumber, and rope loops, but it led up. She scrambled up, almost losing a shoe as she threw herself to the trap door sealing the tunnel. She dropped her oil lamp to free her hand and slammed up on it.

It didn't budge. A crude pin latch kept it bolted shut. She grabbed at it, trying to yank it free.

Then a djinn wrapped his scaled hand around her ankle and pulled.

She screamed. She also stabbed him with her knife and felt the blade sink through something dense. The djinn grunted in pain and let go of her ankle. She had stabbed through his hand, lifted to shield himself, and as he twisted away he ripped the knife from her grasp.

Lily ran, abandoning the knife. With mud splattered over her, she followed her ears and bolted for the confused words of people. The djinn and rakshasa were behind her–she could hear the demon shouting to not kill her and that relieved her—which meant the voices ahead were strangers.

It only took a few turns to find the source of the echo. "Where is up?" she screamed, scaring two opium smokers almost out of their skulls. One, an old man with a greased goatee and no hair left on his head, pointed up. Not out of confusion, but because there was a rope ladder right next to him. "Thanks," she said, leaping onto it. She knocked through the door overtop as the djinn came barreling after her.

One of the opium smokers said, "You're supposed to knock," before he was thrown against the wall.

Lily had to push through a rug covering up the trap door and she scrambled through before the uninjured djinn caught up. With her heart racing, she crawled out from under the rug and got to her feet in the musty basement. She spotted a crate and in a snap decision, shoved it atop the trap door. Immediately, she cursed. The thing was empty; it wouldn't hold them. The room she was in was dark, more shadow than light and she didn't have her lamp anymore. By the time she spotted the staircase up and ran for the door, the djinn had shoved through.

"I'm going to have to hurt her!" the brute roared as Lily threw the door open.

For a moment, the shop beyond the door bewildered her. She couldn't tell if it was trinkets, jewelry, a sundry shop, antiques, or some combination. She couldn't even see a path through the overflowing debris of useless junk and knick-knacks. For a moment, she finally realized how such useless stores stayed in business. The clerk reading a book behind the counter looked up and tried to ask who the hell she was. Before the sentence even got out of their mouth, Lily was running for the back and the djinn came in behind her.

She threw her shoulder into the door.

He picked up a porcelain statue and whipped it at her.

As the door was opening, the glossy replica of Ganesha shattered against the side of her skull. Little ceramic arms exploded across the back alley and Lily staggered. The world tilted. She stumbled into the wall as heat dribbled across her back. Silence was replaced by a ringing in her ears. She knew she had to run, and tried to force her feet forward but they buckled on her. The ground felt soft as she landed on it.

Three shadows loomed over her. The rakshasa knelt down and shook his head. His mouth moved, but she couldn't follow the words. He pulled something off his chest, a scarf or a handkerchief maybe, and wrapped it around her head. Then everything grew hazy and dreamy. A rolling of her body. The smell of horse droppings. Light and dark. Water on her lips and rope on her wrists.

They were kidnapping her, obviously, but hadn't properly checked her body. The unusual modesty on their part meant she still had her bodice knife. She tried to hold onto that thought as she slipped in and out of consciousness and dream. Eventually they blindfolded her, making the distinction between oblivion and waking slim—no more than the dry taste of the linen gag in her mouth. Then she learned to focus on the scent of salt. Ropes creaked around her and the world rocked.

Someone pulled off the blindfold, leaning over her and shaking their head. "These idiots," the man grumbled. "Hey, speak up, speak up. Come on. Can you hear me? I'm a doctor," the man said as he fished the gag out of her mouth.

Lily tried to ask, "Where am I?"

The doctor frowned. "Oh, that's no good. You've lost a lot of blood, lassie. I'm going to get you stitched up proper and then we're going to get some food in you, alright? Try not to hold it against old Job, will ya? He's paid for muscle not for brains. Hold it against Abdul."

Lily blinked and blinked, trying to focus her eyes on the doctor and form her own words. After a bit of effort, she was able to keep up with his questions. The effort brought clarity back. When he tried to give her some broth, the spoon slipped out of her hand and clattered to the deck, adding new stains to her dress.

The doctor sighed. "I'd ask them to stop the rocking if I could, but the world don't work like that I'm afraid. The dizziness should be clearing up. It's the blood loss that's getting you now. See if you can't just, here, take it in both hands. I don't have no nurse on this ship so you're going to have to tough it out a bit. There you go, no shame. Slop it up and get it in your belly. Now, don't do anything stupid so I can go get you some rum to put some fire in your body, yeah?"

She drank the broth and idly thought about how clean the cooking station on the ship could possibly be. She was in a cabin on the ship so small she could touch every wall. At sea, her options were limited, but she forced herself to think through them while she waited for the doctor to come back. She was rubbing the exposed nub of her knife when the cabin door swung open again.

The half-familiar face of the doctor did not look in on her. It wasn't a man at all, but an older woman with her skin nearly cooked by the sun. Her face was carved by age and worry over centuries, but Lily recognized her at once. The woman had met with her brother on half a dozen occasions, always in a mix of civility and tension. Her captor, the goddess Haraswatti, shook her head and asked, "What did those animals do to you my dear? I swear they want war with the Blutengels. I'm so sorry. We'll have you back in your brother's care soon."

Lily grimaced as the ship hall became a congestion of bodies and bottles, the doctor trying to bring her both liquor and water while she wondered what price they would ask her brother for her freedom.

29

∾

John

Lily texted me that she was off to see her brother, and I couldn't help but chuckle at the synchronicity. I made it back to the apartment only a moment after I got the message but she was already gone. I found my text blinking on her phone, unread, as I hid the Garand in the closet. Technically, I might have been committing a felony. I wasn't exactly sure where university campus grounds began, but I also didn't care.

Still, she couldn't have gotten far. I changed into Alfheim attire and stuck my head out into the port city. I figured I'd be able to find whoever was guarding the neighborhood and just ask. Before I could find the djinn, or whoever was stationed at the apartments, the guards found me instead.

"You're that Martin fellow, aren't you?" one of the elves asked.

"I don't think I have to answer that?"

He sneered at me. "Lady Virent wishes to speak with you. I'm to bring you to her at once."

I looked around at the three other armed guards encircling me and my shoulders slumped. "Am I being arrested?"

"You're being detained," the elf said as they grabbed my arms and hauled me over to a traditional horse and carriage. Part of me was relieved to see that they did have some normal transport options, but the rest of my brain was in shock that once again I was being hauled off. Visions of the dragon almost blinded me to the blood and gore filling the trench beside the apartment building. There was a dead lastkan troll still being cleaned up and the stench was already horrific. No, there were two dead trolls.

Someone yelled my name and I turned to see the djinn hobbling toward me on a sturdy crutch, but then the door slammed shut. The shaded interior was hardly pleasant relief as I shrank in on myself. I hung my head as the horse started pulling us and gripped a hand over Tyr's mark.

When they opened the carriage and I saw I was at the prison dig site once again, I shoved myself to the opposite door. "What the hell? I didn't do anything wrong! I'm a free man!"

The elf rolled his eyes. "You're not under arrest. You're being detained for Lady Virent."

"Detained in a prison!?"

Then they opened the door behind me and hauled me out. I almost threw a punch. I really considered throwing a punch and making a break for it. Nevertheless, I found myself shuffling along with the elven guards, grateful they hadn't manacled me. The door they brought me in through wasn't the prisoner loading gate, but a simple flap of fabric. We passed what looked like off-duty guards who barely even grunted at me.

Then one of them shoved my shoulder and sent me stumbling up a walkway to some kind of overlook. I saw the trim figure of the high elf in front of me. In disbelief, I checked my wrists and found that I really hadn't been manacled. Maybe they didn't need to restrain me when so many armed men were around me. Clinging to a hope of freedom, I mounted the steps and stood behind her.

"I owe you an apology, Mr Martin," Lady Virent said. She didn't turn around to look at me, keeping her hands clasped behind her back as she stared at the work below.

The prisoners, the ones who had very clearly set me up to be their fall guy, were pulling at hemp ropes big enough to be mooring lines. A marble slab was attached to the other end, doing a far better job at digging its corner in than they could dig their heels in. They seemed to be trying to brute force it instead of building some kind of mechanical advantage. I couldn't even tell if they had properly dug a leverage hole for it. Not good engineering at all.

She said, "You weren't meant to be in a real fight. I should have been able to pull you out after the show matches. You weren't supposed to fight the dragon. I'm sorry. Lily told me you were her friend and I should have taken better care of you."

She still wasn't looking at me, but it felt like her attention was completely on me regardless. The threat of ending up back in that sweaty pit again haunted the back of my mind as I said, "I survived. Everything's fine. Even got a healer and all that."

"That's not why I called you out here, however."

"Oh? Okay. What is it?"

Finally, she did turn around. "Are you aware of what happened this morning? The rampaging trolls?"

My eyebrows rose. "I saw the bodies, but no. I was completely unaware."

Silence hung. "It was quite loud."

"I'm a heavy sleeper."

"We think someone caused it."

"Okay? Do you have a suspect?"

She turned away. "The usual suspects, of course. Mr Martin, where is Lily?"

"Off to see her–" I caught myself at the last moment, and tried to remember how friendly Lily and Lady Virent were. Loki was a huge secret, but hadn't Lily and her brother grown up with Lady Virent? I thought I remembered Lily saying that Lady Virent was a progressive about that. I couldn't plead ignorance anymore though, my tongue had gotten ahead of me. "Brother."

She turned back. Both of us stood for a moment, me trying to see the color of her eyes through the slits in her lacquered mask. "Is that so? You may leave, Mr Martin."

I blinked. "I can?"

"Unless you want to climb back down there and help. Lily says you're a master of mechanical problems."

My cheeks colored as stress began to fade. "That was a jest... but... well, there are some things you could improve down there."

"Such as?"

Feeling supremely uncomfortable giving an engineering lecture to a noble lady, I did my best to lay out some basic advice, and in so doing essentially confirmed that she had let the prisoners rig it up themselves. Lady Virent's idea had been that if there was an easier way to do it, the laborers would be the one to figure it out. That led to my final question, "Do you think they're slow rolling the dig?"

The elf shook her head. "I can't imagine they would. All of them will have their sentences reduced as soon as the relics are recovered. They have ample incentive to get this done as soon as possible."

Not wanting to outright accuse the criminals of incompetence, because that would reflect on her, I simply agreed and excused myself. Another guard was called up and given different orders that I didn't hear because I was shown the door. No carriage ride back and short on funds, I put one foot in front of the other.

Then I realized I was running back to the apartment as fast as I could weave through the morning crowds. I made it back drenched in sweat and gasping, but no sign of the djinn. A grey haired fellow walked over as I was sucking air. "You the boy with no tail?" he asked. "My blue patient told me a bit about you before I had to put him under. My name is Dr Henderson."

That had to be Minotaur; he was injured somehow. The knot in my stomach grew heavier. "John."

Dr Henderson made some vague gestures around the city. "Miss Hagen has taken it upon herself to do something dangerous and I was asked to tell you, on behalf of our common friend, to tell you that if you do not find her and help her, that he will destroy you and if not you directly, he will destroy your apartment at the least."

The demon was threatening my computer. I didn't even

know if he knew what a computer was, but the threat was unnecessary. "Your patient? You put him under?"

"He has multiple sucking chest wounds. He needs to recover."

I shook my head. "Guess I'm on my own then." Except, I wasn't completely on my own. I had options. I thought about contacting Lance and Hilde. They were at least familiar with the issue but neither could speak elvish. They would also take a while to arrive. Still, I ran back up to the apartment and sent them both texts. I didn't outright state what I was worried about, but I said it was urgent.

I never say requests are urgent. Rather than wait for them, however, I tucked my brother's pistol under my shirt and went looking for the only man in the city I figured could actually help me in the worst case scenario. Going to Thorn's Tap Root And Room was a logical way to find my way to Lily's brother, if they trusted me, but first I needed backup.

I texted Lance, but there was no guarantee he'd see the message soon. So I went to see Tyr. The people at the Last Resort gave me the side eye, but must have been told I was in the god's good graces, because they told me he was at the bathhouse.

I'd never been to a bathhouse. At first I assumed it was something like a public restroom. Part of it was, and stank like an open sewer, but the other half was what it said on the sign: a house with a bath in it.

You know, I say that like there's something wrong with that, but there really isn't. As a man living in an apartment with a standing-room-only shower, I could completely sympathize with wanting to lounge in a huge pool of questionably clean, hot water. There was some idea of scandal to it, but the bathhouse was divided between men and women, and one look at the clientele dispelled anything lewd. They were overwhelmingly middle-aged and up, hairy, overweight, and interested in their own business. The only hint of culture shock was the small children running around naked, but they were all pre-pubescent, and when I accidentally looked at one kid's tail too long (it was remarkably long and it was the first time I had really seen how it connected to the tailbone) half a dozen men furrowed their brows at me.

I ducked my head–for all it did me at my relative height –and approached the employee. I almost lost my train of thought when I saw his eyes, iris and sclera both, were emerald green. He had a gaunt look to his face, but I didn't have time to wonder what kind of aberration, mutation, or curse caused that look. "Fee is one silver coin, sir."

"I just need to find someone."

"And? The fee is one silver."

"Can you just tell me if an old guy with one arm is."

"I can, but the fee is one silver."

"For the love of..." I paid him one silver.

"He's in the steam room. And don't track dirt!"

I kicked my shoes off, I was more comfortable barefoot anyway, and marched into the steam room. The heat was intense, how they afforded to keep so much steam billowing out was beyond me. Maybe they had some primitive form of coal or natural gas, or some magical reagent. Either way, the heat sucked the breath out of me as I peered around. The room, what I could see of it through the haze, was like a mustache club. One man after another, some old, others young, some fat, others ripped, and all of them seemingly of the opinion that I didn't belong.

"Kid," one of them said. "What are you doing with your clothes on?"

In the time it had taken to close the door behind myself, the linen shirt had matted to my body and was baking me like foil for a potato. "I'm looking for the guy with one arm."

"John?" Tyr asked, and I spotted him in the back, laid face down on a bench getting a massage. "What the hell are you doing here?"

I saw the mustache club hold a moot to decide what to do with me, all through the waggling of their eyebrows. I marched past before they could get up to bar my way. I took a quick glance to confirm the massage giver (I had no idea if the term was massage therapist or masseuse) was not an elf. He had a tail, but it had been cut off near the base.

"I've got a problem."

"What kind of problem?" Tyr asked, letting the male succubus work a knot out of his right shoulder.

"The missing person kind of problem."

"Which person?"

"Lily. She meant to go to her brother, but I think that went wrong."

For a moment, Tyr laid there and thought. Then, he said, "Right," and pushed himself up. "Guess there's no laying around then, is there? Time to get the present."

I gawked.

Tyr had gotten a shave and a haircut. The bushy mess of overgrown facial hair had been expertly trimmed down until it was precisely long enough to cover his jaw, and waxed into shape too. His hair had been trimmed slightly shorter, just enough to take off the damage. Now it was swept back and apparently the grime was cleared out too. What had been dingy brown hair now seemed like firelit wood. He stood tall and muscular, glowing with life and grinning at the prospects of the day. "It seems to me that we'll have quite the valiant day."

"I think you mean violent," I said, turning my head away as he wrapped a towel around his waist.

"Often the same thing. Now, there are two places the young miss could be if not with her brother: with the guards or with the Black Fingers. If they wanted to arrest you, they would have just done so though, so I suggest you go and politely ask Lady Virent. You might even get some help out of her, if she sniffs blood in the underground."

"I already spoke with her. You know who she is though, don't you? We need to find Lily ourselves."

Tyr's gaze flicked off me. "Hey! Where are you going?"

I spun to see who Tyr was glaring at, and saw a man hesitating at the door out of the steam room. He had a tattoo of a hand across his breast. I kicked myself for not even thinking about that. The man was scarred up too, and under normal circumstances he wasn't someone I would pick a fight with. Thankfully, he just shrugged. "Respectfully–" His voice sounded like he had throat cancer, which was strange because I hadn't figured out what the smoke of choice was in Alfheim. "If the one-armed one just set his gaze on us, it's my responsibility to tell the Fingers."

Tyr shoved past me, strolling across the room as the worker threw more water to the fires. "What if I don't want you to do that? Your bosses might just give in if you warn them."

"Well, what can I say? There's shit for honor to be had in fighting someone who wants to surrender," the gangster said.

"I suppose you're right there, and there's some to be had in having powerful men bend the knee. Alright then, begone. Tell your leaders," Tyr ordered, and let the man vanish out the door. He nodded, and turned back to me. "Don't worry about that, I need some time anyway."

"Time for what?"

His grin could only be described as wolfish. "To get you a weapon."

I didn't get any more of an explanation than that. He headed off with a promise that he would meet me at my place, then went his own way. I was shoved out of the steam room, barely given time to drink some water, and then I had to head back to my apartment.

Surprisingly, I found Lance already back, and on the street no less. He was talking to a young woman carrying a basket of food. I couldn't hear what he was saying, but well before I got close I could see the way she was twisting some hair around a finger, how she swayed her hips and laughed as he spoke.

"To learn to speak, beauty. Big fire–" he thumped his chest and tapped his head.

Whatever he was trying to say came through to me so garbled I couldn't understand how she was able to follow him at all, and yet she said, "How to speak, you missed that word you know. But you pronounced beauty quite well."

Lance grinned. "Beauty is a beauty."

"Lance," I said. I couldn't afford to let him stand around flirting, and he needed an exit strategy that didn't fizzle out. "You got my message?"

"John! Been looking for you," he said, falling back into English.

I smiled at the woman and nodded my head to her. "Sorry, I have to steal my friend from you."

"Oh, no, it's fine. I'm running late anyways. My husband will have my ear for this," she said, taking some reluctant steps away and winking at Lance.

He smiled and waved, and asked me, "What did she say?"

"She said her difficulty class was higher than average," I said. When he stared back at me, I elaborated, "She's married."

"Ah, I should wait on that one then. Great lips to stare at though."

"Learn the language some other time. I need your help."

"Of course man, I'm here. What are we doing? What's the situation?"

I cleared my throat. "I don't really know. I've been running around for hours trying to rouse some troops. Is Hilde here?"

"On her way," Lance said, and he gestured to the pedestrian bridge spanning the trench where dead trolls had been hours prior. "He one of the troops?"

The man striding toward me was flanked by a squadron of thugs, all of them armored and scarred. They carried weapons openly and everyone got out of their way. I even saw elven guards pointedly turn and march down different roads. The leader was handsome the way movie stars were handsome, and he had his eyes set on me.

Before even closing in with us, he asked, "So, you're my sister's roommate?"

I glanced around his cadre of thugs and tried to recognize

any of the faces, but I couldn't say for certain. None of them were Minotaur. "So, you're my roommate's brother?"

Lily's brother didn't seem like a thug. Not a young one at least. He wasn't twitchy or itching for a fight. He stood straight with a sword on his hip and the muscle to use it. He was nearly the only person beside the town guards that I had seen walking around with a weapon and his was gilded. His beard had been waxed, his eyebrows trimmed to fierce lines, and he cocked his head just so to let me see the scars more clearly.

I said, "We split the rent, yes. She mentioned she had a brother, but didn't tell me anything about you. I believe the phrase is, you have the better of me."

"That's often the case. Where were you?"

"Just now? Getting help to find her."

"I meant when she was taken."

I almost said running errands, but that felt like it might end with me in a shallow grave, or buried at sea most likely. "I'm her roommate, not her bodyguard."

He folded his arms. "No, her bodyguard was found gutted and strung up like a crucifixion. They draped his intestines like ribbons. Then they poisoned the hauler beasts and had them rampage and injure our resident djinn, leaving her no protection at all except what little you provide."

The blood was slow to drain out of my face, but I was processing the danger. It just took a while because the concept was so foreign to me. Dragons and boars and bar fights were one thing, but intentional slaughter was another. The weight of my brother's pistol suddenly felt very comforting. "I'm sorry, can we start from the top? Hi, I'm John. I live with your sister because of some circumstances. And you are?"

"Chrysthans. I'm the leader of the Blutengels, and clearly I should have kept my sister close. I should have come in person the moment I heard about you... John. I was occupied with other matters and now look what's happened?"

I took a step back. "Hey, look, if this is about the fight–"

"It's about more than the fight, you twat. I'll give you some leniency because you picked a fight to protect Lily, but you stuck your hand into the tiger's maw when you did."

I shifted on my feet. "I don't suppose I can still pull my hand out, can I?"

Tyr said, "No," as he came strolling to meet us. He was sharply dressed, but he had fetched something while we were separated. Whatever it was, he carried it under his arm and had it wrapped in a dirty cloth.

Chrys (I hoped he didn't mind me shortening his name) turned halfway to face him, one hand going to his sword as he cocked his head. "Well, if it isn't the expert on the subject."

Tyr laughed. "Are you trying to threaten me? A poor old man who doesn't even have his sword arm anymore?"

"You're butting into somebody else's business. Why are you here?"

"Why?" Tyr asked, dramatically looking around at the half dozen other thugs that had appeared from the alleys. Apparently the Blutengels had a presence in the city. "Because my pupil is standing right there." He tossed me the package.

Whatever it was inside clanked when I caught it. The moment I felt the heft, I knew what it was. I unraveled it with the best flourish I could manage, it seemed appropriate to do so when my martial art master gifted it to me, and revealed the sword inside. The scabbard had lines of gold etched into it, forming layer upon layer of celtic crosses from tip to grip. Letting the cloth fall, I reverently took the weapon in either hand, drawing the steel out a hand's span. Damascus Steel glittered back at me.

Tyr grinned, chuckling to himself as he leaned in. "Dwarvish. Very nice, isn't it?"

I snapped the blade back into its sheath and whispered back. "Is this actual Damascus or cheap knock-off shit?"

"Actual Damascus. Come on, what do you take me for? A peasant?"

"You were groomed like one."

"Until this morning!"

"What–" Chrys interjected, "Is an ancient like you dealing with some punk who met my sister for?"

Tyr straightened up and stepped in front of me. "Bring us along, and you'll find out. You're a man of faith, aren't you?"

Chrys held the god's gaze and nodded. "Fine then, if you're vouching."

"Hold on," I said, "Do you know where she is?"

"No," Chrys said. "But I know how to find her."

Tyr threw his arm around my shoulders and laughed. "Fantastic. Let's go fuck them up."

Everyone fell in line together, a tide of thugs, rogues, and brutes with me in the middle like I was one of them. We were heading off not just to get into trouble, not to be victims of trouble, but to deliberately cause it.

Lance slapped me on the back. "Chin up," he said, with his implacable grin. "We're going on an adventure."

30

∽

Lily

"Oh, don't pout like that," Haraswati said, waving a goblet of wine at her. The two of them were in a perfectly pleasant garden, aside from the multiple armed guards ready to physically restrain Lily should the need arise. They had been told to shut their ears, but respect for the goddess could only go so far. "The dress looks good on you at least."

Lily grimaced and couldn't help but think of the relative cost of the silk dress the goddess had given her, compared to the patterns and cuts that had been one step from thrown away back on Earth. She would have preferred staying in her typical dress, with a knife hidden in it, but between the blood and the raw sewage, that dress was likely destined for a fire—unless John's clothes washer could really work miracles. She'd have to give it a try. "More wine please," she said, thrusting her goblet toward the serving girl.

Perhaps twelve, it was hard to say with purebloods, the girl struggled with the half-empty amphora. When the wine sloshed inside the ceramic jug, it seemed to weigh more than the little waif, tossing her about. The girl was a true succubus, the god-made demons of beauty that had beguiled mankind so many generations ago. Lily was just a shadow of this sheltered girl. The waif's glossy horns glittered in the noon sun like a tiara, which in turn made her eyes look like amethysts set in obsidian. The black sclera fit her well, which sent Lily's thoughts back to herself and her own judgments of her appearance, whether her sliver of demonic blood skewed her perceptions of beauty away from what humans on Earth preferred.

Really, she was thinking about Hilde and that group of friends. She tried to sort them and stack them up and decide who stood where. Their mingled and mangled network was quite a conundrum because it seemed like the less attractive girls had more sway over group opinion. Maybe they were the better gossipers. Still, it was something to think about with comparatively few consequences. It was a safe distraction from reality.

Haraswati patted the succubus on the head, whispering encouragement to the girl and sending her off for cookies or something. The goddess turned her attention back to Lily, unduly amiable. "Remarkable, isn't she? I swear it's like the wine boy crafted her himself."

Lily shifted in her seat to bring herself closer to the goddess. "Do you all talk about each other like that?"

The goddess shrugged. "What? Flippantly? It's not like we're friends, you know."

"You're all, we're all in this together though, right?"

Haraswati tutted and shook her head. "On the same side

doesn't mean we like each other. Far from it. Besides, Dionyssus is a polyamorous heartbreaker. You should consider him the enemy of women the worlds over."

"I suppose you do all have different opinions on what you're supposed to be doing here. Say, if you were to bend the knee, would the big guy let you back?"

The goddess sneered. "I'm sure he would, but you know what I say? He's not even the problem. Going back to Earth would mean having to deal with those peacocking, backstabbing, so-called angels. Nothing but bad blood and also, what would we do with all you children, hmm? You wouldn't be allowed over. Come now. Do you think we're going to abandon you or something?"

Lily swirled her goblet. "Well you did abandon your temple." The wine was getting her drunk already. She must have still been low on blood.

Haraswati sighed and downed her drink. "A strategic retreat. I may not be a fighter, but I am wise and wisdom is knowing when to pull back your forces to fight another day, another time, and win! Why are you asking about Earth anyway? Been listening to rumors have you? About that... Martin fellow?"

Lily almost jerked out of her seat. "What?"

The older woman laughed. "Ah, you're blushing! So you have heard of... what was his name? Charles Martin? They say he might actually be a human, you know. How he got here I can only imagine. Maybe one of the angels is chafing. Wouldn't that be something? Could you imagine a second falling after so many centuries? How would the big guy explain that?"

Lily sighed, but only halfway relaxed. It wasn't John himself, but his brother in the spotlight wasn't much better, all things considered. "You're sure nobody on this side could do it?"

The goddess sighed. "History. You want to talk about history? Shouldn't a girl your age be talking about boys and money? You live in the city, aren't there pastry shops that tickle your nose and wage war with your corset? Fine, fine, I won't let you say I didn't treat you well once I had you."

"Once you had me," Lily agreed. There was still blood stuck in her hair.

"The barrier between the realm is like a contract between companies. In a sense, that's exactly what it is, because in a sense, companies are daemons just like us gods. Now, we live a bit higher in the abstraction than a mere company, so we technically have the capacity to destroy such a contract governing travel between the worlds. However, those of us here essentially have no employees. That's why we could grovel and ask for an amendment because it really takes no effort at all if both parties wish it, but it would take a lot of effort that none of us can muster to change the contract."

"No... loopholes?"

"My dear, even if there was a loophole, the otherside would simply tear up the contract and crush us. They do not want for power in the least. We are here by grace alone. No, enough of the sad past."

Lily smiled sourly. "Shall we talk about the sad present then?"

"How about your happy future?"

"You made me a damsel in distress."

The guards glanced over, their annoyance at the babysitting ever more obvious. Haraswati snarled at them. "And I do apologize for that. Your brother is an obstinate man and worse than that, he's a hopeless optimist. He is, however, completely mistaken in thinking he can trust that Lady Virent to stay true to her word."

"He just needs a good enough contract with her, no?"

"Sapphire!" the goddess called, and the cup girl ran back over to refill the goddess's drink. After wetting her throat once more, she said, "He misjudged her capacity. She doesn't have the political strength to do what she has promised to do. Why, I hear a friend of yours was just arrested the other day, no? She can't even control the local guards to know who is who! Oh, what's this reaction?"

Lily cleared her throat. "So am I missing something about the girl? Why is her name Sapphire if her eyes are purple, not blue?"

Haraswati waved it off, muttering, "The color changed as she aged. What is this reaction I'm seeing? This is the youth I've been looking for! Come, come, indulge an old lady would you? I'm in a world surrounded by children. Let me live vicariously. You called yourself a damsel in distress, that means you're thinking about a hero coming and saving you, right?"

Lily looked away. She scanned the garden, the rocks and statues. There were flowers, both tended and wild. Beyond, the island broke apart in wonderful cliffs, barely muting the crash of waves. "Obviously, my brother is going to save me."

"I saw a blush. My eyes didn't deceive me. That's the second time too. Come on, tell me. You're thinking of a boy, aren't you?"

Lily huffed. The wine was getting to her. "He wouldn't show up. He's not a fighter. Perhaps we should get some tea?"

Haraswati turned and barked out, "Sapphire, a kettle please? Now you. Not a fighter doesn't mean you don't want him showing up."

"I don't want him showing up because he'll get himself killed!"

"Bah, that's your big stupid brain talking. Lay your heart bare, girl."

"Aren't you a goddess of wisdom?"

The goddess rolled her eyes. "Yes, and? Answer the question."

Lily turned away again. "You know, I hardly see the merit in me telling my captors what kind of attack to be expecting."

A new man appeared, walking up to them with a tea set steaming across his beard. "It won't be an attack. Or, if it will be, your brother won't be the man I think he is. The point of taking you hostage like this is to prevent a fight. Just going to be an exchange. No heroism needed."

"And what are you going to be exchanging me for? Do I get to know that? If I'm to be a damsel in distress I'd like to at least know the price I'm worth. Doesn't that seem fair to you?"

The man set the tea kettle down and poured three cups, handing the first to the goddess. He took a second for himself and left the third just barely within Lily's reach. He walked around the two of them and leaned against one of the corinthian-styled pillars, where cultivated acanthus clung like the tongues of fire. "His sword," the vice-commander of the Black Fingers said, sipping his tea.

Lily sighed. "So that's why we're sitting here, doing nothing. The sun has to go down." Her brother's sword was a relic, and a very powerful one at that, but it was nothing special at all beneath the stars. When he could set the time of the fight, he was untouchable with it, but it was the Black Fingers calling the shots, and they were able to do that because she had gotten herself captured.

"When the sun sets, the exchange will be quite peaceful."

She already knew the answer to the question she had to ask, but she voiced it anyway. "And if he doesn't show up?"

Haraswati shrugged and set her cup down. "We'd of course confirm there wasn't some kind of simple misunderstanding, some loss of communication. He might not believe we actually have you. If that's the case, we would have to do something like send your bloody clothes as proof, maybe a lock of your hair. But, if you really must know–it's not a polite thing and you can see I'm trying to be nice to you, dear–if he has actually abandoned you to keep the sword instead... Well, nobody will be allowed to say that we are paper tigers. We'd have to follow through on the basic threat of a hostage situation. Do understand that nobody here wants it to come to that."

Lily picked up her tea and sipped it to compose herself. Cooly, she glanced at the goddess from behind half-lidded, calculating eyes, she asked, "Even if that means offending another god?"

The ripple that sent around the garden almost put a smile on her face. Haraswati seemed most perturbed of all. The joviality vanished. "Depends on the god in question. How would you have run into one of them? Blue Rock Bay is deep, enemy territory as far as we divines are concerned."

Lily smirked. "Well, what's the saying? The closer you are to danger, the further you are from harm? The elves are looking in distant places like this to find you people. Why would they ever look right under their feet?"

"Who? I know where just about everyone is and almost all are accounted for. If you're lying–"

"Tyr," she said. She smiled as every armed guard stood upright suddenly. They gripped their swords and checked over their shoulders.

Only the goddess kept her composure. She waved it off. "That drunk? He's a gambling addict nowadays, and he spends his winnings on more wine. What interest would he have in you? Going to claim you seduced him?"

"Not at all. Our relationship is purely business. You'll understand I can't tell you the details, but it certainly has to do with the odds in the fighting arenas, I can tell you that much. So, you should understand that he has a stake in my well-being and would be rather upset to learn how I've been treated."

The men of the Black Fingers spoke quite clearly with their glances. Tyr may have been missing his dominant hand and nearly wrung dry of his divinity, but that didn't mean he would lose a fight.

Haraswati shook her head and rose. "Well, my dearie, if you're not lying, that is quite the problem for us, now isn't it? You'll forgive me if I have you prove it? Come, I'll prepare the divination."

Lily lost her smile.

31

∾

John

I had been with my brother the last time I had seen the sea, years ago. Lake Huron and Lake Erie were plenty big, enough that you couldn't necessarily see across, but they were still fresh water lakes. The biggest difference, bigger even than the presence of salt or not, had to be tides. Back home, the shore line hardly changes across the day. I could barely believe the floating constructs of lashed bridges and ramps that Blue Rock Bay had to contend with just to let ships dock.

We emerged before a forest of timber posts, like I was looking at a Venetian parking lot for gondolas but magnified in scale. The bridges were all built by segments, floating atop barrels that buoyed up and down the posts as rolling waves knocked against the rocks. And we were inside the breakwater. The monsters smashing into the line of rubble and rock crashed louder than a rock concert.

"What the hell are we doing?" I asked, watching the Bluten-gels carry supplies aboard an unassuming vessel.

Lance shrugged and pointed at a metered post. "Seems that we're at low tide right now. I guess they can't leave safely until the sea level is higher."

I turned my head and stared at him like a barn owl. "What do you know about sailing?"

"Oh, I was on the sailing team at my high school. Didn't get a scholarship or it though, so you know, just had some fun with it when I was a kid."

"I thought sailing was expensive."

He shrugged. "You know what they say, the best boat is your friend's boat."

"There's no Coast Guard here."

"So? Coast Guard's primary job is making sure people aren't smuggling across the border. Just don't sail in a storm."

"But, there's no GPS to know where we are."

"You can navigate by the stars, especially if you keep in sight of shore."

"But, there's cannons. They're going to shoot at us."

Tyr strolled over and said, "They're not going to shoot the cannons. The entire reason that Flower Boy knows where his sister is, is because they want to meet."

I looked between the two of them. "But, that means it's almost certainly an ambush!"

They laughed at me. I couldn't understand it. They didn't say I was wrong, or that I shouldn't be worried, they just didn't care. There was something broken inside the both of them, and I thought that obviously Lance should have been the one to take up Tyr on his mad mentorship.

I didn't know what I was doing. I was literally in another world filled with elves and dragons, smuggling a 9mm pistol and an heirloom rifle like they were magic wands. I had already been imprisoned, gored, and picked a fight with a gang. How had I not learned my lesson by now? All the signs had been slapping me in the face, one warning after another that by being in Alfheim I was going to get myself killed for nothing.

I didn't know what I was doing this for, the entire expedition into Alfheim. A drunk exploration? Some kind of rescue mission for my brother who was here by choice for all I knew? The wildlife would eat me if I didn't starve to death, or contract some horrendous disease. I couldn't believe I hadn't had a bout of Montezuma's Revenge by now, given the beers I had drank already.

I couldn't believe I had ever thought this was a good idea, that anything here was cool or exciting. It was primitive. The arena wasn't even a third this size of the Big House, and far more brutish than the Coliseum. That was something worth seeing, not the rings of concrete the elves had put up to watch prisoners fight to the death. The only thing I couldn't say was worse in Alfheim than d'Amaranth was the guards, but that was only because I had no love for the police back home either.

I had been, for a week now, stumbling from one mistake to the next and only keeping my head on my shoulders by pure luck. The dragon would have killed me if Tyr hadn't happened to be there (and I still needed to figure out just what he was doing to make his advice so good). It wasn't like smuggling spices was something I could do forever, or even particularly lucratively. Setting aside the issue of exchanging the gold for dollars, I'd eventually break the market. Merchants might start hiring assassins to pressure me out, or at least to find my trade routes and contacts. That would obviously get the portal exposed and then the contract would be null–possibly with me stuck in Alfheim forever!

I had been willingly throwing away a safe thing back on Earth. I just had to go through the motions of finishing my degree and then I could just meld into the automotive industry somewhere. It was like half the economy in Michigan, and the other half was the service industry built around them. Motor City, the motor capital of the world, sure it had some ups and downs along with the global economy but it was a damn steady career. No risks, plenty of money to live on and raise a family with...

Lily was in Alfheim though.

Specifically, she had been in Blue Rock Bay and now was out there somewhere in the sea, on some landmark cove waiting for this whole crew of militants to pull up and rescue her. This was a world that didn't have police to call for help. Big Brother sat in a castle and counted his tax money, spending it on wars of conquest, not on stamping out trifles like this. There weren't even real borders, just regions where people pledged loyalty one way, and regions where their loyalty went another way.

It was a world where respect trumped personal gain, if the attitudes towards Tyr and that Hindu goddess were anything to go by. I didn't need an ID card on me at all times, to drive a car or to buy booze. I could just do whatever I wanted, so long as I had the money and the will to do it.

That went for everyone else too. That's why there was so much crime. It was one step away from anarchy, only held at bay because the gangs, right down to the street urchins, self-organized. Like Yakuza branches organizing against foreigners, or the Mafia jockeying for control of Chicago, self-generated organizations had grown out of the freedom and they only cared about other people when those people stuck their hands into the mess–like I had.

I really did have one hand in the shit though, and maybe Lily would have been grabbed with or without me (her brother was surely to blame) but that didn't change the fact that I had meddled. I had changed the dynamic and couldn't say I wasn't involved. That gave me some degree of moral weight. I wasn't just a passive observer, watching other people fight and die. I had already stuck my finger onto the scale.

And, I really didn't want to lose Lily over something like this. If she just went missing one day and I never heard from her again? Didn't go try to find her? How would I live with myself? No one back on Earth would ever know, but I would know, and there was no getting away from myself. I couldn't even imagine that death meant oblivion anymore. Maybe it wasn't the Christian heaven, but it was something if I was literally talking to Norse gods.

I might have an eternity ahead of me regretting the things I didn't do.

And if I did go and rescue her, if I did put my life on the line to do what was right, if I came out in one piece I knew that was something I'd be able to smile about for the rest of my life. I'd be able to cherish the memory, keep it close to my heart until I was a dementia ridden old man. And, just possibly, I'd do it with Lily at my side.

Standing there, on the docks of Blue Rock Bay, watching the tide roll in, I couldn't imagine even a theoretical woman

I wanted to be with more than Lily. Standing around wasn't going to give me anything I wanted. Staying still wouldn't leave me in the same spot. It was obvious when I thought about it. Motion was always relative. I learned that in Physics 101. Motion is defined by the reference frame, and her moving away from me was indistinguishable from me running away from her.

I couldn't stay still and end up where I wanted to be. I had to run as hard as I could and hope that was enough.

Lance was already down on the docks, having descended an entire story worth of steps to get to the low tide floats. I could see that platforms were lifting up once more though. "You coming?"

When I looked at the ship, all I could imagine was getting sunk by a storm, or pelted by cannons. Things that would kill me with no recourse. "Far be it for me to want my fate to be in my own hands at least!"

Tyr came marching back up the steps and stood in front of me. It felt like I was facing a school principal as he looked down at me. "John, I get the feeling this isn't my place to say. Your father should have told you this, but apparently he didn't. Fate is never in your hands. If it were, it wouldn't be fate. It's not even in the hands of the gods. Look at me–" He held up his one hand and his stump. "Come on, I couldn't hold onto your fate if I wanted to. Men and gods, we're all along for the ride. The only thing you can do is steer your ship."

I frowned. "I think you confused your wise sayings. Can I control fate, or can't I? I'm pretty–"

"Oh, come on, we're about to get on a ship. Of course I'm going to use a ship analogy. Look, what you're doing is conflating your fate with your future. You can change your future, and right now you've got a choice. You can turn around and leave. You'll lose Alfheim forever, I figure, and go back to whatever you had going on back on Earth. Or, you come with us on an adventure. Now... if you ask me... only one of those will make you feel alive."

He left me standing there. Apparently, he figured there was nothing more he needed to say. He just marched back down, and I saw him get Lance another package like the one he had given me. That made me fondle the pommel of the dwarven blade. The blade had a gold puck at the bottom, shifting the weight to the middle of the grip. I wanted to draw it out and play with it, swing it like a child in the woods playing make believe with sticks.

I knew I'd look like a damned fool if I did that with an actual sword, a notable sword at that. But, god damn it, it felt like Tyr had handed me a chance to go be a hero. I'd already killed a dragon, now I could go fight a villain. I could go on an adventure like my brother had and do something I'd be proud of.

"Damn it."

***

"Don't even think about drawing that blade!" Tyr barked, swinging a mug of ale at me. "You haven't earned it, not till you know which side is the sharp side!"

I squeezed the mop handle tighter. The growl in my throat, barely restrained by gritted teeth, was louder to me than all the snapping sails and straining ropes. The break of waves against the hull was just background noise as we sailed north aboard the *Austere Compromise*. "You seriously think now is a good time for this? For... for practice drills?" I knew he was a god of war and training was a way for him to activate his magic, but it still seemed ridiculous.

"Damn straight I do." Tyr leapt up and marched around me. The crew peered over, running between ropes as the captain barked orders at the back. The prow of the ship had been given over to us out of respect to Tyr, not because the Blutengels would say two words to me. "You're like clay."

"Easily shaped and taught?"

"Soft and useless. You're about to get thrown into the fires of violence and that's going to harden you. It always does. No way around it. I have to make sure that when that happens, you're hardened into a usable shape. I'm not making art here, I'm going to make you a weapon."

"I've been in fights before!"

"Bah." He swigged so he could swing his mug around even more. We hit a roller and the deck lurched. I didn't see him so much as acknowledge the leap in the deck that almost sent me sprawling. "You've been in brawls. The closest you've gotten to killing though, was that dragon and animals–caged animals no less–barely count. You ain't a warrior yet. If you were, you would have killed that boar!"

I straightened up to get my balance and lowered the mop. "I didn't even have a weapon!"

"You had your body, didn't you?" he barked back, and then he kicked the end of the mop up. "Keep your guard up too! Who said you could stand up straight?"

"My thighs are going to give out before we even get there!" Both muscles felt like they had been baking in an oven.

"Fuck your thighs. When the adrenaline gets going, you

won't notice them at all. What you'll notice is someone shoving you over and gutting you because you were standing up!"

I squeezed my hands around the mop, reminding myself of how many blisters I still had from chopping wood. He had forced me to stand in 'mid-guard' ("middle guard, you idiot, not Midgard!") for what felt like hours. I couldn't tell how far the sun had sunk in the sky because just lifting my head made sweat break off my brow and flood my eyes. Definitely a long time though. "Is a long sword even a good idea on a ship?"

"Normally? No. But you're going to be using it like a spear."

"Then why didn't you give me a spear?"

"Because!" He shrugged. "Reputation is important."

"To me surviving or to you getting your... whatever?"

He strolled around me, looking at the horizon as he selected his words. "On a long enough timescale, it will be for your survival as well. You want people to be afraid of you, in awe even. That makes them less confident in their attacks and will let you set the pace of fights. That's a huge advantage. But, yes, in the immediate term, the primary focus is on what you can do for me in exchange for all this wisdom I'm giving you."

I narrowed my eyes at him when he called basic martial arts wisdom. "Shouldn't we be sparring?"

He held his stump at me and asked, "How would you propose I do that? Left handed?"

"Then get Lance over here!"

Lance was at the back of the ship tying ropes into bundle cords for storage. To my surprise, he seemed to be chatting with one of the younger crewmen, and how he had picked up enough elvish to do that amazed me.

Tyr nodded his head at him and said, "He'd kick your ass.

I gave him two axes to fight with. Given his size and build he won't even be getting into fights. He'll just close in with someone and split their skull. Not the most defensive strategy out there, but in this kind of melee he'll do fine."

"Speaking of splitting skulls, shouldn't I have a helmet on? Or armor for that matter?"

Tyr looked at me, then he laughed. "Heroes don't wear helmets. Don't worry about that, for as long as you're with me, that kind of so-called common sense won't matter. As for body armor, you don't want that at sea. Nobody is going to wear armor on a ship unless they're suicidal... or blessed by a sea god I suppose. Not sure any of them are in the area though."

"Hold on, there are sea gods too?"

"Don't worry about that," Tyr said, and drained the last of his beer. He set it into a nook beside the stairs down, and picked up another mop handle. "Now, this isn't sparring, but show me what you've got. Come on, hit me, head!"

I stepped at him, lifting up the mop handle to smack it down onto his smug face.

"No!" he screamed, and he stepped in at me. Pain erupted in my fingers.

I shouted, dropping the mop and hopping away, flicking my hands like the pain was grime I had touched. "Fuck, man!" The fingers still moved. Nothing had broken.

Tyr flicked my mop back at me. "Don't pump! How many times have I told you to not pump. When you cut someone down, you just do it. You take the shortest distance between where you are and where they're dead and you cut them down. This isn't chopping wood!"

"Well, forgive me for not being an expert!"

"Again! Belly!"

I stabbed forward, and my mop twisted in my grasp. He had twirled his own shaft, catching mine and shoving it away. Then he flicked the mop head at me, splattering salt water into my eyes. "I told you to hit, not stab. That means a cut. What kind of sword do you think I gave you? A super-sized stiletto? It's not a butcher's ax either, it's a long sword. That means you need to drag the edge through the flesh to cut through it."

I straightened up and scowled at him. "But, you just said I was supposed to be using this like a spear!"

"If I want you stabbing, I'll tell you to stab!"

"Why don't you make up your damn mind?"

Tyr rolled his eyes. "Oh go take a break. Get a beer from the kitchen and come back when you're ready. I've clearly jammed too much between your ears. Clear your head and let my godly teachings heal your body."

So, a few moments later, I sat down on a fixed bench in the galley with a watered down mug of beer. From the moment I relaxed, I felt my body going numb. The blood flowed and all the pins and needles jabbed through my skin. My feet gleefully announced new blisters and I sank my head back against the hull.

The chef said, "You're lucky you're not sea sick. Isn't this your first time?" He was an old sailor, wrinkled and warty, and I had the impression that he would have been fat had he lived ashore. Whenever the ship rocked, he swayed like a linked pendulum with his cauldron.

I didn't ask what he was cooking. I had seen the feed pellets of processed something he had carried aboard. In my mind, somebody in the city was taking agricultural waste and grinding it to dust then packing them into little briquettes. The taste would either be non-existent, or revolting. "Not everyone gets sea sick. I think, maybe, I'm too tired to be sea sick."

"Best not to think too hard 'bout it. Count your blessings, I say."

"Not much of a blessing to be here at all, I say."

"Ah, well, the gods can't always watch over you."

That saying seemed profoundly wrong, but also completely coherent in a world where a war god was drinking on deck, swinging a mop around. I looked over at the chef, watched as he snuck himself a nip of rum from a pocket flask, and I asked him, "Do you trust Chrysthans?"

The chef knocked his liquor back and shrugged. "'Bout as much as I need to, aye. I wouldn't trust him to patch an arrow wound, but I would trust him in a fight."

I leaned my head back to the hull once more and let my mind go dull. I was tired, and worn out from juggling worries. I just wanted to relax, but I was on a sailing ship in another world, heading to a fight and–

I cut that train of thought off and focused on the room around me. I could smell the stew, and found that it genuinely didn't smell too bad. The chef was cooking out of a sand barrel, burning some kind of wood–or maybe peat?--that gave off just enough heat to boil water without setting the ship ablaze. The old man was working between two struts. It reminded me of rib bones for a whale, but I couldn't remember the actual name. Everything on a ship had a name, and I didn't know them. Gunwales? Bulwarks?

"Isle Rocha sighted!" someone screamed, his voice carrying in through an open window.

My musings stopped. We had arrived already, like a sea god had blessed our voyage. When I emerged to the deck once more—sticky with sweat from the practice—and saw the shadow upon the horizon. At first, I thought someone had built a castle in the sea, but the walls were cliffs, and the tower keep a mountain peak. I hoped it wasn't volcanic. Islands in the middle of the sea had a habit of being volcanic and that was just my luck at this rate.

Chrys marched past me, stopping at the railing. He pulled out a telescope and snapped it open. "I can see their ships. Two of them, anchored."

"How are we going to meet them?" I asked, squinting my eyes at the horizon.

He turned to me, lips pressed into a frown. "The same way everyone meets on Isle Rocha, at the black sand shoal. Come on, we've got a plan to go over."

32

~

Lily

Communing with a god was in a sense, very easy. It was also very difficult because the knowledge of how to do it was heavily restricted. Theoretically, if the elves figured out how to do it, the gods–while their positions wouldn't be revealed–would be in danger of being harassed day and night. Lily suppressed a chuckle as she realized it was the equivalent of spam calls on a cell phone, something Hilde had warned her about.

Haraswati had the coals smoldering soon enough, the brazier sizzling as she sprinkled water in. The steam spattered and hissed, swirling about the two of them while she shut windows and doors, blotting up the leaking light with curtains and such until they stood alone with the glow.

Naturally, they had taken her bodice knife, but Lily allowed herself a moment of thinking she could have perhaps taken the goddess hostage. That probably would have been a hollow threat. "It's a bit of blood, right?"

"That's one option. How long have you been working for Tyr? Your hair might suffice."

"A couple weeks?"

The goddess tutted and produced a pair of scissors. "Maybe, maybe if we go to the root. Lucky for you dear, we can just peel your bandage back a little bit."

Lily sighed and offered her head. A moment of pain later, that the wine couldn't quite suppress, the scissors rasped shut and a few strands of her hair were dropped into the brazier. Bottle after bottle came next, dashing their contents into the bowl. One smelled suspiciously like cooking wine, but the next started a fire, and then there was a sticky sap smoke that stuck in her nose.

"Breathe it in, dear. Just not too much unless you want to go on a bit of a journey. Let's save that for another time though, yes?"

Lily nodded and leaned her head over the smoking bowl. She had to close her eyes to keep it from burning and she could only manage one breath through her nose. Then she panted, huffing more of the narcotic smoke until she felt sweat rolling down her neck and her skin flushing. The room swam beneath her feet and she had to grab onto the stone table for support. When she was prompted, she said, "Lily Hagen seeks her sponsor."

Moments crept by in silence as Haraswati stared at her and waited for a response. If she was lying, then no connection would be made to her hair, but there was always a bit of a delay.

Then a male voice returned her call, oozing from the shadows around them. "Lily, what an unusual way for you to contact me."

"Tyr," she said quickly. "I wanted to let you know there's been a bit of an event."

After a pause, Loki's voice returned an octave lower and a degree rougher. "An event? Would that have something to do with the fact a magic-less girl like you has somehow communed with me?" His impersonation was flawless.

Haraswati shook her head. "What do you think you're doing, you slot machine? You make a contract with a girl then let her run about?"

"You've caused me quite a bit of trouble actually," Lily said.

After a moment, Loki said, "Well, if it isn't the temple runaway. Playing revolutionary already? But, before you answer that... My dear little head of sunshine and not much else–"

"Hey."

"You just implied something else happened, didn't you? Haraswati here has you because of your brother so what did I get you into?"

The goddess looked up sharply, her brow furrowing. "What's this now?"

"None of your business," Lily said.

The goddess reared up. "You are my prisoner, like it or not. If you have–"

"She's mine!" Loki cut in. "Where do you get off picking up someone else's contractor? Huh?"

Lily cleared her throat. "So apparently you have a smell?"

Silence gripped the room. Eventually, Loki said, "Ah. That was faster than expected. Montu is sniffing around already, is he?"

Lily frowned. The woman was not a fragment of Montu. Namely because she was a she. She tried to think of an encoded way to say that, but Haraswati spoke first. The old woman had to steady herself on the pedestal as she said, "Why are you mixed up with that brute?"

Loki said, "I don't see how that's any of your business."

"Did you bet against him and win or something?" she asked.

"You're on Isla Rocha right now, aren't you?"

The goddess hesitated. "How do you declare that?"

"Call it caller ID," Loki said.

"And what is that?"

He chortled. "You just hang tight. You know I don't care about your little games of politics. My ears are deaf to your pleas for the people. But you'll be seeing me soon. Very, very soon. I'm on my way, you hear that? I'm going to come and get my girl here and if I find even one cut on her I'll be taking it out of your hide to fix her. Lily, don't you worry about the bloodhound sniffing around, not until after I've gotten you back home. Haraswati? See you soon, m'lady."

The communion terminated suddenly and the two of them stood in darkness. Haraswati took longer to recover, eventually asking, "Who says m'lady?"

Lily shrugged and straightened up from the brazier. She twirled hair around her finger. "Apparently, you can ask him yourself. I guess you really should have chosen someone else to be bait to drag out my brother, and for that matter, you should have sent more competent bruisers to get me. Really, djinn? I can't name a more anti-intellectual breed of demi-human than what remains of the djinn. I'm probably lucky to be alive."

Haraswati composed herself, looking down her nose once more. "Well, forgive me for wanting to right some of the wrongs done to them, hmm? Now, if you will accompany me,

I shall have a fresh bath drawn up for you. I think you've made your point about your head wound quite clear, girl."

On the outside, Lily smirked. In her mind, she wondered just what was going to happen when Loki arrived instead of Tyr. At least the god of trickery couldn't hand over one of the most powerful weapons in the world to a group of revolutionaries. Whether or not Loki could save her was another matter. She probably needed the actual Tyr.

Hours later, as the sun began to set across the sea, Lily was helped into a rowboat and taken to a barge tethered off the side of Isla Rocha. The sea was gorgeous sapphire with schools of glittering fish. The air smelled of fresh salt and gulls cawed playfully in the wind. The growing shadow of the cliffs reached over them, cutting the heat from the day as she sat beside the goddess. Someone with a spyglass high atop the mountain had already called down that a ship was approaching.

The white sails bobbed across the waves toward them and eventually the name of the ship was called out. "*Austere Compromise.*" It was her brother's ship. She sank down, burying her face in her hands as she realized her brother was capitulating.

Haraswati snorted, her expression foul ever since the communion. "So much for Tyr's boasts. It seems we'll be over and done before he arrives. So much for that."

Lily didn't respond. She felt the knot growing in her stomach until she felt sick. She didn't even want to think about what the Black Fingers would do with the Prayer Blade, but nobody would be able to stop them once they had it, and it was going to be her fault.

Unless some kind of miracle happened, but she knew

there was no reasonable way her brother would have any kind of help.

33

~

John

Tyr stopped me. "Don't."

"You don't even know what I'm about to do."

"I do," the god said, grabbing hold of my shoulder. He stared into my eyes. "I have given you the help you need. If you use a relic here, they will think you have something worth stealing. They will break into your house and you know what will happen then."

"I brought it! I'm not a swordsman after a few days with you."

He flared his nostrils and leaned in. "You have to be, though. This isn't just about saving Lily, it's about saving her perfectly. About tying up the loose ends. Be a hero, not a trigger puller."

Somehow, he made it sound convincing. "What about the pistol?"

His brow furrowed. "The what?"

I pulled out the 9mm and he snatched it from me. "Well I'll be. I was wondering how I could help you out there."

"You were wondering!?"

He laughed. "It all worked out, didn't it. Look at this thing though. Earth made, huh?"

Chrys barked out, "We're moving." I fell in with the rest of his crew like it was natural, armed only with a sword and the confidence instilled in me by a literal god of war. That had to count for something.

One by one, we jumped into the water. The Blutengels had given Lance and I leather boots and thick socks—told us to lace up as tight as possible and hope for the best. I only understood when my feet hit the black sand. It was obsidian dust, fresh from the fires of the volcano. The tide liked to shift and pull, dragging the glass around but the shards were huge, like fat snowflakes in the water. Not only was wading difficult, but one slip would shred half the skin from my body.

I was very thankful I had listened to their advice and tied the laces as tight as I could.

The Black Fingers descended from their ships much the same as us, wading over the barren expanse and not seeming to mind the sulfur in the air. I tried to tell myself it was a good thing we had met here, because I couldn't imagine how someone could fight in such conditions, and yet everyone had their weapons ready.

Their leader stepped out in front, at least I assumed he was their leader. He was the same age as Chrys, and me for that matter, but darker in skin tone. His facial features had hardened, like weathering from sun and sea salt, which made his scars stand out more. I couldn't take my eyes off the tattoo across his cheek. From jaw to eyelid, he had a hand etched into his skin. Black Fingers indeed.

"What a pleasure to see you again, Blademaster-who-isn't," the man said, snickering with his henchmen. Our numbers were even, which felt like a disadvantage for us.

"For you, maybe. I was hoping to never see you again, Urdao," Chrys said, stepping out to meet the leader of the Black Fingers. "Where's my sister?"

The leader of the Black Fingers, Urdao, pointed with his thumb to the secondary ship. Evidently, it had been waiting at Isle Rocha for some time. Enough to lash together a full barge platform in the shade of the cliffs. Unarmored men and women strolled about, like worker bees to a queen. Two women sat in the middle, one older and regal, her silk dress glittering with gold as she sipped wine. The other, also in a gold threaded dress but not at all pleased to be there, was Lily.

I almost lunged in her direction, then Urdao said, "Safe and sound with the lady Haraswati." One of Chrys' subordinates turned around, cupped his hands around his mouth, and bellowed the news back to the *Austere Compromise*.

I hissed a question to Chrys. "What is a goddess doing on their side?"

"None of your concern," he hissed back. Then he faced Urdao again, as he unlaced his sword belt. "She should be on a rowboat, ready to come home. That was the deal, wasn't it?"

Urdao laughed and nodded. "That it was, that it was. And I see you have brought the Prayer Blade. I look forward to putting it to much better use than you ever did."

So it was a trade. I had been wondering why no one else thought we were all going to die, and why Chrys even knew where to meet the Black Fingers. As the pieces of the puzzle began to fit together in my head, tension waned. I was able to take a breath and see that Tyr was gliding across the water to join the women on the barge.

That meant our backup plan was coming together. Tyr was no good in a swordfight, but his left hand worked just fine, and he was a war god, just a very impoverished one. The instant violence broke out, with his mark on me, he would have the upperhand against any mortal, especially ones from Alfheim. He had the 9mm pistol hidden in his pocket and just needed a bit of magic to help his aim.

"Yo! Hara-sweetie! It's been too long!" he called, and we all saw the disgust on her face as she watched him approach.

With some mild variations, everything was going to plan, just like Chrys had said. Lily's brother had gathered us all up the moment the ships were spied and almost perfectly foreseen the entire event. Which meant that Lance and I were edging to one side, closer and closer to the barge Lily was hostage upon, though she seemed more like she was at a party she didn't like than a prisoner. Fighting in the shoal was a fool's errand if there ever was one, without some form of magical intervention.

That of course meant something was going to go wrong. Murphy's Law dictated it would, I just didn't know what. In a sense, Lily getting kidnapped was what had gone wrong, but that didn't feel like the thing.

Urdao looked over his shoulder, at the crimson sky as the sun began to set. I hadn't even noticed the time passing. I had been up all night subjectively, but fatigue hadn't set in. I must have been completely wired. Urdao said, "You know, the nice thing about dawn and dusk is that you can make plans around it, you know? Big plans, with people in very different locations."

Chrys cocked his head. "And here I thought you were just afraid of a fight."

"True, true," Urdao said, glancing at me. I froze in the water, not taking another step. He looked back to the leader of the Blutengels and said, "I'd be a fool to provoke you while the sun was up, on a battlefield you arrived at. People don't call you a blade master for nothing, but that'll change, and soon I'll show people just how powerful that weapon really is."

"If the Prayer Blade was as powerful as you think it is, we would never have gotten in this situation. Don't you see that? We're on the run! We've been stripped of our legacy, our homeland, even our gods are no better than us now."

Haraswati rose and strode to the edge of the barge. She was distant still, but voice carried well over water. "Times change, Chrysthans Hagen. The world has seasons, cycles of power that ebb and flow. We have been surviving through a winter for a very long time now, longer than you've been alive. You are so close to it that you can't even see the shift, but I can. Soon, it will be spring, a burgeoning of new life, industry, creativity and fecundity."

I glanced at Tyr, and saw him nodding along, getting closer to Lily. I couldn't tell whether he was agreeing or just playing out the plan.

Haraswati lifted a hand to the setting sun and continued like it was her show, and I wasn't sure it wasn't. "The paths between worlds are opening once more. We will have the chance to assert freedom once more, to cast off the elves. What we must focus on now is proper preparation. It tears me up inside that we had to resort to this kind of measure, but you made it necessary."

"I thought you were a goddess of wisdom?" Chrys shouted back. "You're awfully fixated on war at the moment."

Urdao waded closer. "No use preening your feathers when someone has their boot on your neck. Now, hand over the Prayer Blade. The sun is going down, you're no threat to me if the sun is down. That sword will be useless."

Chrys frowned at the weapon, playing for time as Lance and I edged further to the barge. "Relics like this are such a curious thing, aren't they? Unimaginably powerful in some respects, but so very, very limited. Haraswati, you lost your grand treasure, didn't you?"

"Not for long," she said, smiling at him.

Lance and I glanced at one another. That comment pretty much eliminated any doubt. Urdao had made a point of it: a setting sun was a good synchronizer. And to think just that day I had been helping dig out the temple. My gut had tried to tell me: the prisoners were intentionally slow walking the dig. They wanted to finish it exactly when they felt like it.

I didn't know what to say to Chrys that wouldn't screw up the plan though, and didn't have the time to either. The sun kissed the horizon as he turned back to his ship, somber faced and holding the weapon up. With his back to Urdao, he said, "Blutengels! I thank you all for following me. I know you've put your faith in me, and I would never want to betray that faith. This is indeed the Prayer Blade, a relic of incredible power. It won dozens of battles for our ancestors and has been passed down with the instructions. He who bears this blade and arrives at the battlefield before dawn, may he pray for protection and steel will never hurt him all day long. It makes you almost unstoppable for the day."

"But it's night!" Urdao said, and his men laughed in chorus. "You should have made your dramatic speech while you were sailing over. Stop wasting time, Chrysthans."

The sun sank through the horizon. Dozens of hands gripped weapons, cold sweat beading on more necks than my own. The Blutengels had to wait for the sun to set before they could start the plan. Chrys had to stall longer, but before he could open his mouth again, light flashed on the barge.

Two figures appeared, entangled together like dancers. One dwarfed the other, but both were familiar to me. The smaller figure clung to the man, almost climbing up his frame to reach what he held high in the sky. It was Hanz Grimner. I recognized the backstabbing bastard at once, then my eyes flicked back to Lady Virent. Held overhead, the thing she was struggling to grab just barely out of her reach, was an hourglass as ornate as a crown jewel. The moment the light had faded, depositing the two of them so far from the dig site by pure magic, sand began flowing from top to bottom once more.

Evidently, their plan to slow-walk the dig had included arcane theft at the end. It also hadn't worked quite right.

Everyone stopped and stared, even the Black Fingers were caught by surprise, except Tyr. He scratched his beard and said, "Well, if it isn't the warden. Aren't you a surprise."

As Lady Virent gawked at the change in scenery, Grimner planted his boot into her gut and knocked her right off the platform. She hit the water as everyone started asking each other what was going on. "Kill her!" the escaped prisoner bellowed, jerking his hand against the hourglass which seemed to be stuck in the sky with his hand glued to it.

No one knew what to do about a third party appearing. Had it just been Grimner, he would have clearly been an agent of the Black Fingers, but Lady Virent? None of the workers on the barge seemed to even know who was responsible for killing the elf, if anyone. They stared at one another and looked to Haraswati for guidance.

One person didn't hesitate to act, and it wasn't the man ominously standing behind Lily. My eyes caught the glint of steel he had pulled out, as well as the confused frown as he tried to determine if he was supposed to stab Lily. That drove fresh rage into my body, but rage could only make me start wading. The person who acted was Lance.

Lance dove into the water, swimming through the obsidian murk.

Lady Virent bobbed back up, shouting obscenities as she grabbed for the platform edge again. Water like gunmetal streamed off her and she threw her head, whipping her hair around as she tried to clear her eyes. She didn't see the spear as she climbed back onto the barge. Some young thug stabbed at her like he was doing nothing more than checking the water depth. Not even a flicker of emotion, he probably hadn't even thought through what he was doing.

Maybe he knew he had to act before he could process that he was killing someone.

Either way, he didn't succeed because Lance's hand grabbed Lady Virent by her coat and threw her to the side. He rose from the water bleeding like a demon. Thousands of tiny grains of volcanic glass, yet unsmoothed by the tide, had dug into his skin like a howling sandstorm. The warcry he bellowed was the same scream he used in rugby scrums; enough to shake the bones of the thug in front of him. When he swung with one of his axes, the steel bit straight through cloth, flesh and bone, snapping the man's leg with a spout of red.

That had not been in anyone's plan.

Urdao shouted for archers.

Chrys shouted, "Fire!"

I saw half a dozen men pick up bows, pulling them from hidden spots on the barge and from the Black Fingers ship. The thugs on the barge swarmed to Haraswati, covering her with their bodies like Secret Service agents. Tyr shouted, "Go, now!" as he began firing with the pistol. The Black Finger archers fell one after another as I clamped my eyes shut and dove into the water like Lance had, diving into the dark as arrows began flying through the shoal.

I didn't get very far before I had to throw my head back above the surface. The glass sand had gotten everywhere, ripping into my skin. I screamed and thrashed, seeing the world in a blurry haze, but I did see the world. The sun had sunk beneath the horizon and yet there was light in the sky. For a moment, the backdrop of the heavens sprawled across the world like the glowing branches of a tree, dripping with glittering gems. The next moment a ball of burning magnesium overwhelmed the backdrop.

Someone aboard the *Austere Compromise* had a relic of their own: a flare gun to put an artificial sun into the sky above the battlefield.

"Come here, Urdao!" Chrys bellowed, wading across the

shoal like a kaiju, Prayer Blade drawn. "I just wanna have a talk after you kidnapped my sister!"

The obsidian shoal was like a scene from a nightmare. Not quite hell (not enough fire and brimstone) but close enough that I wanted nothing to do with it. The facial exfoliation that felt like it was grinding my armpits to mush definitely had something to do with my opinion on the matter. "This was a horrible idea!"

Torches had come out, little swinging spots of light like fairies in the air. I barely saw the spear tip in time to swat it away with the dwarven blade. I had ripped the thing free of its sheath already. Holding it felt good, the way a hammer to a problem felt good. I just tried to not think about the consequences of fixing my problems that way.

They were criminals that had kidnapped an innocent girl afterall. The most beautiful girl I knew.

"Come and get some!" Lance bellowed, and did exactly what Tyr had suggested he do. He closed with the men of the Black Fingers and he hit them hard–smashing through interposed blades to split skulls. He was lucky the closest thing to a shield was a buckler here and there; discs of wood the size of dinner plates. That meant he tore through the men with berserker rage.

Grimner was still stuck to the hourglass. He must have wished to escape with it and had to continue paying the price. His mouth worked just fine though. "Surround him! Are you idiots?"

Lily had jumped to her feet–she really did look stunning in the dress. Not so stunning when she screamed, "Look out!"

I would have died trying to grab onto the barge if Lady

Virent didn't shoulder ram the thug from the side. He tumbled into the water and I took a wild slash at him. Whatever I nicked must have been important because hot blood squirted into my face. I almost wiped my eyes before I remembered I was covered in the equivalent of industrial cutting fluid.

Someone said, "Take my hand," and I did see a hand in front of me, so I grabbed on. They helped a bit, enough to say they helped, mostly I hauled myself out of the water and managed to blink my eyesight back. It had been Lady Virent. She grabbed me by the shoulders, pushing me to my feet to ask, "What are you doing here?"

"What am I? What are–" a gunshot popped off next to us. We all turned to see Tyr grinning at the corpse he had just made out of the spearman that had come back for us. I really had to figure out if my valorous combat, if it could be called that, had anything at all to do with his ability to pull a trigger.

"This thing is great," Tyr said, and shot another man straight through his buckler. I was able to see the thug's confusion as blood poured out of his chest.

Lady Virent ducked around me with a shout. Someone was charging us, ax high. I threw up a parry, twisting my blade high and at the head of the weapon. Before he could pull around it, I stabbed down and ripped his neck open. Not a lethal wound at all, but enough to stop him.

Lance finished the guy off with an ax blow to the back. As he passed by, I finally realized all the blood on him was because he didn't have a shirt on. I asked, "When did you strip?"

"Before I dove." The two of us forced a pair of thugs back from charging us, claiming space with wide swings. It was Tyr that finished them off. "I figured," Lance said, his words labored with breathing. "That the sand can only cut me if it's rubbing. So... off came the shirt and my arms are up... legs wide too."

Somehow, I had avoided that.

Lily screamed as she ducked beneath the chair she had been sitting on. Her would-be executioner made a grab for her. We were lucky he hadn't blindly stabbed her the moment things went wrong. Or maybe that was because Tyr would have put a bullet between his eyes first. The bastard was right overtop Lily though, fighting to pull the chair off the top of her and cleave a sword into her.

I closed with him before I even realized I was roaring. My blade swung down on him. Steel glanced off steel as he retreated, taking a clumsy parry. I reversed the swing and cut back, stepping in hard. Again, my blow glanced off his weapon, knocking off his crossguard as he held it between me and him. Then I was close enough to lift my handle, to drop the tip, and I thrust. The tip scraped across his wrist as he tried to push it away but still it found his chest. The resistance I felt was like I was stabbing into a pillow.

Thinking I had failed, I tried to twist the blade out and attack again, only to feel it arrested. The two of us stumbled before the blade ripped free of his chest and he fell back. His own blade clattered away as he collapsed in a pool of blood.

"John! Arrows!" Lily screamed.

I couldn't spot Haraswati. I scanned the barge as my free hand found Lily's arm. With a twist of my body I hauled her to her feet and started running. Arrows were falling on us. I swore and sprinted for the rowboat Tyr had taken. Unlashed, it had floated halfway around the barge, like it was running away from us. One by one shafts slammed into the barge around us.

Lady Virent screamed. I spun and saw the blood. One of the arrows had clipped her in the head and ripped the mask off of her. It left a trail of open flesh but I finally got to see the prison warden. It took the span between the blinking of my eyes to recalibrate and understand why Lance had jumped into the fray for her.

For one instant I saw her face and realized she was gorgeous. She was exactly the kind of mature beauty an elven noble lady should be.

Another arrow landed right between Lily and I. Part of her dress was ripped, a ribbon of silk flapping. My breath caught, but she hadn't been hit. She must have torn it on the floor of the barge. Lucky, but I couldn't press our luck. My hand cupped her chin and turned her away from the arrow. "We have to go," I said, and took her by the hand, pulling her to the rowboat once more.

"What are you doing here, John!?"

"Who would save you if not me?"

I gestured out to the shoal. The signal flare overhead was getting low, casting long shadows that danced over the churning water. Urdao hadn't managed to get into a rowboat, Chrys had driven him off it. The fight wasn't going well for the kidnapper. I could see blood in the water around him, and one of his arms hung limp. Chrys hadn't killed him though, and the flare would land in the water. It had a parachute keeping it up, but gravity could only be denied for so long. Theoretically, that didn't mean Chrys would lose the fight, but he would stop being untouchable.

The chair in my grasp thudded. I blinked. I had been holding it up, over Lily's head just to give her the room to yell at me. Two arrow heads broke through the planks of the seat back, vibrating in front of my face. "Uh, go go go."

"Go where?" Tyr shouted, and I saw the *Austere Compromise* had begun sailing around the shoal. They were looking to pull up on the Black Finger's ship, cannons at the front.

I roared in frustration, but that at least meant another volley likely wouldn't come. Haraswati was escaping in a small craft, getting rowed away by her attendants. No point in chasing her. I tried to find who was left.

Only Grimner was, as he ripped his hand free of the hourglass. The grisly thing floated in the air, half covered by the bloody skin of his palm. The escaped prisoner roared, squeezing his wrist and puffing. He squared up with Lance and shouted, "She knows too much. She has to die."

"What is even going on right now?" Lady Virent demanded, a few steps behind Lance.

"Move," Grimner demanded.

Lance shrugged and shook his head. He was breathing heavily and I couldn't tell if he had been cut or not. I wanted to run over and help him, but I had something I had to do. He had chosen to fight for the elf. I had to get Lily into the rowboat.

"And to think!" Grimner shouted, grandiosely strolling across the barge. He kicked a spear into his grasp as Lily and I dove into the drifting rowboat. "I took you for a godly man."

Lance, of course, barely understood what the man was saying. He must have caught some words though, because he shook his head again, and said, "Sorry. Christian."

Having declared himself a heretic to all sides, only Tyr acted quickly because he had heard it before. "He's all yours, kid," the war god said, and ran for a tethered rowboat that Haraswati's ship had left behind. The crew were almost certainly dead on the barge and now that the hourglass had arrived, the platform had served its purpose.

I didn't know what I was supposed to do. Lily and I were in a rowboat, sitting ducks for the archers but the archers were distracted by the ship sailing at them with cannons in the front. The cannons being low poundage, like Tyr said, didn't seem to matter much when the muzzles were aimed at the deck with gravel to act as grapeshot. I saw the *Austere Compromise* blast an early salvo, enough to put the fear into them, as it came sailing up on them. They'd have to reload, but the ship hadn't gotten much to speed since it had been anchored.

So where were we supposed to go?

"What the hell is your plan?" Lily demanded, ripping the hem of her dress off strip by strip to wrap around her bleeding belly. The dress had been nice, I figured worth a few thousand dollars easily, but the arrow had already ruined it. We could get her something else back on Earth anyway.

"I don't know."

"What do you mean, you don't know?" she shouted, crawling into my lap. The two of us were almost prone in the boat, her atop me. She suddenly didn't seem small, not at all like a thing to be protected. She eclipsed the sun–

No, that was the moon. The so-called sun was the flare, cross-lighting her red and then it went out. I jerked my head up to see the dark waters. The flare still guttered beneath the waves, but it was a dying light and the shoal had turned to shadows. I barely saw the silhouettes of Urdao and Chrys.

Their blades were locked together. Urdao had been driven to one knee and his left arm bent in the wrong spot. But he hadn't been killed.

"Now!" the leader of the Black Fingers bellowed.

I didn't flinch as a dozen arrows loosed, because I knew not one was aimed at us. Chrys shouted, and I saw him go down beneath the waters.

"Row, we have to row and get him," I said, scrambling onto a bench as I grabbed the oars and floundered with them.

"Do you even know what you're doing?"

I set us gliding to where Chrys had been, to where Urdao still was. "Fuck, take it over, can you?"

"You've gotta be joking!?"

I sprang to my feet at the prow, holding the dwarven blade up in the mid-guard Tyr had taught me. I was trembling. I was also about to get tossed out of the boat as Lily haphazardly shoved the oars through the water in the dark and the wind was picking up and the waves were getting rougher and there were archers about to shoot me and—

Chrys popped up from the water, sucked in breath, and made eye contact with me. "This way," I shouted, and moved my attention to Urdao. I puffed my chest up as menacingly as I could, and still the bastard marched towards us. Chrys had butchered him by the looks of it, but that had just pissed him off more.

He was looking down on me. I was just some guy come to help his enemy. I wasn't a threat. He must not have realized my sword was dwarven. He was staring up at me as Chrys tossed himself into the rowboat behind me, shouting something as we continued to glide at Urdao.

I had a cold realization as I stared at him: I was able to kill him. It wasn't a heated swing in a brawl, I was pretty sure Urdao wouldn't be the first to die by my hand if I killed him, but this would be something different. Over twenty years of moral education leapt up in my mind to stay my hand.

But, I guess it really didn't amount to much, because I discarded all of it the moment I asked myself what he would do if I spared him. He'd already kidnapped and held Lily hostage.

Urdao held up his saber with a war cry. I feinted around it and sliced through his face. I felt the jarring impact as blade bit through bone.

34

~

Lily

The fight died down like a storm passing. Here and there people still clashed, but the brunt of the forces had passed. Too many people had died. Others had been pulled into the retreat. John had cut the head of their enemies and won the day. He had come to save her through no begging, no transaction, no promise or debt.

He had come for her. Maybe not elegantly or expertly, but he had come and fought.

As the two of them dragged her brother into the rowboat, she almost couldn't look at him. It made her chest tightened and her cheeks flush. Her body warred with her rational mind because she knew there had to be some catch, some misunderstanding. Loki had lied, or perhaps been privy to what was already happening. There was no chance they could have made it to Isla Rocha in time if they had set out after she communed with the trickster god. Clearly, that meant John had known nothing of the bartering, of the balance of revolutionary forces, or why she had been abducted at all.

He probably thought it was because of the bar fights. Their worlds were only rushing against one another, overlapping and entangling more in body and space than in mental force. Still, it overwhelmed her mind. She heard herself babbling, repeating herself and saying nothing at all of importance. She fussed over her brother and helped turn his shirt into bandages while glancing over her shoulder at the retreating ship of the Black Fingers.

John spoke in a daze as well, like he had been struck in the head and left in a daze. He had cut down Urdao without hesitation, but didn't seem to realize what he had done. He drifted, afloat on the simple action of retreat. His eyes kept passing over her without coming to a focus. The strength of his body seemed to be melting away. The further they drifted from Tyr, the more literal that probably was. He was human, a champion of a god of war, he hadn't won the fights on his own merit alone.

No, she knew that was a lie. He had done it all on the force of his will. Tyr had only helped his body; had made up for the years of his life spent in study instead of practice. Lily wasn't stupid or unworldly. She had seen plenty of arena fights, martial tournaments, and back-alley brawls where the larger man had lost because he simply didn't have the right stuff. That was what John had brought to the table.

The will to defy the world, to cut down his enemies. It was his power that had come and saved her.

"Hey," Chrys shouted as they passed into the shadow of

their ship. He reached forward and knocked his fist against John. "You only finished him off. I did all the hard work."

John slammed the oars back, sending the rowboat bouncing over shallow waves toward the side of the ship. He gestured at Lily and said, "I was a little preoccupied while you were dealing with him, you know?"

Chrys laughed. "Yeah, I saw. And? That was my victory against Urdao. You just put the mercy blow on him. That was me! I killed him, you got that?"

John rolled his head side to side, muttering and mumbling and hiding his face as her brother began heaping praises on him.

Lily's heart skipped a beat as she realized John had her brother's approval. Chrys acknowledged him as a good man, a reliable fighter, an honorable hero. He had risked himself for her and fought when it mattered. More than that, he had always instinctively protected her without expecting anything in return. A man who acted on what was right without making excuses.

It was like all her selfish thoughts and hopes had manifested into him.

"Are you okay?" Chrys asked, putting a clammy hand to her burning forehead.

"Ah, yes! They didn't do... I mean, the one guy hit me over the head but he was just a brute, you know? Once they had me, they were very polite actually. Except you know, keeping me captive and all that. They didn't hurt me or anything."

Her brother's hand found the blood still scabbed into her hair and his face darkened. "You'll have to tell me how exactly this happened."

"They broke the door."

The rowboat knocked against the ship and ropes were cast down to fetch them up. Her brother didn't take his eyes off of her. "Those pieces of shit. I should have killed more of them. They broke the door? Do they think we can just make more of those?"

"I was stupid. I should have gotten Finnegan's help first. You see, ah, well... you know, I'll tell you later," she said as she looked up at the crew almost pouring over the railing of the ship to rescue them.

"Wouldn't have helped," Chrys said as he shoved John toward the ladder. "They got Finn first."

Her stomach dropped. "They what?"

Her brother shook his head and stood up in the ship carefully. "We'll have his funeral soon. You know how it is," he said, taking the bottom of the ladder.

Lily hung her head and tried to hold onto the sadness. She could feel it inside her heart, that bit of responsibility for a good man. Finnegan hadn't been some saint, but he had always helped, he understood good from bad and worked hard, and he had been a casualty of Urdao's scheme. Finnegan had been between Urdao and her, and he had died for it.

She knew she couldn't quite hold onto that sadness though. It was a small rock within her breast that she wasn't afraid would go away. It wouldn't fester but it wouldn't fade too quickly. She could tease it out and deal with it in due time. Far grander than that pain was the warmth within her. It fluttered whenever she looked at her hero, her rescuer. She looked at John.

The feelings were vague and swooning. They threw

themselves about her latent hopes and memories, twirling and swirling into an explosion in her chest that had her stealing glances up at his fatigued face. Even when their eyes seemed to meet, she rationally knew there was nothing but an exhaustion fit for the dead; a fighter who had put his all in the battle and had nothing left within him. That emboldened her. It whispered in her mind that she could look as much as she wanted and he wouldn't even remember. She could even do more. Could draw closer. She could touch him and do everything short of kiss him and it would be like a private blur of memory in the haze of victory. So she stared at him.

The feelings were immature, childish, ridiculous. She was one step better than a besotten, lust-addled teen. The danger of death, of disaster for her brother, and the excitement of death had stirred her instincts to a frenzy, but was that so bad?

It was too bad she couldn't go ask her mother if that was normal, but she'd have to figure it out and trust herself. Her heart had fallen for John and she just needed to carefully make every other part of her, and of him, fall into that entanglement of souls. It would take effort, sacrifice, time, everything, but there, rocking across the chop of Isla Rocha, she couldn't imagine a better hero.

He slipped on the ladder to the ship and had to be grabbed by the crew, throwing him over like a fish, but that just made her laugh.

35

~~

John

The three of us flopped onto the deck of the *Austere Compromise* with the flash of cannons still seared into our retinas. Chrys sprang to his feet, shouting, "Go, go, get us out of here! Urdao's dead."

The crew cheered and slapped him on the back. I think he corrected them, but I didn't watch nor listen. I had crawled over to the fore mast and begun stripping my sand coated clothes off. Every time I closed my eyes I saw Urdao's face. He had been surprised. I had been too. It felt like Tyr's rudimentary lessons had synthesized with what fencing skills Hilde had tried to give me in Freshman year. Neither of them had taught me what it felt like to actually cut someone.

Lily clasped her hands around mine. I didn't realize how cold I was from the water until I felt her warmth. "Are you okay?"

I forced out a scoff. "Shouldn't I be asking you? You're the one who was kidnapped. And shot."

She shook her head. "Haraswati isn't a bad person. She forced Urdao to do the whole thing in good faith. Also, you're bleeding."

"I am?" The adrenaline was wearing off. The pain sensors in my body got the all clear to begin firing off and I finally felt what had become of me. The shirt I had just taken off would never recover; it looked like I had sweated red; armpits of blood. Now the salt started to burn and I felt it in my scalp too. "Oh, holy fuck..."

"You're going to need a doctor."

"I ain't gunna die but... shit, hey! Tell me you've got some liquor!"

The ship chef strolled past us, with a tray sticking off his gut like a stadium concession worker. He slapped a bottle into my hand, gave Lily a nod, and moved on. The swill was unlabeled, probably moonshine, and–after I bit the cork out–smelled like it could run my car. It was exactly what I needed. "Great service," I said, and took another swig.

Lily laughed. "John, what the hell are you doing here?"

"Rescuing you."

"My brother could have done it himself."

"Yeah, maybe. But, it's not like I'm uninvolved."

"You're not a fighter though. A brawler maybe, but this? What do you think you are?"

I was not childish enough to say a hero. "Your roommate and co-owner of a certain magic device. Also, I already got in a fight on your behalf. I'm not uninvolved."

She sighed, and I immediately realized I had missed a chance.

Whatever the chance was, the words didn't come even after the fact. "John, I've seen your life. You're a normal guy. That was actually a stipulation I gave when signing up! This violent world isn't something you're supposed to be a part of!"

"You know, I always wanted to go on an adventure. I guess I just didn't really process what it meant. I thought I did for a while, and that's why I never went on one. It's dangerous. You end up bleeding out of your armpits apparently."

Lily leaned over, almost into my lap to peer at my cuts and scrapes in the darkness. "Hey, can I get some bandages?" she called to the crew.

"I think maybe cartoons lied to me? That might be it. I used to watch a bunch of shows where people would fight and blow things up, but no one ever got hurt. It was this bizarro censorship that tried to appeal to kids who want to be heroes while hiding the downsides. You know, like, monsters are monsters because they kill people. And the hero is the hero because he kills the monster, only the monster. But, that's kind of the... the presupposition of the heroic journey; that there is a monster or a dragon or a crime lord to go kill. That some evil has been manifested into a body that can be slain instead of just the pervasive crap that is Earth."

Lily listened while picking up my shirt. She kept turning it around and around until she found a clean spot, then she started dabbing at my cuts. "Are you seriously complaining that your hometown is too peaceful?"

I grunted as she touched the open wounds. "You know, it's peaceful but it ain't pleasant. Something inside of me was withering until I met you Lily... so of course I would fight to protect that, to protect you."

She pulled back and the two of us stared for a tense moment. She was blushing.

I had to say something. There was something that a dramatic, charismatic hero would say and then we'd kiss and– "Also, I'd have to be crazy to not fight for a girl as cute as you that wants to play Capu-mon with me."

She did not kiss me. That was stupid enough of me to say I was ready to slit my own throat in shame. Of course that wouldn't mean anything to her, she had only learned what the game was two days prior. I had to put it in terms that matched her world, her preconceptions of romanticism not fucking nerd fantasies.

Then she kissed me on the cheek. She held it for a moment, only slowly taking her lips away. Whispering into my ear, she said, "I'm not that easy of a capture target, but consider my flag raised."

I blinked and didn't even have the wherewithal to hold onto my liquor as she pried it from my grasp. "Capture target?" I asked, watching her gulp down the moonshine. "When did you learn that term?"

She grinned at me. "That's for me to know, and you to–"

"Kill her! Are you people insane?" someone shouted, and I saw two more figures had flopped over the railing, sopping wet and glistening red.

I was jumping to my feet before I even realized the new arrivals were Lance and Lady Virent. I hadn't actually been stabbed anywhere, but Lance had been. He was covered in bleeding wounds that needed to be treated, and yet he stood his ground between the elf and the crew. I arrived at his side the same time Chrys stepped out from the crew.

"Step aside. I'll sort this out," the leader of the Blutengels said.

"No," Lance said, apparently getting the gist.

I saw Lady Virent glancing around, weighing her options. In the middle of the sea, there was no escape for her though. Before she could open her mouth to beg, I said, "The way I see it, she was never supposed to be here. She got tangled up when their guy Grimner... is he dead, by the way?"

Lance shrugged. "He was alive when I left him."

I didn't see the large man's corpse on the barge, but we were sailing away fast now. "What do you think you're doing?"

Chrys frowned, rubbing his thumb against the pommel of the Prayer Blade as he thought. "You're a bold man, Martin."

I stepped closer to my friend, shoulder to shoulder and in front of Lady Virent. "Lance is my best friend. When I said I needed his help, he showed up, no questions asked. What kind of man would I be if I didn't return the favor?"

Chrys rolled his head, stretching his neck and looking to the sky as he thought. He smirked. "And if I said she knows too much?"

"Knows what?" I asked. "That there are radical elements among the underclass? That the hourglass thing has been stolen? I'm pretty sure they know all that already."

Lily marched over, coming in from the side. "Oh, haven't you made enough of a bloodbath tonight? Are you really going to get in a fight with the guy who saved both of our lives?"

"If I may," Lady Virent said, and Lance and I parted. "Chrys, I have known you since you still wet the bed. I can't say I'm surprised you've been in contact with the exiles, but I am appalled by how you're acting now."

"Auntie Anya, don't you know me better than that?" Chrys responded as he crossed his arms.

Lance and I locked gazes for a moment, finally learning the elf's first name.

"I know you've spent your entire life with a well-deserved chip on your shoulder that nobody else would ever give you a fair shake, that you have a frankly frightening level of focus that would make you the head of the King's Guard if you had been born with pointed ears. I also know the only reason you've ever cracked open a book was for a girl who you drove off last year and that was the biggest mistake of your little life."

"Don't bring her up!" Chrys snapped at her.

"Go get her back!"

"I'm busy!"

Anya Virent planted her hands on her hips, almost pressing him back with her presence. "Fighting over relics?"

"I'm still committed to the deal. They took my sister. What the hell was I supposed to do but come here? Hold up, pause. Where is the relic?"

All of us looked down at our hands, at the ground, everyone. Except for Lady Virent. She sneered. "The one-armed god stole it."

Chrys shook his head. "Well, that's that then, isn't it?"

The crew grumbled, but their leader had given his orders and they didn't question him. Lance was finally able to relax, and his axes fell from his hands. They bit into the deck and stood upright as he heaved out some breath and said, "So, can I get a doctor?"

Anya put a hand on his arm and said, "As soon as we're in town, I will get you the best healer in the city."

I cleared my throat. "Uhm, he's still learning the–"

"Thank you," Lance said, a moment before he dropped to the deck and passed out.

I had to step around him, interposing myself between him and the railing just in case. Lily joined me, watching as the crew dispersed to their duties. Ropes had to be tied. Boom arms had to be swung. Telescopes had to be pointed into the night to find the port. Some men eventually helped wash Lance off and wrap him with some cloth, while Chrys escorted Lady Virent below deck.

As the commotion waned, I retreated from the boom arms before the crew could get them swinging. Lily followed me and I finally got a good look at the bandage around her head. She at least didn't seem in much pain from it. "Your brother is a rather extraordinary fellow, you know that?"

She shrugged. "I suppose so, but having a brother like him has its downsides."

I laughed. "Well, I wish we could have met under better circumstances."

"Hard to do, when he's never around." She realized what she had said the moment after it left her mouth. "Oh, I'm so sorry."

I had turned my head up to the stars. "No, no it's fine. Actually, I'm going to go find Mr Chad Paladin. Should be less eventful than this."

"Really? When?"

"Soon as I heal up, I think. Winter break? It will be an adventure if nothing else."

She smiled. She had a way of grinning from ear to ear and

I had only seen a glimpse of it while she was playing in the apartment. "Sounds like a plan."

36

~

Lily

Snow blew across d'Amaranth, pushing down the din of cars and college students. It howled across concrete crenelations and tacked-on air conditioners. Flags whipped here and there as cracked windows emitted as much noise from televisions as they leaked marijuana smoke. The night was young and light burned through the roads, out from homes and apartments, and up toward the sky.

Somewhere, either above or in some mis-labeled building, were gods, angels, and who knew what else very interested in Lily not being on Earth, nor her brother.

"Well," Chrys said, shrugging his shoulders in an exaggerated motion to get his puffy parka to replicate the motion. "I have to say that compared to Thorn's bar, the risk here has got to be a lot lower."

Lily tugged her coat tighter around her and laughed. The two of them were on the top floor of a parking garage where the ice-laden wind bit at her nose and cheeks, but they were quite alone. "I wouldn't call it perfect, but I highly doubt I'll be abducted. The people here have a strange way of making themselves miserable, and their homes are tiny. It's very strange."

Her brother nodded. "I'm surprised. You screamed at me about wanting a regular life but here you are possibly doing more to save our people than anyone else."

Lily hid her face in the fur of her coat collar. "I just wanted to get away and he offered me a way. Honestly, if I had known it would end up like this, I don't know if I would have signed the contract."

Her brother laughed. "That man John is pretty impressive. I swear, watching him was like watching a horse realize the gates were left open. Like he had been told he shouldn't go out there but knew he had to. The man's got spirit."

"You didn't bully him into coming, did you?"

Chrys leaned on the short wall separating him from a long fall. People streamed by far below, flowing through the city with no sign of police or hassle. "All I did was let him understand the situation and gave him the chance to act. He did the rest."

"Did you tell him it wasn't his fault?"

"Sis, I didn't know what the reason was at that time. How could I say it wasn't his fault?"

She slugged him in the arm. "You told him it was his fault, didn't you!?"

Her brother relented, dancing away from her blows. "I may have implied a bit of responsibility, but he did get in a fight on your behalf! He involved himself."

"I got kidnapped entirely because of you! All he changed was maybe the timing."

Her brother rolled his eyes. "Oh yeah? I have it on good authority that he was working hand in hand with Grimner to screw up the digging rate at the temple. You know the whole thing was done to synchronize with that hourglass, don't you? I'd say he was very involved!"

"You didn't know about that till after! You totally bullied him into it."

Her brother groaned and smacked her fist away. Then he flicked her in the forehead and said, "You can't bully someone into heroics unless they had it in them in the first place. He should be thanking me, you got that? I broke off some of the shackles of civilization."

"The shackles of civilization," Lily parroted. "Listen to you. Which playwright are you obsessed with this time?"

It was her brother's turn to flush. He crossed his arms and turned away. "None of your business."

"It's a girl, isn't it?"

"She's a woman."

"Close enough!"

Her brother threw up his hands. "How about we focus on what's important? If Loki has found a loophole to create these portals, then we may no longer need to beg favor from sympathetic elven ears. We don't need to be one step above slaves. We will finally have an advantage in negotiating. You've just proven that those other rumors, of the dragon slayer and the miracle doctor, are probably real: they're probably of humans."

Lily slumped. "But is that actually a good thing? What if

it's people like the Black Fingers that win them over? We'll have another great war on our hands."

"At least we'd win," he said, leaning once more on the wall and looking across the city. "Did you see the power of that weapon John had? The one he gave to Tyr?"

She shrugged. "Tyr's a god of war. Of course it was–"

Her brother waved her off. "He did hardly anything. It was all that gun. It punched holes through armor like it wasn't even there. You'd need a relic to stop it and there's not many of those. The possibilities are exciting."

Lily stared at her brother, the far off gaze not quite focused on anything. Then he noticed her looking at him and a grin appeared on his face. Before she could react, his hand was on her head, tussling her hair. "Hey, stop with the long face. I know you want out. Obviously you didn't want to be dragged in but it wasn't me that did that. I'm not going to ask you to start smuggling weapons over or something. You're free to live your life, okay, Princess?"

She sighed and stopped worrying about the future. She couldn't help but grin as she looked up at him. "Thanks."

"If John gives you any trouble though, just let me know," he said as he took her by the shoulder and started back toward the stairs.

"He wouldn't dare, knowing I have the great Blutengels ready to swoop in and save me. Not that I'm particularly worried that someone who risked his life to save me would be bad."

"If he does though."

"He won't."

"If though."

"Would you stop?"

He laughed. "Fine, fine. Now come on, I'm going to freeze over here. When does it become summer?"

"In like eight months," Lily said as they descended the concrete stairwell.

Disgust twisted her brother's face. "What kind of inhuman hellscape is this place?"

Lily laughed as she used her back to push through the door to the sidewalk. She spread her arms and said, "D'Amaranth, my new home."

37

~

John

Elven bathhouses were much better than the lower class steam room I had found Tyr in. They were also the preferred working room for Lady Virent's preferred fleshcrafter. I had thought it wouldn't be a very big deal when I watched Lance sit through the process without making a noise. Only after the fleshcrafter made my skin feel like fire ants were eating it did I realize Lance had simply been in shock.

I was shouting and yelping like a child as she slapped my raw, bleeding skin.

"What kind of man wins a fight and then cries because of a little rash?" the doctor asked. My brain wanted to say she was a cute girl, but that was just misinterpreting her elvishness. She had crows feet despite looking almost like a teenager. There was something she could do that no teenager could though: fucking magic.

"It's a shock reaction," I said, scooting away from her. "I was fighting for my life back there!"

She huffed. "And what everyone's going to remember about you is this."

"Bullshit!" I said, almost pulling my arm out of her grasp as she fingered my armpit. "They're going to remember how I valiantly saved Lily and Lady Virent!"

"Hey," Lance said, face down on a bench and so covered in raw flesh he couldn't even move. "Keep to your half of the glory. You saved Lily. I saved Lady Virent."

We weren't alone in the bathhouse, and the one other guest finally spoke up. He was the other guest of the manor, carelessly sitting cross legged on a bench near the steam vent. Mr Smythe continued his flagrant disregard for concern over his identity as he spoke, "You're both wrong. What people will remember is whatever the bards tell people. They're the people whose palms you have to grease." Loki winked. "I've been trying to get a hold of you. Very hard when I can't just... I don't know, whisper in a bird's ear and send it off to your pocket?" That earned him a confused look from the doctor. "I felt I had to do something to let you know the currency problem has been taken care of, thanks to a mutual friend."

I rolled my head back and closed my eyes. "Fuck. I forgot about that. Well, taken care of? So we're good?"

Loki strolled across the bathhouse and ladled himself a cup of water. I could only imagine how hot it must have been. "Yes, I imagine your business ventures will be much improved now. New ideas to be explored? Opportunities to be exploited? Money to be made? I do hope you'll keep it up. You see, somebody had to begin buying all those spices you've been importing, and... assorted other goods, and I thought I'd lend a hand. You did, after all, bring such a flaw to my attention."

After ripping up a few hundred tea bags, the cheapest money could buy, they had poured the leaves into a satchel and sold it for two gold coins. Clearly, not enough to pay rent, but doubling their money was nothing to sneeze at, and it got them in the door. Being able to give her servants tea and coffee regularly was also a status symbol that Lady Virent had proven quite interested in, given the low cost.

Before I knew it, Loki (and his fabricated elf ears) had a full ledger running and the entire rent would be taken care of so long as we brought everything on time. Unfortunately, that left a certain sticky political situation we had managed to insert ourselves into. It was basically the same mess the Blutengels were in, but we weren't part of their freedom fighter gang, or however they wanted to style themselves. Lance and I, after we were cleaned up and presentable to a noble lady, were summoned to meet with the madam of the house, Lady Virent.

"You saved my life," Anya Virent said, gesturing to Lance and I with her cup of steaming tea. "Doing business with you is the absolute least I can do."

I cleared my throat and fidgeted. The doctor had also been complimentary for saving her, but I had to say, "That's great, certainly, but how about keeping us from getting arrested and stuff like that?"

"Ah, right." She rose from her desk. The three of us managed to make her study feel quite small, despite the bay windows behind her. The meeting room was leagues better than the open air cell I had first met her in, but it lacked a certain charm. The bookshelf existed, but was very small, and mostly filled by scrolls instead of manuscripts. The walls had portraits of women that looked just like Anya, but I could tell their age by the cracking of the paint; her ancestors I supposed.

Half my mind was considering the implications of cheap paper, but the machine regularity of printer paper was surely right out. We'd be exposed. Then, she said, "Since you're a mercantile group, my suggestion is to leave town for the time being. Go somewhere, perhaps aboard the *Austere Compromise*. Let things cool off. Keep your heads down. Now that it's known the Black Fingers are conspiring against the crown, there will be crackdowns, arrests. You don't want to be caught up in some form of revenge."

I nodded. "Makes sense to me. As I recall, you were going to furnish me with certain paperworks?"

"Ah, yes," Anya said as she leaned against her desk. Reaching back, she produced a scroll and a bronze medallion. "Your passport, Mr Martin."

It wasn't quite a medal or a trophy, but I supposed it was better than something useless like that. Not a gift, but a prize. I was holding the spoils of victory. It felt really good, even if it was just a cast thing of metal she had scratched my name into. "Great, I'll be needing this."

She smiled. "As long as you're going to keep selling me your products, I'm happy to have given it to you. Even if you are a troublemaker who doesn't respect authority, gets in fights, and seems to be one step from causing a civil war." She smirked.

I had to remind myself that the elves had slaughtered every human in Alfheim, and she simply thought the two of us had been maimed of our tails. "I'm not trying to get into trouble, I swear. Trouble found Lily, and... well, I guess I went and found that trouble, but you know what I mean."

"I do, and please know, I appreciate that the both of you exist in a world of principles, rather than of race." She smiled at Lance as she said that. I swear she batted eyelashes at him too. Lily was constantly harassed and desired by male elves, and now I was wondering if the same was true for female elves snatching up male dreamers. That would get him found out in a night.

Lance grinned and said, "John, could you translate for me that I'll strive to learn her language by the time we're back?"

I wasn't about to get in his way, so I repeated, "Lance is looking forward to speaking with you when we get back. He says he'll learn the language quickly."

"That would be lovely," she said. "As soon as he does, I'd like to thank him without need of a translator."

I looked over and watched Lance smile and nod. I could only guess how much he was picking up from the conversation. I was pretty sure he had never heard most of those words in conversation before, and as far as I knew had no magical aid. I said, "I'm sure the sentiment has gotten through."

"Well then, I'd love to chat more with you, but I did get magically abducted, and I am expected to report in person to explain what happened. I'm stalling so Mr Hagen can get out of town, but there are limits to what I can do before I stop being trustworthy. Do you need a guard escort?"

I laughed. "I'd be surprised if the Black Fingers could retaliate this quickly, wouldn't you?"

She shrugged. "It's a nicety. Your weapons will be returned to you by the servants. Stay out of trouble, and if you can, some honey to go with the next batch of tea?"

Soon enough, the whole crowd of us assembled outside Lady Virent's manor. Lily pulled Loki aside to negotiate something, and I turned to my friend. "I've been meaning to ask, how did you act so fast?"

"What? At the barge?"

"Yeah, you had your shirt off and dove before the light went away. How did you act that fast?"

He shrugged. "I didn't think much about it."

"You just dove into a fight?"

"It was the right thing to do, wasn't it?"

I wasn't sure I could say it was the right thing to do. Lady Virent seemed to be a good person, but I hadn't exactly interrogated her beliefs and the elves had committed genocide centuries ago. Of course, humans were attempting it every few years as well. "How did you know?"

"I just did."

"Just like when you agreed to help me get Lily back?"

Lance laughed and poked me in the chest. "You have got to listen to your heart more, man. That's one of your smart person problems. You spend too much time thinking about what you don't know. Just do what's right. Simple as."

I could only shake my head. "So you're seriously a Christian? After meeting literal gods?"

"False gods, I guess. Plenty of those in the bible, ain't they? Hell, meeting that slimebag has made my convictions even– John, where did he go?"

I spun. Lily was talking to Hilde, I think they were debating getting a carriage to go back to the apartment. They had both taken their eyes off Loki and he was nowhere to be seen. "Motherfucker, he never explained the money exchange!"

38

~

Lily

Loki threw up his hands and Lily and Hilde cornered him in the apartment between a rack of theater costumes and a floor lamp draped with what might have been lingerie. Just approaching him risked tripping over beer cans and landing on sewing kits. Even Loki couldn't move quickly through the mess. "Calm down, calm down ladies!" He swung plastic bags around, burdened with bottles within. He used them like warding cruciforms against evil, and it somewhat stayed the two furious women.

Lily planted her hands on her hips, snarling at the trickster. "If you just had a way to contact you, I wouldn't have been abducted!"

He pressed his back to the wall, stretching his neck like a startled chicken. "A literal god of war went to rescue you! And besides, our contract has nothing to do with your brother's enemies."

Hilde jabbed her thumb to her chest as she shouted. "My brother almost got killed fighting for some over-aged elf."

Loki huffed. "First of all, she's very young for a high elf. Second of all, your brother accompanied John with no knowledge whatsoever of Lady Virent."

Lily clicked her tongue. "Hilde, steal his coat."

"What?" Loki demanded. He had gotten his hands on a leather jacket that still glistened with snow, melting and dripping across the apartment carpet. It had been left by the door.

Lily rolled her eyes. "Hilde, you're not his worshiper and I'm not human. He's totally powerless. Just a man. Let's get his coat."

"Now hold on! If you women force yourselves on me like a pair of barbarians I will have no choice but to drop my fine gifts! I may not have brought frankincense and myrrh but I did my best to suit your palettes. I understand the two of you had quite the ordeal. It's only right I help facilitate a feast."

Hilde scoffed. "You want a feast? You should buy us dinner at Italiano Five."

He paled. "That's a Michelin Star restaurant!"

"Like I even know what that means," Lily demanded.

Then he pulled the bottles out from their bags, letting the plastic flutter away to reveal the lemonade liquor within, the neon candy brews of eighty proof hooch. Lily hesitated, scanning the bottles over. She glanced to Hilde for a cue and saw the older girl back down. Hilde asked, "How the hell did you get a fifth of Birthday Cake? That stuff is hangover in a bottle."

Loki grinned. "But I have it on good authority that you like it. That Arab guy at the liquor store has a memory like a steel trap. Knows damn near every student in your school right now and what their favorite booze is. Barely speaks english, but that's not a problem for me, you know. He gives great favors to anyone who bothers to use his native tongue. Favors like this."

"What's special about it?" Lily asked, stealing a glance over to Hilde. She glanced at the door too, locked, bolted, and chained. The Trickster's only other way out would be the window.

"It's good. So good nobody can keep it in stock," Hilde said.

"I've got this too, but I don't think the two of you will want to drink it right now. Still, it's a token of apology, you see?" Loki said, pulling another bottle free. This one Lily recognized and her breath stopped. It was slender, dark, and rippled like the shape of a woman. It had no label, but the cork was sealed in place with mottled wax, red with white dots.

"That can't be," Lily said.

Loki chuckled and eased his stance. "Oh, but it can. Come now, you think something like this is beyond me? I'm a god after all."

"What is it?" Hilde asked.

To even speak its name gave Lily pause. It was the wine with no name. It was the draught of communion, of heavenly bliss. It was Dionyssus' blessing. "It's good," she said.

"Call it Soma if you prefer."

Hilde's face scrunched. "The Brave New World drug?"

"The man's inspiration."

"Hold on," Hilde said, but she eased her posture as well. "How do you know some mid century British novel?"

Loki sighed and shrugged. He shook his head theatrically and moved like his bones had turned to snakes. "Really, if you're going to be questioning how I import my own entertainment, after all this time, I'm going to begin questioning your intelligence. Now can we have a drink of this liquid tooth rot and discuss our future?"

Lily locked eyes on the bottle of soma then let the tension out of her body. Then shot glasses hit the table and the Birthday Cake began to flow. Loki held his up and said, "I'm very sorry, of course. Not just for the mixup with Haraswati but for the woman sniffing around for me."

They drank. It tasted like frosting and then it was gone and she wanted another. Lily gasped. "Holy crap, you weren't kidding."

Hilde smirked then glared at Loki. "I don't want to hear your apologies. Clearly, if I need to bring you to justice, I can just ring up the local PD."

The Trickster paled. "Now, now, no need to get them involved. That's what we're here to discuss, isn't it? And we only have a bit of time before your brother shows up. We don't want to be doing anything when he gets here, do we?"

"Doing what now?" Lily asked, pouring another round of shots.

Hilde downed hers, but the burn in her cheeks couldn't have been from the alcohol already. "So, you've got like a list of candidates over there, don't you?"

Loki bridged his hands together and grinned. "That I do, that... I... do. We don't need to beat around the bush, do we?"

Lily blinked, remembering hearing this conversation herself. She gaped as Hilde mirrored the god's posture.

"Look, unlike most girls, I'm flexible on height, but he does have to be smart. Athletic too. I don't want some shlub that's going to pack on a hundred pounds in the blink of an eye."

Loki asked, "Would you prefer a bard? A poet? Or a scholar? The latter I've the least of, just not many options to work with."

Lily grabbed her friend's sleeve. "You're signing a contract with him?"

Hilde gritted her teeth and almost exploded. "Do you realize how badly I want a new apartment? Oh my god, the clothes! The clutter! The noise. They drink my liquor and don't do the dishes. They make plans and cancel on me. These women are driving me insane! I've been watching you and John hit it off this whole time and somehow you're like perfect roommates too. Do you realize how jealous I am?"

Lily took a breath and realized a laugh was bubbling up inside her. It ballooned her chest and made her head faint as she tried to not insult her friend. "After all we've been through, I can't believe you still want to go to Alfheim."

Hilde crossed her arms and declared, "As the only one of the four of us that managed to not cause a disaster–"

"You did break that sword."

Hilde continued, "I'm not the one in danger over there, now am I?"

"Not to mention," Loki said as he topped off their drinks. "A second portal doesn't have to be to Blue Rock Bay. The doors are magic. They can connect wherever I wish. Come on Lily, you should be supporting your friend here. Why don't you name some lovely cities and I'll see if I know anybody over there?"

Rumors, songs, poems, and tall tales danced through her head, darting across her mental map of the continent as ideas sprang to her. They grew ever more exotic until she realized she was thinking of one particular city far to the north. The journey to it would be long and imperiled by bandits. The elven kingdoms splintered to robber barons along the way and made travel more trouble than it was worth, unless there was some deep, personal reason to risk it all. The city was said to be among the most beautiful in the world though, if the colder climate could be tolerated. "Well, I'd probably say Fjord's Fall."

Loki chuckled, seeing right through Lily's attempt to be aloof. "I have some options there. Perhaps instead of describing what you'd like in a partner–"

"Roommate," Hilde corrected him.

"Perhaps I should take a cue from your Earthly dating apps? Go and fetch some images of the prospects for you to look at?"

Hilde nodded. "That could help, yes. It won't take long though, will it?"

The god shrugged. "A few days, maybe a week. Now then, I think I hear the thundering steps of the most bullheaded man I've met in ages."

Lily grabbed the bottle of soma. Hilde's hand shot out and grabbed it too. "Whatcha doing?" the human asked.

Lily blushed. "This really shouldn't be sitting out."

"It's wine, isn't it? We can share."

"We should not," Lily said, putting as much stress on the pronoun as she could. She tried to pull the bottle over.

Hilde didn't relent. "We're sharing the Birthday Cake, aren't we?"

"That's different."

"How so?" Hilde asked, jerking the bottle back toward her.

The trudging boots of Lance were getting closer. She

scanned the apartment, looking for a cabinet to stash it in. "It's not wine."

"Then what is it?" Hilde asked, rising as Lily rose but still not letting it go.

"It's a... religious thing," Lily said.

Loki laughed. "It's a love drug, at least that's how I expect you'll be using it."

Hilde froze just long enough that Lily was able to yank the bottle from her stunned grasp. She darted over and through the kitchen straight to the linen closet. She scanned the junk: cleaning chemicals, party supplies, batteries, lightbulbs, clean towels, and then a bleach-damaged beach towel. It was crusty with something she didn't want to think about, hoped it was poorly washed detergent or something, and stashed the soma in it just as Lance threw the door open.

"Knock knock," he declared, hefting a thirty rack of beer into the apartment. "John here yet?"

Hilde sank into her chair, the image of nonchalance. "No, but grab a glass. We've got a treat."

Lance stared at Loki as Lily returned as though she hadn't just hidden a near priceless drug. "You're not an elf anymore," he said, and Loki shrugged.

"Not a good idea to be one here on Earth," the trickster said, swirling his liquor. "Now then, I believe we are celebrating everyone's good health and your first successful rent payment?"

"Shouldn't we wait for John?"

Then his voice boomed down the hall, rolling through the still open door. "I'm coming, I'm coming. My project has been a mess. Dealing with gangsters was easier than this shit," John said as he came jogging down to join them.

Lily's head still itched where her cut was, more as her heart began to flutter. It had been days and Hilde had cleaned it up with some stolen supplies from the college clinic, but it wasn't quite healed yet. It still reminded her of what the Black Fingers had done. That was not something she was going to complain about to her hero however. "Now we can celebrate," she said as Lance distributed beers. She cracked hers open and held it up. As everyone else lifted a drink, she said. "To..."

Loki offered, "Prosperity and camaraderie?"

Hilde said, "How about to sheer survival? Good health and good humor!"

John set his eyes on Lily and said, "To the biggest adventure of our lives."

Lance cleared his throat and added. "So far."

Lily beamed at John and agreed, "So far."

"Cheers!"

39

John

My group project was not going well. Two weeks to go before presentation day, and we'd be tested in front of everyone to see how much weight our crane could support. Naturally, this was when half the group came down sick with the flu and the only other member was worse than useless. A whole week practically living in the engineering building's machine shop, pulling all-nighter after all-nighter had produced a crane.

It would hold an amount of weight.

It was my crane and there was no way in hell I was going to let anyone else in the group try to improve it. They'd probably strip a bolt, or shave an angle, or stretch the cable or something. Who knew what they could do to botch it before the presentation day, so I wasn't going to leave it in the locker.

Thus, I had to hoof it back to the apartment, carrying the forty pound mass of welded steel in front of me. I couldn't reach the doorknob. I gave the door a thump. "Lily! Let me in!" I could hear her playing a game. The noise was cranked so loud we might get a noise complaint.

"Just a sec!"

My fingers were burning, but I didn't want to put it down and have to pick it back up. The ground was a grimy, salty mess of snow slush. "Lily, just pause the game!"

"Just a second! AH! NO no no no no no noooooo!" I heard the fanfare from the game, the out-of-tune whomp-whomp of last place in Super Kart.

"Lily!"

She groaned and trudged over. The deadbolt clunked open and she pulled the door for me. The bags under her eyes were even worse than mine. While I had been getting by with an hour a night thanks to her, she was the one playing video games instead of sleeping. It was not a cute look, but had an appeal all its own with her wearing one of my old hoodies that reached halfway to her knees. "What the heck is that?" she asked, backing away as I barged inside.

"This," I said, setting it on the table and shaking my hands out. "Is at least a three-point-oh."

She blinked, then perked up. "Oh, the project thingy!"

"Yeah, I'm gunna have to keep this in the closet or something until presentation day, and then–"

"So you're going to do it?"

I nodded. "Yeah, I've just got to square some things away. I've now got school basically done, two weeks to prep, and then I'll more or less have a month to find him."

"That's wonderful!" she said, throwing her arms around me. We embraced for a moment, which brought up other things I needed to say and to do.

Naturally, that was when my phone rang. We both felt it buzzing in my pocket, so Lily broke off and went back to Super Kart. I plugged my ear as she restarted the grand prix so I could answer, "Grandpa! Interesting timing."

He chuckled. "Interesting, huh? Would that be unfortunate-interesting or peculiar-interesting?"

I glanced over at Lily as she played the game. She had her tongue stuck out one side of her mouth and kept throwing her hands from one side to the other as she needed to curve (I still didn't know if that actually helped drift with the console's motion controls). I caught her glancing at me, checking if I was still on the call.

"The former," I said.

"Ah, I'm sorry, John. You coulda just hit ignore if it was something like that."

"No, no this is important too."

"Is it? I'm just returning your call. You didn't leave a voice message."

I hadn't left a voicemail because his inbox hadn't been set up yet, after seven years, and I literally couldn't. "Well, we're talking now, right? Could we do Thanksgiving on Wednesday?"

"Sure. It's no difference to me. I'll have to tell–"

"Just us actually. I don't think I'll be joining on Thursday."

I could hear his sigh, the almost heartbreak in his voice, as he said, "John, it's a holiday. Being with your family on the holidays is important. It's one of the only times–"

I cut him off again. "Remember when I visited you a couple weeks ago? About the missing person?"

That gave him pause, and I could picture him scratching his chin. "It sounds like someone's there with you now..." Sharp ears for an old man. Or maybe he just had his phone volume maxed out.

"Yeah, I'm going to bring her over and explain what's happened. Just the three of us, if that's alright."

"Oh? I get to meet someone before your parents do? She must be quite the girl."

Lily caught me staring at her and she stared back, about as long as it took for her to get hit by a rocket in Super Kart and lose first place again. "Yeah," I said. "She is. But, she also knows what happened to Charles."

After a pause, my grandfather asked, "Knows the story of what happened to him? Or... knows what happened to him?"

I almost said it all right then, but he would have blabbed to my parents the moment I hung up. "There are some circumstances that make things complicated, but I need to talk it out with you. So, that brings me back to Wednesday. Is that good for Thanksgiving?"

"Leaving me in suspense, are you?"

I laughed. "Only for a few days."

"Wednesday it is. I'll cook something special. I don't know what, the grocery stores are a mess already, but I'll figure something out."

"Hold on." I put the phone to my chest for a moment. "Lily, you're not allergic to anything, right?"

"What? You think I'm a vegetarian or something? I literally had pork ramen with you last night. Some of the processed food scares me, but you think you can put me in a world with meat this cheap and I'm not going to eat it?"

I turned away and put the phone back to my ear. "Right, so anything you can whip up will be fine. I imagine you're going to barbeque for Thursday, and I don't want to make you do that twice in one day. Honestly, takeout would be fine."

"No, no. I won't have you worrying about that. So what if I have to cook twice? Your grandmother would roll in her grave if I let you go hungry because of something like that. I'll take care of it and I'll see you Wednesday. Do well in class, alright?"

I glanced at my crane. The mere force of my attention on it seemed to make one of the metal limbs flop over, knock a bolt loose, and fall off. "I'll be fine. I've got time. Plenty of time."

"Good talking to you, John. Is there anything else?"

"No, I'm just looking forward to seeing you." We went through the ritual of saying four different variations of good-bye and finally hung up. I had a grin on my face as I wandered over and took the second player controller. She was between attempts on the grand prix and we were able to start up a 2-player race. Right after the green light, while I was just going through the motions of the classic drinking game, I asked, "Lily, does the concept of dating exist in Alfheim?"

She frowned. "We call it courting."

She used the elvish word for it, which forced in some context through the magic, and I nodded while lining up a rocket to knock her into the sand trap. "Huh, that usually precedes living together, doesn't it?"

"You bastard!" she screamed, her kart crashing into the sand pit as I blew past her. "And yeah, usually. Unless like, you're house servants I guess."

"Or sharing the rent on a magic portal?"

She glanced at me from the corner of her eye, still digging her way out of the pit to catch up. "Are you asking for permission to court me?"

"I figure I should, before you meet my family."

"Isn't it usually called forgiveness when you ask after you've already started?" she asked, smiling at me.

"Well then, would you forgive me for courting you?"

"Yeah, I suppose I could do that... for the hero who saved me," she said, and leaned in to kiss me.

It was a ploy, a distraction and a trap all in one. She hit my Kart with a heat-seeker missile, knocking me into the out-of-bounds reset area right before the finish line. She blew past me for the win before I could even accelerate again, stealing the win with the most underhanded of ways. I was going to have to get her back for that. I was going to–

Someone knocked on the door. Faces flashed through my mind of who it could be, and I was about ready to punch Lance for interrupting when I threw the door open. A woman in a dress shirt and aviators stood outside: the fed I had met the other night. She smiled at me. "Mr Martin. Sorry to trouble you."

I closed the door halfway behind me, hiding Lily from her. "I didn't realize you knew where I lived, Officer."

"It's on your ID," she said. "I just had some quick questions and was in the area. The man we're looking for, I was wondering if you had seen him again? Since that night in the bar?"

A knot grabbed hold of my throat. "No, can't say that I have."

"Could I ask you to come into the station to look over some composite images we have of him? The sketch artist is struggling somewhat. The reports have all been conflicting. We're worried he's some kind of makeup enthusiast or something."

Never talk to cops. The internet was very clear about that advice. "Sorry, I'll be out of town soon."

She stared at me. I couldn't tell if she was even blinking, not from behind her glasses. "Could you give me the best number to reach you at?"

"Sure, but I can't make any promises that it will get through to me. I don't bring it with me everywhere."

She scoffed. "A kid your age doesn't bring their phone everywhere?"

"Makes it easier to live in the moment," I said, and gave her my number.

After she jotted it down, she tucked her pad away. "Right, just one more thing then."

"And that would be?"

She grabbed my arm and tugged it over. Before I could react, she shoved my watch up and exposed the mark Tyr had given me. "Huh," she said, looking at the arrow mark. "Not what I was expecting."

I jerked my hand back, heart racing. Quickly, I tugged my sleeve down to cover it up once more. "Is having tattoos illegal now?"

She considered her answer, and said, "No it's not, Mr Martin. Have a nice day."

I didn't return the sentiment, and chain locked the door for good measure as she walked away.

"Who was that?" Lily asked, walking back from the kitchen with two beers.

"Trouble." I cracked one open with her. The room felt stifling after that exchange. Too small for us. Even with a whole world on the other side of my bedroom, we couldn't go there yet. But we had all of Earth to explore. "Do you want to go downtown? Spend some of that spice money?"

"Sure, I can finally wear one of the dresses I bought with Hilde."

"Sounds great. I could text them. Maybe we should go bowling or something?"

"Orrrr we could go to that video arcade."

She really had become a gaming fiend. "Sounds like a... date?"

She pouted playfully. "Hmm, depends. Do I really want to go put on the date dress?"

"And which one is that?"

"Remember that white one I wore last week to the jazz concert?" she asked, disappearing into our bedroom.

"Wait, if that was your date dress then why am I even asking?"

"For forgiveness, not permission!"

I shook my head with a grin and muttered, "Well, excuse me, Princess."

If you enjoyed this book, please consider taking the time to leave a review. Word of mouth is the strongest form of advertising and the best way to support independent authors.

You can also check out my website jameskrake.com for more info about my other publications, my current social media accounts, and what future projects you can expect from me.

Thank you for reading!

Milton Keynes UK
Ingram Content Group UK Ltd.
UKHW020727080424
440801UK00013B/587